P9-DTB-445

Rise the Euphrates

CAROL EDGARIAN

RISE the EUPHRATES

RANDOM HOUSE
NEW YORK

Rise the Euphrates is a work of fiction. While the Armenian genocide of 1915 is a documented historical event and some actual historical figures from that period are mentioned in the book, all other characters and events in the novel are wholly the product of the author's imagination. Any resemblance to actual events or characters living or dead is purely coincidental.

 Published in the United States by Random House, Inc., New York, and simultaneously in Canada by Random House of Canada Limited, Toronto.

Library of Congress Cataloging-in-Publication Data

Edgarian, Carol.
Rise the Euphrates / Carol Edgarian.—1st ed.
p. cm.
ISBN 0-679-42601-9
1. Armenian massacres, 1915-1923—Fiction. 2. Women—Fiction.
I. Title.
PS3555.D464R57 1994
813'.54—dc20 93-6323

Manufactured in the United States of America on acid-free paper
24689753
First Edition
Book design by Jo Anne Metsch

ACKNOWLEDGMENTS

The author wishes to thank the following for their care and generosity during the writing of this book: Albert and Maclin Guerard, Victor Esclamado, Laura Glen Louis, Becky Smith, Leslie Edgarian Sindt, Der Hyre Datev Kaloostian, Tamar Hajian, Amanda Urban and Kate Medina.

And particular appreciation to Tom Jenks, whose first gift was belief, and whose love and abiding attention are inextricably part of this book.

For
Araxie Anna Bagdasarian Edgarian,
who lives not in these pages
but in my heart

All the rivers flow into the sea,
Yet the sea is not full.
To the place where the rivers flow
There they flow again.

—Ecclesiastes 1:7

Բոլոր գետերը ծով կը հոսին, բայց ծովը չի լեցուիր·
Այն տեղէն որ գետերը կու գան, հոնկէ կրկին կը դառնան ծով։

Ժողովող Ա. գլ. 7

Prologue

These are the things that were not lost. My name is Seta Loon. I came to this world through the blue grace of my parents, George and Araxie Loon, and the concise desperation of my grandmother, Casard. It was Casard who named me Seta, after her mother; my father gave me Loon. By these gifts of name I became my grandmother's shiny hope, her Armenian girl, the one to hold her legacy of Turkish massacres and nights on the road of death, a legacy of the shame she suffered at the banks of the Euphrates River. I became Loon: daughter of my father, an American, *odar:* outsider.

I was raised in the town of Memorial, ten miles from the capital of the Constitution State of Connecticut. Here, among the factories, my grandparents laid their roots: in a place where a person could have one opinion in the morning and another in the evening and dismiss them both by saying, "It's a funny thing."

The Memorial I knew contained Main Street, with Connecticut National Bank on one end and, some three miles farther on toward the highway, Jimmy's Smoke Shop, where the best-selling items were Camels and Bazooka gum. Between the bank and Jimmy's there was downtown, and to the south and west the park, and beyond the park, nearly to the reservoir, our house.

My parents, George and Araxie, were both raised in Memorial, though they did not meet until after they had left town for higher education—my father to Massachusetts, my mother to central state—and returned home. They met at the assessor's office, where my mother worked and where my father, an aspiring real estate broker, transacted his business. They courted briefly and married, beginning their new life in an old place, even though my mother had spent a summer in Europe, and so dreamed of grand boulevards and rose-windowed cathedrals and palaces with high gilded ceilings. She chose George Loon and stayed.

My parents were married three years when they began having children: first my brother, Van, then me and, last, Melanie. We three entered this world believing as our father did that we were the lucky ones, for we had been privileged with the most beautiful mother, a mother whose troubled soul only heightened her outward beauty: her black swath of hair, her deep pooled eyes, the lethargic ease with which Momma made even the smallest gesture seem infinite. Countless mornings I stood beside her to watch the wand of her lipstick slowly, painfully describing the O of her mouth.

Momma's beauty had, at its core, an aspect of departure, which promised that nothing about her would ever become mundane. From the time we were toddlers, Van, Melanie and I scrambled to catch the brim of our mother's affection, for at any moment she was likely to clutch a child to her breast, and gasping, as if the lost had been found, she would kiss and kiss me—sometimes it was me, sometimes Van or Melanie—a thousand times behind the ear, as I stood before her still as stone, praying her kisses would never end, and of course, knowing they would.

I grew up with my father, a willow of a man—benevolent, fair—whose gangly limbs reminded me always of roots. In his large, capable hands I believed he had once formed a cup, and in this cup gathered the troth of his charms for the satisfaction of my mother. By turns Momma studied that cup, peering over its rim with wide luminous eyes. Dipping her finger inside, she burrowed to the bottom, where she found that part of George Loon which was most essential. Gazing into his happy, unsuspecting face, she replied, "Well, yes! All right."

Before I knew anything much I knew that by marrying my father my mother had committed a terrible betrayal of her community, and that my grandmother, in particular, deeply resented my mother's abdication. The Armenians, most of whom lived northeast of town in proximity to St. Stephen's Armenian Apostolic Church, did not think much of marrying odars. And while my generation sprang up alongside shopping malls and fast-food emporiums, Memorial's Armenians shunned change, preferring to keep within their own crowded, Persian-carpeted rooms, in which they spoke the old language, ate old-country food and married their kind.

Van, Melanie and I were part of this community. Our grandmother, Casard, was a pillar in the church. Even so, we were treated like distant relations. Our hair was light, while Armenian hair was black; our limbs were lanky, like our father's, while Armenians' were short and compact. At school we kept to one friend, maybe two, while the Armenians moved in packs, the girls dressed like tiny mothers in old-fashioned crocheted vests and long black braids tied back with plastic balls. It was the girls who vexed me, peering from under their thick lashes and dark brows at my light, wavy odar hair. However much my hair would darken with each passing year, it would never be blue-black like Momma's or theirs.

The part of me that was Armenian belonged to Grandma Casard. She taught me that the half that was hers made me special. In me was the first Christian nation on earth, a nation where God himself had settled Noah's ark. In me was the mountain Ararat and the songs of the poets and scholars and the soul of every Armenian slain by the Romans up through the Young Ottoman Turks.

Our Armenia was gone, Casard said and, tucking me close beside her, showed me her empty right palm as proof. As she taught me I taught others: See my fingers, they are Turkey, and Russia is my thumb. And my wrist? Persia. The flat of my palm is the plain of Anatolia, and each line a river, and the rises, mountains and hills. And if asked, Where is this Armenia? Casard taught me to spit in my hand and answer, *Gunatz*. Gone.

Momma's betrayal was not the first in our family. Before Momma ever thought to marry an odar, Grandma Casard committed a betrayal, which, though she spoke of it only twice in her life, bound our family in a miasmic web of shame.

I learned of Casard's betrayal when I was just forty days old. Before the baptismal font of St. Stephen's Armenian Apostolic Church, my grandmother presented me with my name and the Der Hyre priest made me a Christian. Then, as the ceremony concluded, according to Momma, Casard took me from my parents and brought me to the farthest pew, where she whispered the tale she had been saving for many years.

Gar oo chugar, she began. There was and there was not.

There was, in the spring of 1915, a group of zealots, the Young Ottoman Turks, who set out across historic Armenia to purge the land of the Armenian race. Casard was nine years old. Her father and brother were murdered, and she and her mother, Seta the first, forced on a death march into the Mesopotamian desert of Der el Zor. They marched eight days until, finally, they reached the Euphrates River, and it was there, at the river's bank, that the wretched betrayal occurred, leaving Seta the first dead, and young Casard, having lost everything, losing one thing more: her name.

The parts of us lost in childhood—innocence, wonder, youth—we are apt to value most. Casard valued her name. And to this end she waited some forty years, and when at last, on the day of my christening, she whispered her story to me, she wept. Peering into my empty soul, she asked me to find the name she had lost.

"Se-ta, Se-ta," she sang. "You."

• • •

I was eleven when Grandma Casard died—when the betrayal that she had so carefully husbanded, her cross and her strength, having no center, set down upon the rest of us.

Soon after, my mother, sad Araxie, began looking out the window to find the color of her despair. I looked too, and I saw myself as two halves: half Seta, half Loon. I saw my family as shivering fragments and my grandmother falling like a wingless bird. I saw Memorial as a strange, thwarted place, having at its center a grassy knoll where the town's ancestors had been raised on pedestals of granite, alabaster and marble. Around this plot of statues my grandparents settled and my parents after them and here under the watchful eye of the dead I was meant to grow. Lafayette. Bassett. Elliot. Lasalle. Polanski. Squaw.

I was fifteen when I took up my grandmother's legacy. That year, the story she had planted in me—a haunting, tremolo note—which I carried throughout my childhood as a pit in my belly, ripened, in the same way that my hair turned from yellow to brown. I was fifteen: no longer half Seta, half Loon, but something else. Who I was I did not yet know, but my task seemed clear: I found my grandmother's name, and once found, I reached for the window of my escape. Each turn in a life defines, but movement without clarity means nothing. I knew I had to find the name, but I knew not how to heal. I knew not that in families the worst betrayal is the withholding of forgiveness.

When I was just eighteen I left Memorial.

I am now thirty-three. After many years I have come home. For a few days I will pass through town, the woman in palazzo slacks, her heels snapping briskly on the walk. Others will see me, and the child pushing out from under my shirt. The people who knew my grandmother and my mother will find Seta Loon, pregnant, unmarried, smiling: a peaceful, inward smile that will seem commensurate with expectant thoughts. What they will not know—one can never really know—is that I am smiling because, at last, I have learned something of forgiveness, and, at last, without shame, I hear Casard's voice.

Gar oo chugar, she says. There was and there was not.

There was Casard, mother to Araxie and grandmother to me. A child of massacre; an old woman with gray tie shoes. Her dark legacy she neither understood nor could manage, and so she passed it on to my mother and me, along with lessons regarding cleanliness, an obsession against outsiders, a jealous craving for dignity, and a respect for what has been and what might come. My grandmother's truths were never simple, and in the end they failed to equip me for much. Even so, she filled my heart with her murky warnings and crude love delivered inside her dimly lit house, where the predominant shade was mauve. Yes, I remember.

Remember, too, that voice, which stuck to my belly, offering me no grace or escape. It was a broken, unwieldy song, it was a song in a minor key. It spoke of a world existing only in lyrics; Armenia, bearer of Noah's ark and Turkish massacres, a place so ancient that its monks memorized the Bible from stories told. The heroes of Casard's dusty, mournful tune were the artful weaver, the judicious king, the wise chicken, the workers with sweaty backs, and the fields of red wild poppies swaying to a divine beat under the great Mount Ararat.

And still she sings. Casard's voice is backbone, nothing less. The story she tells is mine, though I believe there are other tales of families that pass every day along invisible threads from mother to daughter to daughter. Our tales are what bind, they are the spiraling—the vicious, wondrous spiraling—which, if never questioned, lock the generations in a web of infinite expectation, lies, shame, hope.

For my unborn child, I am after hope. Hope, and the chance for a new story that will put to rest the lies and shame. And so I listen cautiously to Casard, who says: To make a new life, you must hope for the future, and you must remember what has already been. Hope I have plenty of to give Unborn. Hope grows inside me, it could pour any minute from my breasts, gold threads of light. It is that much hope.

For what has already been, I have returned to Memorial, to press my face into the blue-black unending well until our story is told. On the other side Casard, mother to Araxie, grandmother to me and dead, calls out. And though I am listening as I did long ago—saying Tell me about the river that flows through me—not for one minute am I fooled into thinking Casard gives her song for free.

Casard's Truths

Who after all speaks today of the annihilation of the Armenians?

—Adolf Hitler,
Obersalzberg, August 22, 1939

ONE

And God rested Noah's ark on Mount Ararat, in the land of the Garden, where the voice of Abel's blood cried up from the ground. The first king was Noah's great-great-grandson Haik. His people called themselves Hai, and their land Haiastan, Armenia. Through centuries, when conquering tribes of Medes, Persians, Greeks, Romans, Mongolians, Russians, Arabs and Turks claimed the land, no king or empire could claim the Armenians; they knew themselves as Hai.

Upon the ancient soil of Armenia, a girl called Garod lost her name and became Casard.

I close my eyes and I see her, nine years old, dressed in a long gray skirt and starched white blouse, a pair of blue-black braids, thick as horsetail, falling down her back. She is not the pretty girl but she is bright, with large brown eyes and lips that hide tiny square white teeth. She is the sensitive girl, and when her story begins on an afternoon in June 1915 she is tired, having spent the day in the bustling markets of Harput, of the Ottoman Empire, Turkey.

She had gone from the Christian quarter to the market in behalf of her mother, Seta, who was home recovering from the recent birth of a son. The little girl, Garod, and her aunt had set out at dawn in a horse-driven cart with high ambitions and too much on their list. It was now dusk. The blood-red sun illuminated Harput Castle and the city built around it, high up in the craggy hills, where it was possible to look out a window and see clear across the fertile Anatolian plain.

The cart bearing Garod and her aunt lurched along the city's main dirt road, then turned down a narrow lane lined with shops. At the last building on the left the cart pulled up and Garod was dropped at the doorstep of her father's office, while the aunt went on in a flurry to finish.

Garod called her father Hayrig—Little Father, Dear Father—and so he was. Eager to have him to herself, she bounded into Hayrig's office, and, finding him busy, drooped in his brown leather chair, limp as a leaf. All at once her feet ached, her hair hung in strings, and only her slender legs, swinging between the legs of the chair like pendulums, hinted at the bright spirit with which she had entered the room just a moment ago.

Hayrig, a doctor, was with a patient. For this reason Garod's legs swung: he was paying no attention to her. He went on washing his hands in a round tin sink, soaping, rinsing, hand over wrist, they would never be clean enough. Garod's eyes burned into the back of his fine woolen suit. She badly wanted his attention, and any minute she was likely to turn childish and cry. The day had been endless, and now, at its very end, she must wait.

Hayrig's patient was the sister of the powerful Turkish provincial governor, Vali Sabit Bey. Many prominent Turks came to Hayrig, though he was Christian, and he treated them courteously, and, with a few, such as the Vali, he made friends. Trained in Constantinople, Hayrig was considered the best doctor in Harput.

The Vali's sister was complaining of pains in her stomach. Hayrig nodded and, wiping his hands on a towel, let her trail on, as if he had not heard this story ten times before. When she finished, he took a brilliant-blue bottle from a cabinet and handed it to her.

"But it's empty," she complained, waving the bottle in his face.

Hayrig held the bottle to the light as if to see for himself. "Yes," he nodded apologetically and, bowing at the waist, handed the bottle back.

"But—I want one that is full," the Vali's sister whined, and when the doctor seemed not to understand, she gestured at the cabinet on the far wall, its locked shelves full of secret medicines in blue, brown and clear bottles.

"Those?" he said, cocking his head. "My lady, those are for people who do not wish to be sick. No, I'm afraid there is no medicine in there for you. For you I can offer nothing, except an empty blue bottle to remind you of how much better your stomach would feel if it, too, were empty. If only you would do as I say and allow your stomach to rest."

Hayrig tucked his chin, measuring the woman with his eyes.

The Vali's sister stared back at him. At last she shrugged, dropping the empty bottle into her bag.

Hayrig helped her down from the table and escorted her into the foyer.

Alone, Garod took possession of her father's office. Its walls and vaulted ceiling were rich with amber light from the fading sun. In a corner, a mahogany screen partitioned the space where the patients removed their clothes. On the far wall, charts of the body revealed that in the middle of the woman were two figs and an upside-down pear. Garod glanced at the drawing, then at herself, pressing a hand in the space between her hips. She imagined an empty space that would fill with fruit when she was grown. She tucked her hand under her ribs and felt the beating of her heart.

Flattening her palm on the worn leather blotter on Hayrig's desk, she swiveled the chair in a circle and, kicking her foot, gathered steam. Round and round she whirled. Then, dragging her foot, she stopped; something out the window had caught her eye.

Across the road, Franciscan sisters were herding a pack of boys and girls through the orphanage yards. She had watched them before, the orphans seeming to her both pitiful and exotic: the conspiratorial way they clung together, chattering, lurching into the yard, their loose muslin frocks and bare ankles sticking out of black shoes. She saw them laughing and carrying on and, suddenly, her belly tightened with loneliness.

The orphans reached the playground and dispersed in all directions, and the missionaries swooped after them, clucking hens gathering their brood. One boy escaped; Garod saw him dart behind a tree. His freedom, she knew, was illusory, for beyond the tree stood tall iron gates. Perhaps she could help him, and in this way insinuate herself into that strange, cloistered world. Perhaps she would unlock the gate and set the boy free. Then he would think of her as a hero. She saw herself at the gate, standing on her toes.

Hayrig's hand dropped like a heavy hat on Garod's head. Startled, she looked up and there he was, her impossibly handsome father, smiling down at her. Yelping with delight, she sat up in her chair, lonely and tired no more.

In another part of the city, a Turkish muezzin called the Muslims to prayer. The streets teemed. Beyond the gates of Harput City, and its nearly two hundred neighboring villages, across the fertile plains of Anatolia, east and west throughout the Ottoman Empire, criers called the Muslims to prayer. It was sunset, June 14, 1915.

Hayrig picked up his hat and leather attaché case, and they left his office and went out into the street. A Kurd driving a cart of melons nearly plowed into them, but Garod cried out and Hayrig placed his palm in the small of her back and swooped her to safety. She had only to lift her feet and float to the edge of the road.

Dusk brought out the bright flags of Harput. Garod eyed with curiosity and amazement the colorful pageant of villagers and city folk, both Muslim and Christian, hurrying by her, heading from the central markets toward various quarters of the city. To the south went the tiny Tiriki Kurds, their richly colored vests billowing in the warm afternoon breeze; the tall, pinched-featured Zasa Kurds pushed overflowing carts as Arabs zigzagged about them calling out to one another. A group of Turkish gendarmes from the 11th Army Corps rode by on horseback, as several Yezidis, thought to be devil worshipers, with their long dreadlocks, stood to the side and let them pass; an American missionary, probably a teacher at Euphrates College, dressed entirely in white, then crossed the street like a billowy sail. On all sides, the Armenians—intellectuals, tradesmen, farmers—talked excitedly (they never seemed to stop) as they passed through the streets, the farmers in brightly colored homespun, the intellectuals, like Hayrig, in European dress.

Hayrig was careful to place himself between Garod and the activity in the road. She peered around him as the horses and carriages clopped by, laden with goods from as far west as Constantinople, and as far east as Bitlis and Alexandropol. Hayrig had traveled to these places, for pleasure and with the Turkish army. He had distinguished himself not only on the battlefield but in school.

Garod tugged on his sleeve, and as he bent down, she whispered in his ear, "Tell me, please, the story of Lake Van."

Hayrig straightened suddenly, pleasure a ripe fig in his mouth. She gazed up at him as though staring at a bright constellation.

"Well," he began, "my friend Petros and I spent one perfect day at the lake. We were training at the hospital in Van and were allowed only one day off the entire month, so, of course, we had to make that day special. Petros and I had very little money, but we managed to borrow an old cart and a donkey from his father, and loading it with all the wine and food we could afford, we set out for Lake Van—"

As Hayrig spoke they made their way toward home. They passed two older girls from school, Nevart and Jilla, and Garod smiled and shyly waved, proud to be seen with such a handsome father. Hayrig spotted an acquaintance and his eyes lifted in greeting, but he did not stop. He was keeping it all for her, spinning his tale as they walked on, his palm tucked in the small of her back, thus guiding her in two places—along the streets of Harput and the shores of Lake Van—the two winking before her, like promises.

He told Garod of the feast he and Petros had made, so that she could nearly taste the sweet, ripe figs, the cheese and lamb and wine. She pictured herself on the yellow clay bank, gazing into the cool alkaline water and then, suddenly, she began to shiver, for the truth was she could not swim and the thought of the water, any water, frightened her—though her fear excited her, too.

Hayrig frowned. "What is the matter?"

"Nothing!" she said, attempting a smile.

Hayrig glanced at his daughter, and then at the blazing summer sky. "You're not getting sick," he said decisively, and as he tucked her close, they passed from the Muslim district into the Christian quarter.

As they approached the Armenian church, Garod stared up at the building in which she had been baptized by holy oil and by grandeur. Craning her neck, she gazed at the steep pyramidal roof set upon walls of ruddy volcanic stone. Beneath these, the round hidden dome that was the signature of the Armenian architect. She wanted Hayrig to keep talking to her, so she asked about the weight-bearing columns, the piers and apses. Her father patiently explained that they were predecessors to the flying buttress. And what was a flying buttress? she asked. Hayrig explained that, too, drawing in the air the vaulted forms of the great cathedrals of Europe. Garod imagined these mythic churches and the more modest example before her, and was reminded of the charts in Hayrig's office—that is, the church seemed to her like the human body, a vessel with bones and curves and breast-shaped domes, with hallowed chambers covered by ruddy skin. Each Sunday, as Garod passed through the church portals into the sanctuary, she was struck by the holy aura radiating from the columns and beams, and the priest in his vestments of gold, the priest pacing before the altar, illumined by scores of burning tapers. Safe in their church, she kneeled alongside her parents and felt her insides hushed.

And hushed by the holy magnificence she remained, years later, when, as a child, I went with her to church and knelt down in the pew as she whispered to me, as though revealing a secret, the word in Armenian for priest. *Der Hyre*—Dear father—she whispered, her eyes shiny with amazement. I repeated: *Der Hyre,* as the Der Hyre priest talked of a beginning, a death and a rising. And all around us the hymns played, the men and women of the choir straining to hold the minor chords, the women modest in their lace veils.

The doors to the church were closed. Garod and Hayrig turned the corner, past the gates of Euphrates College, and Garod squeezed her father's arm. He glanced at her flushed cheeks and proud, defiant smile and he could not help himself, he nodded: Yes, if she was special, if she proved herself outstanding in school, one day she might attend.

They had gone as far as the government building when they saw the angry crowd. A government decree was being passed out on leaflets. Hayrig got hold of a copy.

The decree, signed by Talaat Pasha, the Turkish minister of the interior, announced that all Armenian males between the ages of twelve and forty-five were hereby drafted into the Turkish army. They were to report for registration by noon the next day. Those resisting would be hanged as traitors or shot.

Garod could not understand what was happening, though she was painfully aware of an inscrutable tension flowing from Hayrig's hand into her body. She looked up at her father for clarification, but his face was the picture of consternation, and so she said nothing. Hayrig knew what his daughter did not: that east and west of their remote city, on the far borders of the Ottoman Empire, two conquerors, the Turks and the Russians, were at war. On this day, the doctor understood, the war had arrived in Harput.

The street erupted with commotion. Garod tugged on Hayrig's coat and pointed to the window of the government building, where the Turkish police chief, the mudir, was keeping an eye on the burgeoning crowd.

The unruly mob numbered several hundred when, suddenly, a

large stone sailed overhead, exploding onto the wooden steps of the government building. The police chief appeared at once, accompanied by several gendarmes. Soldiers with rifles flanked the steps while the chief stood among them, hands hidden behind his back.

The crowd erupted, hurling accusations.

The mudir shouted, "One at a time. One at a time, you will all have your turn."

A voice called out: "When will we be called upon to march. Will it be a matter of days or weeks?"

The mudir, known for maintaining good relations with the community, and for his insatiable appetite for paklava and other Armenian pastries, seemed particularly agitated by the question. Garod noticed that above his uniform collar his pudgy face ran with sweat.

He motioned for a gendarme to bring the man forth.

But the specimen brought to the steps displeased the mudir. The questioner was young, a student perhaps.

"What?" the mudir boomed, for the crowd's benefit. "You say you won't fight, is that it? You won't fight for the mother who has kept you warm and put food in your belly? Is that what you say?"

The student stammered. "No. No, Effendi, please. You misunderstand. My question is one of timing. My wife is due with our first child, and if I were to have a bit of notice, I could make arrangements, perhaps a relative to come care for her."

The chief glowered. "And I say ready today, if today is when you are needed."

"Effendi, please. I am merely asking: Will it in fact be today, tomorrow, or next week? You see, my wife—"

The mudir groaned and the soldiers nearest him stepped back. He swung his other hand from behind him, revealing a pistol. Leveling the gun at the youth, he nodded and said, "What will it be?"

The student raised his arms. "No. Please."

"Today, then," the mudir said, and fired. The student doubled over and fell to the ground.

For an instant the crowd was stunned. Then all around Garod and Hayrig, people began to move. The crowd surged onto the steps.

"Remember, the rest of you," the mudir cried, waving his gun. He disappeared into the portico as gendarmes swarmed the front of the building.

Hayrig propelled Garod through the crush. "Doctor," he barked, and the people made way.

The wounded man lay on his back staring up at the sky. Blood leaked from a hole in his stomach; Hayrig touched fingertips to the man's throat and, eyeing the ground, concentrated on what his fingers heard. The crowd seemed to hold its breath. When Hayrig stood and the crowd caught sight of his anguished face, his lips pressed tightly together, they all began to speak.

Hayrig called to several men to carry the body, and Hayrig and Garod made their way behind it through the crowd. All around her, Garod saw faces twisted with grief and rage, men and women standing in the street, weeping. They wept for themselves, for the dead youth and for the unnamed misery they knew was coming. It was as though the same bullet that had killed the student had passed through their bellies, too.

Garod felt sick. She marched alongside her father, his hand a fiery iron pressing into her back, and her thin shoulders heaved as tears dropped from her chin onto her dress.

Hayrig told the men to take the body to his office while he escorted Garod home. Father and daughter walked on in silence, Hayrig seemingly unaware of Garod's presence. She felt frightened and crushed by his inattention; she yearned to wiggle free of his hold, and then—she yearned to run. But she no sooner saw herself flying down the road than she heard Hayrig's voice, calling her back, and the stern reprimand that would follow.

So she walked on, a little soldier, and tried to get close to Hayrig by guessing his thoughts. No doubt he was trying to anticipate the Turks' next move. Hayrig understood the Turks; often enough, he had bested them at their game—a game established centuries ago.

The Turks had swept across Asia Minor in the fifteenth century, conquering one ancient state after another—Greek, Arab, Kurd and Armenian—to whom they offered the choice of converting to Islam or becoming segregated from mainstream society. Armenia, the first of the Christian nations, refused to forsake its roots and thus functioned as a separate state within the state, its people "protected," but without rights.

As a leader of Harput's Armenian community, Hayrig understood the price of such protection—the Armenians enjoyed relative freedom from other conquerors so long as they bolstered the Turkish economy and kept money flowing into the government's pockets. In an unfair game, Hayrig often told his daughter, to succeed, you must work smarter than your opponent.

Hayrig trusted that he had done everything to succeed, but this vile incident with the student suggested otherwise; clearly, the Turks were on to something new. Hayrig's failure to anticipate the changing tide infuriated him. He had to admit that for some time he had been aware of trouble brewing in other parts of the country. Letters from colleagues in Van and Constantinople revealed that the extremist Young Turks were in dire shape, their economy collapsing while their military took a thrashing at the hands of the Russians. In short, the Young Turks were desperate for an excuse that would divert attention from their failures—hungry, that is, for a scapegoat.

It had happened before: in the massacres of 1895 entire villages of Armenians had been wiped out in a sudden sweep of ethnic cleansing—Hayrig knew perfectly well. But until that afternoon he had been convinced that any wave of Turkish nationalism would pass over Harput. Just a week before, at their monthly bridge game, the Vali, who controlled the mudir, had boasted that Harput's geographical isolation, several hundred miles from the nearest seaport or railroad, allowed him to govern as though he were a sugar king on a remote island. Hayrig and the others at the table were amused by the image of the corpulent Turk sitting on a beach in a loincloth and fez.

But that was then; now, walking with his daughter, Hayrig paled as he recalled something else the Vali said that night—something that, in hindsight, Hayrig should have taken as a warning. They were playing out a hand, and, as usual, the Vali was cheating by talking in Turkish with his partner. Hayrig used the occasion to ask the Vali about a Turkish shopkeeper who, out of the blue, had murdered his friend and fellow shopkeeper, an Armenian, because he suspected the Armenian of selling goods on the cheap. Hayrig was shocked that the murderer had not yet been arrested.

The Vali waved a finger at the doctor, "Ah, Krikor, what is so difficult for you to understand? Any man can see that in nature there is the strong and the weak. We Turks know this—and let me tell you, my friend, not everyone yearns like you to have the worries of a king. No, each man is content with what he has, and with the knowledge that one day, if he obeys Allah, he will have his kingdom in Paradise. When one weak-spirited man threatens the order and another man takes action, we all must respect him. Again, nature is our guide. As the proverb states: The cat who eats her kittens swears they look like mice!"

Recalling the Vali's words, in light of the event with the student, Hayrig involuntarily thumped his fist into Garod's back. The girl cried out and Hayrig looked at her with alarm, certain that they were all damned, and that, at the very least, his daughter would grow up thinking he was a fool. The War was on the move—he could see that now—advancing toward them like a black train, black as a bullet. First, there was just this puff of smoke, but, underneath, a quickening resonance, a roar that would shake the earth.

What Hayrig and his friends could not have known, what they could not have imagined, was that since the outbreak of fighting the Armenians had been in extreme jeopardy, their historic lands situated on both sides of the Russian-Turkish front. The previous winter, as the Turks suffered crushing defeats on the Caucasian front, followed by Allied landings at Gallipoli, the loyalty of the Armenian minority had come into question. Would the Armenians turn against their Muslim rulers and side instead with the Christian Russians? And what of these relentlessly enterprising Armenians, who managed to prosper while the rest of the empire declined?

During the winter, Talaat Pasha, the minister of the interior, had devised a systematic plan to deal with the "Armenian question" once and for all. The details of his plan would be revealed in stages through coded telegrams sent to members of the Young Turk party: "The government has decided to destroy completely all Armenians living in Turkey. . . . An end must be put to their existence, however criminal the measures taken may be, and no regard must be paid to either age or sex, nor to conscientious scruples."

On April 24, in Constantinople, 254 prominent Armenians—lawyers, clergy, writers, professors and doctors—had been arrested, exiled to the wilderness of Anatolia and killed. Among them, several of Hayrig's friends.

Even as Hayrig and Garod made their way home, new decrees were being sent by telegraph and along the Berlin–Baghdad railway to the Armenian provinces, where they landed like bombs. The first of the day's decrees had arrived in Harput that morning, delivered to the Vali's home by a messenger on horseback. It read: THE MEN SHALL BE TAKEN FIRST.

That night, Armenian men from the neighborhood gathered at the doctor's home. Garod was sent to bed. Through the wall, she listened to the men's thick voices.

"The Young Turks are scared. They're taking a beating and they're worried we'll back the Russians. This registering for the army is just insurance to make certain we're on their side."

Then Hayrig's voice: "You miss the point entirely! I've fought beside the Turks—and you and you—we have nothing more to prove. Yet there was such violence today in the street. Ask yourselves: Is such senseless killing the behavior of one who is looking for partners? Does this look to you like a call for help? It is not good, my friends, not good."

For a moment the room was silent, then a man whose voice Garod could not identify said, "Krikor, perhaps you're overreacting. Perhaps this decree is just a formality to appease Constantinople. We register for the army, then we go on like before."

"Not this time," Garod heard her father say. "This time the Turks are itching for an excuse. Look around you—we run every business, and, of course, the school. We've become too rich, too successful while at the front the Young Turks lose. So what do they do? They call out our men. Ask yourselves: When we're gone, who will mind our businesses? Who will defend our families?"

And so it went on into the night. She fell asleep, she awoke; the men talked on. It was nearing dawn when Hayrig and the others agreed that, come morning, they would register as a group. But they would not submit their guns. Hayrig would pull some strings and find out what he could. They would meet again the following night and adopt a plan. They agreed that at this stage there was little more they could do; the Turks, it seemed, had suddenly become immune to bribes.

After the men had left, Hayrig came to her room and sat on the edge of the bed. The room was dark and for a few moments they were silent.

At last he said, "You never know, at your age, what you'll remember. The first death I witnessed was an uncle: his heart gave out right at the supper table. We stretched him out on the floor, but he was gone. I remember the most astonishing thing was that he died with his eyes open. I couldn't believe it. My father passed his hand over my uncle's face and closed his eyes." Hayrig stroked her cheek. "Try not to be too scared. All right?"

She rubbed her lips together and considered his words. She knew he meant to comfort her, but the weariness in his voice frightened her. She worried about his discomfort as he squatted on the low bed, his knees raised, as if he were perched on a stool. She moved against the wall to give him room.

He stood. "I'll say good night. Your mother, no doubt, hasn't slept either." He moved toward the door.

"Are you," she asked, "scared?"

He turned then, deciding.

"Yes," he said finally, and sighed. "But tomorrow I will try to turn that fear into strength, and make it useful."

He opened the door and disappeared down the hall to her mother.

Long after he left, Garod lay awake trembling; when she closed her eyes, she saw the dead student's face, his eyes wide open, his mouth a shocked O. She saw the student and then his face transformed, becoming like Hayrig's. It was Hayrig lying on the ground, his pink mouth, his blood. Horrified by her thoughts, she pounded her small fists against her skull. Then curling into a ball, she wept. The sun rose over the hills of the city and still she cried, until, exhausted, she fell into a fitful slumber, her dreams inconsolable, chaotic, dark.

She awoke fearing her father had died, and when she realized it was but the work of her own wretched imagination, she cursed herself and climbed out of bed. She marched off to school, her hands balled into fists, her mind set on censoring shameful thoughts.

In the afternoon, she returned bearing gifts. She burst into the house, tumbling an armful of ripe figs, Hayrig's favorite, onto the table. At the sink, her mother, Seta, watched with raised brows. Garod quickly explained: she had picked the figs in old man Aram's field, taking those already on the ground, so it would not be considered stealing. The fruit would have rotted before the old man had a chance to collect it.

"Wash those hands," her mother, whom she called Mayrig, said. Mayrig, her face slack with worry and fatigue, stood at the table slicing beans into a large bowl.

Garod went to the sink and washed.

"How was school?" Mayrig asked.

School was fine. "Mayrig?" Garod began.

"Mmm."

"I didn't steal. They were on the ground."

"We'll see."

"Mayrig?"

"Mmm."

Garod revealed her plan: she would hide the figs in the center of the table under a large bowl, like this, and how long did Mayrig think it would take Hayrig to look under the bowl?

Mayrig laughed sharply: it would be the first thing he saw as he came into the house. "But," she added, "right now, there are more pressing things to think about. Here, take these dirty figs from the table. Put them in a bowl, that's it, now come help me with the lavash. We'll talk about taking other people's things later."

Garod dropped the figs into a large white bowl, set them on a chair and then wiped the table clean while Mayrig brought over the ingredients to make the flat bread.

To the outside world, Mayrig, the handsome daughter of a sheepherder, had made a good match for herself when she married the learned doctor. Among the Armenians of Harput City, Mayrig was seen as a sensitive yet proud woman, deserving of respect. But to her daughter, she was remote, pensive, mysterious, and, since the baby, pain-ridden and oppressed. Garod resented Baby Sevan, who took Mayrig's attention: eating and messing his pants, that was him. She watched her mother move about the kitchen, her limbs heavy with fatigue, and for the second time in as many days, the girl felt trapped and yearned to flee.

As if guessing her thoughts, Mayrig turned and looked into her daughter's face, but instead of seeing Garod, Mayrig saw her own worry—of how it was for Hayrig, who had gone with the other men to the government building at noon.

"He'll be back soon," Mayrig said, trying to convince herself.

Garod felt ashamed, for the truth was she wanted not to hear of others, not even Hayrig; she wanted her mother to focus on *her.* When had she, Garod, become so small? Since Baby Sevan, that's when, and now her parents and the baby were a closed unit. At night Hayrig and Mayrig often read from the same book, trading it back and forth while the baby slept nearby in his bassinet. Or Hayrig studied while Mayrig nursed the baby. Holding Baby Sevan to her breast, she sang, and Garod was meant to play quietly by herself or go to her room. Garod felt certain of her place only on those rare occasions when she was alone with Hayrig.

Mayrig checked on Baby Sevan, who was asleep in the corner. He was a month old and already had a full head of black hair. She cooed at her son. "Siroonig," she sang. Dearest one.

Garod made a sour face. "Mayrig, don't we have to fix the bread?"

Mayrig sighed and turned to the table. Her hands darted quickly, assembling the lavash. In the crease of her palm, she measured the flour and poured it onto the table in the shape of a cone. With a finger, she formed a crater in the top, into which she poured warm water. Working quickly, she blended the dry and wet ingredients a little at a time with her palms. "Here," she said, giving the girl a turn. Soon the two were covered to their elbows with flour.

Neither spoke of that which preoccupied them. In fact, they did not speak at all. Soon, their silence assumed a language of its own, composed of arms and breath. They worked vigorously, kneading the bread, and afterward, using the sides of their hands, they cut the shape of the cross into the dough. So absorbed were they that when Hayrig appeared in the doorway, they looked up with complete astonishment, as if he were a ghost.

He had come around the back, leaving the garden gate ajar. He stood stiffly in the doorway in his dun-colored army uniform. They studied him: his face pale with fury, his hands knotted into fists, his breath short labored puffs. Garod had never seen her father enraged, yet she knew instinctively to keep back.

Hayrig moved toward them as if to strike, and then he stopped when he spotted the figs.

"Don't," Mayrig burst. "Krikor, my God, you're scaring us. What is it? What have they done?"

But he seemed not to hear her; he lunged at the table as Garod and Mayrig jumped back to the wall. Hayrig grabbed his chair and threw it to the floor. Hayrig picked it up and tossed it down again, dashing it on the wooden planks. With his boots he crushed the spindles and legs.

"Stop!" Mayrig cried. "This isn't you! Tell me what happened?"

"This—" he shouted, kicking at the pile. "*This* is my chair. *My* chair. You see? I'll be the one who decides when it breaks."

Garod was stunned: it was crazy, Hayrig ruining things.

He fumed over the wreckage, jostling pieces with his boot.

"Krikor," Mayrig said softly, in a voice that made clear she did not expect him to answer. Cautiously, respectfully, she approached her husband and, taking his hands, smoothed the skin with her palms the way she might smooth the creases of her skirt. Intently, lovingly, she studied what she had made of his hands. When she lifted her eyes, he would not meet her gaze but glared at the floor. She jerked his hands, just once, like reins, and his gaze lifted and fell upon the girl.

Mayrig stooped to tidy the mess, and he said, "No, get up. Leave that." Lifting Mayrig from the floor, he clutched her to him.

"Where's the baby?" he asked.

Mayrig pointed with her chin. "In the bassinet. I can't imagine how he slept through—"

"Good," Hayrig nodded. "And the bread, you two are making lavash for dinner?"

"Yes!"

"And after dinner, you will feed the baby, and then, sew?"

Mayrig peered into his face and what she saw confused her. "Why are you asking? You know perfectly well—"

"Good, good." He nodded, as if she had said the right thing. "And tonight, you will remember to bolt all the doors—"

"Stop," Mayrig cried. "Stop this." She pried his hands from her shoulders.

"Quiet!" he barked and glanced at the door. Then he said, "Now, I taught you about the gun. Let's remember together. Where is the ammunition?"

"No!" she cried. "Tell me—"

"Where!" he demanded, shaking her.

Mayrig swallowed hard. "In the drawer of the chest."

"That's right. Now—" He gripped Mayrig around her waist, and Mayrig felt him tremble and saw in his face that he was terrified. Her eyes implored him to explain.

"Shh," he pressed. "One thing more. We won't be victims; let us promise, whatever comes, we will not think of ourselves that way."

Frightened and confused, Mayrig shook her head.

"No?" he insisted.

"No," she said, "we won't."

"Hayrig!" Garod shouted as a Turkish gendarme appeared in the doorway.

"It's all right," Hayrig said, and nodded at the soldier. "You remember this man, don't you? He was a patient of mine. I treated him for typhus."

Mayrig and Garod stared at the soldier and nodded, recalling that after the soldier recovered he brought them a butchered lamb as a gift.

Hayrig glanced at his daughter, and Garod saw that his eyes were stony with fear. "Now," he said, "promise you will do like your mother."

Garod was too stunned to speak.

"Doctor, please," the soldier said.

"Yes," Hayrig answered, and he strode to the corner hutch, where he kept the guns. "You see, I've just been allowed to come home and collect these."

He lifted the rifles from their rack, but left the pistol hidden under a cloth in the back of the larder. The soldier took the guns and stepped back as Hayrig pulled his wife and daughter to him. He pressed his lips against their necks. "No crying," he whispered. "No victims."

Garod dug her nails into Hayrig's back, but before she could breathe again he was gone, the door closing, and the last she knew of him was the shivering rage that flowed from his flesh into hers.

They waited three days for word of the men. Garod and Mayrig went to the government building, they talked with neighbors, but the news was sparse: the men were being processed for the army.

On the third day there was a knock at the back door. It was the errand boy, Mahmoud, who performed odd jobs for both the mudir and the doctor's wife. Mayrig received the small, filthy boy as she would an important guest, offering him tea from the samovar and a plate of pastries. As he talked on she filled his cup. Garod sat quietly to the side, listening, while the boy told her mother what he knew.

The Armenian men of Harput, who had reported to the government building that first morning, had been led into the building single file. Inside, they were processed through a series of rooms, so none could see where the man before him had been taken. They signed papers and checked their arms. Next, they were put in cells, hundreds of men to a room. The intellectuals, teachers, clergymen and professionals were singled out.

The beatings began that first night. Some were bastinadoed, some whipped, others had their nails torn out and the hair on their heads and beards. That first night many died, so many, there was a question of what to do with the corpses.

As the errand boy sipped his tea, Garod had to fight the urge to spit at him or smash the teacup in his face. Mayrig sat very still, palms tucked in her lap. She refused to look directly at the boy and, likewise, the boy did not look at her; it was as though they had agreed not to let their eyes meet, lest the anger and shame connect them.

As she listened to the boy, Mayrig drew with her finger an invisible circle in the crease of her palm. "Please," she said, "my husband. You have news of him?"

"Yes, madam." The boy glanced at Garod, then went on with his story.

It seemed that the gendarme, whom her father had saved from typhus, had pulled the doctor from a group of professionals to question him about his guns. The soldier explained to Hayrig that should the doctor's home be searched—and it surely would be—and weapons were found, his wife and children would be killed on the spot. The policy was explicit.

Mayrig inhaled sharply, bowing her head, her lips pursed. The day before, Garod had overheard her mother say that she feared becoming one of the frightened ladies, so filled with terror they could not function. "No victims in this house!" Mayrig had said.

Garod watched her mother drawing circles in her palm, taking what the boy said into her hand and shaping it, making it round, before taking it into her heart.

"Sorry"—the boy blushed—"please, it is, of course, too much to bear. It is beyond reason, surely. Shall I come back another time?"

Garod had had enough. "Talk, fool," she snapped, with such venom that Mayrig turned to her with an open mouth. "You have something to say about my father, then talk. Otherwise, get out."

The boy shrugged and continued. The soldier had convinced his superior that he must escort this man home in order to seize hidden guns. He would make an example of the doctor and his family. The soldier had taken a great risk in bringing Hayrig to the house. Neither the soldier nor the doctor had since been found.

"Lies," Garod hissed. "Turk lies."

"Please," Mayrig begged, "can't you see he has come to help?"

"Yes," the boy replied, eyeing her mother's ring. "To help."

Four days after Hayrig disappeared, the men were marched at night from the city. Mayrig and Garod stood in front of Hayrig's office and watched them go. Among the ranks of filthy, blood-soaked men were merchants, bankers, doctors, dentists, lawyers, carpenters, bricklayers, tinsmiths, bakers, tailors and shoemakers. They carried only the clothes on their backs. Those, like Hayrig, who had served in the Turkish army were, by the new decree, stripped of rank; they marched as common *ameles,* laborers, south toward the Syrian city of Aleppo, where, they were told, they would build new fortifications and roads.

The men flowed from the city, as from a wound. Garod could not find her father, though she searched every face, every row. The men were bound together at their wrists and waists; many were badly cut and bruised. They seemed weak—she could not help thinking so—weak and already doomed; the sight of them filled her with profound shame. Though she was just a child and could not assess such things, she believed each had failed her personally and that they were the worst kind—victims. She watched their retreating backs, not a sword or weapon among them.

In the days that followed, Mayrig refused to listen to rumors. The rumors said: As far away as Bitlis and Van, throughout historic Armenia, cities and villages were being systematically bled of men, the men killed outright or drafted into labor battalions. Next, the women and children were "relocated." They were given just a day to pack, the belongings they left behind were looted by Turks, the thieving Turks filling their own homes with Armenian carpets, furniture and crystal.

The rumors said: Harput was next.

The rumors said, but Mayrig forbade Garod to listen.

On June 26 a town crier ran through the streets accompanied by a small boy beating a drum. The crier announced that the government had ordered the deportation of every Armenian man, woman and child in Harput and its neighboring villages. The Armenians of Harput City would go on Monday, July 5.

That night, and all that week, Turkish soldiers gathered in the central mosque and prayed to Allah to bless them in their efforts to kill the Christians.

On Sunday, the day before they were to leave, Mayrig prepared a supper of kuftah soup; they ladled the thick soup into their mouths like zombies. Afterward, Garod went to her room while her mother nursed Baby Sevan, who fussed and cried. Mayrig sang to the infant, trying to coax him to sleep. Garod lay on her bed, her mother's mournful song passing through her bones, filling her with dread. Garod pictured a man in a field dragging a worthless leg. She pictured a girl with dirty pants; and a woman with empty palms, searching the floor for where she had dropped the baby.

Garod could not keep her mind from such wretched dreams; she was merely responding to the feeling passing through the wall. She tried to think of something else, of the places in Hayrig's stories—Ararat, Constantinople, the blue-green Araxe River, the feast at the shores of Lake Van—but it was no good. Miserable, she curled in bed, as an eerie orange light passed through the window, and a strange percussion joined Mayrig's song—a sound unlike any Garod had heard: soft yet firm, like fists beating feather pillows.

Garod was asleep when the soldiers entered the house. Rough hands grabbed at her; as she screamed and kicked she was tossed into the street. Mayrig was there, kicking, biting, crying out for the baby. The Turketa silenced her with the butt of a rifle; she fell like sticks.

Garod ran to her mother and helped her to her feet. Soldiers were everywhere, blowing whistles, breaking glass. A cannonball exploded onto the roof of the house, drowning out their cries for Baby Sevan. Within minutes, flames consumed the house as Mayrig, mad with anguish, writhed and pulled at her hair. It was Garod who had to hold Mayrig back from the Turketa. But her mother was strong, and as Garod struggled to restrain Mayrig, the girl's tears ceased. She clasped her arms around her mother's waist and, bowing and scraping, the two cried out for the lost baby, "Se-van, Se-van, Sevan—"

So began the night without end. Throughout the Armenian quarter, the Turks went from house to house, evicting women, children, old men. The people of Harput stood in the street, shivering in their thin nightclothes. Those unable to move quickly were shot in their beds, their bodies burned with their homes.

Garod and Mayrig became part of a group of several hundred led to the steps of the church, where they were met by still thousands more. Turkish soldiers on horseback and on foot packed the Armenians into the square, blowing whistles and jabbing at them with bayonets.

Mayrig fell into a stony silence, tears streaming down her cheeks. "Mayrig," Garod whispered, petrified of losing her mother, too. But Mayrig did not seem to hear, for louder still was the deafening noise of a city on fire. Garod was Harput's witness; she took into her heart the black, black smoke, the multicolored tongues of fire.

To the steps of the Armenian Gregorian church, soldiers brought forth the bishop and his priests and deacons, all of whom had been missing for weeks. The soldiers stripped the bishop and tied him by his hands and feet onto a makeshift cross. Then, as Garod looked on in horror, the soldiers set upon the holy one with knives. Blood spilled from the bishop's limbs and genitals. With each cut the Turks mocked, "Now will your Christ save you?"

Garod's eyes and throat burned. She longed to shout, Stop! What have we done? But when she turned to Mayrig, the look of terror in her mother's eyes kept her mute. Garod searched about for a familiar face and found herself surrounded by Turkish soldiers—strangers—the Vali and mudir nowhere in sight.

The soldiers pulled a pregnant woman from the crowd. The woman was close to term, her belly as large as a melon under her print shift. The woman was crying, holding her stomach as they beat the child in her womb. When she fell to the ground, senseless, they lifted her up and gave her more. Only then did Garod recognize the sound she had heard earlier in her room—the percussion accompanying Mayrig's song had been clubs pounding flesh.

The soldiers pulled more victims from the crowd. In Garod's circle the old men nudged the women and children to the center, for those on the periphery learned about the clubs. A hand grabbed Garod from behind and caught hold of her hair. Panicked, she bolted deeper into the crowd, her hair ripping from her skull. She pushed and shoved until there was no more room to move. Then she turned and discovered she had lost Mayrig. Frantic, she pushed back through the crowd, calling, "Mayrig, Mayrig, Mayrig!" But so many others were bellowing, and above their cries was the din of whistles, shots and cannon fire, and the clubs cracking bones.

Garod recognized her neighbor, old man Aram, from whose field she had liberated the figs. The next day Mayrig made her return the fruit and the old man solemnly accepted Garod's apologies, then gave her candy and sent her home. When the men marched, Aram lost two grown sons. Garod moved toward Aram as soldiers pulled him from the crowd.

"You, big nose," a soldier said, slicing the old man's nose with a knife. Blood spurted from the wound like a fountain, staining Garod's dress. "You have the ears of an ass," the Turk taunted, cutting Aram's ears and tossing the bloody remnants into the crowd. Before each cut, the Turk demanded, "You Armenian pig, spit on your Jesus and save yourself."

When they took to flensing the old man as though he were a sheep, Garod began to vomit. As she retched, a gentle hand touched her back and she shot up, hoping for Mayrig, but it was someone else, a woman looking at her through blue tearless eyes. The woman lifted a corner of her nightgown and sucked on the material, then wiped Garod's face. They did not speak. The woman cleaned the girl's face, then turned her to where, just a few paces away, she caught a glimpse of Mayrig.

Garod forced her way through the crowd. Mayrig turned and clung to her, pressing the girl's face into her bosom. The cotton of Mayrig's shift was soft and vaguely damp with milk. The girl pressed her lips against her mother's gown and cried bitterly. "Sevan," she cried, vowing never to forget her brother, nor old man Aram, who turned his back to his wife so she would not remember him disfigured—Aram, who bled the red that was the center of the fiery orange tongue.

During the next hours several thousand Armenians were killed or maimed, their bodies left where they fell. It was nearly dawn when the gendarmes selected five girls and tied their arms and legs with rope. They strung them up by their thick black braids from the rafters of the government building. There was Ani, Shushan, Chortz, Nevart and Jilla, the eldest, just fourteen; Garod knew them all from school.

A jester among the soldiers pushed the girls so they bobbed, to and fro, knocking into one another as they hung in a row by their black braids.

Garod was stunned; her child's mind tried to grasp what terrible crime her people could have done to deserve this. And what was next?

The soldiers had an answer—it was a game they had perfected in the other cities. Their leader, brought in for the massacre, mounted his horse, then trotted a hundred paces away. He turned and, with a wave, motioned for the girls to be stilled. Then, holding his bloodsword high above his head, he spurred his horse and galloped toward them. With one deft stroke, he severed four heads. The bodies dropped to the dirt like sacks of flour.

The troops cheered and blew their whistles and, clapping their leader on the back, helped him from his horse.

The fifth girl, Jilla, fainted. The Turks cut her down from the rafter and a young soldier raped her in front of the crowd. Her mother, who went mad at the sight, ran at them. They shot her in the face and tossed her body into the fire. When they finished with Jilla, a soldier in a maroon fez twisted her neck in his hands. The other girls' heads were left dangling from the rafters, so that as the sun rose over the hills they appeared as darkened lanterns hanging from black rope.

By dawn the streets of Harput were choked with smoke and the stench of charred flesh. In the gray light, even the gendarmes appeared tired.

But it was not finished. The Young Turks in Constantinople had decreed it so: swift annihilation or, for those remaining few, deportation into the wasteland of the Mesopotamian desert.

Garod and Mayrig became part of a caravan of several thousand, driven by bullwhip and bayonet from the city gates south, along the route taken by the men.

All that day they marched, single file, along narrow craggy roads, past villages and fields, then down into the dry, hot plain. They passed fragrant streams flowing from the mountains, but those who tried to drink never made it back to the road. They were shot, water glistening in their hands.

Garod opened her eyes wide, determined to awaken in her bed. She looked about her and found herself surrounded by a group of tattered, filthy beggarwomen. How fast and irrevocably the matrons of Harput Christian society fell. Garod looked among the faces, trying to find those she knew: the women Mayrig had entertained for tea. But these women looked like strangers. It was as though the Turks had removed the women's faces and replaced them with grotesque masks; in the course of a single day, they had all become plodding mutes, with matted hair and sunken eyes, staring blindly at the road like maniacs.

At dusk, halfway between Harput and Diarbekr, they came upon the remains of the men. Stripped of their clothes, they had been tied in groups of twenty and shot, their naked bodies rolled into shallow graves, out of which elbows, boots and stumps of limbs protruded. Corpses pocked the landscape: everywhere, hills of dead. The Muslims had taken the Armenians' clothes before killing them, believing that clothes off a dead man were defiled. Other scavengers had their turn, too. Bones littered the landscape, and as evening neared, Garod spotted a pack of wild dogs tiptoeing about the periphery, waiting for their feast.

When the women saw what had become of their men, they cried out. Some ran toward the graves, as though seeing their mates rise up from the dead; these women were hacked by bloodswords the instant their feet left the road.

Garod watched the soldiers grimace as they swung their hatchets or thrust their swords. She looked into the soldiers' faces and saw that they did not even hate their victims. They were poor men. They killed not for hate, but as ordered, spurred by a belief that the man who kills a nonbeliever secures himself a place in Paradise. But if this belief comforted their souls, it did nothing to ease their circumstance. They rode on horseback but had little food, and for both Turk and Armenian the sun was merciless and the blanched desert road interminably long.

The corpses lay scattered for miles, but when at last they were no more, Mayrig turned to her. "Your father was not among them."

Incredulous, Garod stared at her mother. How could she know? Then the girl recalled Hayrig's words that night in her room, when he stood in the dark and told her of his intention to put his fear to use. When his fear proved futile, he would have turned to rage. It was rage that ran through Garod's fingers when she hugged him that last afternoon.

Walking on the road of death, Garod, like her mother, became convinced that Hayrig never made it back to the government building. Either he escaped or died along with the soldier he had once saved. There was no proving this, of course, but it was what Garod believed: Hayrig would never have allowed himself to become food for dogs.

Like him, she would decide her fate. Hayrig had asked her and she would answer: she was no victim. Yet if she were to survive, and Mayrig too, Garod would have to sharpen her fear so it became useful.

That night the women and children huddled in packs by the road as a biting wind seared across the dry, flat land. Mayrig offered Garod her breast and insisted that she suckle. When she refused, Mayrig hissed, "Stop your foolishness, child. There is nothing left. Don't you see? There is no embarrassment."

Garod closed her eyes and, trying not to bite Mayrig's nipple, imagined she was drinking strength. As she drank, Mayrig cradled her in her lap as though she were a baby. By morning, Mayrig's breasts were dry.

The caravan of bleeding, dying women and children, dressed in nightdresses and slippers, made its way across the stony steppe northeast of Aleppo into the desert of Der el Zor. Of more than thirty thousand Armenians in Harput City, only this group of several hundred remained. Subsisting on bits of bread and foul water, they plodded onward, dazed and sickened. Their tongues swelled in their mouths, their feet cracked and bled, their minds ceased to register sensation, except for the body's anguish.

Eight days from home, Mayrig began to sing. The long march had reopened the wounds from her recent childbirth: blood stained the inside of her legs. Mad with pain, she opened her mouth and out poured her agony. She sang hymns and nursery rhymes, her sad voice inciting fear in the hearts of the others, not least because the noise was likely to catch the attention of the Turks.

"Mayrig, stop. Please. Stop," Garod begged, but Mayrig looked at her daughter with glassy eyes, seeing only pain.

A woman with a face like a crow approached them and, unwrapping a filthy orange calico scarf from her head, tied it across Mayrig's mouth, stifling the sound. "There, now," the woman said, "you want to sing, go ahead. But don't make it any worse for the rest of us."

Mayrig stared at the women through tearless eyes. As soon as the woman turned her back, Mayrig kicked her. The woman with the face like a crow spun around, and Mayrig, ripping the kerchief from her mouth, cried, *"Amot Kezi!"* Shame on you!

Mayrig clutched Garod to her. "All of you—shame!" she cried. "Do you think there is one among us who will not die? At least I swear I will kill myself and my daughter, too, before I'll allow us to be victims of the Turks!" Mayrig retied the filthy scarf over her mouth, and taking Garod by the hand she walked on.

It was afternoon when they reached the Euphrates. The river rushed before them, wide as a lake. They padded to the bank and stared at the water. Garod heard the Turks behind them, forming a wall with their clubs and knives, thus sealing off the Armenians' escape. It was jump into the river or turn and be killed.

The women nearest Garod required no coaxing. One after another they leaped into the brown rushing water. One woman, her skin drawn so tightly that her face appeared like a skull, threw the corpse of her dead child, whom she had carried for several days, into the water, and then herself.

Frightened, not knowing how to swim, Garod recoiled. She stepped back from the bank, pulling her mother with her. But Mayrig would not budge. With a fierce strength, she tugged on Garod's hand and returned her to the edge. Yanking the filthy kerchief from her mouth, Mayrig bellowed one final hymn, her eyes squeezed closed.

Garod, her tongue swollen with thirst, stared blindly at the river. She no longer hoped that she might open her eyes and find herself back home, in Harput. She no longer believed in silly dreams. Harput was another life and in its place was this river. She looked into the water and saw the charred remains of Baby Sevan, and the girls strung up by their braids, and the hills of dead men, their bodies picked clean by jackals. She saw the river before her, swollen with corpses. Garod watched the woman with a face like a skull as she tried to swim against the current, and then, exhausted, gave up. The woman floated a ways, a small boat heading out to sea, but at last she rolled over, onto her belly, and her face dipped below the ruddy water, as though she were a gull diving for a fish. Her body began to shake, her arms flailed, her feet clenched, trying to grab hold, but the water was heavy and she was tired; slowly, she sank.

Garod turned to face her mother, who cried, "I am Seta, I am Seta—Seta, Seta!" Over and over, Mayrig declared herself with the name given to her by her father—the sheep herder, the poet—Garod's grandfather.

Mayrig pulled her daughter to her bony hip. "Hold my hand," she demanded.

But Garod was already holding. She squeezed Mayrig's hand, terrified of the mad strength in her mother's grip.

The two stared at the river, one seeing heaven, the other, hell. Their hands vibrated with electricity. "We will count together," Mayrig said. "Ready? Begin. *Meg.*" One.

Garod said nothing, but stared at the murky water.

Mayrig pumped the girl's hand and began again, *"Meg . . . Yergu—"*

"No!" Garod burst.

"Yerek!" Mayrig cried, and as she leaped from the bank, Garod released her hand.

The instant she let go of her mother's hand, Garod imagined she saw Mayrig fly, the orange kerchief rising above the river, like the plume of a bird. Then, down Mayrig fell, into the muddy water.

Garod followed her mother's scarf, the only part of her visible on the surface. The sweeping current spun Mayrig around, spun her around, until finally, the soaked kerchief quivered, as though being tugged at from below. Then it sank and Mayrig, too, under the water.

Garod searched the river for some sign of her mother and when she saw none, she looked overhead at the blanched sky. She was expecting an answer or some last sign, but what she found came as no relief.

A child breaks irregularly, like a cup. Garod neither bellowed nor wept; the part of her that broke went numb. Slowly, she turned from the river, prepared to face the wall of bayonets. But the soldiers had abandoned them there. She could barely see them now, riding away in the distance.

Close by, four women were staring at her. She saw what she thought was judgment in their mad eyes; she had betrayed her mother's last command, and for this they would condemn her. It occurred to her that even among the damned she was outcast: she was the girl who stood by and watched her mother drown.

She walked on alone. Her swollen, broken feet carried her miles farther into the desert of Der el Zor. After two days she was nearly dead, when a French missionary found her and carried her on the back of a mule to an outpost in Syria. She was unconscious, a sack of bones. The old nun with eyes the color of blue marbles fed the child, but for weeks the girl refused to speak. Each night, she would cry out in her sleep, and the nun comforted her by rubbing circles in her back. One night, after the child was calm, the nun asked her name. For a long while the child said nothing, and the nun, believing she had drifted back to sleep, rose to leave, when the girl cried out bitterly, "*Kheght-vadz!*"—It drowned.

She could recall everything, the horrors and the life before, and all of Hayrig's stories. But her name was gone. It occurred to her that the name had disappeared with Mayrig, and in its place there was—*amot.* Shame.

She spent hours curled on the thin cot, obsessing on her loss. She was nine years old and romantic. She believed in fairy tales and evil inflicted by an angry God. It seemed to her that among the worst atrocities she had witnessed, none was more terrible than her own refusal to join her mother. Her punishment was that she must live without the most basic possession—a name. In her heart, she believed that Mayrig had taken her name as punishment. It was *haram,* a mother's curse.

Among the Armenian orphans, the girl found few friends. She was sullen and lonely. Her feet, broken and badly infected, brought on fevers that lasted weeks. In private, the nuns took to calling the girl Cafard, the word in French for melancholy of the soul. One afternoon, as she was working in the orphanage kitchen, she overheard the name and believed that she had been given a gift. That night, at dinner, as the orphans lined up in front of a long white bench to receive their soup, she stood on the bench and proclaimed: "My name is Cafard."

Cafard stayed in the orphanage six years, until she was fifteen. She became like the orphans she had seen outside her father's window: an adolescent in a white muslin frock and ill-fitting shoes. In 1921, after the Great War ended, she was placed on a list of refugees sponsored by the Near East Relief Fund and given passage to the United States. She went over on the Boat, which swam from the Old Country to the new, running heavy in the jejunum, filled with a cargo of immigrants.

Later, she would speak of this ship not so much as a vehicle but as a turning point in time. She and I would drink cups of hot, sugared pekoe tea, and she would point to pictures in a magazine. "Seta-honey, see the red in those curtains? That color is what you call cheap gypsy and you don't ever want to use it in your house. That color—it's nothing like the real red we had back before the Boat."

She rode in steerage for twenty-five dollars. A wool scarf in her hair and thick rough clothes. She slept in the hull that stank of urine and shit. She was afraid of so many things: of the water, which threatened cholera, and the dark rancid hull; she was afraid to go up on deck, where the men looked at her and knew she was alone.

On the day the Boat entered New York harbor, the refugees gathered along the rails; thousands cheered as the huge city seemed to rise before them from out of the sea. A young man watched as she tried to climb onto an air vent to see over the crowd. Taking her by the hand, he led her through the masses to the rail. He stood behind her, the push of the crowd pressing his hips into her behind.

They docked at Ellis Island. Single file, she was led with the others into a cavernous brick building, where she was put in a holding cage, a numbered tag pinned to her coat.

There were five thousand immigrants that day. She heard rumors that a single defect—poor eyesight, bad teeth, insolence—could send them all packing home. She was ashamed of those surrounding her—filthy, flea-infested peasants—their immigrant stench revolting. She was determined to succeed and eyed those nearest her with suspicion, certain they would hold her back. In her heart, she felt no tie to their poverty, desperation and crude manners. She was fifteen, after all, and rich, having in her possession a long black braid and the most beautiful word she knew.

When, at last, it was her turn to stand before the immigration official at his tall wooden desk, she lifted her chin and proclaimed herself Cafard. And it was there, in the Great Hall, that she lost her name a second time. The officer mistook her *f* for an *s*. She began in America as Casard.

Later, while still on Ellis Island, she met up again with the young man from the Boat. His name was Vrej Essayan, an Armenian whose first name meant vengeance. Vrej had come over from Russia. His family had been killed in the massacres in Armenia but he had been lucky: he had escaped across the border to work the farms in Georgia. He was educated and he was wily—eighteen, three years older than she. He seemed sure of himself and successful; she admired his new haircut and clean suit.

Their courtship lasted an afternoon. Vrej wooed Casard with the promise of his employment and for her a white kitchen sink. He had been hired by one of the factory recruiters, who made weekly trips to Ellis Island to enlist the cheap immigrant labor. Vrej would make bearings, ball bearings.

He gave her a picture of himself and knew she was interested when she placed his likeness in her pocket. She might first have studied the image and considered the dullness in his eyes versus the shininess of his shoes. She might have considered many things, but her options were few. She was impressed by both his cleanliness and his assured manner. For his part, he found enchanting the unusual combination of her girlish mouth, with its small, square teeth, and her sultry widow's peak. Yet when Vrej told Casard of her beauty, she, unlike the other girls, neither blushed nor acted coy. Looking him in the eye, she bent down and removed her shoe. She kept her eyes glued on him as his glance fell from her face to her grossly scarred foot.

To her surprise, Vrej's face maintained the same hopeful expression. And so Casard went on to tell him of all that had happened to her—of Harput and the Euphrates River and the desert of Der el Zor—and when he did not run or, worse, try to deny her shame, she agreed to go with him. Putting on her shoe, she said, "So, Mr. Vrej, we will not speak of this anymore."

They were married the following day in New York City and spent their wedding night traveling by train to Memorial, Connecticut, where they took up residence in a tenement on Tremont Street.

Vrej worked six days a week in the factory while Casard took in sewing.

That first year she was often sick. Her feet, permanently damaged, required expensive visits to the doctor. There was a question of circulation that affected Casard's ability to walk. She was often in terrible pain, especially in the afternoon, when her legs and feet would puff up like balloons. Vrej took her to the local doctors, but there was nothing they could do, so he brought her by train to a specialist in Hartford. Casard required surgery and, afterward, custom-fitted orthopedic shoes. It would cost Vrej a month's salary just to pay for the shoes. Casard told him not to bother. But two months later, Vrej came home from work with a box under his arm. He made a big production out of putting the ugly black shoes on her feet and tying the stiff leather laces. His one hope was that when he finished, he would look into his wife's face and find her pleased. Casard wept with joy that afternoon, and they both felt enormously relieved. Now, it seemed, better, happier times were possible.

Holding his wife in his lap, Vrej crooned, "Siroonig," Dear One, and Casard's mind flashed on Mayrig singing to Baby Sevan.

Vrej went on, "Siroonig, one day soon I'll buy you pretty ribbons for these shoes. Beautiful ribbons, eh?"

Casard cried in his arms until her head began to pound. Later, as she nursed her headache, it occurred to her that joy was not so different from sorrow—both made her head ache. She sat at the kitchen table, rubbing her temples with her thumbs, and recalled those nights when the throbbing in her legs was worse and Vrej came home from the poker game to find her in bed, writhing in pain.

Ten years and seven miscarriages later, Casard was able to carry a child to term. She named her daughter Araxie, after the river Hayrig spoke of in his stories. Araxie was a beautiful, spirited child, with round brown eyes, which, her mother could not help noticing, turned the color of muddy water when she was sad or frightened.

On their tenth anniversary Vrej presented Casard with the promised white sink. Casard gave him a fifty-dollar savings bond, which he cashed to pay his debts on the cards and the ponies.

By the tenth year of their marriage, Casard could barely recall the days when she had not been Vrej's wife. She was Casard Essayan: Vrej's wife, Araxie's mother. The early years of her life she left on the Boat. No amount of coaxing from Vrej or Araxie could move her to speak of the events that led her to the banks of the Euphrates River. When others spoke of the 1915 massacre, trying to purge themselves, Casard shook her head and refused to speak, referring to those events as the Indignities.

Her loss was untouchable and omnipresent; the family who grew up around her longed to speak of it and thereby release its painful hold. But Grandma Casard refused. Instead, she hid her torment in a closet of Indignities—a closet of miscarriages, immigrant shame and Vrej's gambling debts.

She hid herself, too. Her family saw a woman invested in Old Country customs and quirky beliefs. Casard would have nothing to do with leftovers or drip-dry: these were modern conveniences, store-bought, lazy. Packages entering her home were scrutinized, and anything fresh-frozen, concentrated or vacuum-packed never found the promised land of her kitchen, where the true labors of brewing, kneading, simmering and jelly-making took place. Her beliefs tended toward the practical, a trumpeting of turquoise bathtubs, white kitchen sinks and moral virtue touted in the phrase "A person's greatest possession is his name, and his honor is keeping it clean."

In her previous life, she once told me, she and her mother, Seta the first, had been birds.

"Birds!" I exclaimed. "Grandma, what kind of birds?"

She shrugged then, picturing her Mayrig flying over the Euphrates River. "What kind? Oh, pretty birds—with big fat wings."

Casard's oldest friend, Poppee Krikorian, understood her best. The two friends saw in each other themselves as young girls, precocious and romantic, though their later lives had turned them into markedly different women. Poppee would freely admit that she had a much easier time of it and so could afford to play the optimist. Months before the Indignities reached Bitlis, Poppee's father moved his family by foot over the mountains into Russia. In Russia, Poppee met and married Alex Krikorian, an engineer fresh from the university, who took his young bride on the Boat to New York, and from there to Memorial, Connecticut, where he joined an uncle in the plumbing business.

Poppee and Casard had tea several afternoons each week, and though the Indignities were always present in their minds, they never talked about them. Instead, they sat across from each other, Poppee the more slender and youthful-looking of the two, and, balancing teacups in their palms, discussed the small, daily heartaches that filled their lives.

One afternoon, while they were having tea at Poppee's Tudor home built with funds from copper piping, Poppee's large gray cat leaped onto the sofa and curled like a fur hat on her mistress's lap. Casard disliked the cat, not least because it made a disgusting habit of carting dead birds into the house and depositing them at Poppee's feet. Casard was in the middle of telling Poppee about some trouble she was having with Araxie when the cat awoke with a start, and, stretching, lazily sunk its teeth into Poppee's hand.

Poppee jumped up, shrieking, while the cat slunk out of the room.

"You've got to get rid of that animal!" Casard gasped in Armenian. Both women stared wide-eyed at the drops of blood rising on Poppee's hand.

But the next visit the animal was back on its throne.

"You know," Poppee said, stroking the cat's thick fur, "I read in the magazine why this pretty one bites."

"Ah?"

"Well, she was taken from her mother when she was just a tiny kitten. You see?" Poppee gave her friend a meaningful look. "The mother, Casard, she never had a chance to finish with her."

Casard stared at her friend, and for an instant her eyes welled with tears. "Ah, pssst," she said, and dismissed Poppee with a wave of her hand.

"Ayo, Ayo," Poppee said, wagging her finger, "it's true, my friend. No matter what, it always comes back to the mother."

By the time Vrej, at forty-eight, suffered a heart attack, making Casard a widow, she had become a pillar in the Armenian community. Her child, Araxie, twenty, was away at college. To fill her time, Casard taught Sunday school and honored her commitments as a charter member of the Armenian Relief Society. She saved her money and paid off the house and bought herself a silver-plate service for twelve. Within the community, Casard enjoyed many admirers—some who feared her, and some, like Poppee, who were her friends, and to whom she was fiercely loyal.

Most significant, Casard had Araxie, her beautiful daughter, whom she counted on to finish school and come quickly home.

But in Casard's heart, she was alone—haunted by an orphan dressed in a white muslin frock and ill-fitting shoes. All her life Casard was mortified and shamed by one little girl who let go of her mother's hand, wanting, instead, to live. No matter what else Casard accomplished, that child held her down. She crossed over on the Boat; the child was waiting for her on Ellis Island. Casard married, had a daughter of her own; still the orphan would not go. Casard believed she suffered privately. She believed that no one really saw her, no one suspected her true thoughts. She had told only Vrej of her shameful betrayal, and he was gone. It never occurred to Casard that Vrej would have told my mother, Araxie. Araxie, Casard thought, knew nothing—as if what lay in the mother's heart could be kept from the daughter.

At night, with the house empty and no one to hear her, Casard's thoughts returned to the Euphrates. She placed herself at the riverbank, and gazed once again upon the bodies of women and children, flotsam in the driving current. She felt the blinding sun like a hot thumb pressing down on her head and the heavy, swollen, raw meat that was her tongue. Opening her eyes wide, she tried to trick herself by saying quickly: My name is . . . but her mind refused to release its secret and only clamped shut. "Why, why," she cried, and pounding her skull with her fists, Casard beat herself until the pain in her head made her forget the pain in her feet and tongue and heart. She crawled into bed and, staring blankly at the curtained window, waited for the sun to rise. As the room filled with light and the aching in her head subsided, she felt newly cleansed and bold. And so she pressed on, torturing herself with the question: If it had been Hayrig at the river, instead of Mayrig, would I have let go?

She began each day with this question, whose essence she neither understood nor cared to analyze. The question itself seemed true enough. That it had to do with degrees of love, and the righteous pull of self-preservation, never entered her mind. Each day Casard believed she was deciding her own worth: Was she a good girl after all, and loyal? Did she at least love Hayrig enough not to betray *him*? Each day she asked and each day she arrived at the conclusion that gave her enough hope to press on: If Hayrig, then yes, into the river. Hayrig I loved enough. But Mayrig I betrayed.

Turning to the birds perched on the sill, Casard saw her mother rise above the river Euphrates, a lovely bird with orange plumage and immense wings. To the birds, far and near, she cried out in a childish voice, "Please, please, won't you give me my name?"

TWO

After Araxie finished college and, as expected, returned home, her mother began to plague her with dire warnings.

"Mind my words, Araxie," Casard said. "Marry an odar, and you'll have misfit children."

Odar was Casard's word for George Loon, Armenian for outsider.

Casard said, "That odar will never be welcome in my house. Araxie! You hear me? I mean trouble."

Araxie heard plenty, morning and night. Days she worked downtown, in the assessor's office, where for eight hours she was free of her mother's oppressive warnings. But at five o'clock, inevitably, Araxie returned home, to where trouble festered all day in a hot kitchen.

One evening, as she rode the bus to her mother's house, Araxie decided to tell Casard that she loved George Loon. Yes, that was it, she had been uncertain of her feelings until that precise moment—as she looked out the window of the bus, and thinking of her mother and thinking of George, she knew: she loved George Loon. Araxie spent the remainder of the trip finding the words with which to break the news to Casard. It would not be easy, of course, and worse was the uncooperative nature of Araxie's mind, which, upon being asked to create a speech, flooded with provocative thoughts of George: his swollen lips after they kissed; his smell, soap and musk; the two of them naked on a white white bed, when finally they would make love. This last, she thought of constantly, deliciously throughout the day, and as the bus approached her stop, Araxie was lost in fantasy. Stepping down from the bus, she resolved, somewhat capriciously, to ad-lib the scene with Casard—the proper words, she trusted, would come.

Araxie walked two short blocks to her mother's yard, where she was greeted by a cacophony of birdsong. The birds, many unheard of this far north, came for Casard, who indulged them, believing they were somehow kin to her dead Mayrig. Araxie knew Casard's story—before he died, Vrej told his daughter of Harput and the Turks and the Euphrates River—but because Casard refused to speak of the Indignities, her daughter likewise held them as a secret, and in Araxie's own heart, she felt shame, condemnation and rage stealthily growing, until she feared one day she might implode.

Araxie approached the house, longing for the day when she would finally leave. At the front porch she hesitated and, gathering her wits, set her foot soundlessly on the stairs. Instantly, her mother's voice rang out, "Ar-a-xie! Araxie!"

Casard was in the kitchen, a starched apron covered her print dress and, of course, she was wearing her black tie shoes. Her long gray-black hair, thick as horsetail, was tied back in a bun, anchored by a pair of tortoiseshell combs.

Casard glanced at her daughter with familiar worry. "There you are," she said, as if settling a troubling question. Araxie was Casard's hope, and each day that hope took its sweet time making the trip from the bus stop to her kitchen.

Casard was in the middle of separating a pair of lamb shanks from the bone; inserting a knife into the tendon, she split the shank. Araxie walked over to the table and kissed her mother's cheek.

"There's my girl," Casard purred. "Now let me look at you." Through thick eyeglasses she peered with utter concentration into Araxie's lovely dark eyes. Casard's face fell slack with worry. "Ah, see? What have I been telling you? You give that office too much. Look now—Miss Exhausted."

"Mayrig—" Araxie protested, stepping back.

"Wash your hands," Casard said.

Araxie sighed and turned to the sink. She was twenty-three, college-educated, and still she was being told to wash her hands. She was beautiful, but what good is beauty when you live at home with your mother? When you return home after eight hours of work and the first thing she notices is that your face looks tired and your hands are dirty?

"No, Mayrig," Araxie said, turning to her mother. "And I won't be eating home tonight, either. George and I are—"

"Ho-ho," Casard puffed angrily, "here we go, ho-ho."

During the last weeks they had fought about George Loon with increasing frequency and passion—so much so that years later Aunt Sue, the jealous, would painstakingly recount their bouts for the benefit of the gossips at church. Who would have thought that such a gawky man as George Loon, an odar, with high cheeks and bony hands, could sweep Casard Essayan's beautiful daughter off her feet? When every man with a mustache and an *i-a-n* at the tail of his name wanted her—wanted her and had waited? Who would have thought Casard Essayan such a fool as to alienate her only daughter, when the two of them had been so close. Oh, it was something Aunt Sue, the jealous, recalled, for Casard's efforts to ban the fair-headed George Loon only made Araxie want him more.

"Mayrig, if you start in on George I'm going upstairs. I love him. You hear me? Love. Him. I want you to understand this." For emphasis, Araxie twisted her finger on an invisible blemish in the table.

Casard slapped the shank of raw meat with her hand. "Love"—she sniffed, shaking her head. "What do you know? Love will have you up all night making him boiled meat. English-no-good-shoe-leather-food."

"I'll cook anything he wants," Araxie replied matter-of-factly, for on the bus she had been thinking just such thoughts.

Casard noticed the color rise in Araxie's cheeks. Casard thought: She is so lovely, but it is a loveliness no one can hold. The odar thinks he can, but I could tell him he is wrong.

"Where," Casard began, using the back of her wrist to wipe her eye, "you tell me, does such love come?"

"From George."

"A Catholic? Don't give me that. In the old school, you marry your kind."

"He's Episcopalian," Araxie corrected, dicing a tomato and putting it to simmer in a pot with string beans and ground meat.

"He's not your kind."

"What's my kind? Huh, Mayrig? Those bores at church? Those apes with hair on their shoulders? They don't want a woman, they want a cook."

"You watch your mouth," Casard said, and picked up the pot on the table and slammed it down on the stove. "You think because he takes you for a ride in his car? You think because he says you're pretty and buys you a rose? I'll buy you twenty roses and you stay home. No. You find yourself a good man, Araxie. And that means good Armenian."

"What's wrong with George?"

"Odar. Plain and simple."

"You don't know him."

"You, I know. Him, I don't bother with."

"What, Mayrig, you condemn the man because he's English?"

"Naw," Casard said, waving her knife. "He could be anything . . . Irish."

"He is *not* Irish," Araxie declared. "He never touches a drop."

"Araxie! Listen to me. This man comes from nowhere. Where's his family, where's his job? Where's respect, the man is afraid to look a person in the eye."

"You never even let him in the house!"

Casard waved her hand. "Shifty eyes, I tell you."

"Shifty, nothing," Araxie said. "His eyes say he loves me." There it was again, that word. Araxie invited it into the house as though it were a salty seashore breeze. Love: curling the rim of her mouth. Love: billowing her blue-black hair.

Mother and daughter faced each other, breathing. They were as opposite as two people who are the same can be. They agreed on nothing, but arguing revealed mirroring gestures: a passionate hand chopping the air into shards, fingers pinching an earlobe in self-conscious defeat. Their battle raged, a battle neither could win. Its cycles, like the tides, were seemingly governed by a distant moon—and always to their amazement.

And their breath. It smelled the same, a combination of lamb, pekoe tea, mint and bananas. It mattered not the men they were with, or the children, or how high in the community they might scale. They had the same breath. As a young girl Araxie watched Casard apply her makeup and experienced the odd sensation of her mother's methods and intentions, and yes, the ghosts of the Euphrates, too, planting themselves like a pair of lips on Araxie's white bones. In such moments, it was possible for mother and daughter to find communion and ease, with themselves and each other. The knowledge between them, held rightly, was vast; it extended to children, and women friends and, especially, men. But since George Loon, Araxie and Casard forgot about the essential truths they shared. They forgot, and for the remainder of Casard's life they grew apart, day by day, and had to learn all over again how much they meant to each other in the first place, how close they were; each day they felt the binding inside them tear, painful and fresh as a cut.

Casard sniffed. "There she goes with the lovey-dovey. His eyes say, his eyes say. Honey, his eyes say I'll stuff her with pale, weepy half-breed children. His eyes say I'll take your precious Araxie away, and never let her come home. His eyes say your little girl, she'll never be the same: never go to her church, never be with her family. She'll no more eat her mother's food!"

"Mayrig, stop!"

"Ahhh—" Casard groaned, disgusted, trapped. She looked about the kitchen and, finding the empty pot on the stove, tossed in the lamb shanks; the pot skidded off the burner and crashed onto the floor. Satisfied, Casard turned on her heel and left the room. "His eyes—I'll tell you. His eyes say Good-bye."

Araxie shouted up the stairs after her, "Mayrig, don't you start in with good-byes."

"That's right," Casard cried from the landing, "that's right, no Mr. Good-bye."

The lovers were forced to sneak. On Saturday Araxie left the house, her mother's condemnation a crude black purse strung across her heart. She despised the things Casard said, not so much because they were lies, but because they were lies that contained enough damning truth to plant doubt in Araxie's mind.

Miserable, Araxie walked several blocks to where George Loon waited in the front seat of his cream-colored Chevy. Araxie lifted the hem of her skirt and climbed into the car, accepting George's earnest kiss and a cluster of purple iris. She nodded with practiced pleasure at the picnic basket and tartan blanket he had stowed in the backseat. And gazing at the man, she loved, seeing only what she wished to see, she said to herself: Mayrig doesn't know, Mayrig has no idea what it feels like to be a real woman.

George, eager to begin their day, started the motor and was about to pull from the curb when he noticed that Araxie was staring at him with such lustful intention, he could only answer her with a foolish half-cocked grin. They had agreed to wait until after their engagement, but here it was ten o'clock in the morning and Araxie was making it plain that all bets were off.

George's mind raced with confusion, his heart a paddling dog. He pulled Araxie to him and kissed her. She clung to him and he realized she was crying. Gazing at him through tears, she said bitterly, "I hate her."

George thought he understood. He gentled Araxie's face to his chest. "What did your mother say, Roxie. What now? Do you want to tell me?"

Araxie sniffled and George ran his fingers through her hair, soothing her as one might an animal. She closed her eyes and submitted, letting him stroke her head as tears spilled down her cheeks. When she had cried enough, she sat up. Biting his neck, then kissing it primly, she turned solemnly and faced the windshield.

George understood this as permission to get going, and tucking Araxie close beside him, he turned the car into the street. For a few blocks the lovers rode on, side by side, a single tensile unit, their hips touching, their eyes locked on all that was passing beyond the hood.

But as they neared downtown, Araxie became restive. She slid her hand between his thighs and said, "George, can't you hurry?"

George gunned the Chevy while Araxie, her head tipped back against the seat, contemplated the roof of the car. Another couple of miles and they reached the outskirts of town, and a few miles farther, they turned onto a dirt meadow road. At a sheltered spot behind a chipped green shack, George parked and, taking Araxie in his arms, kissed her. After a few moments there was unspoken agreement that they should get out of the car. At the same time, they both reached for the picnic items in the backseat and knocked heads, making them pant with nervous laughter. George climbed out of the car with the goods and spread out the blanket while Araxie removed her shoes and stockings.

Directly, she started to dance. At first it looked to George like a bit of stretching, but then she really got going. In the dirt, her bare feet kicking and gliding, her pointed toes. George reclined on the blanket and watched, mesmerized. She is amazing, he thought,

Look at her go. I should be scared half out of my wits, but I'm not. No, I'm not.

Araxie bent and curved her body, daring him. Her expression seemed to suggest, Are you big enough? Are you a man? He held her with his eyes and then, all of a sudden, he started to laugh, loudly, crazily, the way a man does as he is about to lose his soul.

Hers was a mating dance and now that she had begun, Araxie took her time. George lay on his back, his hands tucked under his head and all of him vibrating. When he was ripe, so ripe he might burst, George unbuttoned the top of his trousers. Araxie, spinning and gyrating, had her eye on that buttonhole, and when it opened slowly she began to descend, grinding her way down, until she was astride George Loon, riding him like a seesaw, the sharp board straddled between her thighs.

They began slowly, then faster. He cupped her hips as she raised her arms above her head like the wings of victory. She set her eyes on him and leaning her palms on his chest, her blue-black hair hanging between them like a velvet curtain, she peered with wonderment into his happy, happy face. Stricken, she thought, Oh, not yet! and thrust her hips, demanding more.

She looks like an animal, he thought. Here, I'll give it to her: Here, animal with a ferocious appetite.

Araxie tossed her head, revealing a long white throat, and her muscles squeezed him. They both cried out, her voice shrill and voluminous—Oh, George, farther far-ther far-ther!

The day Araxie and George became lovers, Casard developed a pain. The pain began under her ribs, crept up her spine and webbed across her shoulder.

Casard told Poppee, her oldest friend, "The end, here it comes, Poppee. No fooling. Right"—she pressed her heart—"here."

Poppee consoled Casard with tea and advice. "What you've got there is separation pains," she said, "Children indigestion. Ev-rything they got to do themselves. But you wait and see, this business with Araxie: just a passing fancy."

Poppee consoled her friend, but at night she stared at the light fixture above her bed, and, crossing herself, gave thanks that at least her girls were not taking up with odars.

The pain moved to Casard's belly; she began having trouble digesting food. At night she dreamed of a black shape, and when she awakened she imagined the black shape, like a rat, darting across her floor. She believed she was witnessing a manifestation of the dark future, and she promised herself that whatever the price, she would not allow Araxie to marry misery. Casard held this truth like soot on her tongue; every time she spoke, hot ashes fell from her mouth.

"What happens—after?" Casard asked.

"After? After what?" Araxie cried.

"After he gets tired of you and there is nothing, no history, holding you together. What happens the day you look out the window and see his back going down the drive?"

Araxie's eyes burned. "Witch! *Dzour!* You want to curse us. And why? Because you don't have—"

"Oh, is that it?"

"Yes."

"Missy wise guy, you think you'll know forever with a man? Ho-ho"—Casard shook her finger—"forever you only got with your Mayrig."

"I can't talk to you. Who can talk to you?"

"That's right. Go to your room and think about it. What's gonna bind you, Araxie? I don't mean now, but in five years. You think a house? You think children? You think a man ever stayed around for children?"

"Oh, Mayrig," Araxie said, her face lit with a nasty smile, her eyes burning. "We'll always have *you.*"

Casard's protests made all other obstacles seem small. The lovers had no privacy, it did not matter. They developed circuitous routes for lunch dates in the meadows and evening rendezvous at the all-male boardinghouse, where they held palms over each other's mouth and made silent love on George's narrow Murphy bed. Afterward, they mapped out their future. They had no money, but they were rich with plans. George was going to be a real estate broker. He needed just one sale, and then he would buy the ring. With the ring, they would announce their intentions to Casard.

But first, he had to sell a house.

The first Saturday they gave up the meadow Araxie spent the afternoon in George's cramped office, helping him with the paperwork and files. She went over his listings, supplying him with tips she had picked up from her work in the assessor's office. Afterward, they put on the radio and made love on the floor. The next Saturday and every Saturday for a month, they funneled their passion into George's business. George built large promotional signs, which Araxie painted with bold black and yellow letters. Stowing the placards in the Chevy's trunk, they drove around town tacking them to the sides of empty warehouses and foreclosures: BUYING OR LEASING SOON? CALL YOUR HONEST REALTOR, GEORGE LOON.

"What kind of man has no trade?" Casard asked. "You call selling people's homes a trade? The odar lacks dignity. He's a flimflam."

Casard took the pain in her belly to the source of comfort, Stop & Shop. There she met Poppee and the other ladies of the Armenian Relief Society who gathered every morning to shop and visit.

"Loon," the women remarked, as if eyeing a new kind of mushroom, "what kind of a name is that?"

The ladies never openly objected to George Loon—Casard's pride prevented them from being so direct. Instead, they gathered about her and, clucking their tongues, sent Casard home with eggplant, bell pepper and conviction. Casard carted the women's sympathy home to her kitchen, where all day it festered, turning color.

At half past five Araxie climbed the porch stairs. Her mother was waiting for her. Araxie went straight up to her room without saying hello. Casard approached the landing and, blinking into the stairwell, refrained from calling until she heard Araxie's shoes hit the closet floor.

"Ar-a-xie, Araxie," Casard called. "Come down, I have news."

Slowly, reluctantly, Araxie descended the stairs in her housedress and slippers. "Mayrig? What is it?"

"Poppee tells me the odar is selling Myra Cooper's house. Poppee says, they don't even have Myra in the ground yet, God rest her soul. Tell me, what kind of man's this, Mr. Chasing-After-Hearses?"

Myra Cooper's death sealed the lovers' destiny. Two months after Casard spoke the dying woman's name, George drove Araxie to the widow's house. The sign they had made was planted in the center of the lawn. But Araxie's black and yellow letters had been covered by a new banner, one she had never seen before. It said SOLD.

There, on Myra Cooper's lawn, George Loon proposed.

When Casard heard the news, she withdrew. She locked herself in her room and stayed there, all that day and well into the night. Araxie found her mother in the darkened room, curled like a tendril in her chair.

Casard peered at her daughter swaying like some fool whimsy in the doorway, the small diamond on her finger. Casard had been sitting in the dark when Araxie appeared before her in a vision, surrounded by blond-haired children. But that was not the worst. The worst was that the odar had won, and in her mind it became another victory for the Turks.

Araxie rocked on her toes hypnotically. "Mayrig?" she asked. And when her mother failed to answer, she fumbled for the light switch. "Mayrig?"

"Leave the light alone, Missy. Go on now, to your room."

"Mayrig, please."

"Go on. Don't you worry, in the morning Mayrig gives all happy smiles. Tonight? Tonight she sits and tries it on."

"Will you be all right?"

"All right? All right? Listen to her. Now she's the mother? Go on, go on. Back to bed. Go make moons in your sleep, Little Mother." Casard lifted her chin and gave her daughter a limp halfhearted wave.

But Araxie was not yet ready to leave, the light from the hall seeping through her nightgown like the future. "Mayrig, tonight everything feels so new."

"New?" Casard said, noticing her daughter's graceful silhouette. The small waist and shapely legs, the way she leaned her body against the doorframe, trusting it to hold. Casard thought, I was young once, too. Then I watched the girls swing from their braids, I crawled through the desert on my knees, I stood with my own mother at the river, and refused. For what? For Vrej, for Mr. Smile? Mr. Big Teaser? Off he goes and dies. But you, you were my new hope, my shiny new girl. You stand there, some angel with your big pearly wings. How come I never taught you not to leave me.

"Say good night, Mayrig. Please, say good night."

"So-and-so good night."

Araxie sighed and pulled the door closed.

Casard sat for hours in that chair, cursing George Loon with the filthiest words she could think of: first in Turkish, then in English. She cursed him with an American word she knew nothing about, except that it was ugly and evil, what the hoodlums called the pretty girls, shaming them, as they passed by. "Pussy," she said, under her breath, then louder—"Pussy. Pussy"—until she was vaguely satisfied.

As the night passed she felt herself approaching the end. "So this is how it is," she said, not without wonder. The wait since the river had been so long. Her body ached, the veins in her legs and feet swelled. And here it was, her second choice—a bird carries two lives—she must decide, yes or no.

Casard tasted possibility in her mouth. If she died that night, if she willed it so, in three days there would be the Der Hyre priest, the incense and the mahogany casket surrounded by candles and wreaths. The inside of the church would smell old holy. She imagined Araxie's face as they sealed the lid, but inside, she realized, the coffin was totally dark. How was she going to breathe?

By dawn she had decided; she would turn her hand to the odar's children. "Medz-Mayrig," she said, liking the sound. "Medz-Mayrig." Grandmother.

THREE

They lived with Casard for three years and saved their money. These were mostly good, honeymoon years, and if George and Araxie fought, it almost always had to do with Casard.

She was a sharp, ineluctable presence in their lives: a crash in the basement, a thundering of drawers, assiduous hands in the kitchen chopping nuts. She was as abrupt and elemental as wind or cold and they did not think much of her except as a force to push against. In short order, mother and daughter had become of different worlds, Araxie with George, Araxie at work, while Casard remained entirely of the church and the house. George and Araxie could not enter the house without finding Casard on her knees scouring the bathroom floor, swabbing the cavity of a chicken, plucking sheets from the line, or touching a finger of spit to the iron. She was of the house and the house was hers, and when Araxie insisted on doing her own husband's wash, Casard bellowed that she could just go and break her own washer. They fought then, until for the sake of peace Araxie relented, and for the first three years of the marriage, Araxie remained like a child in her mother's house, her mother folding George's underwear and placing it in his drawer.

Truth be told, Casard doted. On the nights George worked late or stopped to have a drink with his cronies, Casard insisted that they wait dinner. She sat in the living room chair nearest the window, and when, from down the street, she heard the Chevy approach, she rose to her feet.

"That's him. Come on, Araxie, here he is." Casard cleaned George's toilet, cooked and served his meals, but there were two things she would not do: look the odar in the eye or acknowledge him by name.

She launched into the dining room, snapping the foil tents from the serving plates, while Araxie went to the door to greet her husband.

Casard heard the couple whispering in the foyer. "Araxie, leave him be, will you? Come in here. Can't he wash his hands by himself? Are you coming? Look, I'm passing the roast. Does he want peppers?"

"Peppers are fine," George murmured as he kissed Araxie. Removing his tie and jacket, he washed his hands, then brought his wife to the dining room.

Casard was seated at the head of the table. George tucked Araxie in on Casard's right and, giving his mother-in-law a perfunctory kiss on the cheek, assumed his place on her left. Casard refused to meet George's smile, but she did manage to raise her brows; on the nights he met with his cronies, George brought home a certain man-of-the-world excitement, to which Casard was not immune.

"So-and-so," she said, nudging the platter with the roast nearer to his plate.

"Looks good," George smiled, allowing both women to serve him. "Hey, let me tell you what I just heard about those Cassenetti brothers."

Casard and Araxie passed the mealtime listening to another of

George's developer stories, which increasingly bored Araxie but delighted her mother, who listened intently to George's gossip, her eyes pinned to his throat.

Later, in bed, Araxie anointed the spot where her mother had fixed her stare. "Here," she frowned, playing the worried nurse, and touching her lips to George's throat, she made a line of kisses that ended below the sheets. "Now, Mr. What's-your-name," she purred, "tell me, is that better?"

Araxie was not unhappy then. Marriage, at least in the beginning, reminded her of the joyous summer in Europe she spent with her best friend, Archie Hagopian. Archie, older by a month, was the maternal one, with an easy laugh and the shiny face of an exuberant washerwoman. The two girls first became close in the ninth grade, when having a woman's body and a girlish mind made them seem exactly alike. They fell for the same blond boy, who, upon choosing neither girl, made the fatal mistake of telling Archie that she was the kind of girl a guy wanted to marry, while Araxie was the kind he wanted to hump. Archie laughed at the boy, and from that day on the girls were inseparable, finding relief in each other's temperament. Araxie, the moodier of the two, escaped the rigidity of her mother's house by spending long afternoons curled on Archie's bed, talking dreamily of a grand life, in which a faceless man in a blue suit and black car figured prominently. Archie, amused by such talk but far too practical to give it much credence, pledged her high school years to finding herself a good Armenian husband and watching out for her sensitive, sassy-assed friend.

When both girls turned eighteen without proper Armenian beaux, they went, at their families' urgings, to junior college, and worked nights as waitresses to save for a graduation trip to Europe. Following commencement, they spent two weeks in France, and when they reached Paris, Araxie knew she had been there before. She had shopped at the butcher's, the horse's head hanging from a wrought-iron hook; she had smelled the café filtre in the bistros, and the pains au chocolat hot from the ovens at four o'clock in the afternoon. Suddenly, she felt confident, as though all her life she had been waiting for the answer to a mysterious question that would bring her home, and the streets, the stone cathedrals, the tiny pebbled walks and crimson geraniums of the Jardin du Luxembourg blended together as a welcoming chorus of Yes, Yes, Yes.

Marriage, at least in the beginning, was filled with the same sweet familiarity and approval, and whenever Araxie had doubts she sought assurance from Archie, who had married Sevan Hagopian two years earlier and already had a baby boy.

"Archie, you still in love with Sevan, after all?" Araxie asked.

They were sitting at Archie's kitchen table, stealing a cup of coffee while upstairs the baby dozed. Archie eyed her friend with exhaustion. "Honey, these first six months with the baby, I haven't had a spark of interest, at least not like you're talking. It's Baby Baby Baby Baby Baby Baby, then Husband, then me. Since the baby started teething, I haven't had more than three hours' sleep a night. Who knows what I feel. Pinch me, I won't feel it." Chuckling, she pointed at her enormous breasts. "I suppose I seem to you as dumb and thick as a Jersey cow."

Archie expected her friend to laugh with her, but when she looked over at Araxie she saw disgust and terror pass across her face. "Oh, Roxie-girl. You and George still got the honeymoon, and that's nice, awful nice, but, girl, eventually things change. They, well, die down a bit. But do I love Sevan? Why, sure."

Araxie made up her mind she was not having any change. That night she made love to George twice, and in the morning she awoke in his arms, their legs entwined, the smell of their sex filling the room. They had gone through a little ceremony and the world had decreed that it was all right for Araxie to lie down with a man. She had not changed, the world had, and by the morning light, the world's good graces struck her as arbitrary and fleeting.

Araxie continued to work in the assessor's office, where she was something of an anomaly in the world of pest reports, maps, property taxes and deeds. In her lilac sweater and cream silk scarf she held court behind the thick oak counter that separated the city employees from the buyers and sellers of Memorial's commercial property and homes. It might as well have been a counter at the butcher's or dry cleaner's, though here the currency was reports done in triplicate, paperwork of every sort, requests for geological surveys, termite inspections, estimates from the office of the assessor. Mrs. Loon leaned across that thick slab of polished oak, on one end a swinging door, on the other a smoked-glass partition. Behind her were five oak desks and a wall of beige file cabinets; before her, buyers and sellers. It was across that counter she had first set eyes on George Loon, there in the world of men.

He had approached with a smile, polite, friendly, curious, asking for nothing. She found herself curious too. When later they became engaged, the men on both sides smacked themselves. "Christ Almighty," they bellowed, "I could have shown her my dandy socks, that's all it took."

Araxie had the gift of making every man feel understood. She leaned across that counter, her lovely, sad face a radiant moon over high-shelved breasts; her lilac sweater was pulled snug about her hips, as if the maker had knitted those curves into the fabric. Without a smile or hint of coquettish charm, she sighed and asked, "Guy?" as Guy Larouche stepped forward and sheepishly handed over a thick folder of documents typed up in triplicate, then watched as Araxie Loon wet her finger and thumbed quickly through them.

She stopped. "What are we going to do?" she asked, pointing to a missing page in the contractor's pest report. She sighed, her brow a spliced row. It should have been a crime, her frowning. It was too painful to see. Guy Larouche looked instead at the papers.

"Guy?"—she breathed sweet, warm air onto his hand. "How bad is it?"

He cleared his throat and, looking down at his hands, said, "Ten thousand, dammit, and that's just dry rot."

She nodded empathetically, her eyes mud-brown pools. "Guy, how about you make some calls and get someone to go over there and give you a new bid. Maybe it's not so bad, huh? I'm sure it isn't so bad. Make the call, Guy, then come back and see me tomorrow."

Of course she would not linger over the fact that he had tried to deceive her; Araxie, weak herself, understood. Her sad eyes absorbed the failures the men wished no one to see—with her they were safe, for she would not judge. Of judgment Araxie Loon was incapable.

On the ride down in the elevator, four floors from the assessor, and later over coffee at Lilly's, the men compared notes. The developers especially had it bad, they were the ones who obsessed. Shiny-eyed, like boys, they glanced into one another's faces. "What is it?" they wondered. "I mean, did you see her? Did you get a look? Jesus H. Christ. Now, there's a . . . woman. Whew. You have to ask yourself—Christsakes, why can't someone put that in a bottle and sell it to my wife?"

She addressed them all by name, but they meant nothing to her. They called her Mrs. Loon, though on the ride down in the elevator she was Araxie, the first syllable of her name sounding prim and the last two hard and suggestive as their dreams. Ar—*rax-ie.*

She knew they talked about her, and though she never let on, their attention had the effect of making her feel exposed. The men who frequented the assessor's office were not the first to assume that a gorgeous woman always knows what it is about her they find so irresistible. The truth was that most days Arxie felt rather plain, and more than once she found herself staring at her reflection in the ladies'-room mirror, wondering what the men saw. Their crushes and advances she bore with grace, and they did not hate her for choosing one from their side of the counter to marry and another from behind it as her friend.

Sal Green was the least likely companion, but for just that reason he was the most obvious choice. Araxie chose him the way a popular, pretty girl will sometimes seek friendship with a homely man. He is so far beneath her, he makes no assumptions, he presses upon her no plans. She can be herself; she can think, We are just two nice people.

Their friendship began the morning Sal Green, wearing his

customary beige shirt, brown knit slacks and brown striped tie, appeared at Araxie's desk. She looked up into his mottled, droopy sad-dog face and felt immediately at ease. Since that morning they shared assignments and gossip, and on the afternoons Araxie wanted to knock off early Sal covered for her. No one assumed anything funny, least of all Sal. Araxie was George's every night, no mistaking, but every morning she was back behind the counter, fresh as though she had spent the night under glass.

"Hey, kitten," Sal said, rapping his knuckles on Araxie's desk, "you meeting the big man for lunch?"

Looking up from her paperwork, Araxie proffered a sweet, miserable smile; nine o'clock in the morning, she was breathing like a souped-up engine. "No, Sal," she said, "not today."

"Then what do you say, noontime we get out of here and not speak of this place and you can look plain and I'll look handsome and no one will think a thing."

Araxie suggested they pick up a meatball grinder and walk over to the benches near the statue of Squaw. As they ate, people strolled by the central square and Araxie made clownish faces that broke Sal up. In the presence of her one male friend, everything struck Araxie as outlandish and spontaneous, and through her eyes Sal could see it that way, too—all of life a chancy throw.

"Except George Loon," Sal said, talking as he chewed. "The first day he came in, I said that's it, he's the one—exactly because he doesn't look like the one. See, on the surface you got just a nice, conservative guy, but what you don't know, what you'd never expect, is that this guy sees himself behind the wheel of a goddamn Ferrari. Excuse me, kitten, but it's true. Nice guy, nothing shady, he just knows what he wants and he gets it. I said to myself that's it: those two—like gas and matches."

Araxie gave her friend a peevish look. "Come on, Sal, you never said such a thing. You never predicted I'd marry George. No one did—" She dropped her chin. "Not even me."

Sal stopped chewing long enough for a curious smile to lift the corners of his mouth. "So what are you telling me, Araxie Loon, you don't believe in fate?" He fixed his droopy eyes on her.

"Oh, Sal," she demurred, inserting a finger into her half-eaten sandwich, rearranging its parts. Sal's quick intensity made her feel pressed upon, vulnerable. She furrowed her brow, trying to find the correct words with which to keep him at bay. All of a sudden, she discovered she was on the edge of tears, overcome by a sudden, wrenching grief. She puffed out her cheeks. "Oh, Sal, I don't know. Don't push, OK?"

"OK, kitten. Next subject," he said, trying to sound upbeat. "But if you really want to know, all this destiny crap comes down to brown pants and brown tie." Sal beamed broadly as Araxie glanced at his outfit. "No foolin'. When I was maybe sixteen, it came to me that I was meant to be the guy who wears the brown pants and the ugly tie. Look around you, there's always one. It's the job destiny puts on me and it gives me peace just to accept. Let the other guy hold up the flashy suit."

As Sal spoke, he kept an eye on Araxie, hoping not to have caused her any harm. His vigilance had the effect of making her feel worse—guilty, as though she had somehow, inadvertently, confessed her most private doubts. Specifically, she felt as though she had betrayed George, though she had no idea how or why.

"Oh, Sal, how can you think there's some great plan? It just goes how it goes. You think the terrible things in this world—fires, murders, earthquakes—are planned? Come on, they're random, and we're random, too. Everyone just goes about doing his thing, hoping for the best."

Her brow furrowed as she tried to put her feeling into words. "There's the part of life we know, Sal, having lived it, and then we spend the rest of our lives trying to cope with the decisions we've already made. Inside we're always the same people, Sal, always hoping for, I don't know, something . . . new. But there's nothing new, is there? Really, there's just different ways of looking at the same thing. As for fate, I suppose it's making the best of it—and, learning to accept." Her eyes filled with tears, she turned to her friend—"You know what I mean?"

Sal gave a pained smile. "Sure, kitten, why not?"

Araxie went home that day depressed. The exchange with Sal had left her shaken. Sal, she knew, was jealous and therefore disliked George. Still, she found herself investing Sal with some grave insight that would bear out in her life with George. After dinner, she phoned Archie, but Archie's husband, Sevan, answered and said she was busy with the baby and could not talk.

Araxie drew a hot bath and lay in the tub a long while, her eyes fixed on the turquoise tiles. She imagined another man, one she had never met. Later, she climbed into bed beside George, longing for someone with whom to share her feelings. George was lying on his side in a fetal position, fast asleep. She felt guilty about waking him, so she spooned him from behind and, kissing the back of his neck, reached between his legs and stroked his balls. He stirred, kissed the air and, tucking her hand inside his armpit, fell fast asleep.

In the morning she awoke early and watched her husband doze, the red-blond hair on his cheek. She considered him as though he were an abstraction, a curious book or cup. She thought about him in English, and then in Armenian. She had never known another man so intimately; the closest had been her father. She recalled Vrej's voice, his smell and, before he died, a cough in the middle of the night when he came home from the cards.

But this man in her bed, this man she chose. Watching him sleep, she wondered what about him she had liked. Would he amount to anything? Would he make a mark or, as so many others, be lost in the crowd? She was amazed by her thoughts, but oddly comforted, too. She and George were supposed to be one, but the morning light exposed their differences—George's skin tone was pink, hers was olive. As he slept she gave him cancer and affairs, riches and bankruptcy. She kissed him awake after dreaming he had been crushed.

• • •

At breakfast George twisted the string of his teabag around the stem of a spoon. He cut his eggs in three strokes, then covered them first with salt, followed by pepper.

"Do you ever try it another way?" Araxie asked.

In the bathroom she heard him peeing, on and on like a horse. How could he hold so much? When he was done in the bathroom, he came into the bedroom to dress. Shirt, slacks, belt, tie, socks, then, at the end of the procession, he addressed his shoes with a deliberateness and total concentration she found unbearable. She felt compelled to induce havoc: "Oh, not the blue socks, George. Definitely the brown." She studied him as he bowed his head and pulled the brown socks from the drawer. There must, she told herself, have been something more.

In marriage, he had become painfully correct; in the morning, in bed, he checked his beard before kissing her. She wished for him to maul her with a sandpaper cheek, she wished he would make love to her whispering filthy words. At the breakfast table he read the paper front to back, sucking up detail as though through a straw, while she saw in a glance everything she cared to know. Any knowledge she truly valued was instinctive, residing just below her ribs. Araxie was constantly having to formulate in her mind what she already knew in her belly. The process was one of hauling buckets up from a well. Her struggle, then, was to put her thoughts and intuition into words, while George measured and pronounced, then studied her face to see what he felt.

They were married two years when Araxie told George that he was about to have financial success.

Smiling, he studied her face. "Gee, Roxie, I hope you're right. I promise I'll keep working hard."

"No, George," she said. "It's already here. All you have to do is take it."

She had sensed the momentum gathering on the other side of the assessor's counter: a new crop of developers was about to capitalize on Memorial's sudden growth. When Hartford's insurance companies expanded, their newly hired executives looked to

Memorial for their suburban homes. The executives wanted houses that were new, sparkling new, and as Araxie predicted, developments soon sprang up to meet the demand. Along Memorial's edges, the young developers trucked in tons of topsoil, fashioning hills and sweeping vistas where previously there had been swamp and scrub.

The homes built on this land were unimaginative: small-windowed Colonials on quarter-acre lots, with cheap brass sconces, cement walks, two-car garages and short asphalt drives. Araxie foresaw that money was to be made on such houses, and if George was smart and if she helped him, cash would pour into their hands.

It was her idea that he take breakfast Tuesdays and Thursdays at Lilly's, where the young players ate their eggs and cut their deals. At Lilly's, George renewed his acquaintance with Angelo Cassenetti, a friend from high school. Angelo was a comer, with deep pockets from his father's contracting business. George bet on Angelo as the man on the inside track.

The following spring the Cassenetti brothers put in twenty homes in less than six months and George had his part, selling. Each day, at dusk, he collected Araxie from the front of City Hall and told her all about his day. He was flushed and brimming with success—five homes sold in a single week. And she was proud of him. They drove back to Casard's, Araxie's hand wedged between his thighs.

After dinner Casard adjourned to her chair in the living room, and if George did not have to show houses, he and Araxie climbed back into the car.

Although married, they still felt a certain illicit spark when driving in the car. They had given up the meadow the day they acquired the bed, so it was not sex they were after on those evening rides but the satisfaction of a newer appetite: they drove through Memorial looking for their dream house.

George steered the Chevy through the new developments. "Factories," Araxie groused. "Houses with no souls."

They coasted west toward the reservoir, where new ranch-style homes were as common as molehills in the once empty fields, then down Shuttle Meadow Avenue, past the old-money estates, the Tudors and brick Federals that rimmed the golf course.

"George," Araxie begged, unrolling the window. "Now go slow."

They drove several blocks and then Araxie asked George to pull over to the curb.

"See that door." She pointed—"Look there. What do you think of that color?"

George studied first the glossy red door, and then the intensity on Araxie's face. "The door is nice, Roxie."

"Our house—" she said, "will have a portico for people to pass under, out of the rain, and a fan window and sidelights around the front door."

George could not himself see the need for such a grand entrance, but not wanting to disappoint her, he nodded.

They drove on, stopping once or twice to discuss the merits of certain homes. In this way they fashioned their perfect house, a composite of parts taken from there and there, for no one house ever came close to the dream.

They were on their way back to Casard's when George said, "Roxie, you know I get a kick out of seeing you so excited. But sometimes, honey, I worry that any home in our price range will be a terrible disappointment."

Araxie sighed and glanced out the window—for her the dream was what mattered.

George could not see Araxie's dream. For him, it was enough to witness her joy and manage the steady accumulation of funds in the bank. He could feel good about that. He could even feel good about the years spent living with Casard. Those years were about building. But George was a realist, and what he could not reconcile himself to was a future he imagined just beyond the headlights, a future where he and Araxie would have to compromise compromise compromise and Araxie, being such a dreamer, would wind up disappointed. George wanted no part of that. If only he could get Araxie to understand that steady growth was what they were after, then all the compromises would not necessarily have to bring them grief. Driving along, George turned to his wife to explain, but when he saw the expression on her face, he lost heart. Araxie was staring out the window—little match girl—her face full of longing, as they drove by the illuminated windows of Country Club row.

In the fall George took on an assistant, a Miss Katherly Dogherty, an Irish girl with a red-blond twist, to help with the paperwork and phones. George's office, in the Strand Building downtown, was a plain room with two brown desks. When he was out on calls, which was most of the time, the office became the domain of young Katherly Dogherty, who oversaw the twin windows, desks, wastebaskets, phones, the pale yellow walls, the worn pile carpet—not green, not brown.

"Real estate office," Miss Dogherty enunciated into the receiver she cradled between her chin and shoulder. She tapped a pencil on a thick white pad, her palm resting flat on the desk, as if any minute she might push off and rise. But rise she would not. For another thirty-five years she would be the voice of George Loon, taking down the messages of buyers and sellers, her red-blond hair first in a twist, then cropped short.

Katherly spoke into the telephone while gazing out the window, as if that were where she found her words. "No. No, I'm afraid he won't be back until *much* later. Yes. Yes. That's right. Oh that would be terrific. Oh, yes. Terrific. I'll see your message is the first thing. Oh yes, he'll get right back."

It was a mild flirtation, the kind that happens in the best of marriages, and if managed carefully, no damage is done. One evening George returned home late, a loaf of orange cake tucked under his arm.

"From Katherly," he told the women. "She's just terrific, isn't she? I stopped by the office tonight and there she was—can you imagine—reorganizing the files!"

The women stared at him. He had brought the assistant's word, *terrific,* into their house. Casard raised her eyebrow, the cake sitting like a bomb on the counter.

"Never mind," Araxie said, and whisked the loaf to the top of the refrigerator, where it stayed for weeks. By the time it turned hard as stone, Araxie had paid a visit to Katherly Dogherty and bought her a "ladies' lunch." Afterward, Araxie dropped the assistant at George's office and collected her husband for an afternoon drive to the meadows. In the backseat she had stowed the picnic basket and the tartan blanket, and when they reached the fields they climbed out of the car. There, in the dirt, with bulldozers and carpenters just over the rise behind a glade of willow trees, they conceived their first child.

They moved into their own house the following May, during a terrible heat wave. Araxie, seven months pregnant with Van, resigned from the assessor's office and devoted herself to settling in. The house they had purchased was practical, far removed from the dream. It was the model home in a development where George had exclusive listings. He could tell his customers that he himself lived down the street. His was the four-bedroom Colonial on the corner, brown shingles, white trim, glossy black shutters and a door painted to appease Araxie's whim: Ferrari red.

The house was a mile and a quarter from Casard's—a mile and a quarter, the measure of their freedom. On the day they moved, Casard stayed in her room, coming out only to warn the movers that what they scratched they would pay for.

After George and Araxie were settled in the new house, Casard came over to inspect the kitchen. Looking about, she pursed her lips. "Well, it's a little dark—you'll need a bigger light, won't you. Where's the sink. Ah, aluminum. Araxie, if I were you, I wouldn't put my vegetables in there—they'll taste like metal. Wash them in a bowl."

The new house offered a good bit of yard, front and back; George immediately claimed the grounds as his area of expertise. On the weekends, he planted saplings of maple, birch and elm, and around these, islands of pachysandra. He seeded the lawn with a costly strain of Kentucky blue. At the corner, and up the back, he put in a row of hemlocks, which, when grown, would create a barrier between the house and passing cars. These hemlocks were as ubiquitous in the suburban landscape as slate patios, station wagons and basketball hoops. When the house next door was finished, its owners planted their row, and the neighbors next to them, on and on, until a car traveling up Reservoir Road needed only to follow the hemlocks pointing, like a lush green arrow, a mile, then another, to the reservoir cliffs.

Saturday evening after dinner, Araxie, in a print maternity smock, traipsed across the lawn after George, who had spent half an hour worrying over the placement of a sprinkler. He set the sprinkler down on the grass, stepped back, then moved it again. Araxie waddled after him. They laughed together—Look at us, they said, Saturday night, two kids playing house.

When George finished with the sprinkler, they took their folding chairs and drinks to the backyard, where they sat until it grew dark. George draped his hand across Araxie's stomach and she moved his palm so he could feel the baby kick. He gazed at the rise of his wife's belly, round like a moon, and at the outline of his roof and the dark stretch of yard where one day his children would spend their summer evenings playing, the sapling trees rising over their heads like shepherds' arms.

Everything was in front of George and Araxie. They had every reason to hope. They believed in their life, counted on it, as surely as when they turned the faucet in their new sink they counted on water to spill out in a gush. They had purchased this view, everything the eye could see: the house, the yard and, yes, that patch of sky through the trees. No one else saw that exact patch of sky through exactly those trees. And following this logic, the life around them was theirs, the life outside, and the new life growing beneath George's palm. They could sit in the dark and feel it between them, stealthily accumulating.

A car passed the corner and they both turned, frowning, until it disappeared and the night was once again quiet. Araxie sighed, leaning heavily into her chair. George gazed at her face, seeing only a glow of skin. She moved stoically now, more than ever reminding him of an animal, a burdened beast. He could not tell her this, of course, nor how, when at night she unloosed her swollen breasts, they reminded him of udders. At night in bed she would ask him to hold her breasts so he might relieve her of the weight that all day she carried. She would lie between his legs on her back and he would cup her engorged breasts. In the same way she once held his balls and, smiling, declared, "King's velvet pouch."

The night throbbed with summer night sounds—the thrum of crickets and streetlamps, the gentle shaking of the trees. He felt the pulse of his own heart and a new heart swishing under his palm. First, it had been just the two of them, making love on a blanket in the meadow. He knew then they would make a very private, special place, a place within. Look what they had accomplished in just a few short years! They had worked hard, for sure—and it was only the beginning. In the moonglow, her skin was the white of bones. They owned a sofa, a toaster, these flimsy chairs. They had a car locked in the garage and in the basement a workbench for his tools. They had a closet for sheets, a pantry, shelves with pictures and books.

And this: at the day's end he came home and found his wife in their house, still choosing him. He loved her for this, he loved her so much he might kill another man if he had to. And it was not for her beauty, not only her beauty, but for a deeper mystery she carried, as some women possess good posture or a weighty brooch. He thought for a moment, and then it came to him, quite suddenly, that Araxie's mystery had something to do with sadness, a profound melancholy he thought their marriage would cure, though he had to admit, as yet it had not.

Still, though neither of them could say how the other really felt—it was impossible to know—he deeply trusted in their vows, which made them partners, and which promised that he would be there for Araxie no matter what came, and she for him. In this way their life would keep growing. The two sitting in their yard on a summer evening, when they could just as soon have gone inside, where the light was beckoning over the kitchen sink.

George Loon squinted at the line of his roof, then at his hand glowing strangely in the dark. He shook it, then put it back on Araxie's stomach. In her chair, she sighed.

Earlier, as he watered the lawn, George had thought of his father, Theodore, and realized how much he missed him. He wished his father could see him: an owner now. A husband. Nearly a father. It seemed reasonable that George would want his own father to be with him now. And though all his life George Loon had felt rushed, this night he was in no particular hurry. He could sit in the dark beside his wife a while longer and no one would think him strange if in his mind he listened to his father's voice: *Save today, plan for what you really want. Put a line of respect between you two, and that line you never cross. Careful with the baby. Take care of those you love. See that the new lawn gets plenty of water.*

FOUR

Into that house, conceived through dreams, got through compromise, we three children were born. Dad was allowed to name Melanie, his third and last child, but Grandma Casard pressed for the honor of naming the first two. Just as she named Momma for the blue-green river Araxe, Casard named my brother for water: Van, she called him, after the great lake of Armenia and of her Hayrig's stories.

"A lake and a river," Casard sang, her eyes shiny with tears, "are free-free."

But freedom had nothing to do with the name my grandmother waited so long to give me. She waited for Araxie to grow and have her own babies, and when the first grandchild, Van, turned out a boy, Casard looked beyond to the first granddaughter. At last I arrived, two years after Van, though it was another forty days' endurance until my baptism, when Casard officially named me Seta and, in doing so, shed her tears of shame.

On that cool spring day my parents brought me to the dark nave of St. Stephen's Armenian Apostolic Church. We were joined at the baptismal font by Casard, Van, my godparents—Archie and Sevan Hagopian—and the Der Hyre priest. The Der Hyre, wearing a golden-threaded cape and gold miter, took me in his arms, and, speaking in Armenian, made the sign of the cross on my forehead with miuron, the holy oil brewed from the essences of forty different flowers.

I am told that I began to cry, and that the thin wire of my voice silenced the Der Hyre's melodic chant, rising over the heads of those gathered, into the highest dome, where it echoed along the stucco walls to the stained-glass windows, to the velvet-cushioned pews.

The Der Hyre lifted me up into the air, so I was level with his golden crown, then swooped me low. He beamed into my face, and as my tearful gaze fell from his shiny miter to his large nose and long black beard, I began to shriek.

Momma took me from the Der Hyre and whispered in my ear, "Tsa-tsa-tsa," but even she could not lend me comfort.

My brother, Van, just two, shot a finger into the Der Hyre's shin and shrieked, "Bang-bang."

Dad scooped little Van into his arms, folding his finger like a wing into his chest, whereupon Van began to cry, for himself and for me, making it two miserable youngsters at the baptismal font.

This much I know from Momma and the photographs taken by my godfather, Sevan Hagopian. What followed I learned through less objective sources: through the terse utterances of my grandmother and my own recollection of those stark images which Grandma Casard planted in me that day and which subsequently grew and grew.

For when it became clear that my tears would not stop, Casard took me from my mother. During the service Casard had spoken just once, to present me with my name. Before that, she had observed the Old Country custom of neither holding nor speaking to me until I was blessed by God. But once the ceremony concluded, Casard seized her moment, and swooping me in her arms, she carried me from the nave to the farthest pew. There without the benefit of another witness, she bequeathed onto me her sad and atrocious tale.

"Gar oo chugar," she began. There was and there was not.

Those at the altar marveled at how silent I became as this woman, nearly a stranger, pressed her mauve painted lips to my ear and filled my empty soul with her truths. Momma and Dad, believing I was in safe hands, led the others out to the vestibule to wait.

Of course it never occurred to Grandma Casard how strange, even silly, it was to expect an infant of forty days to hold a tale of genocide and the shame of one girl abandoned at the banks of the Euphrates River—these truths Casard simply expected me to know.

"Oh, my little Seta-Seta," she said, peering at my pink hairless brow. "The men, you see, were taken first."

And so she recounted her story. When she reached the part about the river, Casard burst into tears. "All these years Mayrig does not forgive. Vrej and I have our own daughter and still I wait! I make myself miserable trying to think: What does she want from me? What more can I do? And then it comes to me: the first granddaughter, I will name the child for her. Here, Mayrig, this one's yours. Look, nothing for me. Nothing for me. Now won't you give me back my name?"

My new eyes gazed at my grandmother's gray tie shoes planted firmly on the floor, heel to heel, toe to toe. I looked above me, at the twin moons of her bosom and her powdered cheek. Her eyes, magnified by thick glasses, peered into my soul, eyes flat as those of fish. Hoisting me from her lap, as though I were a leg of lamb, Casard hugged me close, so close her pounding heart beat in perfect synchronization with mine. And rubbing circles in my back, as hers had been rubbed by the nun in the orphanage, she asked me to find the name she had lost.

"Oh, Se-ta, Seta," she sang, "you—"

And with her tears thus spent and her burden passed on, she

patiently, determinedly set her mind to watching me grow and fulfill her request.

Casard never repeated her story, yet she made certain I would not forget it, either. My grandmother knew from her own experience that what is placed in the bottom of a young soul—be it horror or truth—survives. Instinctively she counted on this, trusting that as I grew, her story would rise from my belly, in my waking hours and in my dreams, and reveal images—a Turkish bloodsword, a muddy river, a child's hand letting go—until, at last, I would recover her name.

Our pact, never agreed to by me, created a formidable, unbreakable bond. The truth was I loved my grandmother, devoutly, as she loved me. And given a choice I always spent time with Casard—in her kitchen, helping knead dough for lavash, slicing peppers for shish kebob, drinking pekoe tea.

Countless afternoons I sat in a vinyl kitchen chair and watched as she attacked a wrinkled shirt with her iron, bending so low to the board I feared that without my vigilance her glasses—gray with metal temples and at each end a tiny silver screw—would touch the hot, hot metal.

For my grandmother's devotion I would gladly have paid, and pay I did, for as I grew, whenever I seemed to forget myself or the task with which Grandma Casard had entrusted me, her disapproval, like her love, poured down on my head, drenching, unexpected and crude.

I recall one afternoon when I was in the second grade. It was the first time Momma allowed me to walk home from school by myself. Wanting to show off my new independence, I eschewed heading directly home and instead walked past the fire station all the way to Grandma Casard's.

The day was blistering hot, the air from the sidewalk whooshing like a blowtorch up my thick wool dress. Sweat dripped from my legs into my shoes. I had a tremendous thirst, and to keep moving I made up a song: "Doctor Pepper, Doctor Pepper, When I'm gettin' home. Doctor Pepper, Doctor Pepper, In a glass with foamy-foam . . ." Left, then right, I moved down the walk, while in my head I sang about the quencher of thirst.

I trusted that Casard would be on the porch waiting for me, for she always seemed to anticipate my arrival. I pictured her smiling, offering me an icy glass of soda. Now, drink up slow, I heard her say, even though I knew she did not allow Dr Pepper near her house, since it was store-bought and therefore not real.

Half a block from the house I heard the birds. As I came closer I saw them perched in the trees and splashing in the lily-shaped baths. It thrilled me that birds were drawn to Casard, for the creatures confirmed that it was right for me to love her, too. To please my grandmother, I had taken a special interest in the creatures; for Christmas, Casard had given me a hardcover volume of Audubon's *North American Birds,* and a pocket guide with which to identify the various species. More than once, I had impressed my peers at second-grade show and tell with tales of wild birds eating unhesitatingly from my grandmother's palm—even the antisocial kingbird and blue jay were not too proud to take seed mixed with grease from her hand.

"Have you ever seen a yellow-bellied sapsucker?" I asked my classmates, for whom parakeets, miniature turtles and seahorses were considered exotic pets. When they all said no, I opened Audubon's weighty tome and showed them a picture of a pair of yellow-bellied sapsuckers. "These," I said, "make their nest in my Grandma's oak." This last bit having to do with the rare yellow-bellied sapsucker was an out-and-out lie, but everything else I said was true. At night the birds were quiet, but in the morning they sang to rouse Casard from sleep, which is why she and I called them her "morning lullabies," that and "the birdies."

I entered the yard of birds, dragging my carcass, all wet dress and stinky shoes, too tired and oppressed to breathe.

Grandma Casard had made a nest for herself on the front porch in a chipped wicker chair. Her Bad Leg, purple and swollen with varicose veins, was propped up on the porch banister, while her other foot was tapping time. Under her chair, Sonny, Casard's black Scottie, curled on a faded pillow. Casard was singing to herself, the dog and the birds, and for this reason the heat did not touch her. Regular and constant as a clock, she dismissed the heat, turning her attention to tapping the day's minutes, as though they were hers to hand out.

As I approached the porch I saw she was slicing up the coupon section of the newspaper, as though carving fat from a roast. Sonny raised himself to a sitting position and barked.

"Hey there, Sonny-Sonny," I called, and the dog, recognizing my voice, whimpered and lay down.

"There she is," Casard said as if confirming my arrival to someone else. "There's my girl." She dropped her scissors in her lap and reached up to touch my face with her hands. Her cool skin smelled of lemon and I felt immediately soothed. But, as always with Casard, there were limits and unspoken rules. If, for example, I were to rush our hello by asking too quickly for a drink, she would think I was disrespectful. And so, dreaming of Dr Pepper, my mouth dry as dust, I sat at her feet and petted the dog.

"So whose idea was it to wear a wool dress and Sunday shoes to school?" she asked, seeing me without looking. She focused her attention on dicing the coupons, placing them in the side pocket of her purse for the next morning's trip to the market.

"Momma told me to," I said, at once regretting the lie, for though I knew my grandmother wanted me to prefer her company to my mother's, I also knew she had a strong distaste for lies—and no canvas book bag could hinder my grandmother's view: without looking, she saw the rolled-up cotton dress and Buster Brown shoes hidden inside my bag.

"All afternoon Sonny and me and the birdies are watching these pretty young girls waltz by in their summer dresses. Nice and cool like ladies, these girls, the heat can't touch 'em." Casard knew heat only because she read about it in the newspaper; otherwise, it meant nothing, since more than once I had seen her pull roasting pans from a hot oven with her bare hands.

"I don't know. Momma just said to wear the wool."

"Ah, then there's nothing more we can say." Casard shrugged, and turning to her coupon page, she went on, shaming me with small talk. "Pot roast on special, in this heat? Tell me, Mister Butcher, who's crazy enough to cook a roast in such temperature?"

"Grandma, I'm so hot."

"Hot, you say?" She looked up, surprised. "The hot drove your Grandma out of the kitchen. The birdies and me are singing to make it pass. Here you go, let Grandma cool you down." And she helped me onto the arm of her chair. With her fingers she brushed back my long hair and wound it on top of my head. My hair was blond then, but at the roots it was already turning dark; Casard told me this was my true self growing out, and by "true" she meant Armenian. From inside her sleeve she produced bobby pins, and wound my true and untrue hair into a bun. Then she kissed the sweaty base of my neck and her love poured over me like rain.

"Nice?" she said.

"Mmmm," I replied. "But I'm still kind of thirsty."

"Hungry?"

"No, thirsty, Grandma. Very thirsty."

"Thirsty, but no hungry. Your Momma was never hungry in heat. You're her girl. Here, Grammy'll fix you a drink."

I had not forgotten about Dr Pepper. "Grandma, I wish you kept DPs in the house."

All of a sudden, her feet tumbled from the banister while the birds, flapping wildly, took flight into the trees. "Filth!" Casard cried, her cheeks quivering. "Where did you get such a filthy word?" The coupons and scissors scurried into hidden places.

"What?" I said, startled.

"You know, you know," she said. "This DP business, tell me where it came from." She removed her glasses and peered into me.

"Grandma, I didn't—"

"Not in this house you don't, girlie."

"Grandma, I'm sorry—"

"Where'd it come—from school, the television?"

The heat slammed into the porch like a hot rag. It seemed as if she were shouting into my brain through a large hollow tube. I had no idea what DP meant to her; I searched my brain, trying to recall, but nothing came.

Casard began to wheeze, her face turning a brilliant red, while her eyes grew huge behind her thick glasses. "You filthy dirty Turketa," she said. "Grandma names you special, after my own holy Mayrig and what is my thank-you? Shame. Filthy-dirty-shame. I told you: Keep that river in your purse, and Don't you ever make me regret. You. You. Break my heart."

It never occurred to Casard to explain that in her day the initials DP meant Displaced Person. DPs were the ones who never made it off the Boat, who never found the proper balance between assimilation and maintaining their own culture. In her day, DP was what the Irish called the Italians and the Jews called the Poles, and so on.

But I would have to learn about DP later, for she had already stormed into the house, taking Sonny with her and condemning me to disrespectful. I had provoked the one feeling that at all times she tried to keep at bay: shame. Shame could kill a person; shame could force a person to leave and never return.

Sitting on her porch, I shut my mouth so that no more shame could escape. I tried to remember all the special things Casard had told me, things she expected me to know. The story of what happened to her in Armenia was inside me, Casard told me so, and I believed her; if only I concentrated, I would recall Seta, the first, and the Turks and the betrayal of a hand letting go. I would understand my grandmother and there would be no mystery regarding her obsessive need to protect herself and those she loved from all Indignities. But it would be a long time before Casard and her past made any sense to me; for years to come, her legacy would seem like a drifting balloon, too far, too high for me to catch, while her temperament—raging, shaming, guilting—weighted my belly with stones.

Inside the house, I heard water running, then the scratch of the nailbrush as Casard scrubbed her hands to remove my filth.

Later, Momma would tell me that by saying "DP" I had called up my grandmother's memory of hoodlums on the corner who used to taunt the young, foreign-looking Casard as she passed by. "Hey, Miss DP. Hey, Princess, how's it with your men so ignorant. You teach 'em how to talk yet? You teach 'em about the bedroom? DPs know plenty about the bedroom, hey, Princess, what? You tell your DP man to keep his ass out of sight." She was a young bride and new to this country, but she held her head high, passing the boys with Vitalis hair, who admired her behind as they pelted it with dirty words.

Inside the house, Casard scrubbed the hoodlums and my filth from under her nails. But on the porch there was no such absolution from heat or thirst or shameful words.

And so I cried—for hours, it seemed—until it was dinnertime and Momma came to the house to collect me and found me on the front porch, sobbing, hugging my sorry knees.

The murky details of our grandmother's past Van, Melanie and I made into stories.

Casard was older than the redwoods in California.

Casard was not born, she was cut from her mother's belly by a Turkish soldier.

Casard spent her first six months living under a bush by the side of the road; the villagers passing along the Street of Death kept her alive.

Casard propped her legs on a chair on account of the clots, large as figs, passing through her veins.

Casard's mother, the first Seta, flew to heaven, an angel-bird, and became holy.

Van, Melanie and I clung to these tales because they were our way of capturing what was incomprehensible about our grandmother. We spent hours idly wondering if Casard ever slept (we never actually saw her sleep); if she had something to do with the lemon tree out back (since even we knew that lemons do not normally grow in Connecticut); and if, when she took down her bun, her secret hair fell to her ankles or just to her knees.

The rest of Casard's story I learned on my own. Inside the sanctuary of her house, my grandmother taught me her truths. In Armenian it was food, greetings, songs, days of the week. In English she taught me atrocity, Indignities and Turk, her word for butchers and thieves. She told me there was no such thing as an Armenian swear; if you wanted filth, you talked Turk. It was not until I became an adult that I actually met a Turk, and, looking into his eyes, was surprised to find just another person, no more, no less.

Had my grandmother been alive then, she would no doubt have refused to believe that I, Seta, her Armenian girl, could ever have allowed myself to become friends with a Turk. For Casard, some things were just not possible. It was not possible to forgive the Turks for attempting and nearly succeeding in wiping out our own. It was not possible to forgive the Turks for refusing to admit their crimes—even the Germans did that. Nor was it possible to live a day without the painful reminder of atrocity; and so, fueled by anger, one must devote one's life to building a new Armenia, in which Armenian language, food, education and—the final imperative—Armenian marriage was preserved. For this, too: it was not possible that an Armenian girl like Momma could ever find happiness with an odar husband.

The war my grandmother waged against my father was fought with petty measures and indirect slights; its battlefield and prize were the children's souls. Casard taught us Armenian; Dad countered with his family crest. Casard served Armenian food and taught us Old Country ways; Dad obliged by hauling out the box of photographs from the army trunk in the basement and showing us the picture of his parents—a diminutive woman standing beside a tall, slender man on the front porch of a white clapboard house. Theodore and Bette Loon died within six months of each other while Dad was away at college. Heart trouble, Dad said. Each time

I heard him say this, I solemnly nodded, as if I knew just what he meant.

A musty photograph and a world of dreams: these were my father's gifts. At night, he tucked me into bed and asked me to make him a good dream. "Start me off," I said gleefully; and tipping back his head and closing his eyes, he would find a picture: "I see a white beach, turquoise water, a gray whale and a gull."

"OK," I said, nodding purposefully, as I rolled my face into the pillow. In the morning I told him my dream.

Memory will play tricks on you; I cannot recall one incident in which my father, a gentleman, ever directed a harsh word at Casard. When harsh words were required, Momma was the one to say them. Casard needled and ridiculed Dad, but everyone knew she was just trying to provoke Momma, who had done the unthinkable by growing up and abandoning her. Dad was the reminder, the excuse.

These two women in my life, from whom I learned most everything, engaged in daily dramas over such matters as the proper doneness of a roast, the price of shirts and their favorite subject, church. Casard wanted us raised in the Armenian Apostolic Church, while Dad and Momma agreed we were Americans first. When Melanie was born, two years after me, my parents and Casard compromised and had her baptized twice, once with the Armenians and once with the Episcopalians. From that day on we alternated our Sundays between the two churches.

I told myself that we were not the first family to fight over divided backgrounds—a fight so fierce, more than once it drove Van, Melanie and me into hiding in the small, unfinished attic over the garage. The first time was when we were eleven, nine and seven, and like most children we knew, we often spent entire afternoons in the backyard playing a spirited game of war. The hemlocks were our jungle, the masonry wall our bunkers, and the slate patio our prison, in which we took turns playing American POWs held by the Viet Cong. Armed with rolls of dynamite caps, a One Man Army plastic rifle, scores of pinecone grenades, two camouflage helmets and Dad's steel canteen, we exploded, pillaged and blew sky-high. Then, when our limbs grew heavy and our minds dull, we trooped back into the house, wholly unprepared for the war therein.

Casard and Momma were in the kitchen, yelling. They shouted over each other and we could just hear bits: Momma saying, "Over and over we try . . ." While Casard thundered, "Araxie, I'm not through. Now, you listen to me!"

We stood in our windbreakers in the foyer, our hands and faces smeared with dirt. Van, the oldest, tugged on my sleeve and we bolted upstairs, Melanie in tow. At the landing, Van opened the linen closet and yanked on the cord hanging from the door in the ceiling. Down tumbled a flight of folding stairs, which we quickly climbed up.

Perhaps our hearts were already guilty, having spent the better part of an afternoon maiming made-up soldiers, but whatever the reason, that afternoon we took flight into the farthest reaches of the attic, spurred by the horrifying conviction that we, the children, were the cause of the real war in our house.

We did not speak to one another in the dark, musty attic room. Like the adults in our lives, we were unaccustomed to thoughtful analyses or explanations; we knew, simply, how to react. Sitting in a circle in the dark, Indian style on the cool, rough boards, we gazed into one another's frightened eyes, and it was Melanie, the baby, who first pressed her palms to her ears. Soon we all had our ears cupped, as we began to chant faster and faster, "We're not bad, we're not bad, we're not bad," while downstairs in the kitchen Momma and Casard raged.

I told myself we were not the only family to fight and then evade resolution by celebrating every religious holiday in sets of two: two Christmases, two Ash Wednesdays, two Palm Sundays, two Easters.

But the truth was we were not like the other families I knew, and in my ninth year I had to give up any contrary illusions.

It was December, and Momma and Casard could not agree on whether to celebrate Christmas with the rest of America or wait until January 6, when the pure Armenians celebrated in accordance with their ancient calendar. In the end, it was decided that we would do both.

Dad announced the news at dinner.

"When do we open presents?" Van shrewdly asked.

Momma and Dad exchanged looks, then Momma said, "How about one gift each, on Christmas Eve, then the rest we'll save for Armenian Christmas."

"No way," Van said. "That's two whole weeks after all our friends. No way."

"Think of it like this," Dad countered, his face telltale red, "Two Christmases mean we're twice as lucky."

"Bull," Van burst out, and was promptly dismissed from the table.

Behind Dad's good intentions we all knew the truth: that instead of twice as lucky, we were only half: half lucky and half unlucky. And during those long two weeks of Christmas, I had frequent occasion to wonder which part was which.

On December 24, we attended the midnight Episcopal service. Dad dropped us off in front and drove behind the church to park. We entered the stone sanctuary, which was decked with giant wreaths and red velvet bows. A deacon handed me a program and a thin white taper in a paper holder. The candle was for midnight, when the congregation would pass the flame from the altar through the pews, and inside the illumined church we would sing "Silent Night."

That Christmas Eve when I was nine marked the first time I was entrusted with my own private candle. I remember quite well. I was always on the lookout for signs that I was moving up from childhood, and the privilege of holding a candle struck me as a special achievement. With the candle aloft, I walked down the aisle, smiling at the grown-ups and making serious faces at the children my age. Van poked me from behind—"Come on, Seta, hurry up."

We sat in front and then Dad came in from the parking lot and took his usual seat in one of the back pews. Momma waved, encouraging him to come forward, but Dad just shrugged and waved back. Finally, Momma stood and smiling wearily at the congregants seated near us, said, "Come on, troops. Let's go."

Van, Momma and Melanie started back, but I lagged behind, reluctant to give up my good seat in front. Fathers, coming in from the parking lot, passed by me, shaking off their camel-hair coats. It seemed they were richer than we, and I found myself eyeing their families with envy. The mothers, sitting alongside the children, wore nubby woolen suits with white gloves, gold brooches and pearls. Most astonishing were the mink stoles that the women had draped across their shoulders, the minks' heads clipped to their tails. The splendor of the women made me uncomfortable and lonesome, so I slipped into the aisle and headed back to my family. As I approached our row, I found myself wishing that just once Momma would wear a snazzy mink, instead of a plain beige scarf.

I was still fretting over Momma's simple clothes when three elderly ladies in pillbox hats and black mesh veils sat down in the pew in front of us. Van, already bored, rolled his program in a tight cone and tried wedging it into the mouth of one of the ladies' minks. The mink's glass eyes seemed to focus as Van pushed the red Christmas program between its jaws, where it hung like a large bone from the animal's mouth.

Melanie, next to me, began to giggle into her palms. She was behaving like a stupid child, employing her recent and most annoying habit of imitating my every move. If I put on a red dress, she had to wear a red skirt. If I paraded up the aisle with my candle, Melanie had to follow behind, clutching her hands as if she, too, had her own candle. When, after finishing my prayer, I bent my head back so my hair brushed the tips of my shoulders like elegant mink fur, Melanie threw back her head like a spastic, rolling her eyes with delight. I turned and pinched her leg, whereupon Melanie slapped me on the arm.

Momma was gazing overhead, at the iron-and-wood candelabras hanging from the vast ceiling, a peevish look on her face. When

Melanie hit me, Momma's eyes snapped back to earth. She frowned at the Episcopalians, then turned on me.

"Stop that," she said.

"Momma," I cried, "*I'm* not doing anything."

But Momma shook her head. As if reading my envious mind, she pointed her chin at the old ladies with the minks. Looking at me with piercing eyes, she said, "Hmm?"

My cheeks burned. "Sorry," I said, not really knowing why.

Momma squeezed my hand and nodded. Under her breath, she murmured, "Holiday Christians."

It was not until a week after New Year's Eve that Momma became excited, our real Christmas celebration commenced and I began to believe we were about to have our luck. That year, Armenian Christmas fell on a Wednesday, and Momma surprised us all by letting us skip school. For breakfast, she made fresh orange juice and omelets with bacon and warm hatsig rolls. Dad put Armenian carols on the stereo and we opened our gifts beside the tree.

When all the presents had been admired, Momma led Van, Melanie and me upstairs to her room. Opening her closet, Momma reached in back to the shelf where the box with her wedding dress was kept—the box Melanie and I were forbidden to touch until it was our turn to marry—and pulled out surprise packages containing new coats and shoes. The last box Momma gave to me. Inside, wrapped in tissue paper, was a white fur muff. "Careful," Momma warned, and by this I was meant to understand that newness quickly spoils.

We rode to the Armenian church in Dad's Buick, afraid to shift in our new clothes. Melanie, coveting my white muff, refused to take her eyes from it until I agreed to let her hold it for one block.

At the church, Dad pulled to the curb, and we saw Casard standing in front, shivering in the snow.

"I told her to meet us *inside*!" Momma said, climbing out of the car. "She never listens. Not once." Momma grabbed Melanie's hand and pulled her up the walk while Van and I lagged behind, mortified that Momma and Casard would go at it in front of the whole church.

"Mayrig, what do you think you're doing?" Momma yelled.

Casard watched Dad's car disappear down the road. "I should have sent him to the bakery" was all Casard said, and turning, climbed the stairs.

While Dad was parking the service began without him, the Der Hyre marching up the aisle in a turquoise cape and matching sequined miter. Two deacons followed the Der Hyre, one with a strand of bells and the other with a lantern of incense. In front of the blue velvet curtain hiding the altar, the Der Hyre recited the classical Armenian service that had been said for over sixteen hundred years.

Melanie, Van and I understood only the words for *we, Christ,* and *God.* We droned on, regardless, pouncing on *Amen.* When the backs of our knees became numb from standing, Casard and Momma entertained us with pertinent facts. Momma whispered to Van that the Der Hyre, originally from Lebanon, was capable of speaking seven languages. Van passed this on. Nine? I asked, leaning forward in the pew. Momma shook her head and flashed seven fingers. Then, as the velvet curtain was pulled back and the splendor of the altar revealed, Momma announced that next year the archbishop from New York planned to stay with Casard when he visited our church. Casard pointed her chin at the altar and nodded.

I pictured the archbishop in his black robes and hood, sitting at Casard's kitchen table. I pictured him asleep in Momma's bed wearing his gilded robe and tall hat. He would lie on his back as though in a coffin, his jeweled slippers hanging over the end of Momma's girlhood bed. Across the hall Casard would pretend to sleep, her long secret hair loosened from its combs, her eyes blinking into the night, careful of sounds.

The organ struck a chord and there was no more time to dream, for we were all meant to rise. Casard, singing the Armenian lyrics in my ear, moved her finger across the page of the hymnal, and I followed along, humming, the organ striking one minor chord after another, the voices of Casard's people filling the holy space like a universal moan.

Casard put her arm around me and I entered the cloud of her Wind Song perfume. My grandmother's smell made me miss her, which was odd since I smelled her only when she was very close. I peered over at Momma, who was petting Melanie's hair. Momma and Casard loved us best when we were in their church, and it was hard not to prefer the place where we received the most affection. At the end of the hymn, Casard whispered in my ear, "You're my little bachig," Armenian for kiss. I beamed up at her: yes I was hers, yes I was sweet as a kiss. Lucky, too. Momma glanced over at us and, for an instant, I thought she might scold me as she had on Christmas Eve, but this time she smiled, and all I had to do was stand in my new clothes and let the love I mistook as Armenian wash my soul.

The service was nearly over when I noticed Dad standing apart at the end of our pew. He had come in late from parking the car and so had to find a seat at the end. His high sandy head bobbed like a buoy among the sea of black ones, but he seemed unaware of his difference. He followed along in the Armenian prayer book as if he were one of them, as if he fluently understood. When the Der Hyre removed his miter with a holy lace handkerchief, Dad nodded. I watched him carefully, my eye moving from his face to the dark faces surrounding him; it troubled me to find Dad so tall and fair.

As we departed the sanctuary, a kindly man in a drab suit handed each of us a cellophane packet of flat holy bread called maas, which was meant to be given to family members who were unable to attend church. At the door, I kissed my maas and placed it on my tongue. As it dissolved into the hollow of my stomach, I made a wish: I wished that I were pure Armenian.

The congregation flowed from the church into the basement, which was decorated with two small wreaths. Van and Momma led the way, while Casard and I brought up the rear. It did not really seem like Christmas, except that everyone was hugging, including the men. Strangers I had never seen before grabbed my mother and shook my father's hand, as if they had just returned from a long trip.

There was a peculiar sadness in the eyes of the adults gathered around me, and in my own childish way I believed that their sadness had something to do with our family and the fact that my father was an odar. Because of him, I, too, was apart: half Seta, half Loon, when all I wanted was to be included among the women, to have their full red lips and brown pool eyes trained on me. Oh, to have them cluck their tongues at my sorrow, open the window on my grace and hoot at my mischief, dark and funny as their own.

That Christmas morning I noticed for the first time that the Armenians were beautiful, while the Episcopalians were just pretty. Momma had called the Episcopalians "Holiday Christians," and Dad countered by referring to the Armenians as "the Tribe." Momma said the difference was that Armenians never went in for showy, but I knew she was wrong. Showy was in their genes, beginning with their prominent noses that arched from their faces like flying buttresses. Among the ladies, even the poorest carried herself with a certain dignity that seemed to say: *I have suffered but I am me.* I stood next to Casard as the women spoke to one another in the old language, their mouths opening wide as if they needed to make their words especially large.

Casard led Van, Melanie and me through the knitted circles of elders, showing us off to the old ladies, who held our faces, and to the men, who pinched our cheeks until they hurt. We belonged to her, the mother of the church, we were Casard's. This meant something to the members, and because it was Christmas they made a special effort to greet us. The elders bent down and offered us wide, wide smiles, never mentioning the full blood we lacked, nor the language, nor the atrocities of which only they knew. The elders patted our hair, and nodded with pleasure at Casard.

"Beautiful little ones."

"And smart?"

Casard smiled and bowed her head. For a moment I forgot that I was different. Painting a foolish grin on my face, I played to my audience, while inside my heart pounded, as though, by smiling, I was telling fibs.

When it was time to leave, Casard waved to us from the parking lot, even though we were heading directly to her house. "Bye-bye," she said.

"Good-bye, Grandma," we called back, "good-bye."

We piled into the Buick. Dad checked behind him to see that we were tucked in before pulling from the curb. Only then, as we drove away, did our grins fade. Rubbing my cheeks, sore from smiling, I glanced behind me—Momma did too—out the rear window at the church, wondering what it was we were missing, what had been left.

Wholeness, I am told, comes from within, but that Christmas when I was nine, as we drove in silence from the church to Cousins Bakery, I thought that wholeness was everywhere but inside us. At the bakery Dad picked up Casard's rye bread and rolls, and no one said a word about the hollow ache inside our bellies.

No one said a word each time Casard attacked my parents' marriage the way a moth attacks wool: making little holes here and there, so that the damage becomes apparent only after it is done.

By the time we reached Casard's house, Poppee and her family had arrived and we were all supposed to be joyous and happy. Casard had set the table with Christmas napkins and plates, colored bowls, silver trays and crystal serving dishes filled with pickles, beans, scallions and radishes; the good china plates were laden with roasted lamb and beef, dolma, kibbeh, bodyjohn pie, green beans, mushrooms and pilaf.

The adults oohed and aahed at the splendor of the feast. Auntie Vart commented on the centerpiece made from pinecones, boughs and ribbon, but Casard wrinkled her nose and waved away the praise. Seated at the head of the table, Casard studied the family gathered about her: there was Momma and Dad and we three kids; Poppee and Great Uncle Alex and their daughters, Auntie Sarah and Auntie Vart, and their husbands and children. While Casard surveyed her guests I observed that Uncle Eddy's brother from Russia, seated across from me, was at that moment picking his bulbous nose. Momma saw me staring and fluttered her fingers in front of my face.

Casard waved for Great Uncle Alex to say the prayer. Great Uncle Alex bowed his head and mumbled something in Armenian; Van, Melanie and I caught up in time to say "Amen."

The women removed the aluminum foil from the platters and served the men, the children and finally themselves. Everyone knew that Casard was a great cook and we heaped food onto our plates as if we would never eat again.

We picked up our forks and were about to eat when Momma noticed that Casard's plate was empty.

"What, Mayrig? What can I get you?" Momma asked.

Casard shook her head at a spot in the center of the table.

"Something from the kitchen, Mayrig? Salt, pepper? You need salt and pepper?"

Casard pursed her lips and, with her chin, pointed at the reindeer shakers on the table. She bowed her head.

Everyone tried to find the one thing Casard lacked so we could all start eating.

"What?" Momma exclaimed. "Mayrig, are you sick?"

"Was only thinking to myself," Casard mumbled, her chin resting on her chest as though she were dozing. Suddenly, her head bobbed up and she stared at Dad's neck. She smiled, squinting, as though straining to see him.

"What—" Momma said, crossing her arms. "What now?"

"It's nothing," Casard assured her, waving at us to begin eating.

We picked up our forks once again—everyone except Momma—but as we took our first bite, Casard turned to Van, who was seated on her right, and whispered loud enough so everyone could hear, "I was just thinking to myself, your father must be disappointed we don't serve none of that Episcopalian Jell-O salad."

Dad's fist hit the table and the ice in our water glasses chimed.

Casard, startled by the noise, looked up. "Don't you worry, Araxie," she said. "I know what those Cath-o-lics like. I see them at the store, buying. Next time"—Casard tapped the side of her head—"next time, Mayrig remembers. We'll serve'em Jell-O right on the table like it was food."

Momma straightened the silver beside her plate. There was not a sound in the room. She took in air, then under her breath she said quietly, "Enough."

Dad combed his fingers through his hair, his face flushed with anger. "You had to spoil it, didn't you?" he said to Casard, his lips pressed as though he were about to cry. "Couldn't leave it be, not one holiday."

Uncle Eddy cleared his throat. "Hey, George, you catch the Knicks last night?"

Momma gave Uncle Eddy a look that left him with his mouth hanging open.

"This is supposed to be Christmas," Momma said to the fork at the side of her plate. "In other families." Momma lifted her glass from the table and, without drinking, set it down. She seemed to be concentrating on her breathing, as though it required special effort just to keep the air moving in and out.

"There's a draft in here," Casard announced. "Seta, go check the door."

"No," Momma said, cutting the air with a finger. "You keep Seta out of this. You're always trying to put her in the middle. There's no draft and you know it."

"On my shoulders, Araxie, I feel blowing." But instead of looking at Momma, Casard gazed pleadingly at me.

"There's no draft," Momma repeated, her voice loud and firm. She pointed her finger to keep me in my chair.

Casard bit her lip and looked at me, but I avoided her gaze. Staring at my plate, my face burned with shame. When at last I looked up again, I expected to find everybody watching me, but they all had their eyes glued on Casard, who had begun rubbing her arms in an effort to warm them, and on Momma, who was concentrating on breathing.

We were not a quiet family, and we certainly never shirked a good fight. But the schism that had grown between Momma and Casard—the thing involving Dad and, I now understood, me—was too deep to discuss. It lurked behind the women's dramatic battles and heavy silences. Until that moment I never knew whose side to be on, Momma and Dad's or Casard's, since both sides were me. But sitting there, I made a decision.

"Momma," I said. Both women looked at me, and when I lifted my eyes to meet Momma's gaze, she inhaled sharply and raised her brows. Then, as though granted permission, she pushed back her chair and headed for the stairs.

She returned with Casard's sweater. "Put it on," Momma said, dropping the sweater in her mother's lap.

Momma took her place at the table and turning to Uncle Eddy, the harmless, declared, "Eddy, I want you to know: my husband does not eat Jell-O salad."

Van says I remember that Christmas because I was finally old enough to see both halves, Seta and Loon, though they had been obvious to him long before. Later, as we drove home in Dad's new Buick, Momma finally let go of the sorrow she was holding. It came slowly at first, then in a great gush of air.

My father steered with one hand and wrapped his free arm around her shoulder. She murmured something to him, something about "So alone." Then she started to sob, while in the backseat Melanie, Van and I bit our lips and braced ourselves.

Dad glanced at the road, then back at Momma and whispered something we could not hear. A moment passed. Momma's shoulders coughed up and down, she burrowed her face into Dad's wool coat.

At the next stoplight he threw the car into Park and kissed her. Again and again, then deeply. He went on kissing her, despite the headlights behind us and then the horns, despite Van, Melanie and me watching from the backseat. We heard the horns, but more shocking was this kiss, like some miracle. We did not know what to do, except hold our breath and grab hands, while the light changed twice more.

The light turned a third time before Dad let go of Momma and, putting the Buick back into gear, drove us home through the snowy, silent streets of Memorial. Dad was turning the car into our driveway when Momma peered into the backseat to find Van, Melanie and me, still stunned by that kiss, still pressing hands.

And if someone says Christmas, this is what I see: the look of surprise in my mother's eyes, as if we were her bonus presents, wrapped in muffs and coats and ribbons, as if we were for her from him and brand-new.

FIVE

I turned eleven in 1970, a year after man first walked on the moon and two years after Dr. Martin Luther King was shot. I turned eleven when the shops downtown began going out of business, one by one.

My father said my time would be remembered for its abbreviation, and although I did not stop to think what this meant, it seemed to me that my time was about endings.

In the city of Saigon, Vietnamese monks doused their bodies with gasoline and set themselves ablaze. At night, after dinner, I sat in front of the television and ate my dessert while watching the monks' orange robes ignite into brilliant flaming pyres.

On the television, I saw protests in Washington and on college campuses throughout the country, but in my daily routine the war seemed an abstraction, something to watch on TV. Then, in the course of several astonishing weeks, all that changed and what had been the steady, predictable flow of my life forever disappeared.

One morning Memorial's shoe repairman, Bob Humms, put a sign in his shop window that read *Until.* Dressed as a soldier in black laced boots, fatigues and a camouflage helmet, Bob Humms set out for Memorial's neighborhoods, where he cried out in a deep, tremulous voice about the burning monks and the dread war.

It was dawn that first morning Bob Humms made his rounds, wrenching Memorial's citizenry from their sleep with calls of "Bur-ning! Bur-ning! My God, wake up! Smell the human flesh burned for you!"

Van, Melanie and I leaped from our beds to the nearest window, where we discovered the shoe repairman, dressed like a soldier, standing at the base of our driveway, a red can of gasoline in his hands. Was he going to set himself on fire?

Leaning out our windows, we called to him. "Hey, Humms," Van bellowed, waving his One Man Army plastic machine gun.

"They're dying for you, son," Bob Humms cried. "And you and you. Look out: the world's on fire!" he bellowed, over the hemlocks and the clipped lawn, the pachysandra islands and Momma's flower garden.

"Do you think he knows it's us?" I asked.

"Course he does," Van replied, wanting to believe as much as I did that we had been singled out. Never mind that Bob Humms was screaming, singing, carrying on at the crack of dawn like some lunatic; never mind the police car, which we heard long before we saw it, screeching around the corner, stopping at the bottom of our driveway; never mind Dad shouting, "Kids, get your heads back inside the house," as he hurried down the driveway in his bathrobe and slippers; never mind that we had seen plenty of protesters on TV, along with a daily dose of graphic footage from the war; never mind any of it, only this: Bob Humms was our first live protester and he had come all the way across town to tell us that the war was wrong.

"Hey, Bob," we shouted, "go, Bob, go!" as Dad, several neighbors and two policemen gathered around Bob Humms, all talking at once, pointing their fingers at the ground. Overnight, it seemed, the cobbler had become a disturbing menace, bent on delivering an apocalyptic message replete with conflagrated monks, napalmed peasants and innocent dying boys. What was it all about? they demanded to know. The elders perceived Bob Humms as a threat to the community. They were suspicious of a man capable, on the one hand, of running a business and owning a home and, on the other, of acting like a radical.

When, days later, it was discovered that in his fervor of conscience, Bob Humms had abandoned not only his business but his home, too, spending his nights in an empty drainage pipe near the river, the police were called in to lock him up.

They found Bob Humms walking in a quiet cul-de-sac of homes. The cobbler gave the officers the same placid, easygoing smile that had greeted them each time they entered his store with their broken shoes.

"Hey, Bill," Bob Humms said, nodding. "Hey there, John, Paul. Hey there, Mitch." The shoeman offered each man his large, callused hand, but the officers refused to shake it, and Bob Humms's hand hung in the air between them for what seemed like an awfully long time. The officers studied the hand, explaining to it that they had their orders to take him down to the station, where they honestly hoped he would get a decent night's sleep and, tomorrow, return to his home, so this whole unpleasant incident would just blow over.

Bob Humms appeared to reflect on what the officers had to say. After a moment, he nodded, and they led him quietly to the car and put him in the backseat, where he rode downtown, gazing out the window.

All night Bob Humms remained in his cell; he thanked the guard for his dinner and again for his breakfast and lunch. At noon the following day he was released. He left the station and walked the short block to Memorial's center, where, among the marble and granite statues, he resumed his protest.

That afternoon established Bob Humms's routine: he would

spend mornings canvassing the neighborhoods and save downtown for after lunch. And when, months later, in June, he was severely beaten by a thug, the police convinced Bob Humms that it was time to stay home.

Bob Humms eventually reopened his store and, not long after, business returned to normal. But the pervasive ire, fear, and foreboding that the cobbler had touched off within the greater community remained, as did the sign in his shopwindow, warning us all—*Until.*

Riding in the passenger seat of Momma's car on my way to ballet lessons at Miss Pat's, we passed Bob Humms's shop and I saw for myself the handwritten scribble taped in the window. For an instant, I wondered about the sign, and what it meant, though I did not wonder about the sinking feeling in my belly. The truth was that suddenly everywhere I looked my eyes fell upon evidence of decline.

Momma and I drove by the First National Bank, where they were trying to lure customers by offering for every new account a red, white and blue alarm clock with a snooze button.

We drove into the Northend and Momma said, "Lock your door," as we passed by the pocked façades and graffitied walls of the tenements. At the near corner, two women, younger than Momma, leaned out their apartment windows, talking to a group of men parked in beach chairs on the stoop below. Across the road several children played getaway driver in the stripped hull of a car, its tireless rims reminding me of burned-out eye sockets. Riding in my mother's car dressed in a royal-blue leotard and pink tights—the colors, Miss Pat informed us, of the London Ballet—it occurred to me, as I pressed my thumb on the metal door lock, that rats also occupied these wretched buildings and would likely scamper up your leg when you sat on the toilet.

On the way home from Miss Pat's, we drove by the Holiday Inn garage, where, in the stairwell, as everyone knew, Big Rita gave herself to any man for five dollars.

In Washington Elementary School, where I attended the fifth

grade, a girl in my class passed through the hall and left behind a smell. My classmates and I called this hovering devil "Theresa." We pointed fingers at Theresa Vartyan's passing shadow, sprayed her fumes with purifying potion and, calling together a group, trod cautiously in her wake. At recess, anyone's unguarded shoulder was fair prey to the condemning tap: "You've got the Theresa Vartyan smell."

There was something too worrisome to take in about Theresa and it was not that she was Armenian, for in Miss Craig's class we were Puerto Rican, Polish, Jewish, Chinese, black, Italian and Irish. We were the sum of our grandparents, many of whom had traveled from distant places, across the wide blue ocean on a nameless Boat. Here, in Memorial, our grandparents settled and made our parents who made us, their pride. But the problem was that it was 1970 and though we were young, proud and hopeful, the world was not.

In Miss Craig's fifth-grade classroom, a brick walled room painted the color of bubble gum, my name hung on the lip of my desk: Seta Loon. In the front row, Tony Dreyfus made moon eyes at Ruthy Kurtz, Ruthy sitting directly in front of me, providing, day after day, a view of fake tortoiseshell barrettes and ponytail holders with lavender and white plastic balls. Ruthy, who thought she was special, always touching her hair. There were Martha and Patty Sullivan, rich girls, and on my left, Glen Morrelli, and on my right, Paul Mahoney, on whom I had a crush. Between them, I sat, in navy bell-bottom corduroys and a favorite lime-green Danskin top with a large white zipper. Sucking on the ring of that zipper, looking out the window or at the back of Ruthy Kurtz's head, I practiced my point and flex, while Theresa Vartyan, the ugly girl in the far row, stank up the room with her smell.

I knew Theresa from Armenian Sunday school, where Casard was teacher of our class. Casard was friends with Mrs. Vartyan. At church school, Theresa sat in the back row, refusing to speak, even when Casard asked in her kindest voice, "*Inch ga chi ga?*" What's new?

Grandma Casard would have to ask three times, until, finally, Theresa dropped her gaze to her lap and, twisting her fingers into knots, replied, *"Pan chi ga."* Nothing.

The world of Miss Craig's classroom was neither so patient nor so kind to Theresa Vartyan. The children begrudged not Theresa Vartyan's heritage, nor the fact that her father had disappeared one June day, leaving behind rumors of a red-haired beautician in upstate New York, nor that Theresa's mother was believed to have some ravaging disease—a creeping fungus, an inexplicable cancer—which made the skin on her face shrink. Specifically, what bothered the members of Miss Craig's class, and bothered me, too, during that hopeless winter of 1970, was that Theresa Vartyan, the ugly, the bodacious, had the mortifying audacity to stand out.

One wintry morning during recess, Theresa walked across the playground and in our minds that was all it took—Theresa Vartyan had changed. Gone was the girl who slunk close to the corridor walls, the last to finish a test, the first to contaminate the class with flu. In her place was a young woman with volumes of black hair falling onto large breasts, wide birthing hips and a strut—plumes on this bird bold as warpaint.

It occurred to some members that Theresa's impudence was detestable and should be punished. How dare she be so different. How dare she stand out. Then, to add insult, she donned hose—hose the colors of the rainbow: orange, teal, emerald green.

Ruthy Kurtz laughed at her, and still others called her names. And when it came time for me to join in or be cast aside I put my feelings of Armenian sisterhood behind me, and stood among my peers on the frozen playground, chanting, "Ter-e-saa Fart-yan wears pan-ty-hose."

But names alone could never defeat Theresa Vartyan. She was too far ahead, flashing her orange nylons while under our winter coats we wore navy tights or Bonnie-Doon socks. And when I thought we would just as soon forget her—in my mind she was nearly gone—Theresa Vartyan came down with the curse.

It was springtime, following Easter break. I returned to school expecting my life to be as newly polished as the school floors. I had said good-bye to winter: to electrified hair, darkness in the morning, darkness after school. I arrived ready for spring: cotton dresses, white sandals, crocuses and forsythia blooms, and my turn at the fifth-grade rite of passage, Nurse Solomon's afternoon series, "Growing Up and Liking It."

Twice each week Nurse Solomon migrated to our classroom, laden with charts and graphs and what she called her props.

"Today's prop," she said, "is this empty Palmolive Liquid bottle." Nurse Solomon placed the clear bottle on Miss Craig's table and filled it halfway with cotton balls. She said, "Let's agree, class, that this bottle is a clean, healthy lung."

Nurse Solomon removed a long white cigarette from inside her purse and held it up for all to see. She said, "Ladies and gentlemen, I don't have to tell you what this is."

Next, she lit the cigarette and drew on it; right there in the classroom she inhaled smoke deep into her lungs inside her starched uniform. We watched, stunned, as she exhaled the smoke, cupping her mouth over the bottle's rim as though giving it an openmouthed kiss. Nurse Solomon knew what she was doing. In and out, again and again—she could not get enough—she sucked that smoke and exhaled its black plume into the Palmolive bottle.

Nurse Solomon sealed the lid with a cap. We leaned forward in our seats to see the smoke lie down like a snake in the bottom of the bottle. The cotton balls sprouted gray fur, the walls of the lung became lined with oily film.

Nurse Solomon waited for someone to say it, and someone did: "Gross."

She scanned the audience. "Class, what happened to that healthy lung?"

She held the smoker's lung at arm's length, as though it were a dirty, contagious thing. Next, she passed it to Roger Wilkins in front, who gingerly passed it on back. With the cigarette still burning between her fingers, Nurse asked, "Class, after today's demonstration, how many of us intend to smoke?"

During the next weeks, Nurse Solomon brought to our classroom props of all types of corruption, including syringes and charts of illicit drugs. They seemed official. We passed a joint through the rows, and she taught us to identify its presence in slang. She said, "Also known as Mary Jane, reefer, bud, doobie and spleef."

We moved on to reproduction. Nurse Solomon announced that we were the first class not to be separated into boys and girls, the first class to learn, in unison, respect for our bodies. Nurse placed a chart of a womb and a dotted-line drawing of an erection against the blackboard. On the shelf nearest the reading table, she placed an orange shoe box marked, *Questions.*

The first question read, "Why do they call it a sperm whale?" Nurse Solomon said we need not be embarrassed to ask. Another card read, "Do you have sex?" She answered, "Nurse's personal life is not why we're here."

Nurse Solomon ended with menstruation. Walking between the rows of desks, she pointed toward the diagram of the uterus.

"Class, soon you will all be entering the exciting world of men and women." She paused beside Theresa's desk and placed her hand on the girl's shoulder. "Some of you may already have arrived."

All eyes turned to Theresa Vartyan, who pretended not to notice or care. Staring straight ahead at the poster of the uterus, from her collarbone up she blushed.

The electric clock hummed, Nurse Solomon clicked her pen as she walked to her desk, but nobody else moved. All eyes remained fixed on Theresa; we studied her homemade clothes and the drape of her hair, black and opaque as a curtain. It seemed to us that the curse was elusive: deep and mysterious, covered by skin.

There are moments in life—only later can you point to them—when it is possible to see a person grow before your eyes. Theresa rose from her chair and, thrusting her shoulders back, headed straight for that uterus. With each step her shoes made not a click, not a sound.

She reached the blackboard and paused. Slowly, so that our eyes remained fixed on her, she began to turn like a cake on a birthday stand.

At first we looked away, but she kept it up. She gave us time to see womanhood from all angles. Bringing our new "Growing Up and Liking It" data to bear, we took note of the pimples on Theresa's forehead, the roundness of her breasts, the curves beneath her fluorescent hose.

At the head of the class she orbited: massive, immovable, elemental as earth.

And when at last her twirling wound to a standstill, Theresa Vartyan cast her cold black gaze on each person in that room. She intended to make certain that the gift she had bestowed upon the unworthy had been received. And when we failed—and make no mistake, we each did—to understand the miracle we had just witnessed, under the picture of the womb Theresa spelled out the word WOMAN.

If, in this life, each person is granted a moment of grace, this was hers. Having had it, Theresa withdrew. Out the door she floated, leaving us once more in her mist.

This spell of hers, however potent, could not last. From up on her high horse, we had to pull her down. And it came to pass that Theresa Vartyan, who first wore hose, bled, in gym class, in the girls' room, silently, disgustingly—in our minds—red. She made us feel foolish and we, in turn, tried to make her feel gross and repellent.

At noon, Washington Elementary School opened its oak doors and released the children. Home we trooped, toward mothers waiting with bologna sandwiches. On our heads we wore baseball caps or barrettes with bows. On our feet we wore PF Flyers, Jack Percell sneakers, Buster Browns. We carefully avoided stepping on sidewalk cracks. Passersby tooted their horns and mothers waved from their yards. We were Memorial's pride.

The other side of pride walked in the shade on the opposite side of the street. Theresa, the celebrated and shunned member of Miss

Craig's class, walked home to an ailing mother with a thick accent, a different kind of sandwich and an odor that breathed. Nurse Solomon said that it sometimes smelled.

In my mind, Theresa's worst crime was that she was a lousy sport. I had proof. Twice each year, at the church children's dance, we performed the *Shourchbar,* the circle dance, and each time Theresa refused to participate unless she was made the leader. The Sunday school teachers, who felt sorry for Theresa, nearly always acquiesced. And so every year it was Theresa Vartyan, solemn-faced and very tall, who stood at the head of our line, and with us all linked by our pinkies, she dangled a white hankie from her wrist and led us in a circle around the room.

Afterward, at the punch bowl, the children avoided her while the old women exclaimed, "She certainly does have height."

The women of the church tried their best to praise Theresa, not because she earned it but because she was the child of a very sick mother. Respect cleaved to Mrs. Vartyan, who had the good sense to suffer alone with her disease in the privacy of her own house. Theresa was driven to church by a neighbor. No one visited the Vartyans, except Casard, who brought them groceries and vegetables from the garden. Casard had no qualms about entering a home with ravaging germs; having survived the Indignities, she believed she was immune from all common contagions.

Casard tried to make Theresa and me become friends. "Theresa Vartyan, now there's a nice, nice-girl," she said. And when such encouragement failed to impress me, Casard tricked me into visiting the Vartyan house.

One afternoon, on our way home from the grocery store, Grandma Casard announced, "I'm going to quick drop off a turkey," as she turned the car into the Vartyans' driveway.

Who just quick drops off a turkey? I said to myself. I said to myself, Get me out of here. But to my grandmother I remained composed. "OK. Go ahead. I'll just wait here in the car."

Casard seemed to allow this. She turned off the motor and left the keys on the seat so I could play the radio.

She walked to the back and opened the trunk. She moaned—I could hear her through the wall of the car—as she tried to lift the turkey; the car rocked as the weight rose and fell back down. Casard came to my window and rapped on the glass. "Seta, turn that off and come help Grandma."

It was not a question, Casard left no room for response. I opened the door and followed her to the back of the car, where I gave a noncommittal glance into the trunk.

"Seta, the meat's too heavy for me. See if you can lift it. That's it, like a strong good-girl."

Just to prove she could not fool me—I knew this was all a ploy to get me into that house—I looked her in the eye and said, "Easy," as I tugged at the bag with one hand.

The dead weight of the turkey nearly toppled me headfirst into the trunk. Eventually, with both hands, I was its master and we shuffled the bird toward the door, stopping to rest twice.

Each time we stopped Casard rubbed her palm into the space between my shoulders. "Girlie, just a little more. Just a little more," she said. "See. They have a special at the market and we buy a little extra for our friends, isn't that nice? That's it. There you go."

Navigation of the front stoop involved four cement steps; I hoisted the bird onto the landing and turned back toward the car. Casard stopped me with a grim look and pointed her chin at the front door. Theresa was standing behind the glass.

From inside the house I heard Mrs. Vartyan yell, "For Chrissakes, open the door, Theresee, open the door. Invite them in, will you?"

Casard gave me a decisive push, propelling me into the house.

We entered a room so dimly lit we had to stand in the foyer and allow our eyes to adjust. This was the home where Theresa Vartyan slept and ate, where she did her homework. The living room revealed itself in stages. First, the walls emerged, covered with pictures that in the dark resembled faint drawings on the sides of caves. As I looked closer, I discovered that the walls displayed a lifetime collection of religious paraphernalia: I saw portraits of

Jesus and the Last Supper; crosses made from shells, porcelain and lacquered wood; I saw the Virgin Mary, in all stages of suffering—Mary at the foot of the Cross, Mary at the tomb.

Then as my eyes grew accustomed to the light I began to make out the other surfaces of the room. There were plant stands, coatracks and, in the corner, hanging from the ceiling, a mobile made of origami swans. There were walnut and cherry side tables, their legs carved with rosettes, lined with doilies and crammed to the corners with framed portraits of Theresa Vartyan: Theresa as a toddler, Theresa on a swing, in a pretty Easter dress, in a Western getup astride a pony. From the top of the television console, Theresa's black eyes peered from our class picture. Yes, in a cheap Woolworth frame, her face and mine were on show.

The real Theresa stood before me, dumb. Not two feet apart, neither of us could look.

Casard took it upon herself to set things in motion. "I keep that same photograph in my house," she said, patting the girl's arm.

Theresa bent down from her enormous height and brushed my grandmother's cheek with a kiss.

Casard, pleased, went over to Mrs. Vartyan, who seemed upholstered in her chair, and the two women patted hands. When Casard pointed to the turkey, which I had dragged into the house behind me, Mrs. Vartyan said, "Oh my." Then she spoke to Theresa in Armenian, and the girl lifted the bag without strain and set it at her mother's feet.

Mrs. Vartyan caressed the turkey as if it were a dog. She smiled at me. "Sweetheart, you'll have to excuse me, these days I'm not much for standing. It's this head of mine. Dizzy-dizzy."

I smiled back, trying not to stare. In the dim light it was difficult at first to discern exactly what was wrong with Mrs. Vartyan's face. Then it came to me as a revelation: she had no eyebrows. Such a small detail, not like missing a nose, but it was enough to throw her face entirely off-kilter. Still, I was somewhat relieved to discover that she seemed to have all of her skin. Trying not to appear too obvious, I peered at her face some more and saw that Mrs. Vartyan's lipstick bled from her lip line in a crooked arch below her nose. The overall effect was that of lips resembling two uneven strips of thick red yarn. With her orange wig, tipped slightly to one side, she reminded me of Raggedy Ann.

"Sit. Sit. Sit." She waved, pointing Theresa toward the kitchen. "Theresee, get them some tea, would you like some tea?"

I said no; Casard said yes.

Mrs. Vartyan said, "Theresa, maybe Seta would like a Coca-Cola." How did she know my name? Mrs. Vartyan eyed me, then, turning to Casard, said something in Armenian I could not understand. The two women smiled and nodded their heads. Oh, Casard was pleased.

Mrs. Vartyan petted the turkey, "Seta, how's your new doggy. Miss America, is it?"

Casard tasted her lip, and nodded.

I glanced at my grandmother in disbelief. In this shrine of Jesus, this home of the outcast and her ravaged-faced mother, Casard smiled. She had told them about our new dog. Moreover, as if we were on a holiday, she leaned back in her chair, prepared to let me rot my teeth with Coke.

The two women resumed their conversation in Armenian, nodding and waving. Theresa caught my eye and shrugged. It was like this: here she almost passed for normal.

We sipped our drinks, then something was said in the other language that caused a shift in mood. Mrs. Vartyan petted the turkey, weighing its significance. She wagged a finger at me. "Do you want me to tell you a story?" The skin above her eyes raised in question.

"Yes," Casard said, speaking for us both.

"No," Mrs. Vartyan corrected, pointing, "her."

They all looked at me and what could I do? I nodded.

"OK. I will tell you an old one that starts out— You tell me."

I looked at my grandmother and shrugged.

Mrs. Vartyan waited.

Casard did nothing; I shrugged again. "I don't know. Once upon a time?"

Mrs. Vartyan tsked, eyeing Casard. "Don't you teach her nothing?"

Casard pursed her lips. "She knows. She knows. She's just wants to be lazy."

I glared at my grandmother, my cheeks on fire.

Mrs. Vartyan studied me. "Seta, honey, it's *Gar oo chugar.* There was and there was not. All our stories begin: Gar oo chugar."

"Gar oo chugar," I repeated.

"Ayo! Ayo!" she exclaimed, clapping her hands and wiggling forward in her seat. She reached out a claw and patted my arm. "Now then. There was and there was not a very wise priest who lived in the mountains outside Bitlis, in the Old Country. A good, big town. Farmers and merchants, your Grandma had family in Bitlis, am I right?" Mrs. Vartyan raised her hairless brow and Casard shifted in her chair to signal yes.

"Well, our story happens in the town of Bitlis. There was this Turk, you see. One day outta nowhere he rides to the center of town and climbs down off his horse." Mrs. Vartyan's hands moved as though she were setting down reins.

"He goes to the big church where at that moment the whole town is assembled for the mass. This Turk is Muslim, don't you know, he has not one ounce of respect for our church. Well, he marches up the aisle to the altar. (They live in filth, these Turks, they spit on their women.) This one, he reaches the priest at the moment that the Der Hyre is preparing communion.

"The Father acknowledges the stranger, but as he turns his back, the Turk pulls out a knife"—Mrs. Vartyan pulled out hers—"and stabs the priest! Right there at the altar. And the congregation? They cry out as their beloved priest is martyred!" Mrs. Vartyan stared at me with amazement. Cocking her head to one side, she gave the story a moment to sink in.

Then she pointed at my chest, and, wiggling her hips, resumed.

"So, Seta, what have we got. We got our priest, see, the Der Hyre, lying on the floor in a puddle of his own blood." Mrs. Vartyan, leaning her elbows on her knees, threw open her hands to reveal the floor. "The Father looks up at the Turk and studies the murderer's face. And what does the Der Hyre say?" Mrs. Vartyan wagged her finger—"I'll tell you what he says. With his final breath the martyr sighs and, looking into the Turk's soul, says, 'But why—why do you kill me, stranger? I have never shown you kindness.' "

Mrs. Vartyan looked at Casard and winked. Folding their hands, the two old women leaned back in their chairs and sighed. For a moment we sat like that, in silence, while I stared at the floor, picturing the priest in a pool of blood.

Casard groaned. Pointing at me with her chin, she said, "This one is too young to know."

Mrs. Vartyan glanced at me, then at Theresa, who was perched on the arm of her mother's chair. "Not mine," Mrs. Vartyan said. "She came out of the womb a baby with an old soul."

The two women reflected on this, and on Theresa and me, as if we were the symbols of their lives. Stories passed across their faces: the Old Country, their fathers and mothers, their youth and their dreams. Nightmares, too. In their minds, they saw girls beheaded and dogs gnawing on the legs of dead men. They saw a desert and a wide blue ocean beyond the deck of the Boat.

The two women sighed. Mrs. Vartyan pointed at Casard. "I tell Theresa stories about home so she knows she has a country. One day she goes there."

"Where?" Casard asked.

"Home, to Armenia."

"Psst," Casard hissed. "What Armenia. Point to it on a map."

"Theresa, get down the book."

"Ahhh, Book-shmook." Casard waved Theresa back into her seat. "The Armenia we know sits here," Casard tapped the side of her head. "After us it's gone. These children, they don't know."

"So we teach them."

"Teach them what, about our shame?"

"It's the Turks who should be ashamed," Mrs. Vartyan boomed.

"You tell that to the Turks," Casard said.

"How can you just give up? How can you not teach this girl to dream of the day when Mount Ararat will again be free?"

"Dreamers, what good are they?"

"What about hope?"

"Hope," Casard repeated, the word sour in her mouth. "Hope. The young children, I've seen 'em, all little blondes. Little Englishes, the whole bunch."

Mrs. Vartyan shrugged. "So it's America. We all melt."

Casard turned and brushed her hand along my cheek. "Sometimes. Sometimes she gives a look just like my little Araxie."

"That Araxie, she grew up a nice girl, and this one will, too." Mrs. Vartyan winked at me.

"No," Casard said, looking through me to my mother. She frowned. "I lost Araxie."

"Lost her? Ahhh, Casard Essayan, what nonsense you are telling me. No child is ever owned—she belongs to the world. We have them but a short time, to borrow."

Casard shook her head. "Che." No.

The two women sat quietly, studying their laps. Every so often they glanced at Theresa and me. We looked at the floor and waited for the moment to pass.

Suddenly, Mrs. Vartyan reached out for Theresa and pulled her onto her lap, the whole long weight of her. It had been years since I was welcome on my mother's lap, yet here was Theresa, the amazon, eclipsing her mother as the moon did the sun. Mrs. Vartyan patted her daughter's leg and beamed lovingly at her.

Mrs. Vartyan began to weep, her tears spilling over her yarny lips. Theresa did not seem to mind. She grinned sheepishly—that is, until she saw me staring at her.

She stood, her face crimson. Camouflaging her mother's weeping with movement, she tidied Mrs. Vartyan's dress and wig.

"Mayrig," Theresa whispered, gentling the woman back into her chair.

Casard looked down at the floor, giving Theresa and her mother their privacy.

The spell soon ended. Mrs. Vartyan waved it good-bye. "It's those pills the doctor gives me," she explained, wrinkling her nose. "Every day, I cry. I pour more water than a teapot."

Theresa was not pleased. I had invaded her house, her place of safety; I had witnessed her mother's disease, her mother's Raggedy Ann tears. Tomorrow, it would be all over school.

Theresa searched for a diversion. She said, "Can you play the duduk?"

"Duduk?" I said, but Casard was already nodding.

From on top of the piano, Theresa took down two pipes made of wood, larger than whistles, smaller than flutes. She handed one to her mother, who, like a child, obediently put the instrument to her mouth. Theresa moistened her lips and sealed them around her duduk. Then, inhaling deeply, she closed her eyes.

They began to play. Theresa blew a single note, just one, and held it, while her mother filled in the melody. Mrs. Vartyan's knotted fingers covered and uncovered the duduk's holes, letting each note have its time, each note its wisdom. Low tones, then high, her fingers quivered and marched, filling the room and me. In my mind I saw a picture of a young girl with no clothes—a sad, naked girl.

The song was "Siretzee Yarus Daran"—"I Loved but They Took My Love from Me." Casard sang it sometimes while she ironed shirts. Sung by my grandmother, the tune became a worker's lament, and although I could not understand the Armenian lyrics, I had always imagined the story to be of men and women plowing a field, their curved backs bent like wheat, their sweaty faces creased with relentless toil. Yet the same song, interpreted through the warm, nasal tones of the Vartyans' duduks, became, unmistakably, about love. Lost love.

I watched the Vartyans and, sucking on a strand of my hair, let their song move through me. I watched Theresa—her black eyes closed, her long nose arched like a buttress, the broad planes of her face pale, as though sculpted from marble. In Theresa's face I saw the music. I saw a room without a ceiling or floor, just four walls of dirt. I passed through the room into a town square, where I saw a row of girls hanging by their braids, their eyes empty sockets, their lifeless bodies swinging to and fro. I passed through the square, onto an open road, where a group of women and children passed, wearing rags. I saw a young girl take hold of her mother's hand, then let go. Tears stung my eyes as the duduk seduced the memory from me, as though it were a thin string being slowly pulled from my heart.

Casard reached over and gripped my shoulder and I leaned my head on her lemony-scented hand.

When at last the song ended, Theresa's droning note resonated in the shadowy room. Inside that chamber with Jesus and suffering Mary, and the picture of Theresa and me, her note, as vibrant and earthy as she, quivered and refused to leave. That note brimmed with the hallowed air of every cathedral and the loam of every grave. It seeped inside me, to a place where things are kept that cry.

Time passed—I do not know how much time—but finally we stood. I hugged Mrs. Vartyan, taking care not to jar her wig, and then, so as not to disturb the room further, we whispered our good-byes. We made our way out the door, Casard holding on to me as we stood in the afternoon light, blinking.

As we passed down the walk, I looked back and saw Theresa watching us through the glass. I knew what she was thinking. "See you tomorrow," I said, to let her know her secrets were safe with me.

Theresa opened the door a crack and for a moment our eyes met and she nodded.

Casard started up the car and drove us home like a captain navigating a battleship, mindful of enemy waters, grim with the burden of carrying life. After a time, she addressed her thoughts to the road. "Theresa's mother has cancer, she will soon die."

Death angered Casard. "This dying," she said, as if someone had robbed the bank and made off with the savings. She pursed her lips and sighed as she turned the great black steering wheel.

I asked, "Did you know that story about the priest?"

"Ahhh, it's an old story, from the Old Country."

"And the duduk?"

Casard nodded. "At home we called it a *srink.* The shepherds used them to call the sheep. My father played with my uncle. Hayrig was the one who held the note. The person with the melody always gets the applause, but to hold that one note—the dam—that's the hardest."

I thought about how ugly and how beautiful it all had been—Theresa, with one breath, holding that note. I thought about Mrs. Vartyan's face and how what seemed at first grotesque came to look rather sweet.

Casard squinted at the road. "It's not my way to talk," she said, "and fill your head with ghosts."

As if these words clarified everything that was between us, Grandma Casard nodded and, gripping the wheel tightly, threaded the car through the neighborhoods of Memorial. At the corners she braked, then accelerated, the sound of the motor punctuating the silence inside the car. We passed by lawns bordered with pageants of colors: crimson tulips, yellow daffodils, the pale green veil of the weeping willow. We passed rows of mailboxes with familiar names: Casard's acquaintances, Dad's clients, my classmates from school. Everything familiar, everything known.

We turned onto Main Street and, driving to the end, arrived at the statue of Squaw. Before I was born, the Indian maiden, alone, commanded the downtown square. But through the years larger monuments encroached—multiplying, it seemed—until statues outnumbered the downtown shops.

So many immortalized dead troubled me. I was, after all, only eleven years old, yet in my short life I had seen so many endings. I had witnessed a cemetery grow beyond its borders, while in town two elementary schools and one junior high school closed. I watched downtown consumed by an arsonist's fire, the burned-out buildings razed, never to be rebuilt, while my father, who years earlier had ridden the last wave of greater Hartford's suburban growth, saw his business dry up, as the managers from insurance companies moved their young families to the pastoral communities east of the Connecticut River. Then every night, after dinner, I sat in my parents' den and watched television footage of an unending, bloody, mud-soaked Vietnam war.

I looked over at my grandmother and longed to ask which ghosts she spoke of—the ghosts before the Boat or the ones here—but fear and habit kept me silent.

Grandma Casard pulled into the driveway and shut off the motor. She lifted her hands from the wheel and tucked them in her lap. Somewhere deep in the engine fluids ran. The car sighed. The two of us sat quietly, listening for something, though neither of us knew exactly what. My grandmother's hands were folded—ladylike, one on top of the other.

She stared ahead, at the garage doors, waiting, and in that moment it occurred to me that one day soon Casard would die. It was a terrifying thought, something I had never before considered, and it made me ashamed to be thinking such a thought while sitting beside her.

I followed her gaze to the brown garage door of the house where I lived. It seemed as if I had never been there before.

Outside, afternoon shadows danced against the garage, but inside the car we could not hear the wind. Only the mysterious clicks of the motor. Then, far off, I thought I heard a horn. The sound came closer and, like the duduk, it held me frozen, unable to open the door and break Theresa Vartyan's spell.

SIX

That note stayed with me, making sure that I would not forget. A week after the visit to Theresa Vartyan's, Melanie and I were sitting on Casard's back porch sucking lemons, and again the duduk found me. It carried me into shifting visions of a cold stone church, where I fell among a brotherhood of black-hooded monks with sooty nails and lamby breath, and then I saw Mount Ararat and Abel's blood flowing down the mountain into a field of crimson poppies. I walked a craggy road, and the duduk sounded in the dirt under the hooves of a passing donkey. Somewhere a baby wailed, its mother frying onions, its father coming in from the street. In the doorway, he scraped his boot with a sharp, flat stone. Dung fell from his shoe. A child's hand grabbed the hand of an elder, then let go.

Melanie, eyeing me, licked the inside of her mouth. "What's the matter with you?" she said.

"Nothing," I said, and she took another bite of lemon and so did

I. The juice trickled down my throat to my belly, where the duduk pulled me like a fish on a line, and I was awash with a sudden, inexplicable shame.

That duduk and the visions it awakened changed my life. Where once I stood comfortably within the ring of fifth-grade popularity, the circle seemed to shift. I no longer possessed the necessary gestures. I was awkward, troubled by a peculiar misery, a weighty threnody playing inside me.

"What's the matter with you?" Melanie asked, but I did not dare tell her.

The next day after school I followed an older girl to the Catholic church across the road. I walked behind her through the heavy white doors and, following her example, dipped my fingers into the holy water. When the girl disappeared inside the confessional, I knelt on a velvet bench and, putting a nickel into the brass box, lit up a row of votive candles. I recited the Lord's Prayer, quick like a droning bee, and then I prayed for my family, for our dog, Miss America, and for myself. I prayed that Casard would not die anytime soon. And I prayed that the duduk, and the memories it evoked, would leave me alone.

Afterward, I walked up the aisle, genuflecting at various pews. I was solemn and grave with religious spirit. At the communion rail I knelt and regarded the Catholic Jesus on his bloodstained Cross. Gripping the brass railing, I stared at Jesus, and for a moment the heaviness inside me lifted, as though my belly were being infused with a clean, watery light, and my heart and lungs, too. This feeling, I suspected, was holy.

Climbing down from the altar, I murmured, "Bless, bless," as I headed toward the rear of the church and the confessional. The girl I had followed was gone and a plump woman carrying a patent-leather purse she hugged to her chest was stepping through the back doors and into the box. Since there was nobody around, I walked over to the mahogany confessional and put my ear to the red velvet curtain.

Right off, I heard the woman confess to slapping her child—just once, she assured the priest, and not very hard. Her voice dropped below a whisper and then she began to weep. The priest said to her, "My child. These desires you speak of, are they outside the marriage?" I leaned in close, my heart galloping, and heard her pitiful, choked sobs.

The effect of the woman's tears on my spirits proved calamitous; I fled the church. It seemed to me that I had witnessed some means of absolution that was heretofore denied me. I was alone; my ersatz holy feeling, gone. I left the Catholics with no idea where to go next. It was nearly four o'clock, I had to be home by six, but until then I grimly placed myself in fate's hands.

I went to the park and walked along the periphery toward downtown, where all day, as I sat in school grinding mathematics problems and social studies worksheets, the real business of life transpired. Behind the gray and brick façades along Main Street, money was counted, packages routed to bins, while in the upper floors of the medical building, remedies for the common ailments of man—bunions, cataracts, tooth decay—were diagnosed. It was downtown where I took my heavy heart, eager to find relief.

At the bank, I turned the corner and walked several blocks to Bob Humms's Shoe Repair, where I paused in front of the window to look at the sign that read *Until.* I was searching for something to shock me from my duduk-induced stupor, and peering through the glass, I found Bob Humms. He was polishing a shoe with a motorized brush. I stared at him and he glanced up from his work and our eyes locked. His hair was matted and he had a black smudge on his left cheek, but his face was sympathetic and kind. On a sudden impulse I blew the cobbler a kiss, then ran like hell down the street. I ran for cover and I ran because it felt good. Crossing the intersection in front of several cars, I ran from the ensuing horns as though into the arms of another world.

I reached the triangular strip of grass at the center of town and sprinted past a cluster of adults waiting for the bus—they were behind me now, they ceased to exist. Into the small park I flew, nodding my respects to the statues of Lafayette, Elliot and Polanski, standing on their marble pedestals like hosts from an Arctic sepulcher. I ran from them all, stopping when I reached barefoot Squaw.

She was rooted at the very center of the square, on top of a marble pillar; she stood there like perfection, white, cool, serene. In one arm Squaw held a baby; her other arm was raised as if swearing an oath. Her marble eyes were cast to suggest that she was gazing at the horizon—that, and a row of maple trees. Her dress was plain with a ragged hem to suggest buckskin; in her hair she wore a feather. Resting at her feet was a carved Bible. I walked around her pedestal to read the inscription on the book, and found Theresa Vartyan sitting in the dirt, at the base of Squaw.

The moment I laid eyes on Theresa I knew that I had been looking for her ever since I left her house. Even so, I quickly calculated the risk should we be seen together. If Paul Mahoney or, worse, Patty Sullivan saw us, it would take exactly half a minute for the word to be all over school. By tomorrow morning I would be crowned Theresa Vartyan's bosom friend.

Theresa shaded her eyes from the sun and, squinting, sized me up. "The doctor says my mother'll be better any day now."

"That's good." I nodded.

Theresa unwrapped a tissue from her bag and displayed a row of cigarettes as though they were hors d'oeuvres. "Do you want one?" she asked.

"I don't think so," I said, thinking of Nurse Solomon's Palmolive lung.

Theresa shrugged and, pulling a match from her pocket, lit up. She began to breathe in the cigarette, rolling it between her fingers, making it delicious, like candy. White dragon plumes poured from her nose and mouth. She saw me staring at her and laughed. From a space between her teeth came this high-pitched, wheezy laugh.

"Where'd you learn how to French-inhale?" I asked, longing for a piece of gum or something to put in my mouth.

Theresa ignored me, her face deeply serious. "My mother liked you. She told a story."

"Poor priest," I said.

Theresa shrugged. "Those priests are always getting killed in my mother's stories."

We both nodded as if this explained everything. Theresa tucked her feet under her, so she was sitting Indian style in the dirt. I noticed she had on tangerine-colored hose.

Without thinking, I took the piece of chalk from my pocket and began practicing my name on the granite base of Lafayette. The writing soothed me and made me bold. I drew my name with loopy tails and elaborate swirls, and then I stepped back. "Theresa," I said, "can I ask you a question?"

She lifted her chin in the air like a hyena and tooted a series of smoke rings.

"What did it feel like?" I asked.

"What?"

"You know. That day. In front of the class."

"Oh," she said, dropping her head and jutting her lip. Right away, I regretted the question, which suddenly seemed unkind. I was afraid that on account of my rudeness Theresa would cry or get angry or do something entirely unexpected, even dangerous, but she remained very still, assessing the burning end of her cigarette. She had, I noticed, a way of moving that was different from other people's—slower, but at the same time less controlled; its effect was to make me uneasy. I no longer had any idea what I wanted from her, or why, at first, I had been glad to find her.

Theresa cleared her throat and leaned close. "You," she whispered, her lips inches from my ear, "are you going to the anniversary?"

Not knowing what she was talking about, I shrugged. "I don't know. I don't think so. Why?"

"You know, Martyrs' Day at church. To honor the massacre."

"Oh yeah." I nodded.

"Your grandma hates it worse than anything. Everyone knows

that. You know what I think? I think it's because it happened to her. You don't have to talk about it when it happens to you."

Theresa rubbed her lips together and glanced at me. "The Turks raped girls, you know," she said, matter-of-factly. "They hacked men's balls. They set families on fire and watched them dance. After, they pulled the gold from their burned mouths."

"Your mother told you this?" I said, crouching next to her.

"It's nothing"—she waved.

"What about the anniversary? What's it like?"

Theresa pretended not to hear me, her attention diverted to a couple arguing across the street, in front of the post office. As we looked on, the man grabbed the woman's wrist and pulled her to the corner. The light changed, but as they started to cross, the woman planted her feet and refused to budge. The man turned to her and said something and she shook him loose. When he started across without her, she followed.

Theresa watched the couple and I watched her, trying to find a way to get her to tell me more about the massacre. I studied her, but she was hiding; her hair, parted in the middle, covered all of her face except for her prominent nose. She was wearing one of her bizarre outfits: a clownish purple striped top, black skirt, orange stockings and maroon pumps. She looked to me then like a rack at a thrift shop, though later, when we were grown, I would go to Paris and find on the Left Bank a population of long-legged Theresas in bright stripes and clashing hose, talking excitedly in the cafés.

Theresa lifted her chin and looked at me through her curtain of hair. "Where'd you get that ruby?" she asked.

"Ruby?"

"Under your eye." She fished in her purse for a mirror. "Look," she said.

"What am I looking for?" I asked, peering into the glass. Then I noticed a tiny red dot under my eye. "That's no ruby. It's a cut or something," I said, clawing at my skin.

"Nope." Theresa grinned. "It's a ruby. I get them all the time."

And she lifted her hair from her neck to reveal a throat covered by tiny red dots.

"God!" I said.

"Why, they don't hurt." She pointed a filthy finger at the spot under my eye. "Anooshig," she said. "Pretty."

"Anooshig," I parroted, unable to keep myself from grinning. Until that moment I had never seen a mark on my skin that did not strike me as a blemish. I had never looked into a mirror that did not tell me Wrong, Wrong, yet here was Theresa, the ugliest girl in school, finding me Pretty.

It was already six o'clock when we headed home. The sky was feathers of red. The shopkeepers along Main Street rolled in their awnings and locked their doors. I would be grounded for arriving home late to dinner. As we walked I accepted the loss of a week of television, a week of phone; it was done and I could take my time getting to it. We walked past the barbershop just as Dad's lawyer, Mr. Levin, stepped out of the door and noticed Theresa Vartyan. He paused and, looking her over, hitched his trousers. She pretended not to see him. A block further we passed another man getting into his car, and when he saw Theresa he cleared his throat. For her, the men hitched their trousers, they cleared their throats.

Theresa and I did not speak as we climbed the hill by the park. Instead, we walked and stared at the ground, thinking our private thoughts. When we reached Victoria Road, she said, "See you."

I went on home and later that night scrubbed my face, but the ruby stuck. I lay in bed reflecting on the spot under my eye, like a kiss of red pen.

The strangeness of Theresa's gifts confounded me. She seemed to possess a kind of truth, more compelling than a particular accent or personality or look, a truth that made her repulsive to fifth graders but tantalizing to grown-up men. I supposed her gift was a certain kind of freedom, and while I could not understand such a gift, I knew at least to respect it.

That night I dreamed of breasts coming toward me and nipples swarming like flies, so many I had to swat at them to protect my face. But in the morning my ruby waited. Like the sound of the duduk, the ruby remained. Anooshig, Theresa called it, pretty. But pretty to a woman was not the same as it was to a girl. To a girl pretty meant top of the heap, but to a woman like Theresa it only meant beginner.

The first chance I had, I asked Casard about Martyrs' Day, and just as Theresa predicted, I learned that my grandmother hated it worse than filth.

"Grandma, why won't you talk about it."

Casard snapped the newspaper and stared at me with fish eyes. "Why aren't you outside with your brother?"

"Because I want to talk."

Casard fumed—"I said *Out.* Go on, take your sister." She pointed at Melanie, who was seated across the room. "You know better than to traipse Indignities in my house."

Casard shook the paper, raising it like a wall in front of her, so there was nothing more to argue with—just the hem of her housedress, her Bad Leg resting on the hassock, her gray tie shoes and a wall of print. I knew she was on the other side of that wall, fish eyes blinking.

It was a mystery to me that an event so far in the past could still hold power over our lives now. How could it hurt Grandma just to have it mentioned? Of course, I did not realize that to talk about the genocide was to make it happen all over again, right there on her Persian carpet. She turned her head and piles of skulls appeared, and, in the corner by the fairy lamp, the butcher Turks.

Since my afternoon with Theresa, I had learned on my own about Martyrs' Day. Every year on April 24, throughout the world, Armenians held a service to mark the first day of the 1915 genocide. But each year Casard refused to participate in a public display that she perceived as toxic, worse than public toilets and public buses, worse than money tainted by "people's" hands, worse than dirty feet on the bed.

"Out"—she panted, shaking the newspaper.

Melanie and I marched to the foyer. "Wait here," I told my sister, and ran upstairs to Casard's room and brought down a book. We slipped out the front door, to where Van had propped a ladder against the trunk of the oak. Melanie and I climbed up and onto the garage roof. Over the peak, on the far side, Van was lying on his back. We stretched out on either side of him, our feet braced in the gutter, the sun's rays prickly on our faces, the heat from the tar shingled roof radiating beneath our clothes.

"Check this out," I said and flashed the book I had removed from its hiding place in Casard's room, high up on a shelf above Grandpa Vrej's desk. It was a book about the genocide; I had discovered it the week before when taking a nap on Casard's bed. We rolled over on our bellies to have a look.

On the back cover, there was a photograph of eight Armenian women, naked and crucified, their long black hair hanging to their waists. Inside, a photograph showed men's heads impaled on sticks, and another, a pyramid of thousands of skulls collected in the desert of Der el Zor. The caption read that at least one million Armenians had been buried in shallow graves in the desert of Der el Zor.

There were photographs of the survivors: emaciated children with bloated bellies and deep-set eyes gazing vaguely into the camera. The caption read: "Armenian orphans in Syria."

We leaned in close, our noses just inches from the page and turned to a photograph of a beautiful dark-haired Armenian girl standing against a wall, her shirt open to her navel. The tattoos on her forehead, throat and breasts were the names of the Turks who had bought and sold her as a slave.

"Jesus Christ—" Van stammered.

And then I said what we were all thinking, "Grandma."

Melanie began to cry, and Van and I each put an arm around her. We glanced from the orphaned children to the slave girl, and back again, silently imagining our grandmother with bloated belly and round saucer eyes, with tattoos hidden beneath the bodice of her housedress.

We had been there awhile, a half hour maybe, when Casard began looking for us.

"Van-Seta-Melanie," she called, summoning us as one person.

"Quiet," Van whispered. "Maybe she's just fishing."

"Van-Seta-Melanie, I see you—on the roof. Show your faces."

I peered over the peak. Casard was hanging out one of the upstairs windows. "Get down, you. I said Immediately-Now. You too, Mister Grown."

We all stood at the same time and stared at her. What we had just seen must have been on our faces, for she looked us over and said nothing. After a few moments she tucked her head back into the house and brought the window gliding slowly down onto the sill.

That evening, Casard came over to our house and sat at the kitchen table, waiting for Momma to bring her a cup of tea.

"Araxie. Honey," Casard began. "Those children. They have no business at Martyrs' Day."

Momma stared grimly at the old woman's face and sighed. Momma's face revealed the inner conversation she was having, which went, Will we have to have another fight? Yes, of course. Do I have the strength? Does it matter? Can we get it over quick? With her, is there any such thing as quick?

Momma began patiently, her voice soothing, as though she were speaking to a child. "Mayrig, I understand how you feel. I do. But the children—Seta, especially, wants to go. They have brought this request to us out of their own need. They want to know what happened. I think it's time—this not talking about it doesn't help anyone. Before Pop died, he took me to Martyrs' Day. Don't look at me that like that, Mayrig! It was my right to know. You, even you, can't wish away the genocide. It made you, it made me. And, Mayrig, it's made these kids, too. Seta wants to go—now, why shouldn't she?"

"Araxie!" Casard boomed, stabbing her finger in the air. "What is this ridiculous I am hearing? They're interested. You let them play with guns, they're interested?"

"No—" Momma said firmly, pointing her own finger. "What I'm saying is they have a right. That's all. Mayrig, every kid in that Sunday school of yours knows what happened in 1915. Why shouldn't ours? Here they are: their own Grandma a survivor."

"That's right, that's right, Araxie. Now you've made a good point. Their own Medz-mayrig lived through it and she is the one to judge. I say, Stay out. Don't give me interested! You let them take drugs, they're interested? You let them read dirty books? I say children have no business poking in filthy Indignities."

Momma, abandoning patience, began to shriek. "Mayrig, listen to me! How many times do we have to go 'round and 'round? George and I have discussed this. That's all. You hear me? Final."

"Ho-ho!" Casard bellowed. "So now it's the odar inviting me to my own Indignities. You tell that Mister: Look out."

Tipping forward in her chair, Casard squinted her eyes at Momma. "Araxie. I'm looking right into you."

Momma nodded. "Mayrig, I know."

"I'm looking right into you," Casard said.

Momma tucked in her lips and chin, as if suppressing a burp. She nodded solemnly.

"So-so-so," Casard said.

"So, I already told you," Momma said.

In the end it was decided that we would all attend Martyrs' Day. Casard said she would meet us at the church.

Each of us tried to imagine the event. Van said that the priest would re-create the Massacre on the altar, using fake blood. Momma said she remembered people coming forth from the pews to tell their stories. The pain of the survivors, she said, made her weep. Dad said what he always said, "We'll see."

I told Melanie there was nothing to be frightened of; the service would be theatrical: we would put ashes on our hands and faces and dance the shourchbar, the circle dance, in honor of the martyrs. I wondered if Theresa would insist on leading, the way she did every year at Sunday school, but I decided that it was unlikely.

At one o'clock in the afternoon we piled into the Buick. Halfway to church Momma looked into the visor mirror and touched up her lipstick. "Seta," she said, "I'm counting on you, especially. Watch after Grandma. Take her hand nice, sit beside her."

I flicked the metal lid on the ashtray open and shut, open and shut. Pressing my finger inside, I studied the soot on my skin. All that week I had tried to imagine a million and a half dead. I had tried to picture a million trees and saw only a forest. It was a strange and eerie lesson that, beyond a certain number, everything diminishes to the eye. Everything becomes one.

I could not stop thinking about the girl with the tattoos. Her lonely, melancholy face captured the essence of the feeling in my belly, the feeling awakened by the duduk. I closed my eyes and saw the slave girl's tattooed breasts and her black soul-dead eyes. And then I thought about Casard and felt frightened, convinced that I was about to learn something that would irrevocably change the way I saw her.

Dad pulled the car up in front of the church. As we opened the doors of the car, Momma swiveled in her seat. "Now I'm counting on you," she said. "All of you—best behavior."

We entered the church basement and were immediately confronted by Hitler's famous words sewn on an enormous felt banner:

WHO AFTER ALL SPEAKS TODAY OF THE ANNIHILATION OF THE ARMENIANS?

The banner hung from the ceiling. Beneath Hitler's pronouncement, as if in defiance of the doom therein, the basement teemed with living breathing Armenians, everyone talking all at once.

The women were dressed in navy or gray, the walls draped in black crepe. Bulletin boards with newspaper accounts and photographs of the atrocities were set up on easels along the four walls.

In the center of the room, below Hitler's quote, two aged men were engaged in a passionate discourse, poking each other's chest. The two men looked old enough to be survivors of the Turks' genocide, which Hitler had studied and augmented to suit his own plans. The sight of these two cronies fighting below a banner that proclaimed them wiped out like the buffalo terrified me, and I grabbed hold of Van's arm. Perhaps he was scared too, for he put his hand over mine and held on.

Momma touched her palm to the nape of my neck. Her touch sent shivers through me. "Stay close," she said. "We'll wait for Dad before heading upstairs to the church." Then Momma took Melanie by the hand and steered us through the crowd.

I glanced around the room trying to find Theresa, but she was nowhere in sight. With Momma in the lead, we pushed through the crowd toward the coffee bar in the back of the room. We wound along the side wall, stopping to gaze at photographs of the genocide, the dead captured in postures of sleep, their knees bent to one side, as if the covers had just been removed. I accidentally bumped into an easel, nearly toppling it, and when I saw pinned to it the photograph of the slave girl from Casard's book, I cried out. The caption read, "Armenian Girls Tattooed by Turks Sold as Slaves."

Momma must have heard me, for she touched me on the arm and studied my face, to see if I was all right. She was about to say something when Ani Baboostian, the oldest member of the church, called to her, "Araxie! Araxie, where have you been hiding! We've been looking all over for you."

Momma turned to the old woman and kissed her cheeks. But Ani pursed her lips and frowned.

"Ani, something the matter?" Momma said.

Although Casard was the leader of the church, Ani Baboostian, eighty-nine years old, was its soul. Stout, with lively green eyes, long white hair and a handsome face creased like a good, soft glove, Ani was adored. Her vanity showed in the gold and ruby rings she wore on every finger including her thumbs, and the vibrant scarves she wrapped around her neck, this one orange with crimson tulips. Ani fingered her scarf, straightening it at her throat. Frowning, she shook her head, as if to say the matter was impossible to put into words. "Your mother, in the kitchen" was all she could manage.

Momma dispatched Van to go find Dad, while Melanie and I pushed behind her through the crowd. People cleared a path, eyeing the kitchen door.

We found Casard stretched out on a stainless-steel worktable in the center of the kitchen, a blanket folded under her head. Above her, hanging from the ceiling, was a huge rack of shiny pots. The old women of the church were gathered around Casard, talking in Armenian, trying to decide what should be done.

"Ah." Poppee clapped her hands. "Finally, Araxie."

The women nodded in our direction, their hands clasped together as though they were praying.

Poppee whispered something to Momma. As she spoke, Poppee put her hand over her heart and thumped a quick rhythm. Momma listened with her brow knit tight, the way she looked when one of us was telling her a fib.

Momma turned to Casard, and cupping her palms gently on Casard's cheeks, she whispered softly, "Mayrig," followed by something in Armenian that I could not hear.

Casard nodded weakly. "Scared me awful," she croaked. "My heart: Boom. Boom. Boom. Boom."

Momma placed her hand over her own heart. The women watched her and some shook their heads, while others rubbed their lips together, as though fighting the urge to speak.

Then Dad came into the kitchen, escorted by one of the deacons. He looked at Momma and they each read the other's mind.

Frowning, Dad asked, "Can she sit up?"

Momma spoke to Casard in Armenian. "She says the palpitations are less now."

The old women looked to Dad to see what he would do.

He studied the situation and then he said to Momma, "Come on. Let's take her home."

The old women nodded approval and helped Dad as he lifted

Casard to her feet. With Momma holding her on one side and Dad on the other, Casard shuffled like an aged queen out the kitchen door and up the steps into the churchyard.

At the car, Dad tucked Casard in the front seat and held the back door open for the rest of us. Melanie hopped in, followed by Momma.

"No," I said, backing away from the car.

Van stood with me. "Go on, Dad," he said, "we'll save your seats till you get back."

Dad grimly shook his head. "Seta, Van, I'm sorry, but the show's over. You might as well get into the car."

"But you promised," I said.

"I know," Dad agreed, holding up a hand. "But it's over now. Surely you can see that. Let's take Grandma home and we'll see about next year."

"Next year," I repeated bitterly, as if he had said, Not ever. "No way. I'm going inside."

Dad shook his head. "Now, Seta, I can't allow that."

I hated him then, I hated them all and Dad knew it. He looked away, studying the road. "I suppose you two can walk back to Grandma's on your own, if you want." He swung the back door closed and then got in behind the wheel.

Casard gazed straight ahead as if we were not there, as if the car were already en route.

"Grandma," I snapped, lunging toward Dad's open window. "Give me one good reason why we all can't go inside."

She would not look at me and I began to shriek, "You're a fake, Grandma. That's what you are: a fake. You're fine enough to sit in the car, but you can't sit in the church."

"Start the car," she said, her gaze never leaving the hood.

Dad glanced at us one last time, and was about to start up the engine when Momma reached over the seat and squeezed his shoulder. "We're not going anywhere," she said, "until Mayrig says something to these kids."

"Enough talk"—Casard sniffed.

"What was that?" I yelled.

Casard lifted her chin.

"Aw Jees," Van said, and took off down the street. He went a ways, then turned back and bellowed, "Just forget it, Seta. Forget—her. It's our massacre just as much as hers. She doesn't own fucking any-thing!"

I followed Van down the road. We were careful not to look back until the car had passed us and disappeared around the corner. Then Van and I turned on our heels and headed back to the church.

The bells tolled. The Der Hyre bowed his head, making the sign of the cross. One by one, the old people rose to speak on behalf of the martyrs. Among the seated congregation they rose like pillars from an ancient ruin:

I am Arshag and I speak for my father, who was taken by the soldiers. I lost my mother and four brothers on the road to Aleppo.

I am Sarah and I stand in honor of my mother, who I remember baking the bread. The night the Turketa came, they violated her in front of me and my sister. All night they went at it and all night she suffered without a word. In the morning they stabbed my mother in the throat.

I am Kevork and I speak for our people. I speak for my family. My mother hid my sister and me in a cupboard in two woven sacks. She told us not to move. When the Turks came and took my mother and father away, we were safe. We stayed in that cupboard until it was very dark, the smell inside the sack making me sick all over myself.

I am Yerchanig. You Christian scum, they called us. They corralled our people like cattle into the church. I was a small boy. I ran from the group and hid behind a bush, no bigger than this. My mother and father, and my two brothers, I saw them being shoved into the church. I saw my mother at the last minute turn and look for me. The Turks pushed her into the church with their bayonets. They sealed the doors and threw burning hay into the windows and set fire to the roof. I will not describe the smell and the moaning. I will not tell you what I heard, hiding under that bush. To this day every time I close my eyes I see my mother's eyes searching for me.

I am Khentir. I stand in memory of my brother, Alexan, who also hid under a bush. Only he was not so lucky.

I am Ani. I was with my mother on the death road when the peasant women came down from the hills. First we heard their cry, "Aayyyyeee! Aayyyeee!" and we thought: At last, they've come to save us. But we were very mistaken. You see, they carried knives for killing Christians and securing themselves a place in Paradise. I watched them put a knife through my mother, but they spared us young ones. I was then in my twenties and still a virgin. Now I am an old, sick woman, who has made her peace with God. But perhaps you have wondered why all these years Ani Baboostian wears a scarf. Now you will know."

Ani untied her orange and crimson scarf and raised her chin so the whole congregation could see the letters that covered her from neck to sternum. The tattoos were in the shape of a cross.

"You young ones can't read Turkish," Ani said, her green eyes opened wide. "Look here, young ones. Look at Ani Baboostian, slave girl. These letters are the names of her owners. These are the ones who violated her. Look now and remember what you see."

At first Van and I could not believe our eyes, but Ani lifted her chin and gave us time. Later, when the Der Hyre gently guided Ani to her seat, I could still see her in front of the altar, the writing on her throat irrevocably linked to the brass candelabras and the velvet curtain and the Cross. Suddenly, it made sense to me why the ancient songs were written in a minor key, why they seemed most true when paired with the sorrowful lament of the duduk. The duduk was the keening voice of the slave girl, and the martyred men and children. It was the voice of Casard, the part that could not speak. At last I understood that the trouble in my belly was my grandmother calling out to me, and I was miserable and brokenhearted, listening to Casard.

• • •

From the church, Van and I walked to the park and sat in the grass, reflecting. We did not know what to say; we were mortified, sick with sorrow and revulsion, and all we could do was privately digest what we had learned. Afterward, as it was getting late, we walked to Casard's, and found Sonny waiting for us on the front porch. He whimpered a halfhearted greeting intended for family, and wagged his tail. Sonny did not believe it necessary to make a big show for familiars. The old dog moaned as we stroked his belly, and then stepped over him into the house.

Momma met us in the foyer. She brushed Van's cheek with the back of her hand and circled an arm around my shoulder. "How's mine," she asked, peering into our faces. "All right?"

Van shrugged and disappeared into the living room, where Dad and the other men had the TV tuned to a Yankees game.

Momma gave me a rueful smile. "All this time, were you at the park?"

I did not want to lie to Momma, neither did I want to admit anything. Shamed by what I had seen and could not tell, I hid my face from her.

She sighed, supposing I was still peeved at Casard. "She's upstairs, you know. Waiting."

"Momma, I can't see her right now."

"Seta-Sue, why don't you get it over with, hmm? You know she can stand up to the whole world, but not you. Not you. One minute and it's over. Quick. Go on. I'll be right here. You come down and it's time for supper."

Through the fence of my fingers, I looked at Momma pleadingly, but she read my expression as hurt pride.

"Go on," she said impatiently. "One-two-three and it's over."

I found Casard lying on her bed, facing the wall, a wool blanket spread over her. The shades were drawn and the room held the murky light of cinematic dreams. I stood in the doorway overcome by feeling: repulsion and love, a wish to embrace her and a wish to flee. Waiting, seeing which way my feelings would go, my eyes turned to her vanity table. Beneath the oval mirror set in bird's-eye maple was a silver tray with a silver brush, comb and mirror, and a bowl of tortoiseshell combs. The closet door was ajar, and it occurred to me that in another month, on Memorial Day, she would move the black and navy-blue shoes to the back row of her closet and bring the lighter shades—taupe, cream and gray—up front. In her house, everything had its order, nothing was permitted to be out of place.

"Seta?" she murmured.

I paused before answering, "Here."

She would not ask again. She would blink at that wall until the end of time, yet she would not ask.

I walked over to the bed.

Only then did she turn and take hold of my hand, running a dry palm along my arm.

"My girl," she murmured.

"Course," I said, but it was obvious that I did not think so.

She squeezed my hand, and when I refused to return the pressure she pulled me to her, her touch, her Wind Song perfume enveloping me like a drawer.

"My girl always," she said dreamily. She wet her lips. "You know, I told you that business a long time ago, the day I named you."

I jerked my arm away, "Grandma, I don't remember, OK? I was just a baby and no one would expect a *baby* to remember. I thought if we went, then maybe we could, you know, remember together."

She sighed and rolled over onto her back. I had never seen her face up close without her glasses. Her eyes were a soft brown, ringed by dark circles; accustomed to correction, they appeared unnatural, unseeing, huge. Taken as a whole, hers was the face of a widow and a martyr. Panic rose in my chest.

"Ours already," she said, and laid her palm on my abdomen. "Right here, it sits. See that. Even now. One day, it all comes back and you're the one to tell Grandma—"

"What—" I cried, panic rising in my throat. "What do you want? It isn't fair!"

"Shame-on-you!" she snapped. "You think there's anything at

that church for you? You think you're going to learn anything from them about *us*? Well, this is it, girlie. Right here: you and me. The rest—forget it. You think some genie's going to pop up and tell you who you are. I'll tell you what: Nonsense."

Casard held her palm to my belly and squinted at me with her huge, unseeing eyes. In my stomach the duduk stirred, and faster than I could speak, images passed through my mind: first, I saw a mountain, then a father coming in from the street, and then the severed heads of young girls—I heard their names: Ani, Shushan, Chortz, Nevart and Jilla—hanging by their braids.

Casard looked into me and smiled. "That's right. That's my girl. Patience. You remember Grandma's story, don't you. Little by little, see that. And when it's time, you bring me my name." Satisfied, she raised her arms like a child for me to help her up. "Here," she said.

The white, white skin under her arms and beneath her chin was jelly-loose. For a moment, I thought of Ani Baboostian and her black tattoos. How white the skin was beneath those tattoos.

Casard waved her arms. "Here. Here. Up."

I wanted to run, but did not dare. Instead, I reached for the blanket and, tearing it from her, tossed it to the floor. Casard made a helpless whiny sound and scooted to the edge, then gripping my shoulders, she grunted as she swung her legs to the floor. As she twisted, her skirt hiked up to her panties, exposing the horrendous truth of her doughy, blue-purple thighs. Oh, sweet Jesus, why did I have to look! Blue like a river, purple as a bruise, veins crisscrossed her white, white skin, soft as a baby's. The Bad Leg, the one that pained her, was most gruesome, patterned by a mélange of veins, some thin and spidery, others thick as pipe cleaners, crooked and bulging just under the skin. In the thickest vein, which ran inside her thigh down below the knee into her calf, there protruded a clotted mass, large as a fig.

"Holy Christ!" I gasped, and tried to pry her from me, but Casard held on, her arms tight around my neck, until I thought I would die, right there in her arms, the realization of which sent a rush of panicked blood pumping to my brain. My arms flailed wildly and a string of expletive-rich babble poured forth: "Go to hell, why don't you. Go to hell, you hear me? Find your own goddamn name. You pig-fat bloodsucker. You white doughy-vein-underpanty-grump. Can't breathe. Can't fucking breathe!" And with a final wrenching groan, I tore her from me and ran for my life from that room.

Downstairs, I hid in the living room, where the men sat in the big chairs and Van and Melanie sprawled on the floor. The Yankees were at bat, and all the men, including Van, were intent on the game. Melanie was trying to get my attention by pointing at the men's hairy legs, their ugly shoes, their sausage fingers like Polish kielbasa. Normally, the sight of the men's thick-soled shoes, short socks and hairy legs struck me as funny and slightly grotesque. Melanie tried to get me going, but I had no use for her. I was too miserable and panic-stricken, Casard's death grip still burning my skin, while the question of what I had said versus what I had thought tormented my mind.

When I heard her coming down the stairs, I tried not to look. If I had indeed cursed Grandma Casard, she would no doubt find me, take me out back, shove soap down my filthy mouth, then enact some obscene and ritualistic torture heretofore unknown. At the very least, she would cast me off as an odar, forever unwanted, filthy, shamed. In short, I was through. Her steps thundered down the stairs, and as it was impossible to hear anything above the roar of my heart, I peeked into the foyer, where I caught sight of her, the picture of composure, in her Supp-Hose, gray ties and the housedress with the tiny blue flowers. She headed straight for the kitchen without so much as turning her head.

I did not know what to think. The women's voices greeted Casard, seeping under the swinging door into the living room. Soon the voices gave way to big throaty laughs. Melanie and I darted glances at each other, then at the door. What were they saying? What was so funny? we wanted to know. Paranoia suggested that it had something to do with me. Whatever it was, we had missed it. Melanie gave me a sulky look, then spread out like a dog on the rug.

I looked around at the men, who did not see me. For them, until dinner only the Yankees existed. I looked around me, trapped by the men's hairy legs and sausage fingers, thick as bars on a cage. Someone else might have thought I was tucked in the center of the familial fold, but to me it felt like the end. I was convinced that I would never grow old enough to rise up and claim an armchair, or hold a respected place among the women in the kitchen. In all rooms, I was the foulmouthed uninvited, the tail end.

The women's laughter swept under the door, their laughter dark as gravy saved in Grandma's Tupperware.

"Come on," I said to Melanie, and holding my breath, stormed through the kitchen door, making a beeline for the pantry. With Melanie in tow, I grabbed a bowl of lemons and a sharp knife, then kicking open the screen door, we marched to the back porch.

Melanie looked at me with wonder, but I was in no mood to explain. "Sit," I said, and we sat Indian style on the smooth porch boards. We positioned ourselves on either side of the kitchen window, so we could keep an eye on the women through the screen. I sliced a lemon, and Melanie and I each took half. The rules of the game were simple: we bit and whoever squinted first lost. If neither of us squinted, we smacked our lips and in unison shouted, "Sour!"

I refused to pucker, even as tears dripped from my cheeks and my teeth felt as though they might dissolve. Melanie attacked her half like a pit bull and held on until I spit the lemon from my mouth. Melanie was the lemon queen, nicknamed by Casard Tutoo, Armenian for sour. She smiled at me, lemon peel showing in place of her teeth.

"One more," I said. "And this time, bite harder."

Melanie chose the fattest lemon and sliced it in half. We bit into our halves, as sour juice dribbled from our chins onto our Sunday clothes. Then Melanie began to chew on her rind and, disgusted, I spit mine into the bowl.

"You sure?" Melanie asked, grinning, wiping her face with the back of her hand.

"Yes, Tutoo," I said and, turning away from her, I leaned forward and looked into the kitchen.

The women were seated at the table, waiting for the roast. Even as they casually assembled, each had her place within the group: Casard sat in the only armchair and Momma in the chair she grew up in. Poppee sat at the far end, and though she was no blood relation, she was my second grandmother. Beside her were her two daughters, Auntie Vart and Auntie Sarah. The five women sat at the table with their feet apart, their knees pressed together, their chests tipped forward, like sparrows perched on a telephone wire.

"I hear Archie's going ahead with the operation," Auntie Vart said to Momma.

Momma nodded. "Next Wednesday she goes in. Thursday they put her under."

"No man should cut off a woman's breast," replied Casard.

"They do the breast or who knows where the cancer will spread," Vart said, pursing her lips.

"Ahh"—Casard waved—"those doctors don't know from Adam. You fiddle with the bosom, then problems start with the downstairs."

"Look at Rosie Hoogasian," Poppee said. "They took the breast and six months later her plumbing went kaput."

Momma made a sour face. "Archie's worried Sevan will find her body repulsive."

"What. What is this?" cried Poppee. "She gives him four perfect children and he's concerned with the look of her breast?"

Casard nodded. "You tell Archie, don't be stupid. Sevan's a good lot, he'll stand by her."

"I think I would feel as if someone had taken the woman from me," Momma mused, and they all looked at her with shocked faces.

"The woman?"—Casard puffed—"Araxie, the woman does not sit in your brassiere."

"Ahhh, they could have one of mine." Poppee waved. "They could have two."

"Don't talk stupid," Casard replied.

"These old things? I'm sick of carting them around."

"You liked them when the boys liked them."

"Oo-la-la," Poppee sang.

"Little Miss Cha-cha-cha"—Casard waved.

"Ahhh, Casard, that's for the young girls now."

"The young girls today don't know what they want. Our day a girl had flesh." Casard palmed her breasts like two melons. "Now all those men want is what's-her-name. Skinny."

"Twiggy, Mayrig, Twiggy," Momma corrected.

"That's her, Twiggy. Pssst. You ask me, skin and bones."

"She might as well be a boy," Vart surmised.

"She's no woman, that's for certain," chimed Auntie Sarah.

Casard slapped the table with her palm. "The other day Van says to me, 'Grammy, when I grow up I want a wife just like you. One who cooks.' "

"Now, there's a smart boy," Poppee hooted.

Casard nodded. "And Archie was a smart girl. Good-looking, too."

"Legs like a colt," Sarah added.

"She grew into them," Poppee confirmed.

Momma shook her head. "You talk like she's dead."

The women paused, considering.

Casard rubbed her palms. "Well, she's not so much younger than my Vrej was."

Poppee nodded. "Twenty years ago, God rest his soul."

"Seems like yesterday," Casard said.

"I remember him young," Poppee mused. "I remember you two, Mr. and Mrs. Newlywed. Woo-who." She beamed, rolling her eyes.

"Not Archie—she's too good to die," Momma said, flattening the wrinkles in her skirt.

"Good?" Casard asked. "Who said good's got anything to do with dying."

"Today for example," Poppee offered, "Ani Baboostian made a statement. Now, that was something. She has the gift."

"Gift nothing," Casard boomed. "What did she say? She survived, that's her gift."

Poppee looked at Casard, her eyes shiny with emotion. Softly, she said, "Casard, did you know she was one of their slave girls."

"Who?" Casard asked.

Poppee gazed at her friend and nodded.

Casard flushed. "Ani said this? She stood in the church and in front of her own children, in front of strangers she said this? Oh my God."

"Mayrig," Momma said, "the shame is what the Turks did to her. What they did to you. It was not her fault. She has nothing to be ashamed of in front of us."

"You," Casard snapped, "don't know a thing. You were not there. You did not see. Ani Baboostian should be ashamed of herself. All these years she keeps her respect and, now, at the end of her life she's got to go and tell everybody. Fine. She wants to wallow with Turketa pigs, she wants to filthy herself, go ahead. Be my guest."

"Che," Poppee said, jabbing her finger in the air, "you're wrong, Casard. Today Ani preserved all our dignity."

"Ah, pssst," Casard said. "You think your tears are gonna change anything? You think the Turks will ever admit to what they've done? You know as well as I do what they say: 'Even if guilt were sable, no one would wear it.' "

"Casard, I am not going to argue. Today wasn't for the Turks. Today was for us. My husband can't sleep remembering his father. Can't eat, can't sleep. He still wakes up in the middle of the night shouting."

"What does he say, Momma?" Sarah asked. Poppee and Casard turned, shocked to find Sarah and the rest of them snooping on their conversation.

"Momma," Sarah said, "what does he say?"

Poppee glanced at Casard, who folded her arms and waited for her friend's answer. Poppee glanced at Auntie Sarah, trying to decide. She peered into the dining room to see if any men were visible. Melanie and I ducked our heads as Poppee's gaze swept across the kitchen, then back to the women.

Leaning forward in her chair, Poppee confided, "He weeps like a little boy, your father. Poor Alex. He says, 'The Turks cut my father's sex parts and set him on fire and they're coming to get Momma, and I can't stop them, I can't stop them!' " Poppee bowed her head and pressed her lips.

"What do you tell him?" Sarah asked, her voice squeaky with alarm.

Poppee shrugged. "I tell your father to make those filthy Turks stop—" She looked into her daughters' frightened faces. "He says he can't."

"I never knew—" Vart stammered.

"Your father don't advertise," Poppee said.

While Poppee spoke, Momma watched Casard, a peevish look on her face. "You know what I heard?" Momma said, pointing her chin at her mother. "They say that the difference between us and the Jews is that the Jews are angry and we're sad."

"The Jews," chimed Vart. "The Jews at least had their day in court."

"Nuremberg," Momma corrected, nodding at her shoe.

"That's it, Nuremberg."

"What do we have?" Sarah said, still shocked by her father's nightmares.

"Each other," Poppee said.

"That and a dime gets you coffee," Momma scoffed and bent down to adjust the buckle on her shoe.

"Watch your mouth," Casard warned. Momma looked up and their eyes met.

"We have the language," Vart offered.

"Oh, come on," Momma scoffed. "Do my children speak the

language? No. After today, will my children ever learn what the anniversary means and how it affected their grandmother? No. Will their friends at school?"

"Your children will learn," Poppee said, "in good time."

Momma could not believe her ears. "How are they going to learn"—she pointed at Casard—"when some people get chest pains so they won't have to tell."

"Listen to her. Tell what? What story? There is no story," Casard boomed.

"First you lost your home—" Momma began, counting on her finger. "Then your family. Then your name."

"Ahhh. What lost my name? Me and all the others."

"No"—Momma pointed. "Hayrig told me: only you, Mayrig, lost your name." Momma looked around her, all at once uncomfortable to be revealing such secrets in front of others. Nevertheless, she pressed on, "You, Mayrig, lost everything—every member of your family and the biggest tragedy is that you cannot face what such a loss did to you! And you won't face what it's done to me and now, those kids."

"Ah, you. What has it done to you?"

Momma threw up her hands. "Look at me, look at us. We sit here pretending this is what it's like to be a family. We fight but we never talk—"

"We're talking now."

"Listen to me for once, Mayrig! Just this morning Van asks me, 'Why is Grandma mad all the time?' Kids pick these things up. They have a right to know."

"Know? How can they know?" Casard said. She eyed Momma, judging how far to push. "What good is it anyway, with them only half."

Momma shoved back her chair and stood. "There she goes, starting with the half-this, half-that business. Tell me, haven't you done enough for one day?"

"Araxie, let your mother be," Poppee said. "We old ones have our ghosts."

"Ghosts, nothing," Casard roared, rising to her feet. "Nobody told her to marry the odar. Now she wants to stuff the babies full of Indignities. No, sirree, not in my house. Araxie, you'll have your turn when I'm gone. Right now I'm the Medz-mayrig. End of story."

Momma glared at her mother, but I could tell she was not really seeing her. Instead, she was seeing a wall that she could never penetrate. Momma's face became perfectly still. She nodded once at the vision, then turned and left the room.

Casard moved away from the others and came to the door of the pantry. On cue, the women stood and made excuses of their hands, busying them with bowls of pickles and salad, which they carried out to the dining room table.

The kitchen was empty and still. Casard walked slowly to the pantry and opened a drawer. She stood there, fishing with her hand for the culprit. Perhaps it was in the cupboards? She opened several. Then she reached into the pockets of her apron. Was it there? Without Araxie to push against, Casard could not be sure, and her hands searched in vain.

She approached the back door, and I closed my eyes as the door swung open and Casard came out to the back porch.

Melanie and I, our knees hugged to our chests, braced ourselves. But Casard swung past us, as though we were debris in the road. On the edge of the porch she stopped and looked out over the yard. She removed her glasses and, pulling a handkerchief from her sleeve, wiped her face.

"Grandma, you OK?" Melanie asked.

Casard seemed not to notice us. Her gaze roved the backyard then returned to the porch, settling upon the bowl of lemon rinds. She exhaled and, bending to pick up the bowl, said, "Follow Grandma."

She moved swiftly, swaying, favoring her Bad Leg, as small tufts of earth and grass leaped from under her blunt heels. Melanie trooped behind her, Casard's apron strings fluttering before my sister like streamers on the back of a parade float. I expected to face my punishment at last, and overcome by impending doom, I lagged behind.

Single file we made our way to the fruit trees along the back fence. There were two well-established fig trees and, over to the far right, the lemon. "Peoples always asking how we get this one to grow," she said, eyeing the small tree. "They wonder-wonder, see, and only us girlies are wiser."

Casard pointed to a small trowel set against the tree. "Seta. Now like a good girl I want you to dig." She touched her toe to a place in the dirt. "Pay attention, that's it, not too deep."

I saw no reason to protest, and digging as best I could, taking care not to disturb any of the previous holes, we made our way around the tree. Melanie could not contain her excitement; she started saying, "Grandma, can't I help, can't I, can't I?" until I was about to slap her.

Casard said, "Melanie's Grandma's second helper," and she offered Melanie the bowl of rinds. "Take yourself a good handful, that's my Tutoo," she said. Then, "Now, Sister," and I gladly took some, too.

We dropped one rind in each hole, then cupped the dirt, burying the peel in a shallow grave. Casard bent low to supervise, and as she held on to the tree, it bowed and dipped, and stray leaves floated to the ground. Casard said, "See, when you give some back, it'll make more. That's the secret."

"How come?"

"Because that's how we did it in the Old Country, how come."

"But why?"

"*Y* is some crooked letter."

"But, Grandma—"

"Let me ask you, Seta. Who do you know wants to give up their own?"

The question hung in the air between us. Melanie looked at me and I looked at Casard, who was nodding at the tree. Melanie and I were meant to understand that our grandmother would never let us go, just as she would never let go of our mother. We were bound together in an endless cycle of birth and death and rebirth; we were fruit of the same tree.

Casard, pleased with us, kissed our hair and our cheeks. She pointed her chin at the tree, wanting us to believe in it, and in her power, instead of in mortifying Indignities. "Our secret," she said.

Smiling, she went on. "Your grandpa planted this tree. People told him he was crazy. They told him the first frost would kill a citrus. But it was all I wanted."

"What was Grandpa like?" I asked.

"Your Grandpa? Your Grandpa, well, nobody's saying Vrej was a saint. But he had a twinkle. Some trouble that Mr. Twinkle."

"Was he handsome?"

"Ah, handsome-shmansome. I'll tell you one thing: he had himself style. Every day he put on his tie. See, all the men at that factory wore the open shirts, but not him. No. He put on himself a tie. A nice one."

"Even Saturdays?"

Casard licked her lips. "Saturdays specially."

"Would he dress up?"

"I didn't say dress up. Vrej was no dress-up. I said Style, style comes from inside here." Casard tapped on the center of her chest. "Your mother, she's got it just like him." Casard smoothed the sides of her bun, checking her combs in back; talking about Momma and Vrej made her want to primp. "The two of them, see, now the two of them were something."

Melanie and I looked at each other, grinning—there at the lip of Casard's joy and sorrow. We could not help ourselves, we were hoping for more, in fact we were plain giddy with the prospect of further revelations, when Casard picked a leaf from the tree and, running her thumbnail along the vein, split it in two. Studying the remains in her palm, she said, "He died on me," as if my grandfather had arrived late or been rude.

Casard nodded at the tree, her confidant. Then she turned on her heel and headed to the house.

Melanie and I stayed behind, investing the lemon tree with our confounded expectations. There was nowhere else to go. It dawned on me that the lemon tree, in its time, must have witnessed more than a few dashed hopes. And it seemed that it might harbor a particular knowledge, somewhere in its crooked branches. I looked. There in the tree's crotch my grandfather's black eyes peered back at me, at first, making my skin crawl, for I believed they saw under my clothes.

But when I looked again, I witnessed yet another miracle Casard would not share: out it poured, so that I felt it in my knees. Vrej's love. He would bend and shape her, he would make her forget she was her own. He would turn her to his goodwill and she would feel again, and not just pain. He was the kind of man who enhanced a woman's grace, just by placing his hand in the small of her back. All she had to do was pick up her feet.

But Vrej was no grandfather, and style makes a poor husband.

A man of few talents, Vrej Essayan spent his days working with machines, and his nights betting on the cards. But in the early evening he came through the door with a delighted look on his face and a kind, loving remark. On Fridays he brought home chocolates, or an antique mirror, or a good head of lettuce or a new magazine. In summer he asked for lemonade and produced a flask of vodka. In winter it was vodka in his tea. Every moment was his last, every breath precious, every exchange rooted in amber lust. And when at last he departed, he took with him the air, melting it like the strawberry cones he loved to watch her savor with her small pink tongue. Into the sweet, sweet air he vanished, slick and elusive as style.

Melanie plucked a lemon from the ground and, wiping snot from her face, asked, "Do you wanna?"

"Wanna what?" And I turned back in Casard's footsteps, not waiting for an answer.

Inside the house, there was no relief.

Momma was standing in the doorway between the dining and

living rooms. "Why is it no man ever left a ball game first time I call?" she said, not really expecting an answer. "What do I have to do? Stand on my head?"

"Please!" Dad called, and thrust out his hand in a desperate plea.

The men leaned into the television. "Did you see that?" cried Uncle Eddy, shaking his fist at the screen. "First base is sittin' there with his finger up his ass. Open your eyes, *Eshag.*"

"Chrissakes, Eddy, sit down, sit down"—Uncle Arsen waved. "Come on, Eddy, you're blocking the whole damn screen."

"You want it?" Uncle Eddy cried and stepped aside like a matador. "There. You like it?"

Momma gave a pleading look at the women, who stood in the dining room with Casard, their hands resting on the backs of their chairs. Poppee called out in singsong, "Alex, George, rest of you, supper's cold."

At last, one by one they all came, glancing over their shoulders at the TV. Uncle Eddy waited in the living room with his hand on the volume. "Christ Almighty," he shouted, and the men rushed back to see what they were missing.

The women feigned irritation, though everyone knew this was the way family meals always began. At last, the men returned to the table and the floor vibrated as everyone pushed up a chair. Momma pointed to our napkins and we set them on our laps. I looked around and it seemed to me that somehow, during the afternoon, everyone had changed. Around the table, the women eyed the men, and the men, too, looked among themselves, each somehow surprised to see the other.

Casard tucked in last. Van lifted her Bad Leg onto the extra chair beside her seat. Casard groaned, and Sonny, sitting under her chair, barked once and lay down.

Momma looked up, and I knew she was thinking that she ought to get Casard to a doctor but, still angry, Momma said nothing.

Casard shrugged, looking past Momma. "Now, where's Alex?"

Everyone turned to where Great Uncle Alex should have been sitting at the head of the table opposite Casard. Poppee said, "Oh my, he's wandered off."

"Van," Casard said, waving her teaspoon, "quick, quick, go check the closet."

Van ran upstairs to the bathroom. "No sign of him here!" he called.

Everyone stood. Vart and Uncle Bob went to check the garage while Sarah and Melanie looked in the backyard.

On a hunch, I followed Sonny into the kitchen and found him sniffing at the basement door. I opened the door and snapped on the light. "Uncle Alex?" I called.

Sonny darted down the stairs and I followed him, down past the shelves of canned peaches, tomatoes, pickled cauliflower. The wooden stairs groaned with every step. The smell of mildew, soap, rotting newspaper, metal, grease and coal rose in my nostrils.

"Uncle Alex?" I called.

Overhead, heels knocked across the kitchen floor. A door slammed closed and then a toilet flushed, sending water shushing through the pipes.

Sonny spotted Uncle Alex first, crouching in the corner in the dog's old wicker bed. As I walked toward them, Sonny sniffed at Uncle Alex's mouth, then began to bark.

Uncle Alex pointed at the dog and snapped his fingers. The dog whined and ran to me, circling my legs. Uncle Alex noticed me then and, looking up with disgust, spoke sharply in Armenian.

"Uncle Alex, everyone's looking for you," I said.

Upstairs, the door to the basement swung open. "Seta, is that you?" Casard called. "Are you there? Show your face."

"Grandma," I said, it was all I could manage.

She pounded down the stairs, gripping the railing with both hands. Sonny ran under the stairway, whimpered and lay down. At the bottom of the stairs, Casard paused, letting her eyes adjust to the darkness.

"O-o-h!" Casard exclaimed when she spotted Uncle Alex. "I told that Poppee, I told her."

"Snip, they cut his balls," Alex muttered, by way of greeting.

Casard walked over and put her arms around me. "Alexan! Look here," she said. "Look at me. We have to get you home."

"Turks!" Uncle Alex called out. "Never, never let them catch you running."

Sonny barked and ran up the stairs.

"Alexan," Casard commanded and letting go of me, clapped her hands. "Alexan, stop it."

His eyes roved about the room, then settled on me. He said something in Armenian followed by my name.

"Che!" Casard shouted. "This is little Seta, not her."

Alex laughed crazily at Casard. "The girl who watched, that's you. Soo-sa-da. They're coming for you, too, Soo-sa-da."

"Che!" Casard cried, but when I tried to touch her, she flinched. Hugging herself, Casard approached the old man and slapped his face. "Stop it, weakling. I said, 'No victims.' You stop it right now!"

"Snip. Snip," Alex cackled, his fingers scissoring his crotch. "Snip. Snip." He grinned at her and she slapped his face again.

"Amot-kezi! Amot-kezi!" Casard cried, and I knew the phrase from her worst scolding. Shame on you. Shame on you.

The hair stood on my arms and for a second time that afternoon it felt as though we were about to die. "Medz-mayrig," I called. "Medz-mayrig!"

She turned and looked, but I could tell she was not seeing me. Clutching herself, Casard began to sway. Then Great Uncle Alex moaned, and crouching in the dog's bed, he, too, began to sway. Watching them, I fell in with their gestures, hugging my new breasts, and together we swayed like trees in a great wind, and waited for the Turks to come.

SEVEN

She fell from the sky like a bird.

It was late August and everything was moving slowly—everything winding down, ending like a lullaby. Casard took the dog for a walk. She had on the peach housedress and the gray tie shoes. Sonny, here Sonny, yes Sonny, tugged at his leash, sniffing at the dirt.

It was dusk and the air was thick with shadows dancing like fairies on the Persian carpet. Mosquitoes bounced off the screen door, but I was safe inside.

I was perched on the window seat, watching Casard and Sonny through the window with Grandpa Vrej's field glasses. I was playing tricks with the focus, bringing Casard and Sonny in close, then blurred. I turned the black knob, turned the black knob, and focused on the firehouse down the road with its red brick and pitched cupola roof. I focused on a single leaf, and then a bird.

She had asked me to join them: "Girlie, put on your shoes and come with Grandma and Sonny."

But I said, "No. No, thanks."

I think of that afternoon, the mosquitoes, the interminable heat, and I can't help wanting to change my answer. What if the scene in the binoculars had been different? What if I had seen past the firehouse to the next day? Would I have changed my mind knowing what I know now—that in less than a day Casard would die and little Sonny with her. Would I have said, Wait. Stop. Let me have this to remember.

For there was Grandma Casard and there was her house. A sanctuary, really, smelling of lilac and pekoe tea. There was no rushing there—no teacher, no Melanie, no Van—only Grandma Casard, in whose house the light of day came filtered through venetian blinds. In her house there was little risk in saying No, since there would always be time.

Would I have gone with her? To ask, just once, how she fit all that hair into one comb? Or, when she said Girlie, did she think it in the other language? Did she think Me in the other language? Was it at night that she missed him most? Was it at night that her feet swelled with the heat of Der el Zor, the heat locked under her callused heels?

We dined, just the two of us, Sonny curled in the kitchen corner. After the dishes, she drove me home. I kissed her through the car window and she handed me two jars of grape leaves for Momma. She waited until she saw me wave from the bay window before she put the car into reverse.

That next morning, still in her robe, she pulled a large bowl from the icebox and turned the marinated lamb with her bare hands. That afternoon in the church kitchen the charter members of the Armenian Relief Society would skewer the lamb kebobs and with peppers, onions and tomato, fire them under the broiler. Enough kebob for one hundred of the congregation. Casard and the women would cook pilaf, too. In heavy-bottom pots they would slowly steam the rice, mounding it in the shape of volcanoes.

She turned the meat, her hands wet with tomato and onion and raw lamb. Her hands were the measuring cups for recipes never written that had come over in the belly from Harput. Her fingers were spoons. She washed her hands at the sink, then rubbed them with rose milk cream.

Nine o'clock, the air was thick as gauze. Everything in the house felt damp to her touch. The dampness seeped through the cracks in the window, it festered under the pad beneath the rug. Before leaving, she put the bread in the icebox and turned the cushions on the sofa. She checked the tomatoes on the vine, heavy as baseballs. She put on her lipstick in the hall mirror, followed by her hat, and then she was ready to go. She wanted to beat the rush to the grand opening of the new A&P. The night before, she had put coupons and a list for the church supper inside her purse. She needed walnuts, a dozen onions, a bag of long-grain rice, iceberg lettuce, Roma tomatoes, parsley, garlic. She needed two economy boxes of orange pekoe tea.

She backed the Chevrolet out of the garage. Sonny navigated from the passenger seat, licking the window, sniffing air.

Across town, Lawrence DeFalco turned over the engine of his Impala. "Lawrence DeFalco," we later said, as if announcing the name of the devil.

Lawrence DeFalco was in a hurry—he would be asked in court, Why the rush? Driving a silver Impala with the blue license plate of the Constitution State, he sped from one side of town to the other.

They met at the intersection of Franklin and Pearl. Lawrence DeFalco never saw the red light. He hit her broadside.

Did I say fish eyes can be lovely? Did I say she fell like a bird? That is to say she fell in flight. And the first thing I missed—I missed it at once—was the steady unfurling of the day across her pillow and iron front.

It was Saturday. Van, Melanie and I were watching cartoons when the phone rang. Momma picked it up in the kitchen. The police told her that Casard did not even bleed. "Incredible," they said.

They found little Sonny first, curled on the car floor, stone silent.

Then they found her. Thirty feet from the car, she was thrown clear and clean. On impact, it seemed, the door of the car swung open, wide as the grave. She flew, from the seat, over the road, landing in the grass. Her dress carried the wind, her hair untucked from its comb. Her face froze with a look of perpetual amazement.

"Incredible," the doctor said, "not a scratch."

Casard, who had been Cafard, who lost her first name on the banks of the Euphrates River, was taken by ambulance to Memorial General Hospital, Memorial, Connecticut. Where she lingered for four days. Momma stayed in the hospital, talking, singing, willing her mother to wake up and make peace with her. But the damage was inside. Casard hemorrhaged. Swelling into a fat balloon, she drifted slowly, steadily away.

For the four nights Casard lingered, I dreamed of Momma and in the morning awakened to find her coat folded on the edge of my bed. She had come home from the hospital, wanting to be near somebody yet alone. On the last night, Momma perched on my bed and willed me to waken. I felt her presence invade my sleep. In my dream I saw bony elbows and an arch rebelling from the curve of a shoe; the air of my dream reeked with the stench of cigarettes.

"Momma!" I said, sitting bolt upright. "I thought you quit smoking."

The light from the hallway illuminated her lovely, tragic face. I felt an urge to kiss her. She was not looking at me.

"Momma?"

"Mmm." Her brow pressed into two thick furrows. She was fiddling with something in her hand, a piece of cellophane. She was sitting on my bed in the middle of the night, playing with a cellophane wrapper. She twisted and looped it around her middle finger.

"Momma," I said, tapping her shoulder.

"It's Mayrig, Seta," she whispered. "She's gone."

There is the time when you are sick and waiting for medicine to come, waiting for relief, and in the stillness you can hear energy running through the lights and beneath the floors, the live buzzing air. It was like that, sitting there with Momma.

My bones inside my limbs started to ache. I stretched a leg just to see that it still moved. It seemed miraculous that the leg, heavy as a tomb, budged.

Across the hall, Dad perched on Van's bed, his shoulders hunched. Van was taking it like a man, nodding affirmatively, as if he understood.

I checked Momma's face to see if perhaps there had been a mistake. Something was reckless about her, something I did not altogether trust. For one thing, her hands kept moving. Those hands were making me nervous, they were too busy for grief. Grief was slow and lethargic, it was lying in bed willing your limbs to move.

And there was the matter of Momma's wagging foot. I noticed she was wearing dress-up shoes, as though she had been somewhere fancy, the arch of her foot strained against the thin satin straps.

"So cold in here," she whispered, gliding a weak hand down my arm. Although it was August, the air was dank and chill.

I had to ask, "Are you sure?"

Her brow furrowed, then she began to shudder like quivering mercury.

The light sifted from the hallway. "Are you two all right in there?" Dad called. He and Van were leaning forward on the bed, trying to make out our faces in the shadows of my room. "Seta?"

Momma peered at me, her eyes wet and sad and angry. "We're OK," I answered, keeping my eyes on Momma. In the half-light of the evening's events, I said what I thought she needed to hear. It was the beginning of a new policy; I would find myself, like Dad, trying to anticipate Momma's need. Casard had died on her, without the forgiveness both women wanted most. Momma was ill-equipped to go on alone.

She nodded, reading my mind. "She walked out on me, mid-sentence." Crushing the wrapper in her fist, Momma released it, and we watched as it unfurled in the cup of her palm.

Momma tossed the wrapper to the floor.

Later, after she left my room, it was as if somewhere a singing kettle had been taken from the flame; Casard was dead, and from now on the nights would be like this: each of us alone in her room.

I cried then, for myself and for Grandma Casard, whom I pictured floating above the trees without her sweater. I cried until my tears ran out, and then I, too, commenced to float. I gripped the sides of the bed as my body rose above the covers like flotsam on a gentle sea.

I had floated once before, when I had been caught in an undertow off Cape Cod and nearly drowned. Then, as now, I felt tossed between here and something other, and though I knew my job was to find the elusive sandy bottom, I could not make myself care enough to reach for it. The truth was that, at first, drowning felt delicious: the quiet, glossy water gliding over me, holding me; only at the surface did I panic, and then I was glad to float. It struck me that maybe this was true for Grandma Casard; maybe she also liked to float.

I was trying to form a picture of Casard at peace when Van came into my room and stretched out on top of the covers.

"You're freezing," he said, pulling the blanket and sheet over me. Years before, I had been the one to sneak into his room, stealthily, in the night, just to be near him. We would fall asleep with our backs facing each other, our heels touching.

"They're not gonna tell Melanie until morning," Van said.

Lying together, we observed a space in the middle of the bed. We blinked in the dark, aware of a mysterious passage having transpired that determined we were too old to hug or touch feet, but old enough to be awakened in the night by grown-ups.

"What do you think it's like?" Van asked.

"I don't know."

We turned to each other in the darkened room, and considered. We offered the worst tragedies we knew—the time Sue Berman found her mother shot to death in her living room, or the time Mr. Allen hanged himself in his basement, and then, of course, there was the War—every day on the TV we saw men dying. But it was no good. Van said, "Grandma's different." And it was true, she was our first real death.

Van frowned. "I think it's bad."

"You mean Grandma?"

"No, here. It feels bad."

We rocked on either side of the sheet divider and felt the badness that had crept into our house.

I asked Van if he remembered the time I got caught in the waves and almost drowned.

"Yeah. Afterwards, you kept puking shells."

"One tiny shell."

"You should've seen Mom's face."

"Scared?"

"Uh-uh. More like angry. Like the ocean had gone against her word."

"That sounds like Casard," I said.

"No," he said firmly. "Momma covers it up good, but she's madder than hell."

I considered Momma's power over a wild sea. Never before had I considered my mother's anger, anger belonging to Casard. But that night I noticed the arch in my mother's shoe and it struck me as a new and painful violence. It seemed strange that something as insignificant as a shoe could make you feel differently about a person, not altogether trusting.

"You know, it didn't hurt," I said.

"What."

"The undertow. Everything just turned blue, then white, then the colors got swallowed up by quiet. Quiet as this"—and I pressed my palms to my ears.

Van did the same.

"Press harder," I said.

And concentrating on the *whoosh* inside our heads, we released Casard to float above the trees. Pressing hard, Van and I listened to what we believed our grandmother heard as she flew over the road into the grass. We lay in the pod, hearkening the thrum of heaven.

EIGHT

In the days that followed I heard Casard. "Girlie," she said and then I cried, realizing she was gone. It was impossible to say good-bye to the person who had shaped my world but with whom I never had a full conversation. Her opinions were as clear to me as the hand at the end of my arm, but their meaning and intent were unnamed. Saying good-bye to Casard was like saying good-bye to a vacant room, there was no one to hold on to, only the memories of what happened.

At the funeral parlor, Casard looked so real, so composed. She lay inside the shiny mahogany box on pink satin sheets, her salt-and-pepper hair pulled back in combs. They had removed her glasses, and her eyes were closed. Her face was done cleverly, not like death at all, but they had forgotten to blot her lipstick. Casard would never have been so careless. "Shiny is for Gypsies," she would have said, and reached for a tissue.

After the funeral we went on to the cemetery. It was nearly noon, the wind blowing from the south, hot and wet. I stood between Momma and Van, the hem of my cotton mini-dress flapping in the breeze, and staring at the box, I tried to imagine Casard lying in the dark, which I knew she hated. I tried to imagine her in the ground, surrounded by all that dirt, when, on account of germs, she never allowed her bare feet to touch the floor. The thought of her dirty made me weep, and worse imaginings: night crawlers and leeches. It seemed that death was her final, greatest Indignity.

The Der Hyre made the sign of the cross and started to chant. Momma fell to her knees beside the grave and began running her hands over the thick sod, picking up stray leaves. She tugged on my hem, motioning me to help, and soon Van, Melanie and I were on our hands and knees picking up twigs and dandelion wisps from the lush grass.

Dad allowed this to go on for only so long, then he pulled Momma to her feet. She pushed him away and returned to the sod. Dad bent low, whispering. He lifted Momma's chin so she could see the other mourners staring. She did not care—not about him or anyone; she was in her own private world of obtuse grief, in which litter by the grave was unbearable. She held out her hand, and we dropped our twigs and leaves into her palm.

That night, after I was in bed, Momma and Dad fought. I went to their door to listen. Momma said, "You don't know the first thing, George. Mayrig's got me in knots. She's got me in knots. Maybe I wanted her to die, huh? She made hell for us when she was here, and now that she's gone I feel I'm dead, too. I can't ever win. And you—you don't know the first thing how I feel. How could you? How could you pretend? You think you can just hope, you think you can just love this away? You think you can? Well, you can't. Nobody can. George, please, I'm asking you, leave me alone."

Steady as a refrigerator hum came the mourners. Great Aunt Sue and Uncle Aram, Grandpa Vrej's brother, made the trip from Watertown. Momma sensed their arrival before we ever saw the car.

We were upstairs in her room, helping fold laundry, when Momma cocked her head and said, "My God, she's still driving that jalopy." And we knew by Momma's tone that she meant Sue.

The blue Plymouth tipped into the driveway, black smoke billowing from its hood.

"Momma, the car's on fire," we crowed, watching from the window. "It's on fire."

Sue and Uncle Aram emerged from the smoke, brushing themselves off.

"Oh my God, oh my God," we cried. "She's so—fat." Below us, on the lawn, stood Sue, with her tiny pinhead and enormous bottom. Van tapped me on the shoulder. "*Hast Vor,*" he mouthed. Big ass.

Sue was pointing at the front seat. "I don't care 'bout no fire! It's your own darn fault. Everything I own's in that purse." She pushed Aram toward the car, adding, "Be careful now."

"Momma, he's going back in for her purse!" Melanie cried.

Momma gazed at us and held up a brown sock. "Would somebody please help me fold?"

"Momma, didn't you hear? It's on fire!"

Momma reached across the bed for a stray sock and, finding that it was blue, tossed it behind her. "Brown," she muttered. "Why is brown always missing?"

Downstairs, Aram and Sue were making their way up the walk. Sue was saying, "It would be just like Araxie not to be home." Behind her, the hood of the car hissed like a barbecue.

"Momma! Aren't you going to do something?" I begged, and Van ran to his room to look out the window.

"Step back," Momma said. "Go on. Close the shade."

Downstairs, the front-door chimes ran up and down their scale.

Melanie and I stared at Momma, until, finally, with great lethargy, she picked up the phone and dialed. "Excuse me, I'm reporting a disturbance. No, no, it's a car. A car's on fire." Momma gave our address and hung up the receiver, her voice never rising above exhaustion.

When the fire engine arrived, Momma said, "Don't anybody move." A half hour later Dad came home, and found us with Momma in the bedroom, searching high and low for missing socks.

Momma never uttered a word about the incident. She offered Sue cool civility delivered in a faraway voice. Sue, what are you planning to do about that car? Sue, is that your panty hose in the shower—it says, here, Queen? Sue, bus is leaving in half an hour.

Neither did Momma offer any excuses for her erratic behavior. At the funeral and afterward, at the cemetery, we waited for the release of Momma's tears, but the release never came. Momma kept all her suffering inside. It seemed to her that death was preferable to life, because at least in death there was peace and comfort. Only life was hard—unbearable—the grief never ceasing.

Momma did not say, but during those days she spent in the hospital with Casard, she was racked by pain. It began with a throbbing in her legs. Earlier that year, before Momma's thirty-ninth birthday, she had her varicose veins stripped. She checked her bad veins—the ones she had inherited from Casard—into the hospital and had them removed. Then, sitting at Casard's bedside, waiting for her to die, Momma felt a throbbing in her legs. Looking down, she discovered a new web of varicose veins had risen to the surface above the backs of her knees. She touched a finger to a vein, it bent like a plastic straw. She called the nurse and was given Darvon, which made her woozy and her thoughts dark. Hour after hour, Momma sat in the hospital with her legs propped up on Casard's bed. And with nothing else to do, and the Darvon slowing time, Momma began to think.

She thought about her previous hospital experiences. She recalled being in labor with Van and Melanie and how, on the day I was born, her water broke in the aisle of the hardware store where she had gone to purchase a hose.

The three births went fine, but a year after Melanie was born Momma miscarried and she had to stay in the hospital overnight. She could still see Dad coming into her room; his face, she now recalled, was the face of the lost baby.

For every tragic event Momma had a picture, and sometimes she saw a picture before anything happened. A week before Casard's accident, Momma stretched out on the living room sofa, feeling depressed, not knowing why. The inside of her face felt somehow different—no longer youthful. She was thirty-nine, and for the first time in her life she saw her potential behind her: she was the most she would ever be. Gazing at the living room wall, she announced to no one in particular that her life was a dead end. Seven days later the accident occurred, and Momma spent the next four days in the hospital on Darvon, waiting for Casard to die.

On the final night Momma combed Casard's secret hair and, pulling the loose salt-and-pepper strands from her comb, wound them into a ball she tucked into her brassiere.

I was a grown woman before Momma and I talked at length about Casard, and during the week of mourning we did not speak of our loss. During those long days of company, I watched Momma recede from the world, having decided that while the world put on a show for death, it offered nothing to comfort her grief.

Momma poured her grief into preparing food. Armenian custom decreed that the family of the deceased must not cook for one week, but Momma and I cooked anyway, becoming partners. Then Archie stopped by and found us in the kitchen making apple pies.

Before Archie kissed us hello, she saw the pies and her face froze with alarm. "Oh, Roxie, not this—" she said. "You want to cry, go ahead, but it isn't right for you to cook. Please, honey, in your poor mother's name, honor the tradition. Let the others bring the food."

Archie was saying what everyone else assumed: that capricious Momma, never one for domestic chores, would be more than happy to let the women of the church cook. The ladies of the Armenian Relief Society had already produced lists, dividing menus and chores for seven days of lunches and dinners.

But Momma shook her head defiantly and, taking up her paring knife, started to skin another McIntosh. "Me or nobody," she said.

"I'm the cook now. I'm gonna keep moving and get through this. What comes of it, well, who knows."

Archie, puzzled by Momma's unprecedented display of responsibility, shrugged, then turned her bright eyes on me. Archie's soft presence always evoked good feelings; I loved her, not only because she loved me but because she seemed to understand Momma without trying. Around Archie, Momma was easier.

Archie cupped my chin in her palm. "How ya doin', honey. You holdin' up OK?"

"Sure." I nodded.

"That's a girl." She smiled and kissed my forehead.

I aimed a kiss back at her, just above the dime-shaped mole in the center of Archie's left cheek. Once she told me she had named the mole Coharig, Armenian for Pearl.

Archie peered into one of Momma's mixing bowls. Since Casard's death, Archie was always the first guest to arrive and the last one to leave. Like the rest of us, she was exhausted.

She sighed, punching the dough with her fist. "I don't know, Roxie, what's gotten into you. You've never been one for the kitchen. Now, of all times, you got to get it into your head to cook. What's gonna happen when the women come here and find out there's nothing for them to do?"

Momma shrugged, unimpressed.

The two women looked at each other knowingly, and Archie smiled. "Stubborn," she said.

Momma chortled. "Well, at least I got something of hers."

Archie rubbed her lips together, and frowned. Then she turned to me. "Seta?" she said softly. "Fetch me one of your Momma's aprons."

Archie picked up a rolling pin and leaned into the table, flattening a ball of dough. "Araxie, listen to what I'm going to say. Stop for a minute. Say good-bye to her, or else you'll find yourself doing it later, in front of strangers. One day you'll be walking along and somebody's rose bushes will be blooming just like Casard's and, bingo, you'll find yourself breaking down in front of somebody you hardly know."

Momma pursed her lips and was about to answer Archie when she saw me staring. "You," she said. "Why aren't you watching television with your brother and sister. Go on. Pat butter on those pies, then off you go. Haven't you had enough hanging on?"

"No one's hanging, Momma," I said, and to show my damaged pride, I slapped the table with my hand. Both women stared at me.

Momma cocked her head, surprised. "You know, Archie," she said. "I think Seta's the one who's gonna miss her most. She was Mayrig's girl, weren't you, Seta-Sue?" Momma blinked and tears spilled down her cheeks.

"Oh, Rox," Archie said, and the two women fixed on each other and I became invisible. Momma sucked in air like a child. "It's like she just—"

"There, now," Archie soothed.

"—walked out—the room."

"I know, honey. There now." Standing, Archie scooped Momma in the soft folds of her arms.

"How come we couldn't be nice and let the other be? Now I'm the one left holding."

"I know, honey. Sometimes, I guess fate has awful plans for us, huh? I didn't tell you but ever since my surgery—"

"Am I hurting you?" Momma asked, lifting her head off Archie's chest.

"Don't be silly. Nothing to hurt, just a bra with a pillow." Archie patted her left breast. "But what I meant to say was that ever since my surgery I knew more trouble was coming. Had to. Tragedy in threes."

"No."

"Ayo. First there was me and the cancer. Then Ani Baboostian, God rest her soul, passing away in June. That's two—I didn't tell you but I'd been waiting for a third. Now, with Casard, it's over." Archie folded Momma to her chest like a doll.

The two women rocked together doing a kind of slow twist. They paid no attention to me. They rocked and shuffled along the linoleum floor, Archie lending comfort to Momma's grief, saying "There now, there now." I could not help wanting some part of that comfort as they shuffled across the floor stirring up motes of flour with their house shoes; I could not help wanting, but it was not my time to speak.

When the women had enough, they parted, and Momma turned to me with a weak smile. "You know, you can go blind poking your nose in other people's business," she said. And though I suppose she did not mean any harm, I had to bite the inside of my cheeks to keep from sobbing. I understood that I was just a child and Momma and I were no longer partners. Turning to the table, Momma licked her fingers and palmed the sides of her hair, her moment of shared grief subsiding.

As Archie had predicted, the women of the Armenian Relief Society arrived with plenty of food. They cooked all morning and then, at the stroke of eleven, they set aside meals in the icebox for their families, applied talcum powder under their nylon slips, and over their slips they put on black wool. On their feet they wore sensible shoes. Sealing their food in Tupperware and on serving platters with foil, they arrived at our house hot and flushed, smelling of attics and flowers. I was at the door to receive them. "Where's your mother?" they asked, as they passed through the foyer, plucking starched aprons from their purses.

They found her at the stove, humming, directing. There was no mistaking the change in Momma: she did not greet them—what they received instead was her backside, done up in a maroon dress, the color of plums. The dress shimmied down Momma like a skin. It was no proper dress.

Archie, washing lettuce in the sink, extended her lips and gave bachigs, kisses, hello. "Inch beses," she murmured, How are you. When the women returned looks that suggested that Momma might as well have forgotten her bra and underwear, Archie merely shrugged.

The women sighed, and shook out their aprons. Reaching behind them, they fastened the strings, and tried to think good thoughts.

Momma was arranging a platter of dolma. "Melanie," she said, tapping the counter with a wooden spoon. For two days, since Archie discovered us making pies the rap of that spoon had sent Melanie and me scurrying. Doorbell. Check the sugar bowl. Don't forget the cream. Are those cups there supposed to wash themselves?

Throughout the afternoon and evening, as company filled the house, Momma pointed that spoon, and we skidded across her slick kitchen floor in our white patent-leather shoes, Sunday shoes saved for Easter and now death. We paid her with our smiles and left her offerings of tea. "Momma, we need more pilaf and the dolma's cold." "Momma, I checked: sugar's fine, but the people are wanting dessert." It was the only talk she allowed: the food, the dishwasher cycle, the absence of napkins, the congestion of cars in the driveway. Archie helped with preparation; Melanie and I served. Van carted chairs and heavy platters, and Dad took care of the "folks out there."

Momma handed Melanie the platter of dolma, and Melanie managed with two hands to carry it to the dining room.

The women glanced at the child but their interest was rooted on the mother. "Look at her," one of them fretted. "Exhausted."

Momma muttered, ignoring them all. No more a child rebelling against her mother, in her grief Momma reverted to the only adult role model she knew: Casard. Later, when depression set in, Momma would change again, but throughout the official mourning she brimmed with her mother's rage.

The Indignities, Momma decided, were the people in her house. As the ladies looked on, Momma whispered to the linoleum wall behind the stove, "No parties, we do not give parties. We do not go to Europe, my children have never seen Europe. So what do we do for kicks? We throw a party for strangers—Mayrig is upstairs shaking her head, saying, 'Now, Araxie, what's this for, no dignity stuffing all of these mouths. No sirree, we have our dignity and we feed it to the animals on our best china.' "

Momma sighed, wiping her forehead with the back of her hand. "Seta," she said, "take those plates out to the animals. Let 'em eat eat eat, and leave me holding the bag."

The ladies puffed out their chests.

"Hey, Rock of Gibraltar," Archie shushed, frowning at Momma. "Now stop that, everyone is doing her best."

Momma puffed away Archie's comment. "You know what, Archie? When I'm gone, my wish is to be burned. You tell George, I want to be cremated and my ashes thrown in the bushes."

"Oh, please, Rox."

"Listen: toss me in some backyard breeze and none of this—"

"Ar-a-xie!" It was Poppee. The old woman, unable to contain herself, glared at the one she loved like a daughter. "Enough!"

Poppee took Momma by the hand. "Araxie, why do you have to take it all on by yourself? Listen to me: let the others take care of this. Go sit with your husband and these children. Look, all the people have come. For your poor Mayrig, yes? Me, I'm sick, too. But there is nothing we can do now, is there? Look at you, frail as a petal. Exhausted. Please, please, for Poppee's sake, go sit down with your grief."

But Araxie, named for the river, the girl with thick black curls—the ladies still thought of her that way, as a child—tucked in her lips and furiously shook her head.

The ladies of the Armenian Relief Society looked at one another. What to do? Poppee's mouth twice flapped open and shut. She was thinking that she ought not to allow the others to see Araxie dishonoring Casard. Yet Poppee was not such an old goose that she could not bend. She thought: This rule, no cooking in the house of the deceased, is just our way of giving the grieving family some time. If this little bit of heating up of food makes Araxie feel better, what harm? If this little bit of whisper-whisper is her way of coping, so what? It's just a matter of time before Araxie accepts the inevitable and lets the others take over.

"All right," Poppee said and, clapping her hands, set the women to work. With Momma ensconced at the stove they could at least manage the flow of plates from the kitchen to the dining room. They filled her sink with dishes. They lifted the aluminum lids on her meats and pies. They poked inside her cabinets and drawers for cups and spoons. When they saw her eyeing them menacingly, the ladies proffered smiles, as if Momma were a pugnacious child who must be humored.

So taken were the women with their missionary zeal that at first they did not notice what had become of their food. They arranged meats on platters and desserts on glass trays, but none of the food was theirs. The goods they had brought had quietly been removed—taken, at Momma's insistence, to the garage.

It was Auntie Sarah, hauling a bag of trash outside, who discovered the food. Inside the garage, the hoods of both cars were concealed by an astonishing array of plates, roasting trays and Tupperware containers. Pyrex casseroles were stacked three or four high. Auntie Sarah dropped the garbage bag and hauled a large serving tray back to the kitchen. She stood in front of the women, holding the tray aloft, her mouth twisted with fury.

"Where did you get that—" Momma snapped, waving her spoon at the evidence.

"Roxie!" Sarah puffed, and, lacking further words, stamped her foot.

"That's it," Momma said, banging her spoon on the counter. The women jumped as Momma lunged toward the back door and slammed it closed. Then she walked over to the kitchen table, where Poppee was slicing a cake, and took the knife from the old woman's hand.

"My kitchen," Momma said, casting her eye on the floor. "My Mayrig. My house."

The women blinked, trying to comprehend. They had seen

plenty of misery in their time and not one of them was a stranger to its many forms. But Araxie was different, standing before them in blue stiletto heels—whore shoes—to match her whore dress. Who among them had the nerve to tell her. Who would dare?

"Araxie, please," Poppee begged. "Too much has been taken from us already. Let us be together."

Momma considered this. She bowed her head and the women turned away to give her privacy. I kept my eye on Momma, and saw the flush rise in her face; I knew that look, she was thinking about Casard. Her mother had deliberately left her, without making peace, Casard's sudden departure the final blow. Momma could not let these women see her so alone.

She lifted her head and the fierce look in her eyes spoke for her: the women must go. Poppee, too. It was unthinkable, barring the women from the kitchen, yet Momma did it anyway. To Poppee, Casard's oldest friend, Momma said, "Can't hear myself think above all the commotion."

"Shame on you," said a voice from the doorway. Aunt Sue, in a brown tent dress draped with ropes of gold, swayed in the doorway like a dark-hulled ship fitted with shiny brass.

"Here comes the fire," Archie mused, under her breath.

Melanie and I bit our lips to swallow giggles. Momma, pursing hers, swatted Archie's arm.

Sue loomed in the doorway, hands on hips, feet apart, as if any minute something might drop from under her skirt.

"I remember such a nice girl," Sue said and all the women turned to look at Momma. "I remember such a pretty—"

"Ancient history," Momma snapped.

"—not some rude per-son, won't allow people to pay their respects. Araxie, I've been in the living room—and let me tell you, people out there are beginning to wonder if you've lost your mind. What are they supposed to think?" Sue coddled a thin wedge of pie and popped it in her mouth.

Momma grimaced with contempt. "Honestly, Sue, I don't have time—"

"Well, then, I suggest you make the time. 'Cause let me tell you, what's going on here is crystal clear. You know a person can't help thinking it's ironic—you're acting just like her. I see it, so does everybody. You've stepped right into your mother's shoes. My Lord, before they're even cold."

"Who are you to say one word—" Momma shrieked.

"Who I am is your comeuppance," Sue replied, puffing up her chest. "Your comeuppance, that's who. All these years you've been snubbing your nose at the rest of us. And that whisper whisper don't hide nothing. Miss Too-Good-for-Her-Own-Kind. Miss Pride-Goeth-Before-a-Fall. You broke your mother's heart, you did. And where'd it get you, Roxie. Where are you now?"

"Well son of a B," Momma said, pounding the counter repeatedly with her spoon. When finally she stopped, she looked around, surprised to find us all standing there. "Out," she demanded. "Out of my kitchen. Everyone. And take that Fat with you."

Poppee left first, the rest of the ladies followed. I went with them as far as the dining room. Through the walls you could hear Momma ranting in Armenian, carrying on a conversation with Casard, while Casard's china rattled in the dishwasher, beating like some sacred drum.

Opening doors, fetching napkins, tending to Momma, spying on guests, there were always two of me present: Seta, Casard's girl, and Loon, the observer. Loon watched out the window and noted that the mourners, arriving in their drab suits, brought with them heat. They were a wool parade of grief. Indoors we were as limp as cabbage steaming under a lid, but the elders were impervious. Stepping from their cars, they climbed the driveway in twos, cutting the air like an iron scythe. The bell chimes rang a four-note scale, and so as not to appear too eager, I waited for the third note before opening the door. In came yet another batch of strangers, unknown men who pinched my cheeks as they handed over their felt fedoras. Cars lined the sides of the road and spilled from the driveway onto the lawn. The doorbell knelled like a toy cathedral, until I got so tired of answering it Dad gave the OK to prop the door open and it was serve-yourself.

Milling among the guests, the part of me that was Loon learned firsthand about death's ceremony—how a week of mourning afforded endless opportunities to jabber. Jabber not only about the deceased—in fact little about the deceased—but about whatever caught fire in the cotton of your brain. Death let go a flood of conversation. I passed a plate of paklava and overheard talk of Little League car pools, and cures for whooping cough, mononucleosis and flu. A woman said, "My Daniel—he got mono from kissing the dog."

But while Loon remained outside, Seta tumbled into the whirl, the eleven-year-old party girl. Strangers were kissing my cheeks and pressing silver dollars into my palms. I was heading upstairs to the bathroom when a man with thick glasses forced me to sit down next to him on the carpeted steps. "Clare," he said, placing a hand on my shoulder. "Seta," I replied. "Clare"—he beamed—"let me tell you a story about elk. Now, the elk know a thing or two about how to say farewell to one of their own." And so began a parable on dying; I squeezed my knees together and waited for the herd to abandon its sick. The man, his name was Carl, held my wrist and made me watch his lips as the dying elk thrashed and shivered, and the herd moved on to another field. When Carl was finally through, my hand clutched a crisp five-dollar bill.

Amid the din and clamor, there was little time to miss her. But at night, floating in my bed, the two parts of me came together and I longed for Casard. I missed her voice, her face and the smell of her skin and of her shiny kitchen.

At night, lying in bed, I talked to her. I told her about the pageant surrounding her death. I told her that the mayor himself had slipped Dad funds for two carnation wreaths and that Mrs. Cassenetti brought not one lasagna but two, not one but three tins of cannoli.

Casard, her face illumined, smiled at me. I spoke of myself and, unlike Momma, she had plenty of time. I talked about Melanie, the idiot, spilling juice from a platter of dolma onto Momma's favorite linen tablecloth, and Casard merely sighed. Pressing her soft cheek to my shoulder, her chin furry as a peach, she purred, My girlie-girl.

I went on and on about the food, describing for Casard the platters of hams and turkeys and the bowls of potato salad and elbow macaroni; the dolma, served hot, with tomato sauce, and the yallanchi, served cold; the legs of lamb; the dishes from Anatolia; the Italian casseroles of lasagna, and sausage and peppers; the kielbasa and pierogi; the pound cakes, strudels, fruit breads and angel wings. Last, I told her about the abundance of gathah, the dessert we called gold.

Casard wetted her lips. She pointed a finger at my bedside drawer, where, in a paper napkin, I had stowed one precious piece of paklava. That's a girl, she said. Have yourself a little snack. No rush, no rush. Take your time. You have a napkin: use it. That's it. You finished? Good. Now, tell me what is this business of cooking in the house of the deceased.

Momma, I thought. Gazing at the ceiling, my cheeks burned.

"She means no disrespect, Grandma."

Oh, girlie, poor Araxie, she has not a clue what she means!

"Grandma, I won't tell you anything if you talk like that."

Pssst. You tell me about your sister but not about her? Let me rest my face on this nice soft pillow, while you go on and tell me a little story. OK? That's a girl. Your fingers, are they sticky?

"No. Well, a bit."

Wet them in your mouth, that's it. Now dry with the sheet. Are you hot? Are you sure? OK. Nice and cool—you look a little flushed. Now, tell me about your mother. Tell me how one rule—no cooking—she cannot uphold.

The next day, by noon, the house was full. Between chores, I drifted from room to room, unable to make up my mind whether I preferred being in the kitchen with Momma, or in the living room with Dad.

In the blank beige of the living room Dad reigned over the odars. He was in search of universal comfort for his guests, and to that end he made great sweeps of the room, securing seats for the ladies and Kleenex for their sleeves, and coffee and dessert for the men, who congregated in the den to check on the baseball scores. Dad milled about his kingdom in a dark gray suit, a white carnation fixed to his lapel. The flower was a curious touch; he had made a special trip to the florist. Momma complained that the flower was showy and that carnations lacked smell, but Dad persisted in sporting the bud. I suppose he thought it designated him official host.

The carnation was not the only thing peculiar about Dad. Between ushering, fetching and chatting, Dad had acquired a hunch. In the beginning he had towered over his guests and, I suppose, after a while he began to think that the odd looks he received were a commentary on his height. So Dad compensated by ducking low. Stooping, his face took on an expression of embarrassment and surprise, as though he had just struck his head on a low beam. And with the thankless job of securing comfort for so many guests—the men in the den, the women in the living room, and Momma in the kitchen, ranting—Dad hovered, making himself small because really he felt so big.

I spent the afternoon with my father in the living room, passing cookies among the guests. When my plate was empty, I headed for the kitchen and, walking by Dad, brushed his hand. Turning, he squeezed my shoulder and was about to say something when Poppee caught my eye and motioned me to the velveteen sofa. Vart, Sarah and the other matrons were assembled on chairs or curled at Poppee's feet, petals to stem.

Poppee was shaking her head. "Ahh, there she is. Seta-Seta." Poppee took my hand in her cool, dry palms. She gave a gentle tug and I collapsed at her feet while the ladies made room. The smell of Poppee's skin, a combination of soap, face powder, perfume and pekoe tea, made me lonesome for Casard.

"Seta, you tell us. What is this business, your Momma won't let anybody serve? It's an insult. Sue's right, she's acting just like her mother. I had to know Casard ten years before she'd let me slice a carrot in her house. Such foolishness. You think you could tell her any better? You think she'd listen? Garbage."

The women around Poppee murmured agreement.

"Momma was never like Grandma," I replied, and these words had the effect of making my eyes sting.

Poppee tasted the inside of her mouth. "Let me tell you something," she said. "The mother, the daughter, they're the same—always connected." Poppee grabbed hold of Vart's arm. "This one here. She moves to Timbuktu, it don't matter. She doesn't call, it don't matter. Always, between her and me, there is this thread."

The women murmured their agreement. They were handsome women, they conveyed an earned ease. They were as comfortable in Momma's house as in their own homes, which all looked the same: beige walls, functional mahogany end tables, velveteen sofas, colored candy dishes, Waterford ashtrays, Persian carpets, mauve damask curtains. And throughout, not a speck of dust.

Although I had grown up in these rooms, they always struck me as old-fashioned and dark. The ladies themselves supplied the color: emerald and lavender and poppy red, these daughters of Ararat. Yes, they smiled up at me. Yes, they knew about threads.

They knew how to make a house, raise their children, bury their own. Petal to stem, they commenced to release Casard through talk.

"That Casard," Poppee began, "no one could tell her what to do."

"I could of told her marketing on Saturday was a mistake."

"Saturday's a madhouse."

"You could have told her? Told her what? That a crazy man was on the road?" Poppee waved her hand in front of her face.

"And the dog. Sonny, was that his name? Going with her like he did?"

"She took him everywhere, that dog."

"I hope that DeFalco monster rots in hell."

"I hope for him this life is hell."

"What a way to end."

"They say she didn't feel a thing."

"Says who, the doctor? Garbage. How does he know what you feel? Anybody ever come back to tell?"

"Araxie won't talk about the accident," Vart said, looking to me for assurance.

I nodded.

"Just like her mother, that one," Poppee said, tapping my shoulder. "Head like a bull. Do you girls remember those ribbons Vrej gave her?"

"Pink ones."

Poppee nodded and, closing her eyes, began to sway. "I was with her that day," she said, pausing to taste her mouth. "Vrej came home from work carrying them in his hands like this, like a pair of reins.

"Into the house he comes, the middle of the afternoon, the two of us just setting down to a cup of tea. We see him coming through the door with these long things in his hands. I say to Casard, 'What do you suppose he's got,' but she says not a word. He comes closer and we see that they're ribbons. Ribbons! Imagine a grown man buying such things. Well, he walks over to her and presents them like they was sapphires and diamonds. He does all but kiss her left toe." Poppee chuckled. Pulling a Kleenex from her sleeve, she wiped her nose.

"Well, I don't think Casard knew what to do. She gives me a look that tells me she's a little embarrassed. You know, all this show, even if I am her good friend. But she goes along. She accepts them like she was the very queen. Such dignity that one.

"The next day I come over and you know where she's got those ribbons? She's got them laced up in her shoes." Poppee threw back her head and laughed who-who-who.

"So I says to her: 'Casard, what's that you got in your shoes.' And you know, she puts her foot out and turns it just so—so I get a good look. Me, I'm not looking at the shoe so much as the face. Oh, you've never seen a girl so flushed. Love. Love." Poppee closed her eyes and smiled. Suddenly, she gripped my thigh with her strong hand. "Not to say she ever let him know."

The ladies gave appreciative smiles, first to Poppee, then to me. Then Vart said, "Those legs gave her such trouble."

"The right one, especially," I added, letting them know she was most mine. "Just like Momma."

"Varicose," Vart pronounced, rubbing her own leg and grimacing with imagined pain. "She was always feelin' it."

"You'd never know," Poppee warned. "Casard never bothered no one with oohs and aahs."

Poppee touched the back of her own leg, still shapely and unmarked. She was two years older than Casard, but always she seemed like the younger sister. Poppee ran a hand through her black cropped hair, a woman in her seventies without a trace of gray.

"Seta," Poppee whispered, pulling me close as if she had a secret. "How we miss her, huh?"

I nodded.

"Such a big hole, she left us with, huh?" Poppee looked around to see who was snooping. "Tell me. What are we supposed to do with such a hole?"

I looked around at the women and felt self-conscious. So I cupped my hand over Poppee's ear and whispered what was in my heart. "It's like someone took all the sound."

Poppee nodded, disgust on her face. "You wait," she said. "When you get to be an old lady, you'll see. First the children go. Off to college: one gets married, one goes here. After all these years you're making dinner for two. You think: How nice it will be just to rest, but you never count on the quiet."

Poppee paused, opening the door to that room inside her. She reflected on the stillness.

"Next, it's the men's turn to leave. Your grandpa went within six months of Alex's brother. Six months. Bing-bang-boom. Casard said the men planned it that way so they wouldn't miss Wednesday poker."

Poppee took a tissue from her sleeve and wiped her eyes. "Casard, now, she was my friend. We had each other. We didn't talk about it, but we knew. We knew. These days you young people, talk-talk-talk. We didn't have to say. The other knew how it felt when the children left. She knew what it was like to go over to their house and feel like a visitor. You wiped shit from their bottoms and they put out the good plates like you're some guest."

Tears rolled down Poppee's face but she ignored them.

Vart reached a protective arm around her. "Mayrig, you want me to get you some tea? You want some nice hot tea?"

Poppee smiled but her eyes were full of fire. Her daughter had married, become a stranger; her daughter had done no worse than she—Poppee had also left her parents. During the massacre, after her father moved the family from Bitlis to Russia, Poppee met Alex, and, later, she went with him on the Boat. Her mother and father insisted that she go; it was their final act. They died of starvation that winter.

Poppee crossed her legs and checked her earrings to make sure they were intact. "Oh, poor Seta," she said, nudging my shoulder. "Now I made you sad. OK, be sad. Don't listen too much to old-lady talk. Go make something big of yourself, a big career girl, huh? A rich, happy lady."

I bowed my head and Auntie Sarah rubbed my back. I had always thought that I wanted to be a career girl, but being with the ladies made me unsure. I did not think that I wanted to be a rich businesswoman, if it meant being different from them.

I raised my head to tell Poppee, but her attention had shifted to the ladies.

"The dinner," she said, "we'll make specially nice."

And in this way the women of the Armenian Relief Society planned their meal. At long wooden tables draped with starched linens they would honor her, Casard, widow of Vrej, mother to Araxie, grandmother to Van, Melanie and me. They would cook for days, taking special care, and the Der Hyre would sanctify the meal with a special blessing. The affair would be dignified and honorable, just right for Casard, who had been a charter member of the Armenian Relief Society, the leader of the Sunday school, the organizing force behind the annual bazaar. Casard had been a friend to some of the women, and to all a formidable presence. She was gone now, dying suddenly, allowing them no time to do enough.

I sat forgotten among the whispering ladies and it suddenly occurred to me that I was witnessing a kind of betrayal: the women were planning a dinner for Casard without first clearing it with Momma. I knew that in her current mood Momma would not want a banquet for Casard; it would strike her as too public. Listening to the women, it occurred to me that with Casard gone, and Momma placing herself on the outside, there was nothing left but history to bind any of them to us. Little by little, the women would turn away from Momma; they would turn away from me.

Across the room, Dad saw my stricken face and moved toward me. As he approached, Poppee motioned the women to hush. They knit their bodies in a circle and presented Dad with polite looks and empty teacups. They offered this male their attention as though it were a toll they had to pay to get to the other side.

Arsine Bedrosian was on the periphery.

"Arsine," Dad said, "it's good you stayed. All of you—it means a lot to Araxie."

"Oh, George," Arsine replied, her voice flat. "On a day like this, nothing is good, is it. Poor Casard."

Dad nodded.

Arsine continued, "When my mother died, for three weeks Casard cooked. For my father, she did the same."

"Is that a fact?" he replied, clearing his throat. "Poppee, are you comfortable?"

"Fine, fine, George."

"Is Seta here behaving herself?"

"Oh, George, leave her be. She's a good girl." And the women all turned and gave me their best orphan smiles.

"Yes," Dad agreed.

"And poor Casard nothing—" Poppee added, waving her finger at Dad. "She had a good life. Never put her problems on anyone. She paid her dues plenty."

"Yes," Dad said, furrowing his brow, for it had been Arsine and not he who had called Casard poor.

Poppee's tongue circled the inside of her cheek. She was deciding something. "George," she began, "I don't have to tell you, this mixed-marriage business was hard on her, so hard. Every mother holds her breath—"

Dad exhaled sharply, his shoulders hunching. I looked at him as they did: apart, no relation.

Poppee noticed his discomfort and was satisfied. "I'll tell you one thing," she said, "she was proud of this one," and she patted my cheek.

"Seta, why don't you go help your mother?" Dad said, keeping his eyes on Poppee.

"Oh, George," she said, "let the girl be."

Dad raised his brows.

"I'll go in a minute," I said.

Dad nodded and excused himself. As he crossed the room he flexed his fingers, limbering them, as though he were getting ready to punch something. He was looking for a place to ground his frustration and in the corner he found the piano. He pulled out the bench and took his seat.

"Don't," I said under my breath, but it was too late.

The ladies continued planning their dinner, while across the room Dad lifted the wood cover. He could have stopped then and no one would have noticed. But Dad had to push. He had to give the ladies one more reason to look at me with their orphan smiles.

He began to play "Moon River."

The women shuddered, cocking their heads like startled birds. Shocked by my father's rudeness—American pop culture had no place in their mourning—they puffed up their chests and, squinting their eyes, glared at him across the room.

Poppee stood and the women supported her, their hands hanging in the air like protective gulls. She clapped her hands. "Pssst, You. Quiet."

Dad's hands hovered over the keys, but his foot remained on the pedal and his last chord reverberated throughout the room. He did not turn, and there ensued the longest moment, followed by another, so quiet I could hear Hasmig Ohanesian grinding her dentures. Dad looked at the wall and saw something that sent shivers through his spine. It was as if someone had written on the wall: Odar.

Poppee clapped her hands, calling the ladies to attention. Bending forward, her lips shaped in an exaggerated O, Poppee began to sing. She waved her arms and the ladies of the Armenian Relief Society joined in singing "Mer Hairenik," the Armenian anthem.

Dad tried to catch my eye. "Come. Here," he mouthed, flicking his head.

"Can't," I mouthed and squeezed my shoulders in an exaggerated shrug. I made big eyes to demonstrate how impossible it would be to move among all the bodies.

Dad frowned. "Come. Now."

I stood, and the women reached up, offering support. I looked down at them on the floor, their legs tucked under their dresses. It occurred to me that they had it in them to usher me gently to the cliff, then cast me over. I thought: They will never own me, not the Armenians, not Dad or Momma—not anyone.

I took my place beside my father on the wooden bench. He had pulled the carnation from his lapel. "Here you go," he said.

I accepted his flower but I did not smell it, since I already knew carnations had no smell.

Dad leaned over and whispered in my ear, "Goddamn tribe." Then, grimacing, he put his arm around my waist. It was unbearable, a parent's possessive touch.

The Der Hyre approached and whispered, "This is how our Casard would have wished it. This"—gesturing at the singers—"does her honor."

Dad nodded dutifully and then his expression lightened as he looked across the room. Momma was standing in the doorway. She looked so fragile, covering her mouth with her fingers. Melanie, Van and Archie stood with her. Archie brought Momma over to Poppee, and the old woman embraced her and patted her back, as if to say: Yes. Yes. Yes. Araxie, now you're home—with us. Come, and let us all heal.

Momma turned and looked pleadingly at Dad and me. I felt an urge to go to her, but then Poppee stamped her foot and they all started to sing "Erk Asadouteeyahn," the song of freedom. Momma sang, too. Plates rattled and the fern in the corner swayed its fronds as the singers clapped their hands and laughed at the rest of the world, those people not part of their group. For the Armenians had been suckled on atrocity, and to them death was as elemental as mother's milk. They grieved for their dead, and then, like miserly kings, doled out among themselves the balm of their laughter.

Momma stood in their midst, weeping, a rueful smile on her face. She rocked her arms in the shape of a cradle, while around her they clapped and sang.

I waited for Dad to tire and let me go. When he did, I fled. Sidling past the bodies, I headed for the door. As I threw open the screen, a cool wind rushed by me. I knew that Casard was part of that wind, but for me she was gone. I took Dad's carnation and flung it on the grass. Alone, utterly alone, I put my face into that wind and pushed.

I thought of heading for the grape arbor behind the house or hiding myself in the bushes next to the barbecue. But my feet had a different notion. They carried me down the driveway, past the rows of cars. At the corner, by the hemlocks, I turned and walked on. It felt good to keep moving. My patent-leather shoes clicked on the cement walk. Hours would pass before anyone noticed I was gone.

I walked along Victoria Road, and then I climbed Steele Road. At the top, I turned, up the street to the Vartyans' driveway. Empty garbage cans were tossed onto the lawn and the grass badly needed a trim. The house looked deserted, the blinds drawn.

I was about to turn back when Theresa appeared at the door, dressed in a lime muumuu.

"Hi," I said.

She nodded and held open the door as I went inside. Mrs. Vartyan was propped up in her chair.

"Oh, Seta," Mrs. Vartyan said, not at all surprised to see me. "Theresa and I are so sorry."

Theresa fished a Kleenex from a box and handed it to her mother, who wiped her nose.

"Honey, your mother, did she come, too?"

"She's home," I answered.

Mrs. Vartyan raised the skin above her eyes. "Well, it's you we wanted to see anyways. We were hoping you'd come. Isn't that right, Theresee?"

Theresa nodded. "Have a seat," she said, and pointed to the chair where Casard sat the last time. Theresa squatted on the hassock in front of her mother.

Mrs. Vartyan said, "Your Grandma, oh, Seta, she was my true friend." Tears ran in rivulets down the sick woman's cheeks.

She reached out a hand and with an iron grip pulled me onto the arm of her chair. I looked down at her. She put my hands on top of hers on her lap. We studied these four hands.

"You be a nice girl for your Grandma," she said. "So up in heaven she forgives herself? So she knows whatever was her secret, it was OK-OK."

I nodded, a lump in my throat. I squeezed my eyes closed, determined not to cry.

Mrs. Vartyan unstacked our hands, then stacked them up again. "Seta, honey, don't ask too much of yourself. You want to be angry. OK. You want to be sad. OK. You want to have lots of friends and forget about your Grandma, fine. The day you were born she was at peace. That's all you need to know. Just be sure, when the time comes, you face the dead with an open heart. It's the only way."

As she spoke, Mrs. Vartyan's words caused the knot in my throat to tighten, until I thought I might choke. The air behind that knot, at last having no place to go, flowed out of me and, behind it, tears. I wailed like a child, as the woman with the ravaged face patted my knee. Theresa disappeared into the kitchen, and I was meant to take as much time as I needed.

When Theresa finally returned, she was holding two bottles of cola. Mrs. Vartyan took the bottles from her daughter and handed one to each of us.

"You girls," she said, smiling, "you girls always like the Coca-Cola."

WINTER

Three years passed. Then, in the winter of my fourteenth year, Momma and I found grace, which came not from things most abundant—the cold, my kisses—but from an apparition we found in the snow. We were both looking, Momma and I, though I suppose neither of us noticed the other until things had gone too far, the match had been lit and burned. I know now that what we sought was nothing so fine as grace, but something smaller, more immediate, an assurance or hope we could grow in our bellies, creating a space between us and that awful falling snow, so silent, so chill.

We looked, Momma and I, though our methods could not have been more dissimilar. I shotgunned the world, spreading my shiny new lust like a new knowledge, a miracle that could save lives. While God unloaded white bombs on the roof, inside I rained silver kisses. I gave kisses to the windows above the radiator, wet kisses hovering, steaming off the glass. Inanimate and coarse objects I fixed with my new miraculous lust: doorknobs, car upholstery, pillows, the back of my hand (with emphasis on the soft place between the knuckles), a sheet of fresh paper, Momma's silk roses on the dining table, the inside of my elbow, and my favorite, Casard's sterling spoons.

Momma kept the spoons hidden in the dining room hutch. She took them out for special occasions and for polishing on the first Monday of every month. When Momma polished the spoons, she laid them in rows on dish towels, sparkling precious jewels. If ever I hovered near as she soaped away the tarnish that ate the metal, she put a hand out, saying, "Get away. Don't touch."

Casard was dead three years, and still on the first Monday of every month Momma polished. She tucked Casard's service into purple felt gloves inside a cherry-wood box, where the air and light would not hasten their ruin. The box contained serving pieces, demitasse spoons and spoons for tea, but my favorite were the round spoons Casard saved for Christmas and kuftah soup.

In my mind's eye I saw them lying in rows in the cherry-wood box, their necks curved like those of swans. I wanted them.

I stole. I took just the one spoon that I buried in the sack of my pillow when I was at school. I reasoned that until the first Monday of the month no one would notice, Momma would not miss it. For a month I awakened from sweat-soaked dreams of faceless men, and the spoon lent me comfort. The strings down inside me pulled, and I painted my lips with silver.

Those strings. They pulled me on the bus, and while I watched television, and in the middle of dinner. They pulled and I had to get myself to the nearest empty place where I sat peering into far away, my eyes set on the very particles of air, the buzzing, slipping air, noisy in its aliveness. I rubbed my lips across Casard's spoon, feeling my way like the blind. I was nearly fifteen, nearly a woman. Sometimes, after I had warmed the spoon, I slid it down and held it there against me, rocking slow, just rocking. Afterward the spoon smelled like me and silver. Me and silver. Then I heard my own voice rising within me, always the same words: Kiss me, Kiss me, and I kissed and I kissed my faceless, imaginary him.

Once the strings had pulled, the convex side of Casard's silver spoon revealed my own face, wide and distorted. The strings inside had dropped me untethered, loose-limbed. I tripped about the house, unsprung as a colt, thighs knocking into Momma's mahogany end tables.

It was on such an afternoon that an accident occurred involving the dog. Miss America had spread herself in the hallway, where it was warmest, in a patch of sun reaching from the bathroom window. The dog slept, trusting that the people in her house would step around her, protecting her slumber. She was a lazy dog, prematurely old; she moved only for food and the rotation of the sun. Nights Miss America slumbered with Van, stretched out over his covers; the two of them humping in their sleep, touching back to back. By day she migrated through the house, splaying her body across sunbeams, soaking up the heat, until her fur grew hot and gave off electric sparks if you dared touch it.

I did not see her. The strings had pulled inside, making my limbs loose; I did not think to look down. My foot landed on her front paw, and from out of her dreams Miss America leaped, her tail whisking a vase of cut flowers from the hall table. The dog blinked at the flower-strewn carpet, uncomprehending. She began to whimper—it was mostly pride—summoning all ends of the house.

Momma's tread came up the stairs fast and accusing. Miss America slipped by her, her tail tucked under, taking the stairs in two bounds.

"Who's fooling with the dog?" Momma hissed, rounding the corner. "Seta, that you? Don't you think I have enough to worry about?"

I set the vase and flowers back on the table, but the spilled water would make a ring. Had Momma not come so soon, I could have wiped the table, but there she was.

I said, "All that dog does is sleep."

"Dog can't help it. People should mind where they're going." Momma shook her head, wiping her hands on a dish towel.

"I'm so tired, Momma."

"You've got no sense, that's your problem. Take a nap."

"No." I wormed in my body. "It's my skin. It's too small."

"Too small?"

"The house, Momma. How can a person breathe in this place, it's so microscopic."

Momma sighed, taking in the hallway: the bedrooms at one end, the stairs at the other. "There's outside for somebody wanting room," she said.

In winter, Outside was the universal threat. If the dog cried and would not stop, it was put Outside; Van returned home late from a party, and he was forced to shovel snow until the darkness fitted him like a glove and the wind rose and Outside taught him to regret; you were fool enough to lose your key, they would find you hours later frozen Outside.

"Stupid dog," I said, leaning against the wall.

Momma's eyes fell on me, her mouth thin with worry. She was appraising me the way an impatient gardener might who had gone off to fetch a hose and returned to find weeds.

I chanced a look at her: sure enough, her mouth was fixed, but something had come up in her eyes, some light. She was running fingers through her blue-black hair, then down the front of her dress, smoothing the folds of fabric, as she mulled me over.

"Seta," she said, her voice soothing, "now I'm going to ask you something and it's all right, you're going to answer." Momma wrapped a finger around a strand of her hair.

"What," I said, hiding my hands behind me.

"Honey, you doing your dreaming by daylight?"

"No," I lied.

"Mmm-hmm. Now, take your time."

"Don't know what you're talking about," I snapped. "Seems stupid, you ask me."

"That's all right, now." Momma chuckled, covering her mouth with fingers. "Well, you don't say."

"No, Momma, I don't say."

"Watch the mouth."

I sighed and watched the stairs.

"And—" she said, soft as a hum, "you're doing something new with your hair."

"I'm just trying it on the side, that's all. Momma, quit staring."

"Mmm-hmm."

"Momma, quit."

"I'm just looking."

"Well."

"Well?"

"Well, what do you think?"

"Your hair? Nice. Nice change. Brings out your features." She reached over and ran a dry palm across my forehead, then down the back of my hair. "My baby's growing, that's what I think. Think that means I'm an old broad before I turn around." Momma chuckled and this time she did not cover her mouth, showing me her white-white smile. "Seta, you think your mother's an old broad?"

The air around us was alive, dancing alive air.

"I think you're beautiful, Momma," I confessed, the words spilling from my mouth simple and true, they were the truest words I possessed. "You are the most beautiful."

"Don't be silly," Momma said, but she pulled me to her anyway. Our arms around each other, we found a comfortable place. It had been a long while, a year, maybe two, since we hugged like this, and in the interim I had grown to her height. I had grown awkward, too. I worried about where to place my head. But Momma's smell softened the worry and I was reminded of past comforts as my head found its nest on her shoulder.

"Miss America-the-lummox," I said, making Momma laugh as we swayed back and forth.

"Seta-Sue."

I squeezed her tighter.

"My Seta-Sue."

"Momma."

"You listening to what I'm going to tell you? You ready to listen to your mother?"

"Yes."

"Well? There's something I want you to remember. When a girl finds it's time to become a woman, she's first got to do some things to get herself ready. Some things the body's done. Others she's got to do in her heart. The world's gonna change for her and she's got to get herself ready. You see? She's got to walk through some rooms, inside. Yes she does. She does she does she does." Momma rubbed my back with her palm, making big circles. "Hmm?"

I nodded into her shoulder.

"There's mine," she murmured. "You keep on going. You'll make it."

The way she kept on with the giant circles was making me feel pleasingly small. Her voice made me want to ask about the rooms and confess I had changed my mind, I did not want to go.

Momma kept on making circles, her chin resting on my shoulder. "You know that hunger for touch—well, it just gets bigger. You think it's on account of being young and boy crazy, but it just gets bigger."

I picked my head off her shoulder to ask her what, what got bigger.

"Shhh-shh," Momma said quieting. She rubbed my back and spoke to her thoughts. "Someday you'll know. It gets big and wide as a mouth—"

Maybe it was how the windows shivered in their sleeves, or how the cold air raced up the stairs, skirting our ankles, but we felt the wind before we heard the front door. Momma stopped her circles and the two of us froze. Against my chest I could feel her heart beating fast, faster than my own.

"Shhh," Momma said, as if to quiet her own breath.

We cocked our heads and listened. Downstairs Miss America was performing her welcome dance: moan-crying, tail beating like a switch against the wall.

"Must be Van."

"Shhh—" she said.

Then we heard the closet door. I closed my eyes and listened as one of the good wooden hangers was removed from the bar and replaced with a heavy coat. I could not make out the muffled sounds that followed, but I knew. He would fold the scarf, placing it on the shelf. Next he would drop his driving gloves inside the old fedora with the green feather and, reaching upward, set the hat back on the shelf.

Momma pushed me away by the shoulders and we watched each other but did not say a word. I knew by her look that my father had come home and spoiled our time. I knew then that my mother did not want him in the house and that she was not going to say anything about it, and that I would earn a piece of her wrath if I dared ask why.

Momma, silent, peered into my soul, her lovely eyes flat as stones. After a while she nodded, as though she had communicated all there was to say. She wiped her hands on the dish towel. "Wash up before you come set the table."

My heart pounded. Dread crept up through my fingers, making them twitch. Whatever happened now, I was part of it, Momma had made me part. She had talked about rooms and this was one of them. I did not want to go.

Slowly, deliberately, Momma descended the stairs, her wedding ring knocking on the wooden rail. Voices traveled up from the kitchen, but I could not make out any words. Then the voices stopped and there was only buzzing air.

What had happened? When did Momma stop wanting him, and why? I reached into my pocket for Casard's spoon. The silver had turned chill; I rubbed it with my thumb to make it warm. Would they make up? Of course they would make up. I held Casard's spoon before me and gazed at my reflection. Kiss me. This is how she sees me. Kiss me. This is how he will see me. Kiss me. Kiss, kiss. Eyes like Chinese, nose wide as a pug.

You might say that it was love Momma and I were after, but talking about love is a tricky business. Besides, Momma was years ahead of me in her wanting. After Casard died, Momma's spirit turned, her hunger for escape growing keen. Stealthily, silently, over three long years, Momma had worked her desire to a magnificent perfection, until one morning that winter she awoke and found herself entirely thirsty, hungry, swept up by her own greed—dangerous, too—ready to spend without considering price. The truth was Momma itched to spend that dime, that dime already spent.

Had she asked me, I could have told her not to look outside the house for color. The trees were not giving any. You could see them: stiff and tired of holding up a winter sky that dumped feet of snow in the crotch of their naked boughs. And the roads, they were a lesson in decline. One day they stretched out showy as white French ribbon, and the next day they iced, their banks smudged with soot and yellow patches of urine.

Inside, where we mostly kept, was colorless, too. The furnace blasted air so dry that, if assigned a color, it would have been brown. The walls seemed to lean in close as we moved between them: white-skinned, turtlenecked, slippered, claustrophobic. Then a strain of Asian flu gripped New England, afflicting elders and small children. Melanie lay in bed, her face burning with fever. The doctor came and went, handing Momma bottles of white pills. And in the slowness of that time, I felt something shift inside me. Only later did I realize it was Momma's uneasiness rising up through me.

Momma might have sought relief in oranges. That bright orb of winter you could hold in your hand, the very thing foreign and precious. It was a food that had traveled a long way, its life centering on sun. Color. One could peel the folds of an orange, pop them in her mouth: sweet delicious flesh. One could do this. But that winter Van spoiled the miracle of oranges by reading in the newspaper that the Floridian fruit fell pale from the tree. Van read to us how, in Florida, workers dipped syringes into vats of dye, then injected the fruit. The color, Van noted, had been perfected by chemists.

So without the solace of oranges, Momma had to find color from an alternate source. Had I known, perhaps I could have helped her. But Momma kept her search a secret. Since Casard's death, Momma had been looking for the color of her despair, and when at last she found it, it was in the snowy backyard.

One morning I came down for breakfast and found her peering out the window over the sink. "Morning, Momma. I gave Melanie her aspirin."

Her lips were moving, perhaps in prayer, or maybe she was talking to herself.

"Momma?"

Van came into the kitchen then, and when he slapped his books on the kitchen counter, Momma was too preoccupied to ask him how she was supposed to prepare food on a counter littered with books. That was the first clue.

Van removed the books anyway, out of habit, dumping them in the corner by the door. "Mom," he said, "is that blue jay raiding the feeder again?" but she ignored him too.

"Your breakfast's on the stove," she finally said.

Our places were set as usual. Van and I shuffled to the stove, ladling hot cereal, then butter and brown sugar into our bowls. We assumed our places at the table, and rather than talk or read the paper, we watched Momma.

The next morning it was the same, and the day after, too: Momma remained fixed at the sink while we waited for something to happen.

On the fifth morning, a Friday, Van left without breakfast and Momma never uttered a word about nutrition and the most important meal. Melanie, still down with fever, lay propped up in bed nibbling on the toast that I had made for her. Dad was in the bathroom shaving; the hot water working its way up from the cellar pipes that pinged and rattled as though any minute they might burst. I went down to the kitchen, where I found Momma at the window, offering me her back.

I was halfway through my cereal when Momma, peering out the window on tiptoe, cried out, "Oh my God. Yes!" The ecstasy in her voice was so alarming, I dropped my spoon. She sucked in breath from behind a fence of fingers. "It's Chartres. I knew it, I knew it. My God, it's Chartres."

Chartres was something of a legend in our house: Momma and Archie had worked all through college just to finance the trip to Europe; at the last moment Casard had given Momma an extra two hundred dollars emergency money, which she spent on a fancy dress and a pair of shoes; Momma touched the soil of France and felt she had come home. Then in the cathedral of Chartres, Momma and Archie witnessed a shade of blue in the stained glass that was unique in all the world. The cathedral boasted a prototype of the flying buttress and a rose window, but when Momma said Chartres, I knew she meant blue.

"Seta, come over here." Momma waved frantically. "Hurry. Look. Look, it's all over the yard."

I scooted to the sink, and Momma made enough room, so our hips and shoulders touched. She pointed to all the places. "Look at that," she said. "There. Look at that."

My eyes followed where she pointed, but the yard looked empty to me. I squinted, pressing my face next to hers. I saw snow covering the yard and woodpile, snow forming casques on the lampposts. I saw the trees bathed in the silvery morning sun and a gray squirrel hopping from one tree to another. I saw the tin roof of the bird feeder reflecting the sun's rays like a mirror and Mr. Fat Ugly Blue Jay swooping among the cardinals and sparrows, chasing them away and then pillaging their food. Besides that, nothing, just yard.

"I don't see it, Momma. Point where."

"Well, it's all over!" She turned to me, amazed. "Just look, you can't miss it. Someone's painted it all over creation. Oh my God, don't you see? That's the blue I've been talking about. That's Chartres."

I looked, but the only blue I saw was the bird at the feeder. He ate his fill and flew off and then there was none. I squinted, thinking that maybe there was a little blue shadow coming off the woodpile. But I kept my mouth shut.

"I've got to call Archie," Momma said, crossing to the phone. "She's not going to believe this, she's not going to believe—" Momma giggled as she dialed. "Arshalous, it's me. No, everything's fine. Listen, you're not going to believe this, you got to come over. Yeah, right now. Oh, just put your coat on over your robe. I mean it, hurry."

While Momma was talking, I shifted to her side to look again. When she hung up the phone I moved to give her back her place.

"You see it yet? You see that miracle outside your own house?"

I saw my mother rocking, peering, eyes twinkling like Christmas lights.

In a few minutes we heard Archie's tires crunching the snow in the driveway. Then we heard her gasp as she heaved the heavy car door closed. Archie's steps came around the side of the house to the back, where I opened the door.

"What's wrong?" Archie puffed, kissing me hello. She had on a gray wool coat, black plastic boots and a sheer pink scarf tied about her head. Archie had done as she was told, and under her coat she wore her robe. She stood on the mat wiping her boots.

"What is it, Roxie? Is it Melanie? Is she worse?"

"Everybody's fine," Momma said, waving Archie over. "Just come over here."

"Look at me, I'm indecent." Archie smirked, shedding her coat. She pulled at her boots and they made sucking noises. Archie gave me a wink. "Seta, your mother didn't tell me she was planning a pajama party."

"Come over here," Momma said.

Archie remained moored on the mat, eyeing her slippers and wet boots. Momma's intensity had the effect of making Archie reluctant to move. "This better be something, honey," she said. "I left Sevan and the kids to fend for themselves. Can you imagine what I'm going back to?"

"Archie, look," Momma cried, pointing out the window.

Archie walked gingerly to the sink. She braced her hands on the rim, steadying herself. Lifting her chin, she studied the yard through her bifocals. Momma nodded, barely containing herself.

The album pictures showed two girls in pedal pushers and starched sleeveless blouses, standing in front of the Duomo and, later, at the Eiffel Tower. At Chartres, Momma pointed a thin finger toward a window of blue. The pictures froze the two girls, recording what lay beneath the years, like the first rings on a tree. Both had been slender and fine-boned. Through the years, Momma kept her shape, while Archie's body thickened like a mature tree, becoming difficult to bend.

Archie's eyes washed over Momma's face, and then the yard. "Point exactly where I should be looking," she commanded.

"Archie, don't be foolish. Can't you see? It's Chartres. Or maybe you don't remember."

Archie frowned at Momma. "Course, I remember."

"Well, then."

Archie rose to the balls of her feet like Momma and, putting her nose close to glass, tried again.

"You don't see it?" Momma cried.

"Give me a minute."

"You don't—"

Archie dropped onto her heels and sighed. "Well, I suppose there's a little hint of something by that woodpile, but, Roxie, it's not Chartres. I don't see Chartres." Archie shook her head, "I'm sorry, honey. I am sorry."

"What's the matter with you?" Momma fumed.

"Well, I just don't see it," Archie protested. "Seta, how about you? You see what your mother's talking about?" And the two women turned to me.

"Well," I stammered, "I did see that shadow by the wood."

"Oh, forget it, both of you," Momma said, her face closed, her back guarding the window.

Archie eyed her best friend with perplexity. "Roxie, honey? Now, you didn't ask me to come all the way over just to look out your window, did you?"

Momma backed away to the stove.

"Roxie-honey?"

"Forget it. Just—"

"I thought I heard a car—" Dad said from the doorway. The women turned to him. He was dressed in an undershirt, a tuft of shaving cream clinging to his left ear. "Morning, Archie. What's all the commotion?"

Momma glowered at the floor.

"Seta?"

"Nothing, Dad. Momma just wanted us to see something."

"See what?"

"George, leave it be," Momma warned him, slicing her hand through the air.

"O-kay," Archie said, inching toward the door. "I'll be getting home now. I left my boys all alone." Archie nodded at Dad and me. "Araxie, I'll call you later."

Momma did not respond.

At the door, Archie retrieved her boots. Dad and I watched as she strained to pull them on her feet. At last she was ready. "All right"—she puffed—"Bye. Bye."

Momma would not look at her.

Archie waved at Dad and me, her lips compressed, and then she closed the door behind her.

"We're not going to discuss it," Momma said, raising her hand as if to strike. She turned her back to us.

"OK," Dad said. "Show's over. Seta, you better get moving."

Momma had found the color of her desire when she found Chartres, but I was still looking. And by looking, I, too, learned how suddenly, irrevocably desire can change your life; how, without warning, your life can be pulled in another direction, one you never intended. In the middle of your brain are the words *I want, I want,* and the next thing you know you are saying to yourself: Look here, remember this; this will mark my life. You step from the house and a garbage truck rolls by, followed by a truck spreading sand. Melanie, sick with fever, calls from her bedroom window, "Seta, come back here," and as you turn, your eye falls on a boy—a beautiful, beautiful boy—riding through the snow on his bicycle. From then on, all your life, you will remember that moment as February.

The boy's back curves into his waist, and the grace and power underlying the sinews strike you for the first time. You notice a certain dignity fitted across his shoulders like a yoke. He dips those shoulders and touches your heart, making you wondrous, wistful, already gone. There will be others who will carry themselves with similar grace, but always you will think of him. You will think of that boy, nearly a man, with a soccer ball strapped to the back of his bike and his thin denim jacket and his head of curls. You will think of the girl you were before you first saw him—as you stood in the driveway in your navy pea coat and boots—and the girl you became after he entered your life, stayed for a month, and then was gone. You will think: Adam BenKiki.

Wanting, it took just one look at him and I fell. The next day, I went to school and found him talking with Shari O'Riley by her locker. I knew Shari, she was in most of my classes; her older brother, Pat, was a sometime friend of Van's. In junior high Van and Pat played football together, but in high school Pat had wandered into trouble. He hung out with the meadow kids and in no time managed to get himself expelled for smoking dope. Dad said it was a shame that such talent with the ball wound up having no greater aim than pumping other people's gas.

Shari O'Riley took after her brother; we were not friends. But Shari was close to Adam BenKiki, and I wanted him.

For the next two weeks I searched for Adam BenKiki; he was a difficult boy to find. Shari and Adam and other meadow kids regularly eschewed the ninth-grade curriculum for retreats into the woods behind school. During the moment of silence in homeroom, I would see them walking across the snow-packed football field: Shari in a tight cotton shirt hitched above her navel, flared jeans and only a denim jacket to keep out the cold. Up the hill she trekked behind Adam, the two doing the walk of the meadow kids—part shuffle, part prance—their matching red bandannas tied like flags to their belts.

Pat and Shari's mother had died in a train accident. Mr. O'Riley worked as a nurse in the ICU at Memorial General Hospital. When he was not working, Mr. O'Riley watched television behind the closed door of his room. His kids ran wild. There was an older brother, but he had gone off, no one knew about him.

On Fridays Mr. O'Riley worked the night shift at the hospital, so it was party time at the O'Rileys'. Sometimes Van attended the parties. Adam BenKiki attended them, too.

One Friday Van told Momma and Dad not to wait up for him, he was spending the night at a friend's. He returned home Saturday afternoon and went straight to his room. He slept until dinner, then rose to vomit, then slept again until Sunday noon. When I tried to awaken him, his head lolled from side to side. He began to moan. There was something in the weed, he murmured. He had been sitting on the sofa in the O'Rileys' basement when the walls started breathing. Breathing. He could not move. The inside of his skull felt as though it had been filed by an emery board. His head was thick and sore; his head wished to be left alone.

The next Friday, after promising my brother that I would do nothing foolish or potentially embarrassing, Van let me go with him to the O'Rileys'.

We parked Momma's car on the side of the hill. Tall pines surrounded the yard and inside the house it was pitch-dark. In the absence of illumination there was sound. Music, pulsing up from the basement through the concrete steps into our bodies. Van nodded at me to follow him inside, but when I turned, I caught sight of Adam BenKiki standing on the side porch. The same

Adam BenKiki, who, it was said, never slept in a bed, preferring a sleeping bag under the reservoir trees; whose only friend was Shari O'Riley. He stood before me: golden hair; white, white teeth; entirely aloof.

"See you," I said to Van.

"Hey," Van said and, grabbing my arm, gave me a fierce look to punctuate our agreement.

"All right, all right," I whispered, shaking him loose. Van went inside the house, and when I heard the door close, I turned.

Adam was lit by the streetlamp.

At school people talked about him. How he slept outside even in storms, how everywhere he carried that ball, showing up at soccer practice after school, dribbling the ball up and down along the side of the field, until one day the coach came over and asked him to join the team. He did not say yes, he did not say no. After a while the coach gave up. Adam never talked to anyone between classes or in the hall. He was liked because he was beautiful: golden, disheveled curls and skin soft as a baby's stretched over sculpted cheeks. During lunch he stood next to Shari in the parking lot, her exotic pet. And this: he was the first one I truly wanted but in my heart knew I could never own.

The streetlamp lit him.

We were alone with nothing between us but the music beating up through us in waves. He had his soccer ball tucked under his arm.

"Kick it," I said.

His eyelashes fluttered.

"Kick it," I said again.

The wind blew crystals off the tall pines. The party music pumped beneath our feet. He nodded once, or seemed to.

It happened so fast that afterward I could not be certain that he had moved. His body coiled and—*thunk*—the ball sailed up over the trees. We heard it land—*thunk*—way off in the neighbor's yard.

Adam BenKiki turned to look at me, displaying a row of perfect teeth.

There was not a word in my head. Not a word as he leaped over the railing and made off through the snow. He hopped over a hedge, and when he reached the ball he sat on his heels in the snow. He was like one of those ceramic leopards they put in yards to scare away birds. He sat in the snow on his haunches.

I could follow him or I could go inside and find Van, that much was clear. The trees shook their heads and snow fell from their boughs. Maybe Adam would think I was chasing him. What might he do then? He might laugh at me.

I found a split in the hedge and passed through. The snow was covered by an icy crust, and with each step I had to pull out my foot. Look at me, I thought, making a fool of myself, tramping through the snow after Adam BenKiki. Look at me, sitting next to him and him acting like he does not notice.

We were perched on a steep bank in front of the neighbor's house. The road lay at the bottom of the hill. Behind us, the O'Rileys' neighbor had strung multicolored Christmas lights along the roof—the same lights Casard called "fruit flavor." They blinked, elongating our shadows so we looked like giants bearing down the slope.

Adam studied the road. I studied it too, as the cold wet snow pricked through my jeans. Soon I began to shiver and that is when Adam BenKiki hurled himself upon me in an effortless arc. He stretched me out, crunching my head into the snow. His mouth was hot, and then his tongue. His full long weight lay on me and I thought: He is not heavy, not heavy at all.

We started to roll down the hill, our bodies picking up speed. His lips were against my ear, his weight spread perfectly, warm against the white, crunching cold, and then we arrived at the bottom. We kissed and this time his hand reached under my shirt.

"No," I whispered. "Freezing."

He stuffed his hand into his pocket in a way that suggested wounding. I had said no and now he would pull away. I nudged him closer, trying to erase the No with exuberance. His mouth tasted like Italian dressing, and I kissed that mouth sweetly, learning and giving back more.

But he pulled away from me and stood, so I was eye-level with his crotch. He brushed the snow from his jeans onto my head.

"Hey, stop that." I laughed.

Laughing too, Adam BenKiki pranced back toward the house. I watched him—part man, part boy in beat-up desert boots—as he climbed the snowy slope.

"Hey," I shouted.

At the porch he turned. "Bye, Seta," he called.

I sat in the snow, cold, wet, stunned. For nearly a month I had obsessed about him, tracking him through the school halls, memorizing his locker number, his clothes, the outside of his house. Then that afternoon, in my room, I had decided it would be enough just to see him, and so I had come to Shari O'Riley's to find him. And we rolled in the snow, his tongue in my ear, and then, when my heart could hold nothing more, he said my name. "Seta," he said, as if my name had been on his tongue all along. And it was not the kiss but the name that made me hollow, as though something inside had been torn. I sat in the snow trying to find what it was. Eventually, to my horror, it dawned on me: in all my dreams of faceless men I had never hoped for, nor expected, kindness.

Snow fell throughout January, the white banks along the road climbing higher than the plows. At night, cars passed slowly through these cavelike passages, their headlights illuminating only the patch of road that lay directly ahead. By morning new snow had fallen, and before the plows came through, Memorial glistened, a fresh canvas. Everywhere, white. Then Momma found Chartres and even God refrained; in the wake of Momma's miracle the snow simply stopped. For weeks the sky remained clear, despite approaching storms and the weatherman's insistence, despite dogs painting the snowbanks yellow with urine, despite the neighborhood kids tracking toboggans through Momma's sacred yard.

The sky remained clear throughout Melanie's fevers. She had

come down with the first fever on Christmas Eve. Momma thought it was just the flu until New Year's came and went and Melanie's temperature continued to soar. She lay in bed sweating under blankets, her lips cracked and pale.

Weeks passed with all of us taking turns keeping vigil. Dad carried the TV from the den into Melanie's room, and after school we sat on her bed and looked after her as she faded in and out. Momma brought trays of saltines and peanut butter sandwiches, flat Coke and sugared tea. Sometimes when the fever soared, we got the hammer out so Melanie could suck on chipped ice.

Van and I took turns retrieving Melanie's homework from the junior high, but often she was too weak to hold a pencil. On such days I feared she would die and I stayed by her as much as I could.

At night, while Melanie dozed, I hauled my stereo into her room and listened to James Taylor, Joni Mitchell and Neil Young while I longed for Adam BenKiki. My fantasies all took place in the tropics, for the inside of Melanie's room was warm and damp as a hothouse.

Momma took over with Melanie in the daytime. After the morning with Archie, she stopped sharing her vision of Chartres. At breakfast she ignored us, and when we returned from school late in the afternoon we found her standing at Melanie's window, her eyes peering from a clear spot in the fogged glass. I knew Momma was witnessing what people traveled continents just to see, what she believed was painted in her own yard.

But when Dad's car pulled into the driveway, Momma turned from her looking, busying her hands with folding blankets or chipping a glass of ice. That is how I came to know blue as the color of the space between them.

At night I held Casard's spoon and prayed. Please, God, I said, look on Melanie's fever, make Adam call me, and what about Momma's Chartres?

I dreamed of faceless men with deepwater voices calling my name. They led me to a round house, in which there was a den that looked out over a forest, a kitchen that led to a beach and a bedroom with tall French windows that opened out across acres of vineyards. In each room a different faceless man waited, calling out to me in a deepwater voice. He spoke of things no one else knew, and then, one night, as I approached, he leaned over to touch me and I awakened, my pillow damp, smelling of musk.

I stalked through the house.

Momma was in the bath, moaning a soft dirge. In the middle of the night she went to her children's bathroom so as not to disturb Dad. She lay in the tub—safe, I suppose, with no one to want her.

I knocked. The bathwater shifted.

"Who's that?"

"Me."

"Seta? What're you doing up? You have to use the toilet?"

"No."

"What, then."

"Can't sleep." I shivered in my flannel nightgown. "I keep having bad dreams."

"Dreams," she murmured, as if underwater. "Don't talk to me about dreams."

She fell quiet, hoping perhaps that I had gone back to sleep.

"Momma?" I said, hopping from foot to foot to keep away the cold.

She sighed. "What."

"Can't I come in? It's freezing."

She shifted, her bottom squeaking on the tub. Water fell in buckets, and then, quiet.

"Don't go letting the steam outta here. Bring a towel from the closet. Make it snappy. I'll shoot, if you let in a draft."

She would have just the night-light on in the bathroom. Melanie was old enough to do without the light, but Momma used it to guide herself down the hall, away from my father.

I opened the door. She lay up to her chin in hot steamy water. What she thought about in her midnight immersions I did not know—only that if you awoke during the night, you would hear her soft moans, half song, half cry, bouncing off the tiles like the calls of underwater whales.

A washcloth was spread over her breasts. Now that I was older, we had an unspoken rule: Momma would be naked and I would not look. Her nipples were purple thimbles, that strong, that erect. I found my place beside the toilet on the cool tile floor and focused my eyes on the shower curtain and the rough cement lining the underside of the sink.

"Don't go making yourself comfortable. Middle of the night. Put that towel over your shoulders, hurry up, before you catch cold. You heard me, put it around you."

Momma's big toe played with the faucet. Since Casard's death Momma's voice remained soft, virtually a whisper. At times I could stand next to her and still not hear what she said.

Her eyes were red and puffy, her black hair wet against the sides of her head.

"You're having men dreams," she said.

"I don't know. I guess."

"Starts about now. When I saw you bumping into poor Miss America, I knew. Starts about now and only gets worse."

She lifted the washcloth from her breasts and, dipping it into the hot water, spread it back over her. Steam rose from her chest.

"Tell me, are you in love with this fellow in your dream?"

"I don't know. I don't really know him."

"He's a stranger, then," she said, turning.

I looked down at the fluffy mat circling the toilet. She could not know about the men, they were mine and she could not know and I was not about to tell.

"He's a stranger," Momma said. "The most beautiful stranger you ever saw. He speaks to you of things you never told anyone." She was watching me intently.

"Momma, quit."

"He makes you feel beautiful, understood; he puts salve on all your problems."

"Momma, it's not like anything you—"

"And he doesn't have a face." She leaned over the rim of the tub and the washcloth fell away, exposing a breast that rose above the rim like a veined moon, its nipple the color of plums. How could she know, how could she steal my men, mine?

Her bottom squeaked as she sat back in the tub. "Oh, Seta, now don't get upset. I don't mean any harm. It just never ends. You listen to me, I'll save you some trouble. When you get to be my age, you'll still be hoping for that something special, that big, big surprise. It never ends, see. Circle circle circle"—she made spirals in the air with a wet finger. "To think your Grandma must have had the same thing. When I was your age, she said, 'Wash your head under the faucet, you have men thoughts.' Oh, what she must have felt later on. It must have scared her something."

"Grandma? Men? No way."

"That's what you think."

"She told you?"

"Course not. Told me. You think she told me anything?" Momma pursed her lips. "Scared. You never saw someone so scared as your Grandma, and no wonder. After those Turks, no wonder she was scared. Poppee says part of your Grandma died in Der el Zor."

"I dream about the massacre sometimes," I said.

"That's right. It's part of you, too."

"Last night I dreamed that Melanie died. She's so sick, Momma. Do you think she's going to die?"

Momma frowned and curled her toes around the faucet. "Melanie was never strong like you. The day she was born I kept thinking, Where are the rainbows, where are the rainbows? A ridiculous thought, I suppose, but these rainbows got in my head and wouldn't leave. She was just so weak. You and Van, no problem. I couldn't make enough milk to keep you two happy. But Melanie, she was too weak to suckle. Your father, I looked into his face and saw that he was afraid. I saw in his face that our baby might die. The first couple of weeks, your father stayed up all night putting my milk into Melanie's mouth with a tiny dropper. Still, I couldn't get the rainbows out of my mind. Rainbows?" Puzzled, Momma shook her head.

"Momma, when is Melanie going to get better?"

She looked at me. "There's nothing any of us can do, Seta. It's *anetzk,* that's all, anetzk."

"What are you talking about, Momma?"

"Curse, it's the curse Mayrig left us. She didn't take care of her own business, and now we're stuck with it. Don't you see. Don't any of you see?" Momma slapped her hand on the edge of the tub. "This whole house, all of you, blind."

Water from the tub lapped over the sides.

I wanted to splash that water all over the room. "Momma, I don't believe in your curses. You hear me? Melanie doesn't have to be sick and you don't have to hate Dad. You're just not trying. You wouldn't see Chartres either if you didn't want to, if you weren't always looking out the window asking for it."

"Careful."

"Why should I be? Why should I be the only one? When are you going to act careful?"

"You're a child."

"I am not. Don't call me that. I'm not anymore."

"You're not, huh?" She sighed, looking me over.

"No, Momma. I'm not."

"All grown up."

"Almost."

"What's your hurry."

"People hurrying me."

"People, huh? I remember you. I remember thinking I could dream it and then it would happen. Melanie's age I'd dream Casard died and I'd wake up convinced I'd killed her. Your age, I'd have the faceless men. Later, when I met your father, I started having dreams with *his* face. That's how I knew he was the one. All the different dreams, there he was. I saw him taking me from that house, so I wouldn't have to think about her dying-not-dying, Indignities, sad-sad blah blah blah."

Momma studied the faucet. She bit the inside of her cheek. "I don't see his face anymore."

With her big toe Momma turned on the hot water. She let it run a bit, then shut it off.

"Momma?"

She waved her hand. "Go on now," she said, "I'm going to wash." She dipped the washcloth, then scrubbed it with the bar of soap. "Go on. You heard me. Go."

The next morning, when I awoke, my first thought was of snow. Lifting the window shade, I peered into the backyard: everything was white—the whole yard blanched with snow. I curled inside my comforter, waiting for Dad's slippers to scuff along the carpeted hall. At my door he blew reveille, his fists stacked against his mouth like a trumpet, "Da-du-da-dada, Da-du-da-dada. Everyone up, Miss Seta-Sue that means you."

"Yeah, here I am, up." I lifted my head from the pillow.

Dad smiled. "Shh. Pipe down, your mother's sleeping in."

"She sick?"

"Resting. Honey, your Mom's just wrung out."

"Is it still snowing?"

"Mmm. Couple feet, at least." He looked vaguely in the direction where the shade covered the window. "I'd say it's a safe bet you kids have yourselves a snow day."

"Dad?"

"Mmm?"

"Did Momma check out back? Did she see Chartres?"

He sighed and leaned against the jamb. "I don't know, Seta. I think your mother believes it's disappeared. I never saw it myself."

"Dad?"

"Mmm?"

"What's going to happen—I mean, if it's gone?"

"I don't know, Seta. Don't know."

He had on his morning face, droopy about the eyes and at the throat. Leaning in the doorway, he looked pale and ancient.

"Maybe she'll see a new one, Dad. Bigger, maybe. You think so?"

He gave a quick nod. "Take your time getting up. We'll save the shoveling for later."

Beneath the covers, I rubbed my thumb inside Casard's spoon. I thought, It's all falling down, it's all falling down.

In my father's house we were insulated from the cold, but where Momma looked there was no warmth.

"Dad," I said, "it'll be fine. I know it will."

He attempted a smile. "That's the way."

I closed my eyes as his slippers retreated along the carpet. When he reached the end of the hall, he opened the door and I heard her sobbing.

"George, George, is that you?"

"Shhh, Roxie, I'm here now."

But she cried out anyway, part alarm, part command, "Gone! Gone!"

"No," I whispered, clutching the pillow. "No."

My legs jerked under the covers, my heart raced. Momma and I had only wanted the same thing. A little bit of color, a little bit of hope to keep away that awful chill: cold as a river, bluer than the bluest snow, blacker than night.

Rubbing Casard's spoon, I murmured, Kiss me. Kiss me.

SPRING

What does it take to make a life? More than we are taught.

And when in March, the calendar turned to spring and spring did not come—not the crocus, not the forsythia, not a hint of warm vernal breeze—when spring like a reluctant suitor remained distant and coy, I took it upon myself to go out and find it.

One night after dinner I put the dog on a leash and headed up the hill, for the neighborhood. The torpor of winter I left behind, and a taste of freedom and of things yet unknown inflated my spirits. Miss America and I jogged past the gray-slush lawns and curtained windows of the neighborhood. Once or twice, I heard muffled voices—intimate, house voices—that seemed to call me home, but I put them out of my mind.

At the top of the hill, where we usually turned back, I kept on going, past where the houses and streetlamps left off and the wooded acres of the reservoir began. I had in mind to find Adam BenKiki, and I moved along the moonlit road toward the reservoir, where he was often said to go. My hips led me, as though I were being reeled in. Miss America's nails clacked noisily on the pavement, announcing our presence, as did her occasional bark whenever some unseen creature rustled a leaf in the dark woods.

The road dead-ended into a parking lot, bordered by two enormous treatment tanks, humming and glowing silver in the moonlight like huge Martian spaceships. On the far side of the lot, a chain-link fence blocked the narrow road leading to the dam. Finding the gate locked, we slipped off to the side, between two steel poles—Miss America barking with nervous excitement before dashing through—and onto the road. I let the dog off her leash and she ran ahead into the woods.

Without the dog, the capacious black silence, the white eye of the moon, the call and quake of the throbbing woods spooked me. I could barely make out the road, and I was imagining murderers and rapists, my maimed body photographed on the front page, when just behind me someone coughed. Stiff with fright, I slowly turned. He was standing by the side of the road, hands stuffed into the pockets of his worn, saggy jeans. I saw the white checks on his wool shirt, and then I noticed his grin.

"Hey," Adam said, and that was enough for me. I walked toward him, butting my head into his chest. He put his arms around me as I pressed my face into his neck—his neck smelling of smoke and woods. Then his mouth was on mine, his hands under my shirt and, trembling, all I yearned for was to get down to the ground, to fall down on the ground.

We tumbled onto the paved road, me on top, and then him on top, and then the dog came up and licked our faces. Adam threw his head back, laughing, as the dog pawed his shoulder.

"Lie down," I croaked, and Miss America barked once and sat.

We fooled around, the dog watching over us, until the freezing asphalt became intolerable and we all started shivering. We stood and Adam wrapped his filthy wool shirt around me. Then, too shy to talk or look each other in the eye, we kissed some more.

At last I broke away. "I guess I've got to go," I said, apologizing, each word seeming like a crude and excruciating betrayal of our silence. "You'll be at school tomorrow?" I asked.

He bowed his head and considered his desert boots. "Naw," he said, "I'm taking off."

"Where to?"

"My Dad's livin' in Florida. I might go check it out for a while."

"Your Mom, is she going, too?"

He grinned at me. "What are you, Cathy-question?" And then he laughed, making me feel foolish. "They split up when I was small," he said.

I wanted to ask, Is that how come you live in the woods? but I did not feel I had the right to pry.

We held hands and walked back to the chain-link fence, and beyond to the reservoir, where we looked out over the black, turbid water, which seemed to contain both terror and calm, and, like all things that lay ahead of us, seemed volatile, uncharted, omnipotent. At the center of the reservoir, there was a tiny round house, used for measuring the water level. The house was made of stone, with a pitched shingled roof. In the summer, the round house seemed to float on the surface, while in the winter, the reservoir froze and receded from the house, exposing a bone-colored foundation. Since I was a child I had fancied the foundation as the round house's throat.

"Have you ever been out there?" I asked.

He grinned at me—a beautiful boy with golden curls. "Yeah, me and my brother swam out there a few summers ago," he said. "Why?" I could tell by his sly smile that he was thinking something more, but was not going to say—something that had to do with me.

"It'd be fun to swim out there." I smiled, my body likewise appreciating all that could be done on the floor of that round house.

"Yeah," he agreed, stuffing his hands into his pockets. "But it's fuckin' cold!"

"So-o," I said, giving him a sly, daring smile, and just to make sure he knew I was serious, I cocked my head like one of the tough meadow girls and squinted at him.

He laughed then, enjoying himself, or maybe he did not know what else to do. He kept on nodding. "Well, I got to get going."

"No, wait," I said. "When are you coming back?"

He shrugged. Then, sighing, he swung his arms over his head and his T-shirt pulled out from his pants exposing his taut abdomen. "Maybe sometime I'll see you—out there"—his elbow pointed vaguely at the round house. He leaned over and kissed me, his tongue diving into my mouth. Then he darted into the woods, the dog shamelessly following him until I called her back.

A week passed and then another; Adam did not return to school. I knew better than to expect him, but I kept an eye out for him anyway. When I came home in the afternoon, Melanie was in her room. She had recovered sufficiently from fever to sit up in bed and play tunes on a light birch recorder, a gift from Dad. I sat in the chair beside her bed while Melanie, pale and thin as the instrument itself, drew the arched mouthpiece to her cracked lips, and, breathing stale, feverish breath into the flute, produced one shrill note. The week before, with my encouragement, she had mastered the scale, her milky pink fingernails methodically covering and uncovering the holes. She had moved on to simple tunes like "Three Blind Mice" and "Frère Jacques" before slapping the workbook from her bed and calling for Momma to bring on the contents of the piano bench.

Melanie spread the pile of sheet music across her bed, some spilling onto the floor. There was a collection of Beatles tunes and, of course, "Moon River." There was Bach, Mozart and Chopin from piano lessons, one Episcopalian and one Armenian hymnal; there was Peter, Paul and Mary's *Greatest Hits* and Dionne Warwick's "Do You Know the Way to San Jose," and Christmas carols, the scores from *Mary Poppins* and *The Sound of Music, 500 Easy*

Listening Tunes and the complete works of Mr. Scott Joplin. The day before, Melanie had opened the Beatles collection and stopped at "Yesterday." Note by note she tooted her way through the song. After she finished, she began again. All day and into the evening Melanie toot-tooted "Yesterday" on the recorder.

"That's great, Mel," I said. "Now try something else."

"Uh-uh," she said. "This is my only favorite."

In the beginning, no one had thought to complain. The run of flattened notes, the incessant toot-toot was, if nothing else, affirmation that Melanie had not succumbed. Soon she would return to school and forget that recorder. Then quiet, if not peace, would return to our house.

But when, at the end of March, Melanie returned to school, she did not stop tooting. That first day she came home and headed straight for bed with the recorder and a tray of food. Her thin, spindly legs pounded up the stairs with determination. She ate for that day and for the days she had lost, her cheeks turning rosy. Her snack consumed, Melanie turned to the pile of sheet music on her night table. She flipped through the covers, the thicker collections falling to the floor like heavy boots. But there was nothing of interest. "Yesterday" was her one song.

Miss America was the first to protest. Rising from her lolled position, her snout pointed like a missile skyward, she howled, letting it be known that a certain line had been crossed. This life of hers was just too full of sorrow. In the basement, out of doors, it mattered not. Miss America heard Melanie's music and cried.

Van, sixteen, expressed his own displeasure with no greater refinement than the dog. He had enough to worry about. That winter he had fallen for Lexi Sherer, one of the popular girls in the junior class. He had some limited success in engaging Lexi in a phone conversation in which they talked up the minutiae of teachers, music, her baby-sitting and his after-school job at Stop & Shop. At a certain point, however, in the conversation, Van found himself describing in detail various unsavory aspects of the meat locker, not because Lexi had asked but because she did not stop him. The next phone call he would broach the subject of "going out," and she would either agree or invoke the crushing phrase "just friends."

Waiting for Lexi, Van locked himself in his room, and stuffing a sweater under the door, blasted Led Zeppelin, the Rolling Stones, the Who. But Melanie's toot-toots had the power to seep through any wall. Van jerked open his door and, banging on the jamb, bellowed, "Jesus Christ. I'm going crazy. Does anybody hear me? I said *crazy*. Melanie, do you hear? What are you—*deaf*?"

Van escaped in Momma's car and I went with him. The day was bitter cold. Waiting for the car to get warm, the cold froze our tongues, and so we did not speak of Lexi or Adam, though they were with us in our thoughts. With us, too, was the unease in our house. If only the car could fly fast enough, our worries would fall back into the trunk, and from the trunk be sucked out a hole into the biting wind.

We pulled out of the driveway and the moment the tires rolled onto the road we began to feel easier.

"Let's go to the reservoir," I said, and Van turned that way up the road.

We trolled up Fern, turning left onto Sycamore Drive. Van drove Sunday-slow while I adjusted the dials on the dash. We had all the time in the world. Positioning the vents toward us, I turned up the heater and checked all of the songs on the radio before choosing "Under My Thumb" as the car approached Caretaker Road. Van braked at the stop sign, then turned. As the wheel straightened he hit the gas and I felt the powerful surge of the engine pressing me into my seat as we left the houses for the woods.

The car bounded up the road like a dog off a leash. We lunged over the speed bumps and curves that Miss America and I had navigated slowly in the dark, Momma's green Plymouth wagon gliding along the wing of road, her left tires gobbling the broken yellow line. It seemed we had waited all our lives for a moment like this: Van driving, the engine sucking the air from our bellies, the trees whipping by like so many indiscriminate sticks. We were free, so long as the radio played and gas sloshed in the tank. Before the parking lot by the water-treatment tanks, Van swung a hard right onto a dirt road that went through the orchards, the apple trees barren and wintry, as the heater finally kicked in, sending a warm springlike breeze roaring through the vents. Flicking the fan to high, Van and I simultaneously unrolled our windows and stuck our heads into the cold, bracing wind.

We shouted our names, and the names of our beloveds; then we shouted whatever came into our heads—mostly loud, multifarious whoops. We had never been so free, never been so free, so long as we never stopped. I stuck my face into that wind and shouted the most profane curses I knew.

Van, addressing the road, egged me on.

"Do C.L.," he said, smiling wickedly.

"Uh-uh. I hate that one."

"Do it," he warned, tapping his foot on the brake. "Or I'll dump you home."

"Sure," I said, crossing my arms under my ribs.

Van slammed on the brake, and just as he was turning the car around I leaned out the window and aiming my voice at the top of the trees, yelled, "C-U-U-U-NT L-A-A-A-A-PPING!"

I glanced over at him and stuck out my tongue.

My brother smirked, and dropping his voice low like Elvis, he said, "Well, Daddy's little girl."

Laughing wickedly, we left the orchards and returned to the road, bypassing the woods where Adam slept. I looked out my window expectantly, hoping to see him step out from behind a tree. The car banked to the right, through a grove of pine, then out by the reservoir. The water was icy and slate-black and, in the middle, I saw the round house. Since the night with Adam, not a day had passed that I did not think of the round house and, in my mind, picture what we would do there. Sometimes I went there in my dreams with faceless men, and sparrows flapped in the eaves as we made love on the floor.

Van gunned the engine and I looked back in time to discover

that someone had beaten me to the round house. Just above the waterline, in bold spray paint, someone had written on the foundation: LULU SUCKS.

The words had nothing to do with me, but nevertheless they struck me as a personal slight. My heart sank like a stone. Van slowed down as we left the reservoir and returned again to the houses, down the hill to the back of our lot. My glance fell upon the row of hemlocks that bordered our yard. Seventeen years earlier, Dad had planted those trees, intending them to grow and form an impenetrable wall that would protect his family from onlookers. Beyond that barrier were the walls of our house. It occurred to me that these were the twin walls of a prison. It occurred to me, too, though not so much in words but as twin stones of dread and lethargy rolling in my belly, that I did not wish to go home. That should I stay in that tiny brown house, eclipsed by evergreens, I would soon find myself grown bent, like Dad; or caught up in a blue miasma, like Momma; or lonely, unforgiving and desperate, like Casard. And if not like them, then something worse, with every one of my dreams coming round to Lulu Sucks.

At the stop sign, Van turned to me and asked, "Where to?"

I did not want to burden Van with my doomed vision, nor with the fact that he looked juvenile behind the wheel—juvenile and pretend. I was not going to be cruel, though cruel was how I felt. Looking at my brother, trying to find some good, I decided that he was sort of handsome, though far too skinny. A down vest, corduroys and desert boots could not hide a body that was as thin as a pared reed. Van had Dad's height—Dad's fairness too, which combined with Momma's blood to make dark, striking features relieved of their intensity by a wash of blond curls.

Van glanced into the rearview mirror and I saw blemishes on his nose and forehead, which, that night, he would scrub with a cloth. He was careful about grooming; each morning he meticulously shaved the stray hairs on his lip and chin. Looking at him, I experienced a swell of pride that came with the realization that we were no longer close. Lately, like the rest of the family, we knew each other best as cohabitants: taking turns in the bathroom, turns on the phone. We knew each other as parts from the same source: watching Van drive, I saw our father in the way he palmed the center of the wheel at turns.

Miserable, I thought of Van's new life, which led me to Lexi Sherer, who, I decided, was a yellow-haired fool. Let her fall for him, then let him break her heart. Let him break all their hearts. As his sister I would be there to testify to the sensitivity he inherited from Dad and the flash of temper he inherited from Momma—all of which made him push away the things that frightened him, thus inspiring me to nickname him Buck. We were kids then and knew not why the word, or why it sounded so right. Just like that afternoon, as we sat idling in Momma's car, we understood little of the awful paradox that conspired against us, ensuring that every time we tried to flee, we would somehow find ourselves returned to the corner of that yard, where every bush was a memory of childhood games of gun, Indian, fort.

"Van," I said, deciding, "let's go to the Northend and buy some beer."

He shrugged, meaning the idea impressed him but first he had to think it over. Leaning forward and craning his neck, he peered out my window to see what I was looking at. He took in the hemlocks and, beyond, the line of our roof, and sighed, his breath blowing on the back of my hair. "Shit," he said, conclusively.

"Let's go," I urged.

"I don't know." He sighed, empty as a bag.

"Yep. I know. We're going. What the fuck."

Van looked at me grimly and winced. "You sure are getting some mouth."

I rolled my eyes toward the house, as if to say, Can you blame me?

Just then, a car pulled up behind us and tapped its horn.

"Goddamn it," Van said. "Goddamn it." And palming the center of the wheel, he gunned the car around the corner, heading us north.

• • •

A week later, after Easter, Dad and Momma went to Bermuda to try to patch up their marriage. For nine days we were put with Poppee, who took charge of three sulky orphans, too old to be baby-sat. At dinner the first night I picked a fight with Melanie, and Poppee, waving her finger at me as if naming trouble, said, "You I want next to me, in Vart's room."

That night in Auntie Vart's girlhood bed, I scissored my legs to find the cold parts of the sheet. Such a loneliness gripped my soul, a terrible suspense. My thoughts were like grim soldiers marching through my head: Kiss me. He loves me. So alone. God help me. I love you with all my heart. I'm the only thing I have in the world. This will end. Better. I don't care. Fuck 'em. The world comes down to me. Just wait until I'm grown.

I rolled over, light from a passing car filtering through sheer curtains fringed with lavender ricrac. Sighing dramatically, no one to hear or save me, I got up wearily and paced to the window.

The street was empty, nothing much to see. I snapped on the bureau light—an illuminated confection made from a lacy shade hung on an iron stand. Beside the lamp was a framed photograph of Auntie Vart at sixteen; Auntie Vart gazing at the world, her expression part virgin, part widow. I thought: Our faces tell exactly who we are; they even predict our future. I looked in the mirror and wondered what my face said about me. I saw large dark eyes and light wavy brown hair that fell to my waist and teeth that were straight and small. I saw my face in parts: nose, brows, cheeks, but the sum remained elusive; I wondered if this was normal, if others saw only fragments, too. I thought of Momma and Casard, their faces too close and familiar for them to really see.

I turned out the light, collapsed into bed, and, lifting my night-gown, ran my hands down my torso, as far as they could reach. Picturing Adam, I held my breath, then pushed the air out, lingering, breathless, until I could not see him anymore—until I was certain my heart would stop out of sheer boredom.

Did I think of Momma? Not so much. Her absence meant that

for the first time in my life I was free of my mother's moods. Was she having fun? I could not say. If she were home, I would lie in bed and feel the tickle of her mirth on the inside of my face. Or if she was depressed, then her dark hollow would expand in me like a great balloon I yearned to retch. But Momma was in Bermuda—too far away for me to tell—and the inside of my face was heavy with my own lust and boredom.

It was something I had never questioned: how much of my mind was tied up with Momma. Since Casard's death, monitoring Momma's moods had become second nature—in the same way, I suppose, that after Casard died, Momma felt her mother in the misalignment of doors. "Close the door!" Momma bellowed from her room upstairs, when, downstairs in the kitchen, I lingered too long in front of the open refrigerator. Casard had instilled in Momma a belief that our lives, like food in the refrigerator, teetered perpetually on the brink of spoiling.

Lying there—nothing else to do—I thought about my parents and wished for them to return home happy and in love. I closed my eyes and tried to picture them at breakfast in the hotel, sinking silver spoons into slices of melon, looking out at the sea. Afterward, they would tool around the island on scooters, like the couple in the hotel brochure. Then lunch. Then she would put on her swimsuit and visit the pool while he went to the pro shop to pick up a foursome. She would stretch out on a chaise, and when the heat began to prickle her skin she would walk to the rim of the pool and, pointing her toes, dive into the water. She would swim, once across, plucking out her elbows and her head. But what did she feel when, later that evening, he escorted her down the wide carpeted stairs to their table? What passed through her heart? Was she giving him a chance, when, at night, she lay with him in the hotel bed? As she shut her eyes to dream, did she see my father as a clear light or as a gauzy haze occluding her from the life she deserved? I closed my eyes but could not tell.

On the third day they phoned. She sounded giddy and a little drunk. "Your father keeps trying to teach me to ride a scooter," she said. "They drive on the left here. Did you know that? Dad says my problem is I keep wanting to veer to the right. You kids would catch on in a minute. Next time, huh? What else, I don't know. I think I'm getting fat. We eat all the time. Your father says they're going to have to charge us double for the room to make up for our meals. It's lovely here, not too many people. Tomorrow we're taking a ride on a boat called a catamaran. I got you a present today. Do you like pouka beads? I bought Melanie a ring. Don't tell her, let's have it be a surprise. I would have gotten you both Scotch kilts if I thought you'd wear them. Oh, what else, what else? Seta, your Momma is fat! and we're just about to go to dinner. You're not giving Poppee too much trouble, are you?"

That night, again, I could not sleep. I threw open the windows and spread myself on Auntie Vart's rose sheets like a moth pinned to velvet. An hour passed and then another, the wait elongating, gathering, until any moment I expected a loud deafening noise, a sudden burst. I was fifteen, alone, waiting for the next event to happen. I screamed into the pillow at the top of my lungs, "Go. Go. Go. Go," until, hoarse and exhausted, I slept.

At dawn I awoke to a man's voice—a terrible sound, like a wounded animal crying. "Suzanne! Suzanne!"

I went to the window. Across the road, in the center of the neighbor's drive, where the vernal sun stretched like a yellow tongue, Bob Humms, town watchman, cobbler, crazy, stood. He was wearing camouflage fatigues that blended with his sandy beard, and black army boots; an army canteen was strapped to his thick brown belt. Dressed like an American soldier in Vietnam, he lifted his throat and cried out, "Suzanne! Suzanne! Oh, Su-zanne, come down!"

Such was his call to spring. I clapped my hands and danced a jig on Vart's Persian carpet. Spring! I threw open the window and leaned out. Just a few days earlier, Melanie and I had wondered aloud whether this year, with the war finally over, Bob Humms would find himself a new cause.

As if to answer, he raised his throat to the dawn: "Su-zanne, Su-zanne. Girl? Girl? Su-zanne?"

Poppee called out from her room, "Lunatic! You hear me? Six o'clock in the morning! Pipe down!"

I opened my door and tiptoed into the hall, the morning air buzzing with invisible shavers, the floorboards under my feet releasing pockets of tortured violins. My bones, though young, clicked like light switches as Bob Humms called from the street: "Suzanne-in-the-hills! My girl? My girl? Suzanne!"

I stopped at Poppee's door and peeked in on the old woman swathed like a mummy. Above the mound of covers was her tiny head. Poppee licked her lips and whimpered, "So early. P-lease!"

Then, behind my back, the floorboards moaned. A thin flannel sail emerged from the shadows of Auntie Sarah's room.

"Shhh," I hissed, cautioning Melanie back.

"Shush yourself." She waved, barreling toward me.

Trying to ignore Melanie, I peeked into Poppee's room and found her conversing with the ceiling. "Poor thing," she said, lapsing into Armenian. The cadence of her voice rose and fell. I tucked my arms under my ribs while Melanie, standing on tiptoe, leaned against me and breathed. In this manner, we observed Poppee, an otherwise sane adult, talking to the cracks on her ceiling—an occurrence so spectacularly foolish and, on our part, disrespectful to watch, that for a moment we forgot Bob Humms.

The first night that we stayed with her, Poppee brought Melanie and me into her room and explained to us that the large crack over the bed had first appeared after Sarah's birth. Deep like a groove. Next, Poppee showed us the hairline cracks shaped like Florida. That was Hurricane David. And the linear split, that was the old oak. But the longest scar, the one she measured each day with her right eye (and each day it grew), that was Great Uncle Alex's funeral. According to Poppee, on the afternoon of Alex's funeral, she shook hands with all her guests and kissed her children good-bye before ascending the stairs. Her intention was to lie down a minute. "But hands," she said, "have little minds of their own." It seemed that when Poppee reached her room, she grabbed the door and slammed it with all her might. Again and again, she cried, "Damn you damn you damn you, leaving me alone."

That first night we stayed in the house Poppee waved her finger at the cleft in the plaster, and said to Melanie and me, "This crack belongs to Alex. 'Careful, Alex,' I tell him. 'Talk to me or I'll do the door.' "

And again that morning, as Melanie and I looked on, Poppee sought the counsel of her deceased husband, whom she pictured in a heaven wallpapered with harps and vines. "Hey, Alex. Alexan, listen to me. He's back again. The poor thing, traipsing."

Poppee was about to say more when the telephone next to her bed began to ring.

Melanie yelped and pinched me in the back. I spun and grabbed her wrist.

Poppee plucked her teeth from a glass and, wiggling them in place with her tongue, lifted the receiver.

"Sarah?" She blinked, leaning close to the base of the phone. "Honey? What's the trouble, six o'clock in the morning?"

Poppee held her breath as Sarah spoke.

"Who?" she asked. "Oh, yeah. Mr. Mormon Tabernacle Choir's outside the house right now. You hear him?" Poppee held the receiver out toward the window. After a moment she put it back against her ear. "Sarah. Sarah. You tell Eddy, Bob Humms never once missed our street." She nodded, agreeing with herself, and removed a Kleenex from her sleeve to swab her nose and cheeks.

They would talk for an hour—Poppee loved to talk. I headed for the stairs, Melanie behind me.

"Where're you going?" she whispered, her breath on my back. At the foot of the stairs I reached into the closet for a coat and a pair of shoes.

"You're not going out—" Melanie cried, "this early?"

"Melanie," I said, tying the shoes, "go back to bed."

Melanie waved furiously, pointing to the stairs: someone was coming down.

We waited, hearts pounding, as heavy boots descended the carpeted stairs. But it was only Van.

"Hey, fools"—he grinned—"did I scare you? Watcha doing? You escaping, or is this just some fool parade?"

"Nice outfit," I said.

Van surveyed his attire: coat, pajamas, boots. Then he turned bug eyes on me and, grinning, took note of my nightgown peeking out from under Poppee's coat. "Well, look who's who," he said.

I tipped my head. "You guys coming, or not?"

Van shrugged, as if to say he did not care.

"Got to put on my sneakers," Melanie mumbled, unenthused.

"Go on," I said. "Ten seconds. Hurry."

Once out the door, we all started to run. "Snow day," Melanie whooped, recalling those mornings after a blizzard, when, like giddy Eskimos, we ran through the neighborhood, diving into snowbanks while Miss America went on ahead, desecrating the white snow with dribbles of urine.

"Snow day. Snow day," Melanie crowed, though it was spring and there was no snow in sight. Twirling like a ballerina, her arms reaching above her head, Melanie danced down the driveway and onto the road.

Van and I followed several paces behind her. At first it seemed like a good idea to greet this spring, for which we had waited. But the momentum was not with us—we did not know why—all of a sudden it seemed silly and impossible to run from the house pretending we were goofy kids.

We stopped at the crest of Victoria Road, and watched as Bob Humms neared the bottom. His voice warbled back to us like a mournful horn, "Su-zanne? Su-zanne? Suzanne of the hills!"

"Who's Suzanne, anyway?" Melanie asked.

Van and I looked at each other but could not think of an answer. A light went on in a house across the street, and it occurred to me that someone might see us, standing in the road like fools.

"I'm gonna catch up," I said, and set off down the hill after Bob Humms.

"You're wasting your time," Van called to my back.

"Yep." I waved.

"He's just a kook, Seta, a kook," Van said, his voice high-pitched like a girl's.

I stopped, but did not turn. "What are you afraid of, Van Loon? Tell me why, exactly, you're standing in the road screaming your head off?"

"You guys," Melanie complained, Tinker Bell feet scampering toward me. "You guys—"

I started down the hill.

"All right," Van called, "but this time no talking."

At Steele Road we turned up the hill, tracking the shabby camouflage coat. Bob Humms's agony filled the morning air. "Suzanne. Suzanne. Oh, Suzanne. GirlGirlGirl? Ohh, GirlGirlGirl, Come down."

Suzanne, I decided, would be his lover. Just like the faceless men, Bob Humms would go to her, and in each other's arms they would shiver like new leaves.

We had passed Mountain Drive, when all of a sudden Bob Humms took it into his head to dart across the road. Melanie grabbed my hand; I shook her away but allowed her to remain close. We three crossed the street, stopping at the far curb. Bob Humms walked up the driveway, into the yard, and stood before a large dogwood tree. Clasping his hands behind him, he studied the tree's stark limbs. Melanie caught my eye and shrugged. Bob Humms pulled a branch, thin as a finger, toward him and sniffed its row of knotted buds. Melanie and I looked on, unable to suppress our grins, while Van stood back a pace, his mouth dropped open in contemplation.

Bob Humms released the branch and headed back to the road. Van blocked my way. "Give the guy room," he cautioned, holding me back until Bob Humms was nearly out of sight.

At the intersection of Hickory Hill, we lost him.

"Where the hell did he go?" Van fumed.

"Don't ask me," I snapped. We had followed Bob Humms and,

by doing so, put an end to years of wonder. We had dared do that, go after him. And while the thrill of following him had more to do with shattering the inertia of our lives than anything he might have shown us, it was essential that we not lose Bob Humms.

Panicked, we turned in circles in the middle of the road. "I don't know," Melanie squealed, to a question no one had asked. She flitted behind a green hedge and Van ran off in the opposite direction.

Suddenly, I was alone. Across the road a man in a dark suit got into his car and drove down the hill. I revolved slowly in the street, and found myself standing in front of Theresa Vartyan's house.

As I stepped onto the curb I heard giggling and a sound like snorting coming from behind the garage. I turned the corner and saw, or, at least, believed I saw, Theresa sitting on the ground with Bob Humms kneeling before her, as in prayer. He tipped forward and his bare ass wedged in the V of her thighs. They moved, not in a gauzy, dreamlike manner—not like the faceless men and me—but like dogs, humping and growling. His camouflage trousers bunched below his knees while her feet struggled to free themselves of her chartreuse hose. It occurred to me that maybe he had forced her down, maybe their act was born of violence, repulsive, against her will. Then she pulled him to her, and his buttocks squeezed as she wrapped her legs about his hips. They became one engine, and then Theresa Vartyan threw back her head and moaned.

I hurried back to the road, dizzy, covered with sweat.

Van was waiting. "Seta?"

I shook my head, no.

"I don't believe it," Melanie cried. "How can a person just disappear?"

"We screwed up, that's how," Van answered, spinning.

Melanie jumped up and down. "Fuck, fuck, fuck," she said.

Watching Melanie, I tried to think of something other than what I had seen, but the harder I tried, the clearer I saw them. I decided then that everything I had imagined about love was ridiculous and untrue. Love was not the golden light of faceless men. It was indiscriminate, taking seed wherever planted, whether in violence, despair or the hard-packed dirt at the base of a forsythia. Love was a moment, no better or worse than the intentions brought. It changed nothing, it changed no one.

Watching my sister, I decided that I would never again yearn for this love, which was so much less than I had hoped. Yearning and hoping was what got our family in trouble in the first place—Casard and Vrej, Momma and Dad—all of us waiting for the good, right thing to come. Well, it would never come, I felt certain, and love would never be more than what was in us in the first place. What was in me I did not yet know, but standing in the road trying to forget what I had seen, I had an inkling as to the black bottom of my soul.

We went back to Poppee's and stood, dejected and penitent, in the old woman's driveway, three teenagers with nothing more to prove. Around us, and without mercy, the day began. A bus rolled to the corner and, gasping, received a load of commuters. Cars destined for work stopped at the sign. The weather would turn warm by afternoon, and in a few days there would be a final, brief snap of cold. Then Momma and Dad would return home, the outcome of their unsuccessful reconciliation etched in their suntanned faces. And I would go on living with my secret: each night I would climb into bed, and, closing my eyes, find Theresa and Bob Humms. He would kneel before her as in prayer, and my dreams would begin there, with the soles of the cobbler's black laced boots turned toward me, like an open book I was meant to read.

We are bound by a single thread. Everything comes around, comes around. Everything touches.

The night Momma and Dad came home from Bermuda I climbed into bed and waited for my mother's pain to sink into my belly. I closed my eyes and licked my lips, but nothing came. Then, at midnight, I heard Momma sigh as she passed down the hall. She went into the bathroom and shut the door. The tap squealed as she unleashed torrents of water, filling the tub, filling my belly with despair.

I never imagined hurting someone. But in time, my despair turned dark and hard like a burnt seed and I began to yearn for a place to plant that seed and, removing it from me, put it back into the world. And so my betrayal began to grow.

In my mind I saw them behind the garage so many times. I spent hours during the night wondering why Bob Humms called her Suzanne. I worried this question until it came to me: in Sunday school, Casard had called Theresa by her Armenian name—Shushan.

"Shushan," I said, turning in my bed, as three rooms away, Momma turned in the tub. I kicked the wall with my foot, wanting to hurt someone to match the hurt inside me. I was not thinking about betrayal, but it was what I wanted.

The next afternoon, the popular girls from the ninth grade gathered in a semicircle around the public library wall, and I decided to join them. I was not a regular member of the group, though I had known all the girls since grade school and a long time ago some of us were friends. For old times they allowed me to stand with them, pretending not to notice, so long as I remained on the fringe. One girl, with carmine-colored hair, pale blue eye shadow, and a yellow vinyl miniskirt, positioned herself at the center. She was Lori DeNigres, queen of the moment, the one around whom, with anarchy fisted in their pockets and guts strung tight as drums, the girls gathered and performed. The dance was paying court. It was four o'clock in the afternoon.

Lori hopped onto the stone ledge and we assumed our places around her. In the central sphere, closest to Lori, the confident girls convened. Those girls knew that one day they too would have their turn as queen. Until then, their task was to grace the planet with a divine lethargy. For them everything was a bore. Such a bore for Cynthia Berman, who reclined on the stone ledge as if it were her private chaise. And for Patty Sullivan, inspecting the pink-frosted nails of her sister, Martha. And for Leslie Crumm, who had turned her back, doodling circles in a green spiral notebook. Those girls understood that popularity did not always require the obvious gifts of looks or brains. The hidden skills were what truly mattered: cunning, style and the ability to throw one's observations like darts.

The rest of the girls—girls like me—had to jockey for recognition. We packed in close enough to the confident girls but several layers away from Lori. Like them, I could have committed large, impressive crimes or flung myself singing from the roof of the gymnasium before Lori DeNigres's frosted lips mouthed my name.

Lori reached into her purse and lit up a Kool. Martha removed her own pack from a coat pocket and, placing two cigarettes in her mouth, lit them both, passing one to her sister. There followed a chain reaction of frantic purse searches, flavored lip-gloss applications, lighter clicks, coughs, sniffs, sighs. Patty Sullivan ran a comb through her hair and released the loose strands into the wind. I slipped a piece of gum into my mouth and, keeping an eye on Lori, began furiously to chew.

Lori DeNigres was known for her outrageous attire, as some people are known for a particular handicap or gift. More than once that year she had been summoned to the principal's office for violation of the dress code. Lori was cheap, and though just fifteen, she was nearly spent, from the tip of her stripped hair to her shoes—one of which, that day, lacked a buckle, so Lori had improvised, stapling the strap closed.

Lori never talked about what went on between her and her boyfriend Keith. It was generally assumed that they spent entire weekends locked in his room over his parents' garage, but if this was true, Lori kept it to herself. She and Keith, together since the seventh grade, were the trailblazers of our class. They were the first to pass from hand-holding to French-kissing to running the bases, all the way to home. Or so we assumed. Now there was talk that Lori and Keith were experimenting with S and M. S and M we said, S and M.

Lori, the subject of our gossip, sat before us, swinging her legs as she perched on the library wall, like some kid pumping a swing.

Patty Sullivan asked, "What're you and Keith doing this weekend?"

"I don't know." Lori shrugged. "Just hang out, I suppose."

"Mmm," Patty smiled, inspecting her nails.

"Why?"

"Just wondering," Patty said, picking out the dirt from under her nails with a paper clip. "Heard you guys had some wild Saturday night."

"Where'd you hear that?" Lori squinted. These girls talked so slow, not even a bomb could make them move. I watched closely, studying, memorizing the cunning lethargy of the would-be queens.

"Bud said so."

"Yeah?" Lori exhaled, her torso folding like a lawn chair. "Take it from me, Patty, Bud doesn't know shit." She sighed, and, looking herself over, seemed surprised and comforted to find herself attached to such a body. Gripping the wall, she pumped her legs furiously. "What'd he say, anyhow?"

"Oh, nothing."

"Nothin', huh?"

"I really don't want to get into it," Patty said, gazing about her. "I really don't think I should."

"Say what?" Lori squealed, her face twisted with disgust.

"Lori, I don't think you want me to get into it, all right? Not here." Patty let her hands drop to her sides to show how impossible it would be to explain herself when surrounded by so many listeners. "Besides, Lor, you already said Bud doesn't know what he's talking about, so fine. Anyway, he told Martha, not me." Patty made eyes at Martha, and Martha shot back a pained look, her face flushed.

"So, Martha. What did Stick-up-his-Bud tell you?"

"He didn't tell me anything. And by the way, you don't have to be derogatory."

"Derogatory. Derogatory?" Lori smiled, her eyes nasty.

"That's right. That's what I said." Martha turned to Patty for encouragement. I turned, too, nervous and thrilled at the prospect of a fight.

Lori looked around as if she had just dropped onto a strange planet. "Wait a minute," she said. "Wait just a minute. You're . . . going out with him? Since when's this?"

"Last week."

"Bud Coolidge? The same Bud Coolidge with the—"

Martha stuck her fist on her hip. "Lori, I don't think you want to say anything bad about Bud. Specially if you don't appreciate people talking about you and Keith."

"I don't believe this. I don't. Buddy Coolidge is spreading lies about Keith and—"

Martha's mouth dropped open in feigned horror, but before she could say anything, Patty piped in. "Lori," Patty began, "let me tell you there's nothing wrong with Bud Coolidge." Patty gave Martha a reassuring nudge, which had the effect of making her sister blush.

"No, let me tell *you,*" Martha echoed, and the two sisters squealed, covering their faces with their hands.

Lori observed them, her mouth hanging open. Then she sighed, as if to convey that, really, she had been on the job too long.

"Seta?" Lori said, eyeing Patty and Martha before casting her gaze on me. "Did you know about Martha and Bud?" All the girls turned to look, as if noticing me for the first time.

"Yeah," I admitted, trying to sound casual. "I guess I heard something."

"Last week?" Lori inquired, her manner friendly and professional, like a doctor inquiring how long you have had that cough.

"Yeah. That's right."

"What'd you hear? *Exactly.*"

"I don't know. Nothing big. Just that they were going out." I stole a glance at Martha, who for the first time ever was offering me one of her big horsy smiles. "They're just getting to know each other, I guess."

Martha liked this last part. "That's a nice purse," she said.

"Thanks," I said, "yours too." And just to cover my bases, I pointed to both their purses, hers and Patty's. The two sisters grinned.

"Seta," Lori said, not at all amused. She looked at me meaningfully. "Seta. How's Van? Is he still going out with Lexi Sherer?"

"Sort of."

"He's cute, your brother. Keith likes him."

"He's just my brother." I shrugged.

"Yeah, right," Lori answered. "So, Seta, what have you been hearing about me and Keith? You know, what kind of lies have *certain* people been gossiping about." And she turned as far away as possible from Martha and Patty.

In that moment I realized that Lori DeNigres's reign was coming to an end. I had not seen it coming, but here it was. The new queen was money: Patty and Martha had money. On their wrists the sisters wore stacks of sterling bangles, which they had purchased on family vacations to places like Yucatán, Acapulco and St. Bart's. St. Bart's, Patty said, as if St. Bart were her father's personal friend.

I looked at Patty's and Martha's white smiles and saw the future. They were pretty, unlike Lori, who was cheap.

I opened my mouth and took my chance. "I heard you guys do S and M."

"What!" Lori said, her top lip raised like a ferret's, exposing tiny, square teeth. "What did you say?"

When she was still alive, Casard warned me that I had no idea how to protect myself. That when confronted with a knife, instead of fighting, I would just as soon roll over and expose my belly. Casard, of course, had been mindful of never becoming a victim.

I closed my eyes and tried to think of something brilliant, something that would protect me but please everyone else. But my mind went completely blank, my heart flapping with failure.

"I don't know, Lori"—I shrugged—"I guess everyone's heard about, you know, S and M."

"Seta Loon!" Patty Sullivan called, her face blotched with fury. Gathering the girls' attention, the new queen went on, "Seta Loon, I don't know where you get your information. I, personally, never pay attention to blatant lies about my friends." For emphasis Patty turned to Martha, who nodded vigorously.

"Well," Lori DeNigres declared, looking increasingly like a worn chair.

"Well, nothing," snapped Martha. "Seta, if you hear any garbage about Lori, you just say it's not true. It's crap and everybody knows it. What kind of friend are you?"

The afternoon breeze puffed over the hills, stirring up tiny whirlwinds of newspaper and sand. The girls were watching me, but only for a moment. Soon they would turn and I was meant to disappear. My heart fluttered like a trapped bird.

Across the road, Bob Humms was making his way toward us.

"Look at him," I said, gesturing.

They all turned in the direction I indicated, at Bob Humms. Their faces turned back to me, stern, unimpressed.

"You ever wonder," I said, "why he's always picking at his ears."

Lori cocked her head. "Honestly? No."

"There're dimes in his ears," I said. "He puts them just inside the fold. See? The metal allows him to tune into various radio frequencies."

"Get out of here," Lori said.

"No way," Patty echoed.

"Oh my God!" Leslie Crumm squealed. "Here he comes."

Bob Humms crossed the road, then changed his mind and returned to the far curb. He lifted his mouth to the sky and cried out, "Suzanne. Su-zanne." Then he leaned against a telephone pole and began to sort the contents of his pockets. He pulled out cards, napkins and dollar bills and neatly folded them, and then stuffed them back into the pockets of his trousers. He stuck a finger in his ear and vibrated it, then wiped the finger on his pants.

"Gross," Patty said, making a sour face. She moved closer to Lori.

"Who's this Suzanne?" Leslie Crumb sniffed, directing her question to Patty. "I mean, what must she be like to go out with him?"

Lori shrugged, as if to say she had seen worse.

"I know who she is," I said.

They turned to look at me and I understood this to be my last chance. Looking into the girls' faces, I made the decision to follow through; I told them that Theresa Vartyan slept with Bob Humms. When, at first, they would not believe me, I pressed. I said, "Do any of you know Theresa's name in Armenian?"

"What." Patty insisted.

Twisting my mouth, I said very carefully, "Shushan. Shu-shan. Su-zanne."

Their painted eyes blinked at me. Then I told them what I believed I had seen behind the Vartyans' garage.

Patty Sullivan flipped her hair from her face. "Come on," she said; and Martha echoed, "Get outta here." But in spite of their protests, I did what was most convincing: I bowed my head and shrugged.

As I studied my shoe, waiting for the group's verdict, Theresa Vartyan exited the library and came down the walk toward us. "Oh my—" Leslie Crumm gasped. Theresa was wrapped in a bright green windbreaker; her hair covered her face. She made her way down the walk, looking to neither the right nor the left. At the bottom of the stairs she turned in the direction of her house, and for a moment our eyes met. Then Theresa hurried past.

Across the street Bob Humms began to move, keeping pace with her. The girls watched in wonder and amazement as the two lovers picked their way up the street.

Martha said in a hushed tone, "You really think she fucks him?"

"Oh God, don't even say that," her sister replied, shuddering. "I mean gro-o-ss."

"Definitely," Lori concluded and, bowing her head, studied her shoes.

Patty glanced at Lori, a witchy expression on her face. Turning away, her eyes squinty and mean, Patty looked at me and mouthed, "Yeah—not anything like *her* and *Keith.*"

The girls around me smirked and a few laughed out loud. Lori lifted her head. "What. What's going on?"

No one said anything. All the girls were focused on Patty and me, and on Theresa and Bob Humms, who, by now, were way up the road. Ever so subtly, the group shifted, tucking closer to Patty.

Betrayal is a heavy load to carry home. I told myself that what I had done was not so bad. Obviously, small betrayals happened all the time, and people like Patty thought nothing of gaining advantage by trading private details of other people's lives. I told myself this, and as much as I believed it to be true, I also knew that by telling my story I had sent powerful and, perhaps, largely exaggerated information into the world (for I no longer knew what I had really seen) and I could not take any of it back.

I left them standing by the wall of the library. As I walked away, Lori DeNigres made a special point of waving good-bye. That wave of Lori's was my reward, and having it made me as cheap as her dime-store sandals and yellow vinyl skirt. I thought of Casard and how ashamed she would have been. She would have cried and lifted me up by my hair and then, shaking me, called me a filthy dirty Turk. I was supposed to be Seta, named for her holy; I was supposed to rise above.

Walking on, I wondered why my grandmother had to die so soon, and why her death seemed like the beginning of so many terrible events. I told myself that I hated Patty Sullivan, but I knew the truth about that, too. The truth was that I envied Patty and Martha Sullivan for their total and unwavering conviction that the world would be kind to them, that the world would provide. I could no longer afford to put my trust in their kind of world, though I badly wished I could.

I had gone a block when I looked back and saw the girls huddled close, working over the new information. What they said had nothing to do with me. What they said would grow and grow. By dinnertime the whole town would be talking about Theresa Vartyan and Bob Humms.

SUMMER

And in the land of Haiastan, Abel's blood cried out from the ground: *Murderer! Oh, vile and wicked brother! Hear the cry of my blood and know that you have betrayed me!* And born on the earth was sorrow. And born on the earth was shame. From that moment we were no more keepers, but vagrants and wanderers cast out onto land red with the blood of innumerable brothers yet killed, and innumerable betrayals, small and large, yet imagined. In time, it would seem that around every turn there was a murder waiting for a murderer, and a lie behind every truth, and a betrayal ready to fall ripe from every friend's lips. And it would seem that good required assiduous concentration while evil tripped from every tongue, until the world, shocked by its own unrighteous and corrupt nature, had to cleanse itself through tears and remembrance.

To this end, today, throughout the world a child sits on an elder's knee and is told the story of the Victim and the Betrayer—a cautionary tale, of two lives forever bound by blood and shame and sorrow. The child is told about Cain and Abel and in this manner learns about the duality of human nature, the one hand and the other; good and evil; conscious and unconscious; prodigal and lost; heaven and hell. The child learns about Jason and Medea, and then there is Judas and Christ. For every Victim there is a Betrayer and for every Betrayer the ultimate curse: forevermore his life will be linked to the one he wronged. Think of the Romans and the Christians. Think of the Nazis and the Jews. And when one thinks of the Turks, are the Armenians ever far behind? For a story is a picture of the world, and the world is a picture of our unhallowed and contradictory souls. We cannot help yearning to forget, while recalling with subtle fondness that in every murder there was a bit of love and in every love a bit of murder.

A child sits on an elder's knee and is told a story that begins: Gar oo chugar. There was and there was not.

There was all summer to regret what I had done to Theresa, and there has not been a day since that I do not think of her. I think of the two of them, Theresa and Bob Humms, and that truncated nothing of a spring that lasted one short week, during which the leaves burst, the temperature soared, and the invisible, insatiable gypsy moth laid its silent bombs of devastating larvae onto the trees. We humans, slow to recognize plague, went to sleep in winter, rolled over into blazing, dizzying heat, and when at last we awoke it was summer.

Bob Humms continued to meet Theresa after school. They walked on separate sides of the street all the way to her house, where they sat with the dying, ravaged-faced mother and sipped Coca-Cola.

Mrs. Vartyan called him Robert. "Robert," she said, her hairless eyebrows raised, her mouth a delighted O. "You want something more to drink?"

Robert was not unworthy of her love. He was eccentric, capable, abiding, true. He brought Mrs. Vartyan gifts: a hassock for her feet, which he took from his own house, shattering a window instead of breaking his personal pledge not to enter through the front door until his annual rite of suffering was complete, at the end of June.

Mrs. Vartyan returned the gift of attention. She found Bob Humms not unstable or odd but refreshingly clear. The stories that poured from him about the tragic far-off war were not so different from her own tales of massacre and deprivation. They sat in her dank living room, surrounded by effigies of Jesus and Mary, talking in turns. Never once did they think of themselves as eccentrics or martyrs. By exposing to each other what was most true and urgent—their love and their fear—Mrs. Vartyan and Bob Humms became the freest of souls, and that room, those hours, knew the inestimable relief of hearts having spoken and been heard.

Theresa was not always silent, but it was true she liked best, on those blazing afternoons, to sit between her mother and Bob Humms and allow their voices to pour down inside her, along with the iced cola.

Later, when the light through the venetian blinds turned a certain shade of purple, Theresa rose to fix dinner. They ate their meal on TV trays, since it was difficult for Mrs. Vartyan to get up from her chair. The TV trays, like the hassock, were a gift from Bob Humms.

After dinner, as dusk turned the light in the room to ash, Bob Humms gently lifted Mrs. Vartyan and carried her like a bride to bed, and then he left the room while Theresa readied her mother for sleep.

Bob Humms was thirty years old in 1974; Theresa Vartyan was fifteen. Years later she would tell me about those evenings, when, after Mrs. Vartyan went to bed, the two lovers nestled in a sleeping bag on what had been the grass patio behind the garage and was now hard caked dirt. This was Theresa's time to talk. Bob Humms listened to whatever she had to say, and if she had nothing to say, which was often the case, they were silent. They were like old lovers who understood that time was their friend, if they only allowed it to run through them, if they never pushed.

Those early summer nights Theresa made few efforts to surprise or perform. The best entertainment she could offer was a trail of smoke rings rising above her head, her lips toot-tooting silent O's like a fish talking underwater. She laughed at the rings, and he was gratified to share in her pleasure.

"Come here," he said and, using his fingers, combed the hair from her face. She became terribly quiet, barely breathing. He lifted her face in his palms. "There you are," he said, smiling. "There's you."

Another time she brought a hairbrush from her room and Bob Humms brushed Theresa Vartyan's thick black hair. Afterward, when the time was ripe, they clung to each other like the insects we called sewing needles, which all that summer danced in the blanched rays of sun, performing miraculous and daring feats of copulation while flying. They were two thin blue rods, hovering, hovering.

PLEASE LET HIM COME SOON AND LOVE ME AND PLEASE MAKE OUR FAMILY WHOLE.

I prayed. My earnest wish for better things come summer made better things seem possible.

Then, on a stifling afternoon in May, Momma disappeared into the attic eaves to rummage for our warm-weather clothes. In my room I heard her deck shoes pad across the loose attic boards, followed by skids and grunts as Momma coaxed Casard's trunks, noisy as startled elephants, across the pine boards. Momma groaned, the trunks squealed and the ceiling thundered with a cacophony of lamentations. Then Van's box of marbles broke loose and it was sheets of rain.

At dusk, as a breeze rippled the scalloped trim of the awnings, the attic door swung open. Down flew linen and madras trousers, cotton blankets and floral sheets, bikinis tied in balls, seersucker suits. Leather goods—Momma's black-and-white spectator pumps, Melanie's sandals, Dad's summer belts—landed at the bottom of the stairs like hurled bricks.

Unsettled by the commotion, I left my room and went downstairs. In the kitchen, Melanie, healthy again and just thirteen, was perched on a stool at the counter, making a pitcher of lemonade too sour for mortals. Next to the pitcher she had her snack, a steak bone.

"Melanie, why can't you eat like normal people," I said. "It's disgusting, a person sucking marrow."

"Ars," she murmured, followed by a string of Turkish curses she had picked up from Poppee. "You Kal-ca-nejy-sik-did," she said.

"Lovely, Melanie. Lovely."

Cracking the back of the bone, she said, "You don't think about protein, Seta, that's your tough luck. Someday you're going to wish you had. Old hunchback Seta, never fed her blood. What—you don't believe me?" Melanie plucked a wet finger from her mouth. "Come over here and try to bend one of my nails." She waved ten long polished fingernails in my face, and when I turned away she whined, "What's the matter? Come here."

At six o'clock Momma left the attic just as I was coming up to ask about dinner. I found her standing at the bottom of the stairs. At her feet lay a heap of summer clothes, shoes, belts and deflated beach balls. Momma, her hair pulled back in a polka-dot scarf, her clothes covered with dust, seemed to be thinking hard about something, her fingers dancing across her lips.

"Momma, do you want me to help you carry these down to the laundry room?"

"Hmm?" she said, by way of dismissal. And as I looked on she raised her leg, pointed her toe and glided over the mess, executing a perfect ballerina leap. She walked by me, her sneakers rubbing against the floor like erasers. At the end of the hall she did not bother to turn around. "Wash up," she said. "Dinner's in half an hour."

Dad was at the office trying to make a sale. Days he worked the phone, and nights he chauffeured clients to homes pictured in his three-ring binder, with sections labeled "Multiple Listings" and "Exclusives." Weekends he ran open houses, but no one was buying.

Waiting for dinner, I climbed onto the roof of the den to think things over. It never occurred to me that money was a problem, since it was never discussed. The year before, Momma had gone back to school to obtain her real estate sale's license. She worked three days a week for a company in Farmington; she worked, we were told, because she needed a challenge.

Downstairs, in the kitchen, she was rattling pans. It was Friday night, and when dinner finally arrived on the table we picked around Dad's empty plate like birds. After dinner, Van took Momma's car and drove over to see Lexi Sherer. Melanie and I cleared the dishes; at eight o'clock we went into the den and sat in front of the television. Momma was in her room. Melanie and I watched two half-hour shows, then the nine o'clock movie. We snacked on kosher dill pickles and bowls of chocolate-chip ice cream. By ten o'clock I felt edgy and depressed. At eleven we went to bed.

The hall ceiling fan stirred a late-night breeze that floated into my room on gentle hands. I put my stereo on softly so as not to disturb Momma, and played the saddest songs I could find. In my T-shirt and underwear, I rocked Indian style on the bed and sang my heart out.

I was in bed when Dad's car pulled into the driveway. I listened as he came into the kitchen through the garage door, set down his briefcase and pulled his warm plate from the oven. He sat at the table, and I heard the tines of his fork slowly scraping his plate. It was after midnight. When he was through eating I expected to hear him come up the stairs, but then he opened the garage door.

I climbed out of bed and went over to the window and, lifting the screen, leaned out. Dad was on the lawn just below, fidgeting with some contraption. His hands were cupping a light and the skin shone through orange, lit up like a jack-o'-lantern.

A car passed by and I watched it disappear down the road. I noticed then that the leaves on the maple were turned over on their silver bellies; by morning it would rain. I turned back to Dad, who was wearing the light, fixed to a pilot's cap, on his head. Dad kept the contraption, a relic from some war, in the garage with his tools;

he used it whenever he needed to fix something under the hood of the car, or find an object in one of the garage cupboards.

"Hey, Dad," I whispered. "Hey—Dad."

"Seta, that you?" He looked up, blinding me with the light.

"Yeah, it's me. Can you turn that thing—"

"Oh." He glanced down so the beam shifted onto the bushes before darting back to my window. "We better keep our voices down," he mumbled, eyeing Melanie's window and touching his cap.

"It's OK, Dad, Mel's asleep. What're you doing?"

He cupped his hands around his mouth and talked in a loud whisper. "Your Mom—thought I'd give her a surprise."

I ducked my head back into the room to hear whale sounds coming from the bathroom. "She's in the tub," I said.

He nodded. "Van in yet?"

"No."

He nodded again.

"Hey, Dad."

"Yeah, babe?"

"You want some company?"

"Oh"—his hand flew self-consciously to the light—"that's OK. You better get on back to bed. I'll just be a minute. That's a nice thought, but I'm fine."

"You sure?"

"Sure." He waved.

"Good night," I said, then added, because he looked so lonely, "Daddy."

He waved a second time and I was glad to think I had pleased him. Often it was difficult to know, since he never seemed to require anything from us but our own happiness, a habit that unintentionally made him seem detached and artificially gay.

He returned to the bushes, acquainting himself with the shears, working them open and closed. He must have thought I had gone to bed because when the light shot back to the window, his voice was uncertain. "Seta?"

I shielded my eyes. "Yeah?"

"You know what you can do for me?"

"What."

"Make me something. You know, in your dreams." He paused before adding, "Just for tonight."

I stared into the beam above my father's head, and then it came to me—it was a game we had played when I was small. In the morning, if I remembered, I would tell him what I had dreamed.

"Sure," I said, "OK."

"Good." He nodded and the light swept crazily up and down the house.

It occurred to me that maybe he had something particular in mind. Something he wanted me to work on. "Hey. Dad."

"Yeah?"

"You want to start me off?"

"Oh," he said, and the light shot above my window and disappeared. His mouth hung open as he gazed thoughtfully at the stars. "I don't know," he said. "Why don't we just see what you come up with on your own."

"You sure?"

"Yeah. That's better. Let's run with it and see what happens."

"OK. Night."

"Night-night," he said.

In the bathroom Momma was running the water. After a few minutes she shut off the tap. The house was still then, thin and fragile as a shell. I willed my mind to make him something good. Something to—make him happy.

Tossing the extra pillows on the floor, I tried to think of something I could tell my father, something I could give him, other than rutting dreams of faceless men.

Outside, Dad was attacking the bushes, and the beam from his light danced on my ceiling like a Hollywood opening. He was using Casard's shears, the ones so rusted you had to force them open. I thought I would make him a white boat with broad yellow sails. We would take a nice trip.

But as soon as I had that boat in mind, it transformed into Dad's mouth. His lips hung open, his teeth shone phosphorescent. I wanted to close that mouth, snap that ridiculous hat from his head. Hurry up, I wanted to tell him, Hurry.

I turned over. Come on, I said. Come on. A white boat. Yellow sails.

The bathroom door opened and she padded down the hall.

"Momma," I called, but if she heard me, she did not answer. The tub made sucking sounds as it drained. She reached her room and closed the door. She would climb into bed, prop her legs up on a pillow, and dabbing cream on her palms, she would massage her veins. She would work the pressure points in her hands and be glad for some time to reflect. When she finished, she would spread her moisturized palms on the coverlet, and easing her head back into the pillow, she would turn out the light and dream, sweet Momma, while outside, Dad tried to please her by pruning a hedge.

As I closed my eyes, my father's labor filled the night—the old shears whining, Why aren't you why aren't you Why?

We were a universe of private orbits, unhinged, eclipsed. Momma left the pile of summer clothes where they fell in front of the attic door. Mornings, we traipsed to the landing and took what we wanted to wear, until at week's end all that remained were some old shoes nobody wanted, and a belt and two shirts nobody claimed to own. In past years, summer arrived on our beds, folded, smelling of soap. But that year, it seemed everything had changed; we went into the world creased, stinking of camphor and attic must.

On Saturday night there was a party at Shari O'Riley's, but Van was busy with Lexi, so I stayed home. I turned on the TV, Melanie copiloting from the couch. "How about that," she said, "or that. Come on, that's good," but I turned the knob and kept on going. Soon, I became mesmerized by the turning dial, the curve of my knuckle, the ridged knob.

"Stop it," Melanie snapped. "Seta, cut it out before I scream."

I kept turning.

"You're a jerk. You know that? an absolute jerk," Melanie yelled as she stormed from the room, slapping her magazine against my back.

I shouted, "No, you!" and slammed the den door as hard as I could.

"Eshag!" Melanie hollered, Turkish for ass. "You berserko."

"Leave"—I slammed—"Me. Alone!"

The following day was a Sunday. At supper Dad peered into his glass of iced tea. "I don't know what's gotten into this family. I swear you kids fight more than any other family in America. Why is that. Can anyone give me an answer?"

We each surveyed our plate. Momma adjusted her napkin. At last Melanie said, "How come you guys don't go out Saturday nights anymore?"

"Because your mother—" Dad began, but stopped, surprised by what he was about to say.

"Because Mom what?" I insisted.

Dad waited for a sign, but Momma would not look at him. "Araxie, the kids"—Dad pleaded, his hand smoothing the table—"are asking. It's time we explain what's going on."

Momma touched a finger to the base of the salt shaker. "This family," she began, her brow furrowed. "Well, it's me, really, isn't it. I'm the one in Trouble—" Momma darted a look at each of us—Van, Melanie, me and, last, him. She lingered a long time on Dad's face, giving him a lost, frightened look that ensured he would forgive her, as in the end, we would. Her sad, orphan eyes implored, yet denied: asking for help, yet implying there was none that anyone could give.

A voice said, "I'm out of here." It was Van, pushing from the table.

"Sit down," Momma said.

"Roxie, let him go."

The house rocked as Van slammed out the front door.

"It's all right, now," Dad told her, as if reasoning with a child. "Time is the healer. The doctor said so. Your new job is a first step.

You have to take the steps, Roxie. This depression, it will pass, I know it will."

She shrugged; she did not believe him.

As my father spoke I involuntarily kicked the leg of the table. This was the first I had heard of any doctor, and it made me furious and anxious to hear this news and to realize I had been left out. I knocked the leg again, and my napkin fell from my lap to the floor.

Melanie looked scared. "You dropped—" she whispered and swooped under the table to retrieve my napkin. She gave me a quick, uncertain smile, passing the cloth back, leaving her hand on the rung of my chair.

The sudden movement made us both dizzy; we looked back at the table to see what had changed. But there was no spillage; the moment had passed without breakage.

Momma lifted her fork and began to eat. Dad followed. But I sat waiting, Melanie with me, certain that worse news was forthcoming. It seemed that I must concentrate and be diligent; it seemed I must not move.

A picture formed in my mind, of my parents as children. They were at the top of a windy hill, turned toward each other, their arms open, their shoulders rounded, pleading. On their faces was the question: What do we do? Watching them at the table, I knew they would not find an answer. It was unbearably frightening to see that they were no wiser than I. It occurred to me that my parents had had their chance and they had squandered it, but not me, not me.

Melanie's hand hovered near and I could see that though she was only two years younger, she was still the baby—small for her age, vulnerable, scared. Without turning, I squeezed hold of her hand.

I took a forkful of dinner. "Wish bite," I whispered, and Melanie took a forkful too. Eyeing each other, holding hands, we ate our wishes.

Like sucking lemons, it was a ritual we had learned from Casard. Melanie and I were taught by our grandmother to make good luck by wishing on the first bite of every piece of cake, and on every nickel, eyelash and moth we found. To this list we added our own. We anointed every day it broke 90 degrees, and the first lightning, and every bird in flight. During school I wished on every last bell. And on found tennis balls, empty cereal boxes, sneakers tied and loose, Volkswagen Beetles, railroad tracks, graves. Melanie and I never revealed our wishes, but mine was always the same: Please let him come soon and love me, and please make our family whole.

During the last month of school the promise of a long summer vacation made everyone act a little crazy. Fights broke out, couples got together and then split up, best friends made each other weep. Time was running out, and with everyone wanting to end the year popular and in love, those on the fringe got lost. Gossip about Theresa Vartyan and Bob Humms, having reached a near frenzy, peaked, and all that remained was a stark reputation: the girl who slept with Bob Humms.

"Look at her," Martha Sullivan gasped, bulging her blue eyes. "Look at her nose! How can she—" Martha paused, allowing us to finish the sentence in our minds. How can Theresa be so ugly? How can she exist?

No one wanted anything to do with Theresa, and truth be told, neither did I. Yet, for the remainder of the term, Theresa and I shared a table in Miss Trundell's visual arts class. Together, because we were assigned. The class met three afternoons a week—an endless stretch of time to sit across from Theresa, feeling guilty, while at the same time looking over my shoulder, fearing that one of the Sullivan sisters would find us. Once, at the beginning of class, while passing a paper, Theresa's hand accidentally touched mine; we both drew back as if stung.

We sat by the windows, where the air puffed into the room, hot, full of sun. It was seventh period, the end of the day, four weeks remaining of school. Theresa Vartyan secured her purse under the table by hooking the shoulder strap over her knee. She looked up as our teacher, Miss Trundell, approached, dragging a large garbage pail.

"Reach in without peeking," Miss Trundell commanded.

I went first, plunging my hand into the large pail and seizing a cool, rough stone. Miss Trundell nodded her approval. "That's right. Feel your shape." Her eyes danced as she said *feel* and *shape.*

Miss Trundell announced that our final project would be a sculpting exercise in which we were to find a unique form in an existing shape. "Listen to your stone," she said.

I looked at my piece of black sandstone, flat with one blunt end.

"What do you see?" Miss Trundell asked.

"A turtle," I said.

Miss Trundell asked Theresa what her stone revealed, but the girl shook her head and refused to say.

Miss Trundell set two steel files on the table. "Those of you who really want to challenge yourselves will create something to enter in the art show, next fall."

Theresa picked up the largest file and set to work grinding her stone. Every few minutes she stopped and dipped below the table to check on her purse. I wanted to ask what she thought she had in there that was so special, but my shame over what I had done to her kept me mute.

Ten minutes before the end of the period, Martha Sullivan sashayed into the room with a note for Miss Trundell and my worst fears came true. Miss Trundell initialed the paper and handed it back to Martha, who turned and walked heel-toe, heel-toe toward the door. She was nearly gone when she turned and saw me sitting with Theresa. Martha raised her thinly plucked brows and smiled.

I wanted to be bigger than I was, to say to Martha, So, what are you going to do now? But I knew exactly what Martha was going to do: she was going to tell the others that Theresa and I were a picture, a perfect pair.

Across the table, Theresa cleared her throat.

"What?" I snapped.

She peered to the left and to the right, checking to see who was listening. "Butt pickers," she said, and her face screwed up around that uncle's nose. She began to laugh like a hyena, her shoulders coughing up and down. I motioned for her to be quiet, but she just licked her fat red lips and said, "Butt pickers. Butt—" And all I could do was watch incredulously, as she laughed until she wept.

Across the room Miss Trundell called, "What's going on at that far table?"

Theresa pounded the table. She was hysterical; I had to turn away.

Then tears filled my eyes and I was overcome by an urge to confess. "Theresa," I whispered, "Theresa, I'm really sorry. I didn't mean it. I swear." These were the truest words I could say.

I turned slightly and glanced at her; she looked at me. Very softly she said, "I saw you, you know. Behind the garage."

"You did? Oh my God."

"You said my name. Don't you remember?"

"No."

"Ther-esa, you said. I bet you think it embarrassed me to have you see us, huh? But you're wrong; it only made it better. Like a show." She patted the sides of her hair. "And then you told those butt pickers."

"Theresa—"

"So, what did they say?"

"I—didn't."

"What did they say?"

"Theresa, I feel so bad about this."

"No," she demanded, pounding the table.

There was no point in denying her. "I guess at first they didn't believe me."

Theresa nodded. "They were impressed."

"Well—"

"That I would be with a man. That he would call for me all over town. They never had anyone like that." Her face fairly glowed with triumph. She had outdone the Sullivan girls. She had outdone us all.

"How about you," she asked, and the black eyes narrowed. "*Toon al.*" It touches you, too.

"Ayo," I gulped. Yes.

As I bowed my head she, who had always been ahead of me, went on to name the thing I lacked.

"You have no one," she declared.

Memorial Day: tropical lotion, the opening of Rockridge pool. Cutoff jeans and a white halter top. Linda Ronstadt singing "Heart like a Wheel." Wishes. Van and I with the windows down, driving home. Melanie perched on the roof of the den playing her recorder, Dad watering the lawn; Momma smoking on the patio, eyeing the road.

Memorial Day: Casard cleaning. Casard rearranging the closet, sending the navy and black tie shoes to the back row, and bringing the lighter shades, the taupe, cream and gray up front. In the afternoon the family would come over. The men in the living room, watching the ball game, the women in the kitchen. Melanie and I on the back porch, sucking lemons in the shade, the birds chattering, the humidity making our lives seem as flat as our grandmother's hem.

After the long Memorial Day weekend, only two weeks remained of school. I awoke on Tuesday morning and got dressed. Outside, on the corner, six men in orange jumpsuits arrived to repair and tar the road. As I brushed my hair a hundred strokes I watched them from my window; feeling inspired, I put on pale green eyeshadow and raspberry-flavored lip gloss. At breakfast, Van studied me out of the corner of his eye. "Why are you so dressed up?" he asked.

"Am not," I answered and, leaving the house, set out for the men in jumpsuits. The incessant pulse of the jackhammer extinguished every thought but the conviction that my feet were liable to trip over a crack.

I approached the corner and was met by sudden, abrupt quiet. The jackhammer was summarily jerked from the pavement, its motor whirring; a truck coughed and was shut down; a boot scuffed on the gravel. Someone spit a hawker. Eyes like fingers pried the hem of my skirt.

"Good morning, Delicious. What's your name? What's your name, pretty girl? Come on. We're not gonna *bite.*"

If I looked at them, I would be a tease; if I did not look, they would call me a bitch. I wanted to shout, Leave me alone, who do you think you are? But, instead, I trained my eyes on the sidewalk and kept going.

At my back, someone spoke, his voice gentle, urging. "Spark," he called, his words a blessing. "Spark-FLY-Y-Y-Y." I turned to catch a glimpse of his smile, white in a coal-black face. Then hoots and catcalls drowned out the rest.

The next morning they were gone. I ran my hand along the newly poured curb. A dog crossed the road, tiptoeing through the sand like a lady in heels, then sprang onto the grass. I was about to turn and head for the bus when I saw—right in the middle of the road—my name drawn in the fresh tar: SETA LOON.

I walked to the bus loose-kneed, shiny-lipped, sockless, out of control. It was blistering hot, the backs of my legs tickling with sweat. In my mind, I heard jackhammers and whistles and catcalls. A shiver ran through me. Was it one of them? Was it Adam? Flushed and mortified, I ran all the way to the bus.

At dusk Van came home and knocked up the stairs. "Hey, Seta," he called, bursting into my room. "Someone's carved your name into the lampposts at school."

Van spread his fingers two inches apart. "This thick. You know what cuts like that—a hunting knife. So who's this with a hunting knife advertising your name?"

SETA, SETA, SETA LOON. Spray painted on the backs of the stop signs along the road to school.

Then, on the board in Western Civ., my name was drawn inside a cloud, the handwriting small but fine. Adam, I thought, definitely.

I made myself ready. After school I went into Momma's garden and cut the peonies. I cut the tulips and laid them in bunches on the grass. Clutching her clippers, I stepped among the pachysandra in my new cotton dress, black, with a fuchsia silk-screened dragon.

A week passed. The stems of the peonies blackened, the water in the vase thickened with slime. Then he painted my name on the cliff at the reservoir, the *N* in LOON dripping like a tear. Seta Loon, Seta Loon, a record caught in a groove.

It all went by Momma: the peonies, the signs in the road. She had tossed our summer clothes down from the attic, expecting what? That we would stand at the bottom and catch whatever fell?

And the rest of them: my name was painted all over town, but they did not think to ask. What flavor lip gloss are you wearing? Patty Sullivan might have inquired. Passion fruit, I would answer, just to see the look on her face.

On the final day of school he ventured closer, drawing SETA LOON in chalk at the base of our driveway.

I asked Melanie, "What do you think?" as we folded the laundry.

She shrugged. "I think he's either some really romantic guy, or"—she paused, giving me a goofy look—"some weirdo out there with your name."

"Sure, Melanie." I smiled. "Like your lover."

"Not my lover," she said, Miss Ancient. "My lover would pick up the phone."

"Melanie, your lover hasn't been born yet."

"Yeah? Well, you better hope yours isn't some hood."

As part of our futile campaign to tend house, Melanie and I set the folded laundry on the edge of the beds, but the piles spilled onto the floor. The shirts we ironed hung wrinkled in the closets, and, despite our efforts, we pressed irregular pleats into Dad's trousers. We used the same detergent, but even so, we could not approximate Momma's smell.

Where was Momma? Running errands? In her room? On the phone?

The roses—the Chicago Peaces, Double Delights, the Brandys and the Lincolns, her favorites—all bloomed early, on account of the heat, but Momma never saw them. The roses wilted with aphids and rust, but she was somewhere else.

She was off, allowing the roses to die, when the one who wanted me rang the front-door bell.

"Oh my gosh, Oh my gosh," Melanie yelped, as she ran up the stairs to my room. "He's at the door."

"Who?"

"Frank Agostini!"

Frank Agostini? At school I had passed by him daily but never really saw him. I went downstairs and there he stood, smiling at me through the screen with his black wavy hair and thick brows. Around his neck he was wearing that gold charm all the Italian boys wore—a cross between a snake and a jalapeño pepper.

"Hi," I said.

"Hi. Seta"—he shuffled from foot to foot—"Loon."

I squinted over his shoulder, at the last red rim of the sun falling between the birches. In eighth-grade current events, Frank Agostini's desk was in front of mine, and all year not a word of conversation passed between us. We were tenth graders now. Sophomores.

"Come on, what are you doing here," I said, trying to sound friendly.

He shrugged, as if to suggest he had already told me. Placing his lips against the screen, he said, "Seta Loon."

And then it dawned on me. "You? You're the one?" I cried.

He raised himself on the balls of his feet and grinned.

"Oh my God! I don't even—know you!"

Disappointment did not deter Frank Agostini. He plucked a sprig of flowers from the andromeda and sucked on it to get at the sugar. Right there on my front stoop, as if he knew me well, as if he had a right.

He chewed the stem like a rabbit. "So if you don't know me, who did I have this year for fifth-period math?"

"This is stupid. Mrs. Duga."

"Mrs. Duga." Frank Agostini nodded. "And how do you know that?"

"Because I had her too."

"You had her too," he said, with the measured cadence of a salesman. "And still you don't know me, huh?" He raised his eyebrows. "Up until yesterday you saw me four days a week. That's more than most people who are mar-ried." Frank paused to let this sink in. "Where did I sit in Mrs. Duga's class?" He folded his arms and waited.

I kicked the door lightly with my toe. "Somewhere in the back."

"Somewhere in the back." Frank Agostini frowned. "Somewhere in the back? That's absolutely wrong. Where did I sit? I had the perfect seat. Right behind you." He pointed his finger. "What, you don't believe me? I'll prove it. Two days ago you wore a new sleeveless top I never saw before. It was creamy color. And those little gold hoops. I liked it, you know, the combination."

Listening to him, I self-consciously rubbed my foot against the weather stripping on the bottom of the door. His words made me feel exposed. I glanced at my tank top, checking the parts of skin it revealed, the parts remaining clothed.

"So. You still say we don't know each other?" Frank put his face close to the screen and blinked. He smiled. "Will you go out with me?"

"No." I kicked the door.

He jumped back, startled. "No?" He bowed his head and thought for a minute. "OK," he said softly, holding up a palm. "Will you at least come out here and talk to me for a second?"

"I don't think so," I said, biting my lip so I would not smile.

"You don't think so?" he echoed.

"OK, then no," I said, my foot wagging behind the door where he could not see.

"Would you get me a glass of water, then, would you at least do that?"

"Why?"

"Why?" he asked incredulously.

I did not know what to do. "All right. But stay here."

"I'm not going anywhere, Seta Loon." And the way he said it felt like a hand under my shirt.

I let the tap run until the water was cold, then I filled a glass and took it to him. Frank backed away from the door so I had to step outside and personally hand it to him. "Here," I said, the cement cool under my bare feet.

"Thanks," he said, but he would not take the glass. "Will you hold that for me a second?" He removed his wristwatch. "You want to look at this." He handed me the watch and took the water. The watch had a lizard band and a gold face. In the center of the face was a window that turned from a picture of stars to a sun, depending on the time of day.

"Nice," I said, handing it back.

"Yeah, my father gave it to me. I love this watch, if you can love a thing, that is. You think you can? I mean, is it all right with you?"

"What?"

"The watch. Me. I don't know, me loving a thing."

"I guess I don't care."

"You don't?"

"N-no."

"But you don't think I should."

"I don't know." I shrugged. "Things are just things."

Frank Agostini seemed to consider what I said as he raised the glass and marveled at the sun shining through the water. He dangled the watch over the glass, as if meaning to drop it in. I lifted my hand to shade my eyes. "It's waterproof, right?"

"Nope," Frank answered.

"Then don't!"

"Got to." He shrugged, and turning the watch so it sparkled, he dropped it into the water.

"You're crazy," I said, glancing at his jawline, which I noted was square, like the letters he carved into posts. The words flew out of my mouth before I could stop them. "I can't look at you."

Frank Agostini threw back his head and whistled. "I know, Seta Loon. I know."

For a moment it was just the two of us: Frank Agostini beaming and me unable to look.

He handed me the glass. "Here," he said, and then, as he turned to leave, he darted his fingers into the glass and plucked out the watch, twirling it in the air—Big deal, I thought, let him throw it.

"Seta," Frank called, and when I refused to look, he planted a cool wet finger on my shoulder. Cool as the electricity running up my arm.

The water in the glass sloshed over the rim as I watched Frank pick his way down the driveway. I said to myself: He is not so bad, I don't know, maybe. I said: He doesn't have a thing on Adam BenKiki; he cannot light a candle in the room of the faceless men. But his eyes are blue, blue as a malamute's.

I remained on the stoop, long after he was gone. Wind made of hot, spent air puffed in my face like a breathing dog. It had run, this air, through the turbines of Fafner Bearing, bouncing off the boarded windows of the mills, crossing the golf course along Shuttle Meadow, where it picked up humidity like weighty cloth, and dragging that wet, dirty cloth along the newly tarred road, it blew past the telephone wires and the hemlock fence to find me, shivering on the front stoop.

I never chose Frank Agostini; he took care of that by choosing me. And all that summer we were together. Each day, he picked me up at noon and we rode the bus downtown, where we bought hamburgers and, later, ice cream sandwiches from the vending machines at the YMCA. We zigzagged along the sidewalks downtown, eating our ice cream, Frank peeling off his wrapper and gobbling, while I tried to make the whole business last.

The first time Frank saw me nibbling, licking the ice cream between the two chocolate cakes, he chuckled in a way that made him seem experienced. "That gives me ideas," he said.

"Sure," I said, trying to sound sassy.

"Se-ta," Frank sang, but I made him say it again before I would look at him. "You're really something." He grinned.

"Yeah?" I said, my eyes sparkly. "You're something too."

Then something in Frank's face made me uncertain. Things were running so fast between us, and I could not tell at any given moment what he was thinking. He might be enjoying himself, or getting bored, or sensing that I was too much. In my ear I heard Casard cautioning me: *Tone it down.*

"Now what are you going to do?" he asked, pointing at the two ice cream cakes stuck to my palms.

"Eat 'em." I replied, and proceeded to take tiny bites until I had worked the rectangular sandwiches into squares, then triangles.

"You," he said, shaking his head.

"Me, what?"

"Just you."

As we walked by D&L's department store, we glanced in the windows at the mannequins with their nipped-in waists and dangly wrists. In broad daylight, Frank palmed the small of my back. We passed adults on the sidewalk who knew our parents, and still he kept his hand there, the heat from his palm passing through me in waves.

We crossed over to the statues and drifted to Squaw. Pigeons nested in the crooks of her arms and on her head. Their droppings coated her Bible and the face of the baby in her arms. Seeing Squaw made me think of Theresa, then Frank slid his hand under the waistband of my jeans and said, "Let's go to the park."

At the baseball diamond, Frank circled me with both arms and we walked on that way, as if nothing unusual was taking place.

We followed a dirt path by the swings, and walking in the center, we made others move to the edge. We did not look at each other. We focused our eyes ahead, our minds racing with the question What is going to happen next?

At the pond, Frank and I, legs trembly as colts', collapsed on the bank. We lay under the great oaks and, with nothing else to do, nothing in the world, pulled each other in.

Frank rolled over so I was on top. He smoothed his palms down the planes of my back, each time dipping lower. We held our breath and explored mouths, until our chests tightened and our lungs threatened to burst. Gasping, we pulled apart, divers reaching the surface. We breathed, then finned below, his mouth wet and smooth.

I worried that I was not going long enough between breaths. Other girls could make out for hours. I rolled over, grave, certain he was counting my faults, certain that, just like Adam, he would leave. Then, gently, ever so gently, Frank reached over and tucked a wisp of hair behind my ear. For that tenderness I would have given him anything he wanted.

Frank took off his jean jacket and began waving it in the air. "Flag," he said.

"What?"

"Flag." He waved, sending the jacket floating into the air like a kite. He snatched it and pulled it down over our heads, and from the waist up, we were covered.

"Flag," Frank boomed and, punching the coat, sent it flying in the air.

"Flag," we called and punched it again so it sailed even higher. In the sunlight, we eyed each other, strangers, who on a whim had decided to become a couple.

"Flag," Frank murmured and drew me under the tent of his coat.

He kissed my eyelids, my throat, my mouth. He walked his fingers, spider's legs, across my stomach, drawing slow wide circles that climbed into a spiral, gathering me, until all of me was drawn under that finger—my legs wrapped around his, my face burrowed, my arms about his neck snug as scarves. When I could climb no further, tighten no tighter, that audacious finger swept across my nipple like a chill. I prayed it would stop, I prayed it would keep on going, when all of a sudden he pinched my nipple as if it were a small pea. He was going to make me give myself over, and yes, oh please for heaven's sake yes, nipple, nipple—and then he quit.

I nudged the finger to set it back on course. "Frank?" I asked, my voice hollow and obsequious. "Frank?"

And then he said it. "Yeah, Beautiful?" he said, and the way he paused, I could tell he was smiling.

I punched the jacket loose. You think you have something to be proud of, Frank Agostini? You think you do? Look at you: you have Seta Loon, all wrapped up in a tiny shell.

I kicked Flag with my foot.

Frank lunged after the coat and tucked it under his head. I rolled over on my back and pretended to concentrate on the sky. He had no interest in me. I was a first: a nipple he had rolled in his fingers. Next, he would put it in his mouth.

I could hear him beside me, ticking. Finally, he burst loose—"Ates Nool!" he said.

"What?"

"Seta Loon," he hollered, arms raised like an impresario. "Backwards."

He will crush my heart. I will get desperate and then he will crush my heart. For I am too obvious.

"You sure do like that name," I said.

"Yep." Frank grinned. "My name. My Seta Loon."

"So what if I'd been named—Eunice. What then?"

"Eunice Loon."

"No—Eunice Curd."

"Eunice Curd!" Frank repeated, turning to face me. "Oh, Eu-u-nice," he called, "it's time for your med-i-cine."

Frank pounded the grass with his fist. He was having a grand time and for a moment I was safe. Of course, I did not ask myself why it mattered so much what he felt, or why, when I was with him, my mind centered so much on him. I pulled out a bunch of grass and dropped it over his head like confetti. We beamed at each other, and when it got too much, I turned away, content with the pictures in my head. No one, I was certain, had ever felt this good. Then, just as quick, it came to me: not even Momma.

"Frank?"

"Yeah?"

I chewed on my lip.

"What?" he asked.

I paused. "Say it again."

"What, Eunie?"

"You know. What you said to me just now, under the jacket."

Frank rolled on his side and concentrated on my face.

"Oh God, you don't have to strain!" I cried, rolling over.

"Come on, will you give me a minute." His brow wrinkled, his mouth opened. At last he found the word and his face lit up. "You mean, Beautiful?"

Shy, I hid my smile.

Frank wagged his feet and put his face next to mine. "You mean the most beautiful."

I could not look.

"Oh no, you mean the Absolute Most."

There was no helping it, the tears came. "Seta," he called, and realizing he wanted me to look at him, I focused on his blurry chin. "Hey," he said sweetly, "come here." He took me in his arms and I curled up like a baby so no one would see me.

"You wrote my name on a sign," I said.

"Lots of 'em."

"Would you still? Now."

He paused and I began to panic. His arms loosened. I looked up to find his face clouded, his hand frozen in the air. "Careful," he said. "You have something in your hair—"

"What is it? What is it?" I whined, everything wild, an emergency. "What is it, Frank? Frank!"

They were all over: tiny white inchworms. In Frank's hair, too, and on our clothes. "Frank, are they on me? Ew. Ew, I'm covered. Get them off."

"They're just worms, Seta. Come here, let me brush—"

"Hurry," I yelled.

"It's not like they bite."

"No. *No?*" I said, stomping. "I hate it, I hate this," and I pulled at my hair.

Frank grabbed hold of my wrists and squeezed.

"You're hurting me," I cried. "Let go, Frank. Let me go."

But he held on as I bucked and kicked. I clung to him and hated him all at the same time.

"Seta, why are you so miserable?"

"I don't *know*!"

"Is it me? Is it us?"

Us, what a bold leap, that word. I shook my head, hoping he would say something more, but he was just a boy and already his attention had turned.

"Look at that," Frank said, tugging on my wrist. He pointed above our heads, where the limbs of the oak spread out like the spokes of an umbrella. From every limb, worms dangled like ornaments, millions of them, draping the tree with their nets.

"Goddamn," Frank marveled.

The tree was barren, its leaves mere stalks.

I circled Frank with my arms and, pressing my palms into his back, felt him give way to the spectacle—the gypsy moths would kill the old trees, one by one. Feeling along his shoulders, down his arms, I found the goose bumps, which told me all that I needed to know.

"Big man," I murmured happily. "Big man's got the creeps as much as me."

Later that afternoon I returned home to an empty house. In the living room the radio had been left playing to scare away burglars. Melanie was at the pool, Dad at work, Van bagging groceries at

Stop & Shop. In their absence the sun beamed through the sheers, illuminating dust motes, which all day long floated through the room like wind-borne ballerinas. The house ticked as the walls shifted minutely and settled. There was a world existing underneath ordinary life, and it moved constantly inside empty rooms.

I snapped the TV on, then off. On, then off. Its noise unsettled me, though the quiet did, too. The house seemed different in the daylight; it belonged to Momma. She was gone now, leaving behind clues: her reading glasses on the table, her sweater draped over a chair.

There were secrets and I looked for them. I lifted a picture frame from the foyer table. The photograph was of the day they brought Van home from the hospital; Momma wore red lipstick and pearls. Soon after the birth she had begun having trouble in her legs. The inevitable had come: she had inherited Casard's varicose veins. In the afternoons while the baby slept, she put her legs up and talked on the phone. She had few friends, but every morning, and again in the afternoon, there were the calls to Archie and Casard. Looking at the photograph, I wondered: Is the inability to make friends, like hair color and height, passed down through genes?

During elementary school, we walked home each day at noon to have lunch with Momma. If she was in the right mood, after we ate she would gather us around her to discuss our morning's work. She pointed at our pictures, their colors the most beautiful she had ever seen. Amazed, she said, "Did you make that? Oh, Seta, look at that horse!" Later, when we returned home at the end of the day, we would find our drawings taped to the wall above Dad's desk so he would be sure to see them when he came home.

Now an oil painting that Momma had made hung over his desk. Stacks of papers covered every inch of the leather desktop. Dad had stacks for work, correspondence and bills. I opened the top drawer. Everything was in its neat receptacle: a separate compartment for elastic bands, and for paper clips and pens. I opened the box of peppermint Chiclets and popped two in my mouth.

I went up to their room, where Momma and Dad slept in twin

beds fitted to a single mahogany headboard. Opposite the beds, there was a large wicker hamper. Her side of the room was left of the hamper, with the vanity and built-ins, while his was on the right, with the tallboy.

I sat on the cushioned vanity stool and touched the makeup, the silver horsehair brush and the bowl with Casard's tortoiseshell combs. I unrolled a lipstick and applied it; in recent years, Momma had begun to favor pink shades of lipstick, with names like Cordelia and Gypsy Rose. I glanced into the mirror. This is what she sees. This.

Frank had called me beautiful, and now I wanted to see for myself. I leaned closer, my face nearly touching the glass. Slowly, I turned, examining each angle. Turning, turning, I saw Casard's wide, dark eyes and Momma's chin and Dad's sharp nose. I saw parts; I made no sense as a whole. Frank said it, but he was just a boy. In Momma's mirror I could not find beautiful.

What happened next seemed to be happening to someone else. I walked over to her closet and opened the door. I knew exactly what I was doing, yet I never thought. I reached through the hanging clothes to the cedar shelf in back, where the large box Melanie and I were forbidden to touch until we got married was kept. Inside, Momma's wedding dress was preserved in a special medium that I pictured as the fluid used to preserve embryos in jars. The sight of that box used to take our breath away. Melanie and I were allowed to touch only the lid. It was enough. We did not need to see more, for we had seen photographs of the tea-length dress and the short veil, and beautiful Momma before she was ours. I leaned in, my cheek pressing the sleeves of her blouses, and pulled the box to me.

Something fell. It landed on the floor, the dropping of a plum. I looked down to see what it was, but the closet floor was a riddle of shoes, scarves, umbrellas, leather purses and dust. At the end of a day, Momma opened the door, and, gripping the molding, booted her shoes in. Mornings, she fished with a toe to find mates.

What fell must have been on top of the wedding box. I picked up a wrinkled blouse and tossed it to the back, and dropping to my hands and knees, combed the floor of her closet. At last, I found it, behind a navy crisscross sandal. As I carried it to the light, I saw that it was a corsage made of pink sweetheart roses, tied with a lavender bow. I turned it over in my palm. The corsage meant something to her, and holding it was like holding, what, a piece of Momma? I imagined the corsage arriving in a gold box with a cellophane lid; I saw my father as a young man with slicked-back hair and a new suit, knocking on Casard's door.

A sudden noise downstairs. The back door slammed and then her heels hit the kitchen linoleum. I shoved the box between the dresses but the wall of material pushed back. I shoved harder and a row of blouses dropped like handkerchiefs to the floor. Downstairs, Momma was opening the hutch and taking out the sherry. I hoisted the box onto the shelf and tossed the corsage behind it; the blouses were an accident: Miss America hunting for bones.

When I came downstairs she was sitting on the sofa.

"Oh, my, you scared me—" she said, startled, holding her heart. "Seta, have you been upstairs?"

I stood there, trying to recall something I knew but did not know. And then it came to me: the corsage. The roses were still fresh.

Momma talked on: "Couldn't you have come down here and got dinner going? Just this once? You saw the sauce on the counter. Couldn't you have put it on the stove?"

"Sorry," I said, not sorry at all.

She smelled like cigarettes and perfume. She was wearing pearls.

"Where have you been, Momma?"

"Out," she replied, and bit her lip.

Gingerly she set her sherry glass on the coffee table. "I picked up your sweater from the cleaners," she mumbled. "I must have left it—in the car."

When I said nothing, she turned to look me over. "You look funny to me—"

"Thanks. I do not."

She nodded. "Yes, you do. You're wearing lipstick."

"So what?"

"Frank, does he like that kind of thing?"

"Frank has nothing to do with it."

"Oh, no?" She smiled weakly, gazing out the window. "That boy's got your name all over town."

"So? So what? It's not like you or anyone else around here cares. *Seta, I am very excited for you. Seta, isn't it nice you have a new friend?*"

Sighing, she stood. "Well, are you happy? That's what really counts. Seta, all I'm saying is, don't wear that lipstick: you're fine the way you are." She took a few steps toward the kitchen.

"Momma," I said, quietly. "Can I ask you something?"

"Hmm," she said, her voice faraway.

"Why did you marry Dad?"

Momma turned, her face contorted with fury. "Why—" she began, "do you have to do this! Who asks these things. Crying out loud— What have I done, to you? What?"

"I just want to know. OK?" I croaked, swallowing my fear.

She was stunned. "How—can I talk to you?"

"Just tell me. It's no big deal. Just tell me." I spoke quickly, knowing that any moment she would silence me. "Did you know it was the right thing or did you have second thoughts? The day you married Dad, did you have last-minute doubts or were you absolutely sure?"

She dropped her head and stared at her shoe, her lips mouthing unspoken protests. At last she lifted her eyes and looked at me, tears welling in her eyes. "Who? Where—this afternoon—have you been?"

"Nowhere, Momma. I was with Frank and then I came home."

She squinted, trying to comprehend.

I did not care that my questions made her angry. I was going to keep asking, not because I understood what I was doing but because I could not stop.

"Momma, I'm just asking: you and Dad, were you sure?"

She covered her mouth with her hand. Fixing her eyes on the

dining room table, she touched a finger to the wood and rubbed. At last, she shook her head: No, she had not been sure.

"And Grandma? She didn't like it that Dad was an odar, right?"

Momma nodded.

"But she made the dress—"

Momma nodded again.

"—but the whole time she told you you were ruining your life."

And standing there, I could hear Casard saying: "Araxie! Araxie! You want the odar? Take him. But don't look to me for help."

Momma peered at me, her eyes like a child's. She was waiting to see what would happen next.

"OK, Momma. After you guys came to this house, and you had us, it wasn't so bad, was it?"

She shifted.

"So. Momma. What's so bad?"

Her gaze, furtive, pleading, centered on my neck. Casard, I thought, she is looking at me the way Grandma looked at Dad. Not seeing him, not daring to, a look of—what? Later on, it came to me: guilt.

A stillness passed between us, filling the room with a certain calm. It dawned on me that she was doing the best she could, and soon, much sooner than I expected, it would be my turn to be the adult. Intuitively, she understood this, for just as she was about to leave, Momma turned and a strange, quizzical smile passed across her face. She looked me in the eye and raised her brows.

Years later, when I returned to Memorial, Momma and I would recall that day. I would remember the afternoon with Frank and, later, finding the corsage. But Momma remembered only what had happened to her earlier in the day.

She had gone to find Haig Kazangian, the man who had given her the corsage and with whom she was having an affair. She had looked for him everywhere, but he was nowhere to be found. Haig was a musician, a singer, and on that day he had gone to the capital for an audition at a club. He had forgotten to tell her, and so she drove aimlessly around town, driving just to keep moving. Finally, after she had gone clear into the Northend and was heading back, she passed Martha Hart Pond, and on a whim drove up the hill.

The street ended at the Children's Home. She sat in the car watching a group of orphans playing on the lawn. She did not know how long she sat there. She remembered a terrible emptiness, numbness, really, as she sat in the car, thinking of nothing, the minutes ticking by.

Finally, a small girl with blond hair approached the car, on her way to the main building. She looked at the lady and Momma smiled back at her. The girl had scrapes on both her knees. Momma got out of the car and knelt so as not to scare the girl. She came closer, close enough for Momma to reach out a finger and touch the scab above the girl's left knee.

"Ouch," Momma said, "I bet that hurt."

The girl backed away, uncertain. She twisted a lock of hair and put it in her mouth.

Momma opened her purse to find something to give the child. She had keys, a lipstick, a comb and, in the bottom, a roll of mints—all of which she offered in her palm.

The girl wavered. She wished to make the correct choice. Tentatively she pointed to the lipstick.

"It's a pretty color," Momma assured her. "My favorite."

The girl opened the tube to see. "Can I have a mint?" she asked.

"Of course," Momma said, and handed her the roll.

The girl put a candy in her mouth but did not give back the roll. "I have to go now," she said.

"All right." Momma nodded and ran her hand down the girl's sleeve. The girl scampered up the driveway toward the main building. She had not gone very far when she turned, and asked the stranger, "Are you somebody's mommy?"

Momma felt the ground rush beneath her. She nodded, but the fact was, she could not be sure. She could not quite remember. She drove home in a blind daze, still uncertain when I found her.

• • •

The following night was Friday; Frank and I drove to the meadows in his mother's car. The temperature hovered at 90 degrees, the humidity 98 percent. Frank and I parked by some trees. In the moonlight we saw the outline of other cars parked a short distance away. In every car there was a pair of lovers, passing sweet wine or beer, and marijuana. Mosquitoes danced on the windshields. Hands made their way in the dark.

We were of the age when nothing soothes the body except another body, pressing. We were stuck, urgent, incomplete, in a town with too many funeral homes and pizza parlors, a town where the gypsy moths ate all the color off the trees.

With the radio blasting, Frank removed my shirt.

On the other side of town, two police cars pulled up at the Vartyan house. Acting on the advice of rumor, the police found Bob Humms and Theresa behind the garage, asleep. The police arrested Bob Humms for assault of a minor. They took him to the station in handcuffs and locked him in a cell with drunks and petty thieves. He stayed there for a week, but no charges were ever filed. Mrs. Vartyan, too sick to stand, arrived at the station in a wheelchair. Bob Humms was released.

But the damage was done, the rhythm broken. Mrs. Vartyan was taken to the hospital, where tests revealed that the cancer had metastasized in her lymph glands. Theresa, stunned, withdrew from the world. She would see no one, not even Bob Humms.

I have a photo from that summer; my hair is long. Each morning I gazed into the bathroom mirror to see what it would look like short. Come fall I would finally cut it, but all summer I obsessed about the length of my hair. I obsessed about my baby-sitting job and every moment with Frank.

The gypsy moths ravaged the maple, the sycamore, the oak. Frank tucked me under his arm and we walked, stoned, through the park, marveling at the trees' stark, numinous beauty and the proximity of death all around us.

The elders watched from their park benches. We understood their looks as disapproval, but the truth was they couldn't have cared less about Frank and me. The old people met in the park in the late afternoon to monitor the progress of the gypsy-moth larvae—the millions of thin white inchworms that flew on filament across the broad limbs of the oak, devouring its canopy of leaves. The elders believed they were witnessing a plague—worse than the arson fires, which several years earlier destroyed half of downtown. The elders sat under the oaks, where it was cool, and watched the children in the playground brush off the thin worms like worry.

The park service commissioned Beckman's Nursery to spray the trees, floating the vermin and a toxic cloud of pesticide into the river, south.

The elders pressed their backs against the curved wood benches. "After the fact," they said.

One afternoon in late July, Poppee came to the house to drink tea with Momma. Poppee did not ask how it was for Momma, she already knew. She talked instead about the gypsy moth.

"It's in the air," she said, biting her upper plate.

"What is?" Momma asked.

Poppee made a face. "Death."

Summer ended abruptly on a Saturday in early August. I left Frank and came home. Melanie was rocking on her bed, her legs folded beneath her, her body a tight ball.

"Hey, Mel."

"Get out of my room. Mom and Dad had a fight."

"What about?"

"I don't know. Mom's in her room. I don't know where he went."

"Club."

"Probably."

"Is that why Mom's pissed off?"

"I don't know!"

I went to my room and dived onto the bed. It would be four more hours until I saw Frank again. I went back to Melanie's door and knocked. "You want to come to my room?"

"I don't know," she said.

"It's not me you're mad at, Mel."

"I'm sick of this," Melanie yelled back, and I opened the door to find her hunched on her bed like an old woman.

"OK," I said, "I'm going to talk to Momma. Come to my room later, if you want."

I knocked on Momma's door.

Her voice was sleepy. "I'm lying—down."

"Can I come in?"

She was lying on her stomach in bed, the covers pulled up to her hair. Under the covers, she was rubbing her stocking feet. It made a horrible sound, like a dog scratching. She spoke into the pillow, "You with Frank?"

I nodded but said nothing.

"Archie might come over and join us for dinner. Van, it seems, has disappeared."

"Van's OK."

"No," she said, lifting her head, then dropping it back down. "If your father spent more time, gave him a little direction."

"Van is fine, Mom."

Her feet rubbed furiously. I wanted her to cut it out and tell me what happened with Dad.

"You want me to roll your legs with the pin?" I asked.

She murmured, "Nice."

Momma had read in a magazine that massaging the thighs with a rolling pin improved circulation and muscle tone. She said it relieved her veins. I reached under the bed for the rolling pin and pulled back the covers.

"Keep the sheet," she said.

"Momma, it's ninety million degrees."

"Keep it."

"Fine." I climbed onto the bed, and, straddling her, sat on her feet. Leaning hard on the handles, I flattened her thighs like dough.

"Ow," she said. "Stop." Her hand shot out and flailed at the roller. "Soft or quit."

"How's that?"

The feet wiggled; it was OK.

I rolled the hill of her buttocks, then down the slope to her knees. Momma sighed into the pillow.

I rolled both legs together, then fanned off and gave each its turn. I took care with the right leg, which gave Momma, like Casard, the most trouble.

I rolled my mother's flesh and imagined biscuits, apple pies.

Momma had her eyes closed. "Your father. How's he ever going to teach his son to become a man? Mr. Holiday Father."

"Is that what you said to Dad? Is that what you actually said?"

"What?" she asked, lifting her head. Her hair was bent to one side.

"You know."

She sank back into the pillows, her feet rubbing.

I was furious. "God, Momma, you expect—"

Before I could finish, we heard a car pulling into the driveway. Momma raised her head and motioned me to go to the window and see who it was.

"It's not Dad. I don't know who it is. Some man in a gray—"

She was out of the bed, pulling on slacks, fishing in the closet for a blouse. Downstairs, Miss America barked. Momma glanced out the window, gave a short, nervous wave, then checked her face in the mirror.

"Oh," she said, fussing with her hair, "quick, Seta. Go down, tell him I'll be right there."

"Who is he?" I asked.

"Go on, do what I said." Her voice was pinched.

"Who is it?" Melanie called as I rushed past her door.

"Don't know," I said, bolting down the stairs.

Haig Kazangian had shut off the motor and was leaning an elbow out the window, waiting. He had a strange, handsome face: dark eyes, thick black hair and a mustache. Something about him made me timid.

I called from the front stoop, "My mother said she'll be right down."

He smiled and waved.

Miss America and I watched him from the foyer window. Why he did not come to the door and ring the bell like any other visitor was beyond me. On a Saturday afternoon he was wearing a suit.

Momma swept down. She had tied back her hair in a chiffon scarf and put on a navy blouse with white anchors and tight white slacks. On her feet she wore crisscross sandals, as if this were dress-up. In the foyer mirror she checked her face one last time and, noticing me, said, "Thank you."

"For what?"

"Oh, Seta"—she puffed. She slapped the screen door and cut across the lawn. He must have said something because she squinted at him, then turned back to the window. Momma shooed me—"Go on. Go on," and flashed a smile designed for him. I went upstairs and watched from her window.

She leaned against the car, her fanny waving in the air. I could hear only stray words, such as *Boy* and *Knock around, I tell you, the kids, golf.*

He talked, she nodded, and every once in a while, she covered her mouth with her fingers the way she did when she was embarrassed. Every so often she glanced at the house.

They had been out there ten minutes when Dad's car pulled into the driveway. He parked the Buick close behind them and turned off the motor. Momma raised herself so only the tips of her fingers touched the roof of Haig Kazangian's car.

Out of habit, Dad glanced in the rearview mirror, then opened his door and got out. Haig Kazangian saw Dad coming and he got out of his car, too. Momma backed away a few steps to make room on the lawn.

Melanie rushed into the room. "What happened?" she said, all breathy, kneeling on the floor beside me.

"Shh," I said and moved over so she could look, too.

"You believe this?" Melanie said.

"Come on, Dad," I said, gripping the sill.

"Yeah," Melanie said.

Haig Kazangian offered his hand, but Dad kept his in his pocket.

"Good," Melanie said. "Don't be nice, Dad."

Dad was wearing his golf clothes and his yellow golf cap. Something about his uniform lent him authority, a professional man at his leisure. Dad removed the cap and ran his hand through his hair. He flexed his jaw in a way that suggested he was trying very hard not to yell but to choose his words and actions carefully. He looked at the house, and Haig followed his gaze.

"Get down," I hissed, pulling Melanie's shoulder.

"Shhh," she said. "Wait."

Dad was speaking. He pointed a finger at Haig Kazangian, and at Momma, too. We heard words like *shenanigans, behavior, come and go,* and *hump.*

Haig Kazangian tried to defend himself but Dad silenced him with a wave of his finger. Haig took a step back and threw up his hands.

Momma hugged her middle. She started to speak, but Dad waved like an umpire and cut her off. I had never seen him do that, never seen him so much as interrupt her.

Then Dad tried to speak to her, but she would not look at him. He lunged toward her, and she and Haig both cried out, "No!"

Dad's fist hung in the air between them. It shamed him, that fist; opening it wide, then drawing it closed, he stuffed it into his pocket. Momma turned away, that fist having its effect on her, too. She turned back and looked at him. They stared at each other, but did not speak.

Everything was decided without another word. Haig got into his car, and Dad let him sit there for a minute before he walked over to the Buick, got in and turned on the motor. He backed out of the driveway, then Haig's car followed and disappeared down the road.

Momma remained on the lawn. Dad pulled the car back in and got out, while she stood there, her eyes focused on the grass.

He picked up a piece of rubbish from the lawn and threw it behind a shrub. He walked as far as the front stoop. "Araxie, you finished with this business?" he declared. "Because I'm through, you hear me?" His hand, like his voice, trembled with rage. "No more. I mean it, enough. You go back in the house and you're part of this family. No more pissing on Goddamn everything we have."

She grimaced, each word a blow. It was awful to hear him curse. Yet she did not weep or make any effort to stop him. She accepted his anger, and when he finished she peered at him, her face astonishingly clear, serene.

"George," she began, and by the flat tone in her voice I knew.

"She's not coming back," I said.

"She's such a jerk," Melanie said and started to cry. "Dad should of slugged that guy."

"She's gonna be sorry," I said, hoping. "Really sorry."

"Yeah," Melanie answered. "Only what if she's not?"

Below, Dad said, "I'm going in," but he did not move.

Momma understood, and went into the house first. They would discuss it after dinner like "civilized adults," and then, after talking for an hour or so like civilized adults, Dad would go up to their room and pack a bag. They would gather us into the living room and tell us that they needed time apart to think it through. For now, at least, Dad would stay in a hotel.

But before any of that happened, my father surveyed his lawn one last time and, remembering the piece of trash, retrieved it from behind the shrub. Then, finding everything in its place, he followed her inside.

FALL

My father left, and for several days I waited for the whinny of the screen door that would signal his return. But he did not return, and each footfall in the foyer was a false alarm. I believed that Dad wanted to come back, and during those days apart I felt his longing enter my bones, and it hurt more than anything to keep away from us, to pass by the house and find the grass brown and withered, the hedge shapeless, the windows on the second story, without their screens, lifted wide open.

Dad could have forgiven Momma if only she had apologized and put an end to the affair, or given him some other encouragement or reason to hope. But hope was what she had always counted on him to provide, and now that he was gone, there was no one left to make the repairs.

A week later Dad came back for his clothes. He went upstairs and the four of us waited in the living room. Melanie and I perched on the velveteen sofa while Van sat in the armchair, his lanky body sprouting in all directions, his slender hands—Dad's hands—fiddling with the extra fabric swatch on the chair's upholstered arms. Miss America lay at his feet, the dog blinking, trying to keep awake. Above our heads, we could hear Dad opening and closing the tallboy drawers.

Momma could not sit still. She got up and paced to the stairs, her hands nervously darting and plunging between the balusters. The movement of her hand suggested to me that while Van had inherited the shape of his hands from Dad, he had inherited his motor from Momma. My eye went from Momma to Van and back again. There was no mistaking the fact that both Momma and Dad made my brother, made me, too, and whatever would happen from this point on, they were, like countries, indivisible, at least, in us.

Overhead, Dad walked over to the far wall and opened the louvered closet doors. The doors squeaked and Momma peered into the stairwell, responding to a call that had not—would not—come. She frowned.

When finally Dad came down the stairs, he was carrying a suitcase and a navy duffel with YMCA stenciled in white on the side. He had changed into slacks and a cream-colored polo shirt. Had it not been for the suitcase, Dad would have looked the same as he did every Saturday, heading out the door for a round of golf at the club.

"Did you see the shirts from the cleaners?" Momma asked, soft as a touch.

"No," he answered.

"Let me get them—"

"Really, Roxie, these are fine." He gestured at the suitcase.

"No," she said, palming the rail. "Just a second." And she skirted up the stairs.

We three stood, eyeing our father, as he turned and the familiar look in his eyes of boyish alacrity, game-for-anything, easy-does-it followed Momma's behind as she climbed the stairs.

"Dad," I said, as if by speaking his name I could stop them. Our parents had brought us to this threshold called separation, and every sound, every movement seemed precipitous, filled with dread. "Dad," I whispered, but he did not hear me because I had whispered and, besides, he was speaking to Van.

Dad was a tall man, and having bent so long in the service of others, the muscles in his neck had tightened and it was now impossible for him to straighten. Gray at his temples marked the first signs of age—that and crow's-feet around his eyes as he focused on Van, explaining to him something having to do with keys. Watching Dad, it occurred to me how different he seemed without Momma, who, for so many years, had provided him with a context: Araxie and George.

The successes that Dad never achieved—did he think about them as he packed his clothes? Did he think of himself as a man in his mid-forties, with certain unfulfilled promises and dreams?

His aspirations, at least the ones he admitted, were few: someday he wanted to climb the Presidential Range in the winter, when the summit reached minus 40 degrees; and to see the Yankees beat the Mets in a World Series; and to reel in a marlin off the southern Baja coast; and to own a second home. Of course, he must have had other, secret yearnings—one never knew—since the most he required for Christmas was shaving gel or black socks.

His audacious and lavish dreams had all been for her: a trip to Europe; a '56 Mercedes convertible coupe, cream with lipstick-red interior; a bathtub with massage jets; a maid; a cook; a voyage on the *Queen Elizabeth II.*

He stood at the bottom of the stairs. This man, who had never taken a business trip or gone overnight without her. Yet—and this was the strange part—he did not seem bereft. Standing there, holding on to his suitcases, talking to his son, my father seemed to be a man of possibility. Momma had betrayed him, but it seemed she might have released him, too.

Like our mother, we three had gathered in the living room to see him off. We stood close to him while in our hearts we were putting distance between us, so that hereafter we would count on him less, hereafter he would be less in our lives.

I wondered what he would become without us, as if before we came along he had been nothing, just breath and clay. Would he become one of those men at the airport—a man wearing a gray suit and cologne, who walks to the gate without having to check the monitor; who carries his bags as if they are an extension of his arms; who flies with hotel keys and a woman's name written on a cocktail napkin and buried in his pockets; who slicks his hair in the men's room with a small black plastic comb? A man with a life separate from fixing mowers and doling out allowances and throwing a ball? A man separate from her. From us.

"Take care of each other and your mother," he was saying, "and listen, there is no one to blame. You hear me: no one. Please." He sliced the air with his hand, leveling this no one's blame, making it fair and square.

Melanie plowed into him, sobbing, and he bent down and cradled her face in the crook of his arm. Then Van stepped forward and gave him a manly handshake.

It was my turn, but just then Momma came down the stairs and instead of turning to me, he looked up at her. His face froze with a new look: polite, goshful, but, in the eyes, blank.

It was his look that made things final and kept me rooted to the carpet. "See you later," I said.

"Be good." He nodded.

"Take care," I called.

Momma followed him out the door. She stayed outside long enough to make us believe she had said she was sorry. She stayed out long enough to make us think that they might come back arm in arm, joking about how they had forgotten to appreciate, how this should be a lesson to us all.

Then the car started up and Van, looking out the window, shook his head. "Here she comes."

Momma stepped into the house. "I'm sorry." She sighed, fiddling with her hands.

"Save it, Mom," Van said and headed for the door, fists balled in his pockets.

She spun to face him. "Don't talk to me that way," she yelled. "Come back here. Don't you ever talk to me that way."

"Why not," Van spat. "You let him go, didn't you? Didn't you? You bring your boyfriend here and you let Dad go."

"Stop it, Van," I yelled. "Stop it."

We pulled into a tight ring in the foyer. Momma hugged her ribs and studied her shoe. "You're angry. Well, I don't blame you. Your parents, they're supposed to have all the answers, and then it turns out they don't. I don't blame you. Things you couldn't know."

"I know more than you two do," Van hissed.

"Van, your father and I have had a long history of doing to each other, and then shoving it under the rug. Can you understand that? Don't go picking sides unless you know you're right."

One phrase, yet another in the language of separation, hung in the air: *your* father.

Van wavered between taking off and staying on to fight. "You gonna stop seeing that jerk?"—he hedged.

"She already has—" I said.

Momma, Van and Melanie exchanged looks that said that they knew differently.

"You were out with Frank last night," Melanie explained.

"Oh," I said.

Van made a sick face at Momma. "Seta, didn't you know Momma's pet, Haig Kazangian, picked her up and took her to dinner and a show last night?"

"Oh, Van." She sighed, her body sagging with exasperation. She waved away the distasteful words he had placed in front of her nose. "Poor Van."

"Haig Kazangian: Mr. Goddamn Church Deacon," he said.

She rolled her lips, and, starting with his shoes, inspected him, all the way up till she reached his brow. Momma's gaze offered nothing maternal. She was deciding whether Van deserved the respect of her anger, or just pity. Her gaze dropped to his eyes. She peered into him, and found his heart. A perverse smile spread across her lips, for his was a boy's heart, and she could see herself inside its chambers, its first love.

"So it's official now, huh?" she said. "Your mother's knocked from the pedestal." She squinted at the line of his hair. "No more Big Momma. You hate me now."

Van tried to return a cold stare but his quivering lips gave him away.

"Oh, Van," she said, as if he had hurt himself and come home with a scraped knee.

"Don't," he said, raising his palms to fend her off.

"Van, look at me."

"No."

"Then tell me what you plan to do with this hate, Van? You're old enough, but what will you do with it? What will it make you?"

"I'll think what I think: that my mother cuckolded my father. There's a word, huh, Momma? Cuckold."

"Slap you," she said, her voice pinched with anger.

"Go ahead," he dared, stiffening for the blow. "Come on, do it."

Momma darted her hand, but her fingers merely touched one of his curls. Van closed his eyes, and on his face her touch produced the effect she wanted: he softened.

"Why can't you just say you won't see him," he asked. "Haven't you done enough? Hasn't that jerk done—"

"Shh—" she cooed. It would have been so much simpler if only she had promised not to see Haig Kazangian, if only for a while. But Momma had no intention of cutting off Haig Kazangian, and the one thing she could never do was lie. So she played Van, played us all.

"I'll kill him," Van said.

"Me, too," I added.

"No," she corrected. "Remember, all of you: it takes two. Your father and me, not Haig. You don't want to hear, but maybe it's time you all did. Be careful. Van, Seta, you two especially, be careful. Once you judge, you can't go back. A nail gets put in your heart. Hate, too. And then you are cynical. You're cynical, and then you're nothing. I won't have it. Not any of you kids—your father and I dreamed of many things—and now . . . we never, never wanted for you to turn out cynical."

Momma sighed and, quitting the foyer, walked out onto the lawn. The despair, which she and our father had made, she left behind. It would invade our bones if we gave it a chance, if we did not quickly move. Van raced up the stairs while Melanie hurried into the kitchen, leaving me to find an exit before despair took hold.

The quiet desperation of our lives was like a scream heard underwater. We moved through the house, separate, unable to touch.

The rest of the summer went by, and then, after Labor Day, Van, Melanie and I returned to school. For the first few weeks the weather stayed warm, but in the beginning of October a cold front moved in and the air turned chill. The gypsy moths had devoured the leaves, so there was not much in the way of autumnal color. One day after school Frank and I went to the park, and as we reached the oaks, he turned to me.

"Hey," he said. "Pick one." He offered me his two closed fists.

"What is this?" I said.

"Pick one," he repeated, and, impatient, he opened his left hand, revealing a tiny package wrapped in gold paper. "Here," he said.

I looked at the gift and could not touch it, afraid of what it might be. Frank, eager, tore the wrapping, and then, opening the box, dropped a ring into my palm.

"Here," he said.

The ring was gold with a small square blood-red stone. When I turned the ring slightly, the red stone turned gold. On either side of it were tiny seed pearls.

"Frank, where did you . . . It's beautiful. Where did you—"

"Garnet. You like it?"

"Garnet," I repeated, turning the ring so its colors came up autumn leaves: yellow, red, amber. I admired the stone and its setting, but a pounding fear kept me from putting it on my finger.

"Where did you get it?" I asked, wanting him to talk a bit while I calmed down.

But Frank was through with conversation. He seized my arm and propelled me in a foolish wedding march down the walk, under the naked trees. At the end of the path, before an imaginary altar, he turned, his cheeks red with joy.

Oh no, I thought. Frank peered at me, his eyes sweet and vulnerable. "I love you," he said. He seemed about to cry.

Now it was my turn to say it back. We stood facing each other, waiting for the simple words that would bind us to pour from my mouth. I had been preparing these words for weeks, mouthing them into my pillow at night. But as I looked at Frank, terror, instead of love, raced my heart.

"It's OK," he said.

"No, it's not."

"Don't worry about it," he said, clamping his jaw.

"It's not OK, Frank. You know it's not. Christ!" I said, slapping the ring into his palm. I turned on my heel and started walking.

"Wait a minute," Frank called, furious. "Where are you going? Seta!"

I started running—all the way downtown, until I was convinced he was not behind me. Frank wanted too much: every day there had to be some new experience, some new step. At times I craved to be still, be alone.

"Go to hell, Frank Agostini!" I shouted. "I never asked you for anything. I never asked for a stupid ring. Did I? Did I?"

Afterward, no one noticed that the phone had stopped ringing for me, and that each day after school I came immediately home. I locked myself in my room and listened to the stereo till dinner.

The Sunday following the disaster with Frank, I had a date with Dad to see his new apartment. None of us had seen it, and Momma, especially, was anxious to hear a full report. Secretly, jealously, she kept tabs on him. At the hour Dad was due to pick me up, Momma hid behind the sheer curtains in the living room, waiting for him.

"Your father's here," she called as Dad's car pulled into the driveway and he tapped on the horn.

"Come on. Seta! Don't make him toot again. Please. I can't stand having him toot."

These were what Dad called our "dates." Sometimes Van, Melanie and I went together, but this evening Dad had asked me to come alone. He said he wanted to make a special dinner for me in his new place.

He shut off the car motor, and looked out his window at the yard. Everything was trimmed and neat. That week Haig had sent over a man to trim the hedge, but Dad would not ask. Haig had bought the flowers in the bay window and, on Momma's wrist, the thin gold bracelet. But Dad could not possibly see what was hidden behind the sheers; he could not see Momma, sitting in the window with a drink, her legs crossed, her foot wagging, anticipating his next toot.

Momma's voice stopped me halfway down the stairs. "Those shoes?" she asked.

"What's wrong with them?" I said, looking down at my sandals.

"They're awfully summery."

"So?"

"What about your black shoes?"

"Why," I began, and then I noticed that her eye had barely shifted from the window. "Hello?"

Sighing, she wiped the condensation from her drink and applied it to her wrist. I was the first to see Dad's new place and she felt left out.

"OK," she said. "Have a good time."

I walked to the car, and Dad came around and gave me a good hug. He was fresh from the shower, his hair slicked back, his pants creased. He smelled like mints and soap. Opening my door, he tucked me in.

As we rode toward his apartment, Dad prepared me for what I was about to see. "It's a good deal for me, Seta," he said. "The owner's a friend of mine, Bill Wasnick, you remember Bill. He wanted someone to keep an eye on things and, well, I told him that in the present circumstance I'd be willing to do it—strictly on a temporary basis."

At the light, Dad checked for my reaction, and when I smiled sheepishly he smiled, too, and then he said, "We'll just see how it goes."

We skirted town, past the old high school, from which both he and Momma had graduated, and then we drove by the entrance to the community college. Dad slowed the car. "What you're looking at," he said, pointing at a huge, white monolith on my right, "is a two-hundred-million-dollar medical center."

I bulged my eyes to show that I considered two hundred million dollars an impressive sum.

"Yep," Dad said. "State of the art."

As we headed west of town, Dad kept on talking. I did not feel a particular need to say anything, so I just looked out the window, and let myself be lulled by his voice and the motion of the car.

In that part of town near the community college, the homes were small but well maintained, with neat, trimmed lawns. We passed by a white Cape Cod, just as an elderly couple were walking out the front door. The man was holding the door open for his wife, who gingerly gripped the rail as she stepped down the front stairs. When she heard our car, she picked up her head and frowned at the unwanted commotion.

The Buick passed them, cutting through their neighborhood like a knife. At the end of the block, Dad turned into the driveway of a redwood-shingled apartment building. He drove all the way to the back and pulled into a space marked "29."

"This is it," Dad said, removing his hands from the wheel.

"Great," I said, and smiled.

We rode the elevator to the top floor. Dad was nervous; I was nervous, too. I had never known anyone who lived in an apartment, and it seemed odd, the thought of my own father living far above the ground.

We stepped out of the elevator into a hallway with rust-colored indoor-outdoor carpeting; the place smelled of cigarettes and cleaning fluid. Doors to the apartments ran the length of the empty hall. It seemed like the kind of place where adults go after they have run out of options.

Dad's apartment was the last one on the left. The front door opened on the living room, with a matching beige sofa and chair and an artificial plant stuck in one of the corners. The room was ugly, but very clean and neat.

"Have a look around," Dad said as he went into the galley kitchen to start dinner.

I walked through the living room, down a short hall, to the bathroom, and then I turned back and went into Dad's room. I peeked into his closet and was amazed to find his clothes neatly arranged the same way he had kept them at home. I was opening the drawers of his bedside table when he startled me. "You find anything?" he said, wondering what exactly I was doing, as I wondered myself.

Dad pointed to the framed pictures of Van, Melanie and me he had lined up on his dresser. "You recognize those characters?" They were the same pictures he had kept on his dresser at home. One was missing. I pulled open the bottom drawer of his bedside table and there it was.

"I don't keep that out," he said, easing the picture from my hand.

"Why not, Dad? You don't have to put it away for me. I mean, not if you don't want to."

"No," he said, concentrating on the velvet backing of the frame. He gathered himself before turning the picture over and there was Momma, smiling at us. "It's strange sometimes not to have her out with the rest of you."

"Yeah," I said, recalling the bouquet Haig had given her, which she had arranged in a vase in the bay window, beside Dad's old chair. Those flowers made me ashamed of her, and of Dad too, though I was uncertain what he had done that was so shameful.

"You like it here, Dad?"

He gazed about the room, considering the question, as if judging his new place for the first time. "Well," he said, smiling apologetically. "Why don't you let me show you the balcony, and while we're at it, I'll light the coals."

We ate our meal of steak, corn on the cob, salad and French bread at the small dining room table. For dessert Dad had bought brownies and two kinds of ice cream. "I couldn't make up my mind," he said, amused by his own indecision.

We took the two dining chairs, our bowls of ice cream and the plate of brownies and went out to the balcony, where we propped our feet on the railing and watched the sun fall in the field behind the lot. Dad brought out our coats and wrapped a heavy army blanket around my knees. It was Sunday night, the hardest night of the week, the night that felt most like divorce. Tomorrow I would be back in school, and this apartment and Dad's new life would seem far away.

"Give 'em a year or two," Dad said, pointing at the empty lot next to the building. "Three at the max. They'll come in and clear that lot, then put up a strip mall. What do you bet."

I nodded, because I wanted to be agreeable, though the truth was I did not have an opinion on the subject.

"Yep," Dad mused, puffing air into his cheeks. "That's what you call a crime."

We were quiet then, and I thought it was my turn to fill up the space. I peered over the balcony railing. "There's your car."

He bent forward to check.

"Number twenty-nine," I said.

He eased back into his chair. "Your mother," he began. "She was waiting by the window tonight."

Since it was not a question, I felt grateful not to have to respond. I turned slightly toward him.

He cleared his throat. "Did she say anything?"

"No. Just the usual, 'Have a good time,' that sort of thing." I eyed him before continuing, "I think she was nervous that I was coming over here. I think maybe she's curious, Dad. You know, what the place looks like." And here I had to hold myself back from fabricating a nuance that would offer him hope. "I guess she wants to know that you're OK."

We were silent, thinking it over.

Dad coughed. "About tonight. What are you going to tell her?" His voice was deliberately casual, so as not to put any added weight on me.

I watched his face and knew he meant the business with the picture. "Oh, I won't say anything, Dad. I promise I won't."

"It's OK if you do."

"No—"

"Really. I don't want you kids in the middle, having to censor yourselves."

"No. No way. I'll just tell her you made me steak and then we sat on the balcony and talked." I smiled reassuringly at him.

"Whatever you want to do," Dad said, and leaning back in his chair, he followed my gaze down into the parking lot. Most of the cars in his building were American, some of them fairly beat up. This meant something to me, something I could not put my finger on. It had to do with our pretending that it was normal for a father and daughter to spend a Sunday evening sitting in kitchen chairs on a cement balcony, looking out over a parking lot. I recalled the old lady we had passed on our way to the apartment and the judgment on her face.

I excused myself and went to the bathroom, where I sat on the closed commode and leafed through some magazines. Then I took an inventory of the medicine cabinet. I sprayed a little shaving cream in the sink and washed it down—something I used to do as a kid. Everything in the medicine cabinet was lined up in rows: toothpaste, deodorant, aspirin, steel razor, dental floss, white styptic pencil in a plastic cylinder—the same things he kept at home.

The only other person I ever knew who kept things that neat was Casard.

I was rummaging through the drawers by the sink when it dawned on me that I was searching for some sign of another woman: if Mom could do it, so could he.

When I returned to the balcony, the sun was fading, the sky a brilliant orange. Dad was musing on the view.

"Dad," I said. "You want to hear something incredible?"

"Sure, babe."

"You know who this place reminds me of?"

"Who's that."

"Grandma."

He chortled. "Really?"

"Yeah," I admitted, turning my chair so that it faced him. "Isn't that funny?"

He nodded, thinking it over.

"Dad?"

"Yeah, babe."

"Do you ever wonder about Grandma?"

"How so?"

"Do you think about her?"

He smirked, curling a finger under his nose. "Funny you should say that, Seta. Funny. Since all this happened I don't think a day has passed that I haven't thought of your grandmother."

"Really?"

He laughed, another joke on himself. "I suppose I miss her, imagine that."

In a way, it made sense. Our lives had changed beyond anything we could have imagined, but in the end, we would always come back to Casard.

"I was never close to my own parents," Dad said. "Oh, they raised me fine. But we never had enough in common, I suppose, worth fighting about. Now your grandmother—she could fight over the shape of a loaf of bread." He smiled. "Yet, crazy and angry as she *was*, she had this strength. She really kept things together. I'll give her that. She and your mother, the two of them—well, as you probably remember, they went at it morning and night. But Casard loved your mother—there was never any doubt—and she gave Araxie something solid to push against. That was the nature of their relationship. After Casard, I guess it was my turn"—he nodded to himself. "Problem is, constant upheaval just isn't in my nature."

In the dim light I studied my father's features. He had a good, strong face.

He went on, "Your mother. When I met her, boy, I knew nothing would ever be the same. She was my dream girl." He bowed his head, and I worried that he was going to cry. But he smiled. "She doesn't mean any harm," he said. "It's just her spirit. I thought it would be enough to get her out of that house and give her a new life. We had something, the two of us. Don't let anyone tell you different."

Dad spoke with conviction. I had come to his new place expecting to find him diminished and weak, but instead I found him strong. His gift, though simple, was belief; it was, in the spectrum of gifts, more sustaining than most.

I thought about my grandmother's death, how long ago it seemed. And I thought about the silence that had followed Casard's death, and how, by the laws of nature, something had to come in and fill that empty space.

"Dad?"

"Yeah, babe."

"What's the matter with Mom? How come?"

"Oh," he said. "Your mother's depressed, Seta. She thinks she's missing something—inside. I suppose she is. I suppose I thought I could help her with it. I suppose that Armenian fellow thinks he can, too. But you can't give someone joy, you can't make them feel like they have a purpose in this world. Her mother had the same emptiness. Different, though. Casard was stronger—she had to be to survive those Turks. She protected herself by putting off onto the rest of us a lot of anger. Underneath, I think she was just a scared little girl. Now, your mother, she took Casard's anger to heart, and it beat her up pretty good."

He shrugged, lacing his hands under his knee. "I don't understand a lot of it. It seems to me it goes all the way back to that genocide. Those women drowning themselves and their children, rather than becoming victims of the Turks. Imagine that. How can we? The Turks took something from them, the ones that survived, something more than life—dignity, purpose—something humans aren't meant to do without. That lack just keeps on perpetuating through the generations. A terrific sadness, I suppose, that keeps getting passed down in the blood."

"Dad?"

"Mmm."

"Do you think I'll get it?"

"Oh, babe, I didn't mean—"

"Why not?"

"Oh, not you," he said, and he reached over and took my hand in both of his. They were warm hands, and dry. He rubbed mine like a flint. "Not you." He smiled sheepishly.

I bit my lip and, fighting back tears, nodded.

"Hey," he said, trying to sound chipper. "Would you look at us, sitting here in the dark, like a couple of bears. Look at you, all goose pimples. Come on, inside you go."

On the drive home, we talked about school and then Dad asked if sometime I might like Frank to join us.

"I don't think so," I said. "We broke up."

"No," he protested. "No, you didn't. How long ago?"

"A few days."

"Oh, that's no time. No time at all. You two can still patch things up."

"I don't know, Dad. Sometimes—it's complicated." I glanced at him and he glanced back, and the two of us had to smile. "I'll ask him, Dad. I will."

"That's the way," he said. "Good."

We reached the house and he pulled the Buick flush along the curb. We did not look toward the lighted windows. We hugged and kissed good night and I walked to the door knowing that he would wait until I was safely inside.

Momma was in her room. "How did it go?"

"Fine," I answered, heading to my room.

"Seta?"

"What?"

"Come here."

"What?" I said.

She was already in bed, her face blurry as if she had been dozing. I stood in the doorway as she rubbed her feet together under the covers. She was wearing wool socks and the sound of their rubbing made my teeth hurt.

"So, what did he make?" she asked. She patted a space on the bed for me to sit.

I hesitated, and then I approached as far as the bureau. "Steak."

"That's nice. You have a good time?"

"Yeah. I guess I'm a little tired, though."

"Mmm. Well, I have something to tell you but I guess it can wait."

"What."

She tilted her head, flirting, and smiled. "Frank called."

"He did?"

"That got your attention, didn't it."

"What'd you say?"

"I said you were out with your father. Is that what I was supposed to say?"

"Did you tell him when I'd be back?"

"How could I tell him, I didn't know. And if I were you I wouldn't call back in any hurry. Don't make yourself too available. You'll see him tomorrow." She punched the pillow and propped herself up in the bed. "Now. What was the apartment like."

"Nice."

"Mmm. Did he say anything?"

"What was he supposed to say? God! What do you expect him to say?"

"Don't give me lip. So where is it?"

"Near the community college."

"Over there? Why would he want—"

"Momma, it's a nice place, OK?"

"He said it was small, an efficiency, he said."

"I don't know, it's not that small. Why do you want it to be small?" I paused, to see what she would say. "He's got it furnished, OK? With pots and pans, and everything."

The feet started up again, rubbing together like pieces of steel wool. "Bet he's got himself a neat little system. This pile here, that pile there, all he needs to keep him happy."

"I don't think he's so happy, Mom."

"What makes you say that. Did he say anything?"

"I said it was nice, OK?" I paused, hating what I was about to do: she had pushed and I had to push back—it was just a matter of completion. "He keeps the pictures of us on his bureau, just like here at home."

"Mmm." She nodded.

"But only the three of us. Melanie, Van and me."

She had to work a bit to see the image and then her face darkened with recognition: she had been left out.

Her mouth twisted. "Well"—she sighed, reaching under the covers—"here's a picture," and she tossed it toward me on the bed. "That's your grandmother's wedding day. Some wedding: a gardenia corsage and a Lebanese priest."

I looked at the photograph and was amazed: Casard was young and trim, in her long gray suit. Her hair was tied back, but across her forehead it fell in a luminous black wave.

"Look at the two of them," Momma said, jabbing her finger at the frame.

I looked again, this time with Momma's eyes. Vrej was indeed small, Casard even smaller. He gripped her shoulder as if to say,

This is my wife. The precise moment that the picture had been taken Casard looked up, at something just above the frame, perhaps a bird or a patch of sky, while Vrej gripped her shoulder and gazed downward at his shoe.

Momma was agitated. "Look at that priest," she said. "Get a load of that priest."

The priest stood in the center, dominating the frame, as if he were the one the photograph was really about. With his miter, beard and robe, he made a wall, dividing the picture in half. To his left were the church steps, and to his right, Vrej and Casard—Casard at the very edge, as if at any moment she might altogether fall out of the picture.

"She never had a chance," Momma declared. "That marriage was doomed."

"How come I never saw this picture before?" I asked.

Momma shook her head, ignoring me.

"Momma, she didn't have a wedding dress?"

"Wedding dress! Look at them, will you," she shrieked. "I'm telling you she never had a chance!" And with that, Momma snapped the picture from me and rubbed the glass with her palm.

Momma shook her finger. "Your grandmother specifically told me there were no photographs taken in the first ten years of their marriage. 'Too expensive,' she said." Momma sucked in her cheeks and glared at me. Sighing dramatically, she yanked back the covers, and there, spread out over the sheets, were photographs—ten, twenty, thirty photographs—the whole bed covered. There were pictures of Casard in front of the house, and Momma as a baby with Vrej, the two of them standing by the lemon sapling.

Momma sighed. "I had to find these after she died, when we went through her house. And, this one—" Momma's voice trembled with emotion as she shook the wedding picture. "This one she had hidden in her underwear."

"It's not a very happy picture," I said, feeling numb and wary of fanning Momma's flame. "It's just a lousy photograph, Mom. The photographer probably missed the happy picture."

"Happy?" Momma cried. "Are you crazy! Look in front of your nose! All this time I'm thinking she kept the truth from us, the good memories. Just another example of her withholding, her deceptions. But no—" Momma tapped the frame with her nail. "Mayrig kept this so it would not be passed on."

"What do you mean, Momma?" I cried. "Answer me, what do you mean? That they were never happy? That it was impossible from the start to be happy? That's crazy."

Momma made a sour face and shook her head.

"Mom!"

"Too late!" she shrieked. "Too damn late!"

The hall was dim. Melanie had gone to sleep—she could sleep through anything. Van was out. I went downstairs. Along the way I made a point of snapping on all the lights, inside the closets, too, until I reached the kitchen. I opened the door to the basement and sat down on the stairs by the brooms and shoe polish and cans of soda water. I pulled the phone to me and, cradling it in my lap, dialed Frank's number. At first it was busy, and I had to try several more times before he answered and I could tell him what was in my heart, what had been there the day that he gave me the ring, what I had to say so as not to become like Momma and Casard. "I love you. I love you, Frank. I'm sorry. Please."

SOLSTICE

The old ones said, *Kna merir yegoor sirem*: Go die, come back I love you.

On the first of November Mrs. Vartyan died in her sleep, her last vision being that of Theresa, who was asleep on the bed beside her. It was nearly three in the morning, and as Lila Vartyan passed from this world to the next, I awoke, my heart racing. At first I thought I had awakened from a wretched dream, but as I lay there, black night all around me, a sweet peace passed through my bones, not unlike the *whoosh* of a golden light. Later, I knew the light was Mrs. Vartyan's soul come to bid me farewell, her spirit patting my hand as the ravaging disease ebbed from her sweet, hairless brow.

Mrs. Vartyan died at the beginning of November, four weeks till Thanksgiving, seven till the winter solstice. On the afternoon of her funeral, a warm, salubrious wind swept up from the Gulf of Mexico. The wet, unsettling breeze whistled through the telephone wires and the hemlock boughs.

Theresa was home receiving mourners. The women of the Armenian Relief Society arrived in their galoshes and black wool. Bearing sympathy and food, they organized themselves so that someone was always on hand, helping Theresa in the afternoon and in the early evening. Still, that left many hours when Theresa Vartyan was alone.

She was alone the night Bob Humms came to the house to pay his respects. Theresa received her former lover in the living room, granting him a Coca-Cola, and, for a brief few minutes, her hand.

"Never seen you in a suit," she said, standing when it was time for him to go.

Her hair hung in front of her face. She had eczema on her hands and wrists. He longed to touch her, soothe her, but that was impossible: she had gone inside herself, her heart was closed.

Theresa's father could not be found, despite the persistence of the police and the Der Hyre priest. Mr. Vartyan was gone. The court appointed the church as Theresa's legal guardian. She inherited the house and its contents outright, and there was a small sum in a bank account that if husbanded carefully would carry her several years till she reached maturity. In another year she would be old enough to drive the Ford. Until then it was school and home, and all the hours unseen, behind doors.

Two weeks after Mrs. Vartyan's funeral, just after dawn, Theresa was awakened by the commotion of garbage. They came from down the road, garbage men hanging casually on the back of a truck, hot air shooting up their legs from the tires. At Theresa's house they noisily dragged the cans from the curb. A boy in leather chaps flipped a switch and the truck's huge jaws swallowed.

Theresa shifted to a cool part of the sheet and wished them gone. She stretched out her leg, letting it languish in the warm breeze. She ran a palm over her face, checking her features, scooping her hair from under her neck and arranging it on the pillow above her. She picked up a book and turned to the place where she had left off the night before, then closed the book without reading a word. There was something else she wanted to think about. Smiling, she pictured the self-portrait she had carved into stone, having begun the project in Miss Trundell's visual arts class and then finishing it over the summer. Her delighted teacher had encouraged Theresa to enter the art contest, part of Memorial's annual autumn fair, opening that very day at noon.

During the night while Theresa slept, the limbs of the Ferris wheel were carted from a truck and assembled in the empty lot beyond the statue of Squaw. Under a pearl moon, frames for the bumper cars, air jets, popcorn makers and cotton-candy machines were unloaded and set down on the grass. Tents for the bake sale, the ring toss and darts followed, their spikes anchored in the dirt.

In just a few hours, alongside the grove of willows by the picnic grounds, the high school art department would set up the annual art show. Theresa lay in her bed and imagined clothesline being tied from tree to tree. She imagined rows of paintings hanging like wash from the line. But it was on the long tables—dark, knotty slabs she equated with the word *bazaar*—that the ladies of the PTA arranged the nominees for best high school art. At noon, judging would commence for that year's prize.

Theresa's leg swung along the side of the bed. Throughout the morning a panel of professional artists would run their hands across Theresa's smooth sculpted cheeks and judge the relationship of the features, the artist's eye for detail. Beaming, Theresa thought of how fine and lovely—*siroon*—she had made herself: her nose, delicate; her eyes, wide and luminous. And though it was early, the sun barely a promise, Theresa felt certain she had won. Dreaming of the blue ribbon, she swam toward a cool strip of sheet.

We were caught in a cycle, going around, going around; we were apart, linked by threads.

The garbage men left Theresa's house and made their way toward mine. At the crashing of metal garbage lids on the driveway, I awoke. Lying perfectly still, I tried to recall my dream. The night after Mrs. Vartyan's funeral, I had begun to have terrible dreams in which my faceless men appeared as faceless death. I dreamed of hissing ferrets I had to beat back with sticks and, finally, a wire hanger. And I dreamed of Casard. It had been four years since her death, yet in my dreams she was exactly the same: recumbent inside a polished mahogany box, wearing pearls, her best blue dress and black tie shoes.

"Seta," she whispered, beckoning me with a smile. "My girlie-girl, come here."

"Grandma," I said, rushing toward her, my heart nearly bursting. As I bent down to kiss her cheek, she reached for me and I awakened.

I lay in bed, recalling the dream. After I went back to sleep, I dreamed that I was a medieval bride, in a mauve damask gown and long veil. I was pale and very sad, gazing out a tower window at a wet, barren land. At my feet there was a dog, and when the animal began to whine, I bent down to comfort it, and discovered it was Momma.

I had no idea what to do with such a troubling vision, and lying in bed, I groaned. After a while, I got up, put on my robe and padded downstairs. I opened the front door and walked out onto the stoop.

It was pleasant on the steps, the morning light climbing the naked trees, the morning light dim and uneven. It was nearly seven, and Momma, Van and Melanie were still slugs in their beds. I sat down on the top stair. The unexpected heat wave made me restless; it was sexy weather, a hitch in a grown man's pants. I thought about what I would wear to school and decided on my jean skirt, sewn from a pair of dungarees, and a white halter top that I would hide under a cotton sweater during classes. The halter would be a special surprise for Frank. After school, at the opening of the fair, Frank would put his hand under my sweater and the touch of my bare skin would excite him and make him hard—hard in front of all the people. He would rub his thing daringly against my hip, and, instantly, the wet would drop down inside me, like rain from a second-story window, and in front of all the people, there we would be, right there.

Rocking on the stoop, I pictured Frank in his bed, Frank under his pajamas, his thing curled like a walnut, damp and friendly. For weeks now, Frank and I had spent our afternoons in his parents' basement, where he pressed me like a stem between his body and a Naugahyde couch. "All the way," he murmured, "all the way," puffing his feverish chant into my mouth. His love was wet and insistent—warm like the air passing through the sleepy, naked trees. In the morning light, Frank's kisses seemed like promises—of a future time when we would race, windows peeled, air licking the tires, all the way.

Such thoughts made me hug my knees and hold my breath, and I became as hushed as the bulbs in Momma's garden. I watched the milk truck come down the hill, a white whir, and pull to a stop at the base of our driveway. The side of the truck read PERLA DAIRY. The milkman appeared at the back of the truck and then, carrying a basket with Momma's order, he started up the driveway. I wondered how long it would take the milkman to find me, and I stared at him—at his name, Leon, stitched on the red pocket of his uniform. This Leon had long sideburns and a cowlick over his left eye. He was not bad-looking, just plain, as irreproachable as the day, white as milk.

Leon was only a few yards from me—me, sitting there with nothing on but my robe—when he changed course and headed around the garage. I watched him through the glass portico as he slid four half-gallon bottles of milk and a pint of cream into the silver box by the back door. He pulled a brown envelope from the slot beneath the lid, and checked inside it for his payment. Momma had forgotten once again. Leon searched the back door for an explanation.

Finding none, he came around to the front. I was certain he would at last find me, and I huddled in my robe pretending I was cold. Leon looked up at the roof, at a squirrel hopping from the maple to the chimney. The milkman's gaze dropped back to his envelope. He bit his lip; Momma would cause him trouble at the office.

Shifting his feet, glancing at the roof, he wrote something on the envelope, then went around back and placed it on top of the milk, where any idiot would find it.

He came around to the front once again, and then headed for his truck without so much as a glance at me. I watched with voyeuristic delight as the milkman's buttocks squeezed as he loped down the driveway. I thought about my life and the life I wanted, where men such as Leon would present themselves and I would offer myself, bare under my robe. I liked men—their laughter, their tender dignity, which, I noted, some like my father carried across their shoulders like a flat yoke. Of course, there were foolish men, who wanted nothing to do with duty and honor. They were the dangerous ones—the ones in my dreams I chose.

Sitting on the stoop, I thought of Frank, who would never be a milkman, not with all his fabulous talk. I admired Frank's plans for a grand life, as they corresponded with my own. Still, there was something undeniably sexy about wearing a uniform with your name sewn on the breast pocket, and spending your days delivering a product as elemental as milk. Mine was a romantic vision, maybe that was all it was. Leon started up the truck and I sat there watching him, longing for simplicity. The day was coming soon when I would leave Memorial; I knew this, the same way I knew that the person I would eventually become was already inside me. Until it was my time to leave, I wished only to ripen in the hot sun and indulge myself in fantasies of putting my tongue on the salty ridge of a milkman's thigh.

But the day conspired against me. Leon's truck lurched around the corner. Inside the house I could hear water running.

Theresa cut classes and spent the morning at the fairgrounds, helping the art department and the women of the PTA set up the show. Laughing too loudly, like an overexcited child, she worked alongside her teachers. Her eczema-ridden hands she hid under long sleeves as she arranged the pottery, papier-mâché and sandstone sculptures.

At noon she stepped back into the grove of willows as judges with clipboards made the rounds. Each time they paused to consider an object or jot a note, Theresa thought she was going to die. She had never wanted anything so much as that blue ribbon, and watching the judges decide her fate, she scratched her wrists raw.

At two o'clock the mayor's wife, Luanne Pac, wearing a gray midi-length A-line suit and matching fedora, swept across the lawn to announce the results. The mayor's wife, a former summer-stock actress, blew into the microphone, "Testing, A,B,C," as Theresa stepped from the trees into the small attentive crowd. The tinny music of the Ferris wheel droned in the background, but Theresa did not hear it. She remained perfectly still as the mayor's wife announced the winners of third, then second prize. Yet before Luanne Pac could announce the winner, Theresa was on the move. She walked quickly to the podium, her hair sweeping behind her, exposing her real face, while the mayor's wife giggled and held up, for all to see, Theresa's other face, the lovely one carved in stone. And hiding her hands so that only the tips of her raw fingers peeked out from her cuffs, Theresa snatched the blue.

Later, she stayed and helped the teachers break down the show. Wrapping the unclaimed objects in tissue paper, Theresa stowed them in the back of Mr. Joseph's truck. She took her time, wanting the day never to end. It had been so perfect: the heat, the communion of artists, the ribbon pinned to her chest.

At dusk, Theresa walked Miss Trundell to her car. "I'm awfully proud of you, Theresa," her teacher said. "The portrait is quite true."

Theresa blushed and politely refused Miss Trundell's offer of a ride; she wanted to hang around for a while. She stayed by the grove of willows until nine o'clock, when they shut down the Ferris-wheel lights. Finally, Theresa left the picnic grounds, peering over her shoulder as if to memorize the sight of her triumph. Carrying her stone, she went into town and walked along Main Street, past the illuminated shopwindows. At the center, she saw the cluster of white statues shining in the night like bones.

At the library she turned north and made a loop by the factories before cutting back onto the road, by the park. Drivers passing by, their headlights flashing on her, acknowledged her presence at the side of the road without really seeing her. She was her mother, she was an illicit affair with Bob Humms, she was an odd bird with breasts and an uncle's nose, flashing in an instant through their minds. Theresa climbed the hill of the park, her blue ribbon flapping like a great wing on her chest. She swung her arms, trading off the stone—left, then right.

At the crest of the hill something happened. Theresa accepted the ride offered, perhaps on a whim or her own dare. What did he say to her? What kind of an invitation would deliver Theresa Vartyan three hundred and fifty miles to the coast of Maine?

That evening Bob Humms watched the Vartyan house from his car parked across the street, but Theresa never came home. At ten o'clock he phoned the police, "What's happened to her? What are you doing? Have you found Theresa Vartyan?" Throughout the next day, every hour, Bob Humms phoned, pleading for the police to take action. Each time he received the same answer: it was too soon. There was the requisite twenty-four hours.

That following evening, Theresa Vartyan became an official missing person and a police car was sent to the cobbler's store. The shop was empty, the sign under the shoe: CLOSED. At Bob Humms's home there was evidence of an abrupt departure: the back door was ajar; a roast was left out on the counter. The news of their disappearance spread. Archie phoned Momma: Theresa and Bob Humms had finally run off.

That night and for two days more, police throughout New England searched not for Theresa but for the one who stole her. Six states issued warrants for Bob Humms's arrest. He was found alone, crazed, driving ninety miles an hour on the Massachusetts Turnpike. It took four state police cars to force his car to the shoulder.

Bob Humms was placed in handcuffs and driven across state lines to Memorial. There he was met by Zucky Harris, Memorial's police chief, known by all for his signature crew cut and a reputation for spending evenings parked in a chair on his front lawn, hurling insults at the black family that lived across the street.

"Tell us," Zucky Harris demanded of Bob Humms. "Tell us about the girl. What did you do with her, you sick piece of shit?"

Five officers were gathered in the cork-lined room. Bob Humms looked above the heads of three veteran cops and two rookies, as if unable to locate the precise direction of the speaking voice.

"Here, asshole," Zucky said, grabbing the shoeman by the collar so that the chief's foul, wet mouth was inches from the suspect's face.

Bob Humms turned away toward the one window in the room. Outside, he thought he heard someone calling. A voice that no one else could hear, the same voice that told him of the burning monks and of his beloved Suzanne, now warned him that she was alone and hurt while the men in uniform huddled by him, too close.

Bob Humms moaned. The five officers stepped back, not knowing what to do. For years Bob Humms had awakened each man with his vernal call. They had performed their morning tasks—dreaming, making love, donning the uniform, drinking their coffee to the music of one man's suffering. Teddy Cheney had conceived his youngest child, Emily, to the music of Bob Humms's burning monks. Never before had it been so close. They could not stand having it so close. Listening to it was worse than watching a man slowly cut himself, the torment getting under their uniforms, under their skin, until they thought it was the devil himself in a sympathetic guise, the devil they would later hear in their own voices and the voices of their children and wives, and the wail of the squad siren, and every dog that howled. Bob Humms cried and they would not forget: the sound of a man's heart turned out like a sleeve.

All that time Theresa was in the white truck with the red letters PERLA DAIRY.

Maine police found the truck on a fire road parked between two stumps. For seventy-two hours Theresa Vartyan lay curled in the hold, refusing to call for help. What kind of person could have done such a thing to her? What did he look like? When did he remove her clothes? She would not say. She clutched the stone that he used to beat her—her attacker pummeling her with her own self-portrait. He smashed Theresa Vartyan's skull and body, until blood flowed and contusions sprouted along her limbs and face. The blue ribbon from her tattered shirt, he pinned in her hair.

The next week, Thanksgiving, the air crystallized, hardened, bit. The trees, weakened by the gypsy moth, dug in for cold. The afternoon sky turned clear, so clear that the old people remarked that God was casting his blue eye on the planet and judging all the people.

By five o'clock it was dark.

Alone, in my room, I wept for Theresa Vartyan. Sitting on my bed, hugging my knees, I relived each of the attacker's blows. I imagined the rock and the smell of sour milk mixed with sweat and the cold metal floor of the truck. I imagined his damp fingers on her skin and the wet, sweet blood matting her hair. And I heard the echo of her breath as she was left to die, the inside of the hold dark as a tomb.

I felt responsible for Theresa, not only because I had told the secret of her romance with Bob Humms but because I had seen the milkman that morning, and had lusted for him, making it twice that my filthy desires affected her.

Van, Melanie and I ate Thanksgiving supper with Dad. It was already dark when we got home, and I went directly to my room. Later, Van came to see me and I confessed to him all that was in my heart. My brother's stricken face mirrored my guilt.

"But what about the cops—" Van said, trying reason. "Wouldn't they have questioned this Leon? Sure, they would, a guy like him, working at the dairy, driving one of the trucks? That'd be the first place they'd look."

"What if he slipped by them!" I cried. "What if he did this to Theresa and got away?" I did not confess the other pressing question: What if Leon had seen me first?

Van dialed the phone and held my hand as I told the police about Leon. The officer assured me that they would call if there were any questions.

"What did they say?" Van asked.

I hugged my ribs and sobbed.

PERLA Dairy. PERLA Dairy. The people talked. Many had likewise greeted the milkman that morning dressed in their robes. Children drank the milk that he had delivered. No one could recall seeing the truck later that afternoon. It seemed that the milk truck had been stolen from the lot after five, when the dairy's distribution center closed. The truck's cab had been wiped clean, not a print or clue.

The authorities waited for Theresa to speak. She suffered some neurological damage, which, though slight, included a fair degree of amnesia. She managed to supply the police with only the sketchiest of descriptions, and these changed with her shifting moods. First she said her attacker was "dark," then "ruddy," then "light-light," until the only consistency in her story was the timbre of his voice—"rough," she said, "gravelly."

In homeroom, during the moment of silence, we prayed for Theresa Vartyan. In the afternoon the whole school filed into the auditorium for an assembly that included parents. In the large auditorium, I sat between Dad and Momma, while Van sat apart with his friends. Throughout the proceedings, I braced myself for Momma to cry or create some disturbance, but the gravity of the situation stunned her. When the school psychologist spoke of grief, Momma methodically stroked my arm until the skin became prickly and I had to move.

Afterward, there were two cars to take me home—only I could not make up my mind whom to go with.

"Go with your mother," Dad encouraged.

"You sure?" I asked.

He nodded and, putting his arms around me, gave me a kiss.

Reluctantly I walked over to where Momma was waiting in her car.

She started the motor. "Where to?" she asked, her voice light, companionable. "Where should we go, just us girls?"

"I don't know, Mom. I don't feel much like going anywhere."

"I know." She frowned. "Still, I thought we might take a drive. Do something. I want us to appreciate that we're fine—you're fine. I keep thinking it could have been you. What would I do, then? You didn't know that Mrs. Vartyan and I were in the hospital at the same time having our babies."

"Me and Theresa?"

"Mmm," Momma said.

I considered this information. "I feel so sorry," I said.

Momma adjusted the rearview mirror. "It's this town we should feel sorry for. There's never any good news, is there?"

I hoped she might say something more, something to lighten my burden. Instead, looking in the mirror, she sighed. "Your father looked awful. I told him not to wear red. I told him a hundred times that it washes him out."

"It does not."

She frowned at me. "Of course it does. You saw him."

"So what. What's your point. Who cares if he's washed out? You don't."

"Hey! What's the matter with you!" she said.

"I'm just supposed to agree."

"I never asked for that. What's gotten into you? Are we going to sit here and fight? You can forget that. I'm not Grandma and you're not me. I'd just as soon take you home."

"Fine." I said and leaned back into the seat. "Let's go."

"Seta, why don't we try something—" She turned, giving me her round, dark eyes. "Let's be nice to each other. Can we do that? Can't we go somewhere, just the two of us, and be nice?"

I had no idea where I wanted to go until Momma mentioned

Grandma. "Momma, the place I want to go to, I promise you won't."

"Oh, for Pete's sake. What could be so bad."

"Please, Momma."

"Is it a place you go with Frank? Is it a fooling-around place? Where is it? Is it off the highway? You want me to get on the highway?"

"No."

"Then where?"

"OK, if you're sure," I said, daring her. "I want to go visit Grandma's grave."

We parked under a large tree and climbed up an embankment to the stone. Shrubs had recently been planted on either side of the grave.

"Who put in those?" I asked.

Momma ignored me. Bowing her head, she folded her hands as though in prayer and began to murmur, her head nodding as she took up with Casard where they had left off. Momma paused once, and I knew she was giving her mother time to answer. I left them to their business. There were a few things of my own I had to say.

I was awfully young when Casard was alive. Now I was fifteen, and I did not feel so young anymore. Since Casard's death the members of our family had proved themselves to be no better, no wiser than the people down the street, who Casard always said had no sense. I wondered what she thought of us now. What she thought of Momma, separated from her husband, and of me, a betrayer, standing in a cemetery, talking to a patch of grass. Did Casard see Theresa locked up in the milk truck; did she see Frank and me on the couch in his basement, or Momma with Haig? Did she see Dad in his own apartment and feel glad that Momma had finally rid herself of the odar?

And most of all, what did Casard think of the person I had become and why did she keep haunting my dreams?

It occurred to me that I must have been only five or six years old the first time I closed my eyes and recalled those terrible pictures Casard planted in me at my baptism. We were in her dining room; I trailed behind the hem of her housedress, wanting to grab hold, as she swung through the door of the kitchen. She dragged a chair in front of the ironing board and I climbed up. She began her work; her fist enveloping the iron handle, her blue veins bulging, she hypnotized me with the metronome of her swaying arm. As she ironed, she bent low, and I waited for the moment when her glasses—gray with metal temples and at each end a tiny silver screw—would touch the hot, hot metal.

Casard sang as she ironed, old songs in the old language. She sang of Momma's river. Mother Araxie, blue-green, on its way to the sea, her voice rising and falling like rippled water. After a time, working, puffing, singing, she forgot about the room, and me. I became invisible. And since I was invisible, I was free to stare. I memorized the top of her hair and her glasses and her thick wide shoulder bearing down on the board. Photographs tell that she was actually quite small and trim, but to me she loomed. To me, she seemed as perfect and round as I was inconsequential and skinny. I closed my eyes, and longing to become someone, I became her.

I closed my eyes and saw the child at the river take hold of the woman's hand, then let go. The vision repeated, repeated, repeated, as the kitchen grew hot, as steam from the iron dampened my cheeks.

A cold wind climbed through the cemetery trees. Momma stood beside the grave, her feet apart, as though standing on the deck of a ship. I looked beyond her, toward downtown, where the smokestacks formed walls to the low gray sky. What had this vision in my heart taught me? What about it could I use? Everywhere I looked I tumbled upon perversity: Casard's loop-the-loops, which described the failure of adult lives.

"It isn't fair, is it," Momma said, eyeing me.

"No," I said.

"A long time ago I expected you and I would be different. But no. The daughter must finish the mother's work."

"What is that supposed to mean?"

Momma shook her head, defiant. "If I understood the mess your grandmother left me, then I could tell you. But I don't. Now it's your turn to try. Go ahead and ask her—" She waved at the stone. "Go on, get it over with. Maybe you'll have better luck."

"OK, but stop looking."

"I'll be over here," Momma said as she stepped carefully in her high heels over the grave and up the slope.

I bent down to study the headstone, and using my finger, I traced over Casard's name. I did the same for Vrej because it seemed right, because he was there in the ground with her. His name came first, then Casard's. In between it said, AND HIS LOVING WIFE.

I crossed my arms and stared. Had she been a loving wife? I doubted this, though I believed Casard would have been a fine caretaker, tending to the meals and to the house. But loving? Had she allowed herself to love? The longer I stared at the stone, the less I believed that Grandma Casard would ever have allowed herself to be so vulnerable.

Standing, fists stuffed into my pockets, I said, "I can't."

"Take your time," Momma called, shading her eyes.

"I said, I can't!"

Momma frowned and pointed to the ground. "Then just listen," she offered.

"But I can't hear her!"

Momma shook her head and tapped on her chest. "To yourself. Not at me, to yourself." She turned away.

Sometimes, between shirts, Casard would pause and look me over. I never knew when this might occur, when her eye might rove from the pile of laundry to me. If she found me drifting, she returned to her ironing without a word. But if I looked her in the eye and allowed her to see what was passing through me—the hand letting go—then she would reward me with a story.

Casard sprinkled water on a wrinkled shirt. "This fly-fly-everywhere business. Who needs it? This hurry-up, what's so important?" She touched a finger of spit to the iron. "In Africa they hire grown-up men to carry goods across the desert. These men, they walk with these heavy loads on their backs. Well, hurry-up hurry-up has gotten to Africa too. Their bosses tell the men, 'Walk faster. We'll pay you more just get it there faster.' And so they run, these men, over the desert with great bundles on their backs."

Casard clucked her tongue. "Well, when they get to where they're going they sit on the ground and you can't move them. You can't move them. 'Why don't you get up?' the boss asks. You know what they say? They say: 'Oh, Mr. Boss. We have journeyed great distances very fast. But our souls do not go so fast. It is unsafe for them. We're going to wait here until our souls catch up.' "

She watched my face to be certain that the story had its effect. "See that," she said. "See that. Always be sure to look after your soul."

I looked away from the headstone. "Momma?" I called out.

It was getting dark and she had to squint to make out my face. Had I been closer, I would have heard her murmur, "Mmm?"

"Did Grandma ever tell you about those Africans and their souls?"

Momma swatted the air and said something I could not hear.

"What?" I called, walking toward her.

"I said your grandmother picked that story up from the radio."

"From the *radio*!" I said, incredulous.

"Sure, what difference—" Momma shrugged. "Mayrig probably got it from one of those talk programs she was always listening to. Though after telling everybody, I suppose the story might as well have been hers."

"Why. Why did she tell everybody," I said.

Momma shrugged and began turning in a circle, the way Miss America tested a spot to see if there was room enough for her to lie down. "I suppose it meant something to her," Momma said. "Things were moving too fast for your grandmother. She was getting old and she wanted everybody to slow down."

"That's simple, Momma. God! That's so simple."

Momma's brow arched. "OK. You try."

"What good are you?" I snapped, my mouth bitter. "You can't even answer a simple question. Once you knew. I remember when you knew."

Momma's lips flattened to a seam. "You forget: you were a child. Things always seem bigger to a child. The question is, what do you expect from me now?"

So this was where we had come. I felt an almost irrepressible urge to kick her. "Nothing," I said.

"Yeah?" She laughed. "I should have so many nothings in my pocket."

"You could fix yourself," I said.

"Fix myself! Ha! You make me laugh."

"You mean you won't."

"I mean concentrate on yourself, Seta. You make me so damned tired." Momma swung her arms as if to free herself of excess weight. "Listen. Stop looking to me for everything."

We both knew what was coming next—we looked at each other, and the rage rose up in me and I could not help myself, I had to let it out.

"Momma," I chortled wickedly. "I gave up a long time ago counting on you."

"Oh yeah? Now you're the big judge."

"That's right, Momma."

"Judging my every move."

"You leave no choice."

"You and the rest of them." She nodded. "What have you done that makes you big enough to judge *me*." She flared her nostrils. "You think moony-wishing counts? You're crawling, girl, you got on training wheels. I'm so tired, you three blaming me for what I did to your father, and him letting you go on with that. What left him, huh? You think I left your father? You think *I'm* the one who decided? Answer me." She snapped her fingers.

Hands on my hips, I pretended to look away. "I'm not going to answer that. But if I did, it would certainly be Yes."

"See? Mouth. Him and his bachelor apartment, him and four chairs and a box of oatmeal. You think I'd be content to have three rooms to my name, for crying out loud, all my things in neat-tidy rows? Ugh! Get me out of there."

"So you just quit," I said.

"You shut your mouth. Quit. And I suppose for one minute you'd let me. No. I've got to be a perfect picture for all of you: Momma doesn't do this, Momma doesn't do that, Momma doesn't even clean her closet. You think I don't know when you've been pawing through my things, you think you invented Miss Sneaky? My own wedding dress can't even have a moment alone without *you.*"

There was no stopping her, she was enjoying herself now. She was swaying, the familiar ire passing through her. Cold air brimmed over the hill, air she would use.

"Who do you think you are, coming home and telling me 'Daddy doesn't keep your picture anymore.' A month I've been licking that wound. Well, who do you think you are. Huh? You think you know something? You think you're the only one who knows he keeps me tucked in his bottom drawer. That's right, don't look at me with those saucer eyes, Missy. You asked for it. Let me tell you something: that picture goes out on the bedside table when I come over. That's right—*when I come over.* Your father and I get into that bed and that picture's right beside us. Surprised? Next time you go prissing that lip of yours, you can remember you're no better than those girls at school who won't let you be part of them. They're a pack of bitches—you heard me—I used to worry you'd never see what grace it was that they'd have no part of you. Well, I was wrong. You belong with them. You and those prissy girls high-horsing Theresa Vartyan. It's you who should be ashamed. You're no better. And don't you feel sorry now. Don't you dare feel sorry now."

Clearing her throat, she pointed at the stone next to where we were standing. "Look here. Look at this stone. It says, 'Ani Baboostian.' You remember her? Ani Baboostian was Theresa's grandmother. She was as good as a sister to your grandma. When Mayrig first came here, it was Ani who helped her set up her home. I suppose you didn't know that. Next time you think you're better than the rest of us, go find a mirror. Did Theresa judge her mother? Did she whimper about her lot? Did she betray her friend and tell all the girls something that was no business of theirs or anybody else's? Don't look at me. You think anyone in this town doesn't know from whose mouth that dirty rumor started. Who are you, Seta? Who are you? I can tell you—you're not mine."

"Stop it. Just stop it, Momma." I wept, hating her.

"It's the truth you can't stand. You'd rather stick your nose in dirty underpants."

"Oh, you should talk. Dad only left because you were fooling around. I saw you, wagging your tail. You and Haig."

Her hand glided toward me, I saw the inside of her palm and her gold ring and then I heard the resounding slap. But I did not feel it. "That just goes to show you know zilch," she cried. "You hear me? Zilch."

"This!" And before I could stop myself, I slapped her.

Momma stared at me and rubbed her cheek. The rage had come up in her and by its own force been spent. She was shocked, hollow, the sag evident in her face and dress.

But not me. I was brimming. What was broken could not be fixed, perhaps ever. And I had barely begun. I was dumb, sore like an infected tooth. "Go ahead, Momma. I know what's coming: you're gonna turn your back. That's what you're good at."

"I don't think I like you," she said.

"You're no mother," I replied.

"Oh, for God's sake, Seta. Let me go. I'm so tired of your dozen arms." She cupped her face in her hands. "I can't explain Haig to you. Stop looking for that. You might as well get used to it—I can't explain him." She shook her head at an invisible point. "We share things. Things your father and I never did. Your father thought it was enough to show up and be loyal. But Haig, he takes me—"

"Away," I finished. "He takes you away—from us."

"No!" she cried, stomping her foot; her eyes filled with tears.

"Not you. That—" And waving a limp hand in the direction of Casard, again she cupped her face in her hands.

Some thoughts are too powerful to be spoken, especially in anger. Momma looked up at me with such sorrow that had I been wise, I would have reached over and put my arm around her. Momma had hoped for a grand life—there was nothing wrong with that—but the life she had gone on to make was a terrible disappointment. It was not something you could point to, not one bad incident but a string of thwarted opportunities and missed connections. By Momma's own estimation, she could not afford the sum of such failure.

We stood in the graveyard hugging our coats. I was no longer angry, just sad. I tried to think of a solution, something I could tell her, the way I used to offer suggestions when she got lost driving to the capital. I had wanted us to come to Casard's grave and find peace. But the anger came first and left us spent. It ripped through our bodies, just as the wind rushed down the hill into town. Looking at my mother's face, I saw the sorrow that bound and damned us.

"Momma," I said softly.

She did not move.

"Momma, I didn't mean it about Theresa. You know that. You know I didn't mean it."

"No." She sighed. "We never mean for what happens. We always have something else in mind. We're always going to have a good time."

I nodded. "I feel bad," I confessed, not to her but to myself.

Minutes passed, and then I said, "I've been dreaming a lot about Grandma lately."

Momma nodded. "Me too. All the time."

"What does she want, Momma?"

"Oh"—she sighed, shaking her head from side to side. When she saw me looking at her, she stopped and her round, child's eyes peered into mine, hoping. "Do you remember, when you were just a little baby? She wanted you to find her name."

Looking at Momma, I realized that whatever this name was, she, too, had hoped I would find it and, by doing so, free her.

Suddenly, I realized that Momma had been waiting for me to grow up. Realizing this, I could no longer blame her, nor expect the day to come when she would snap out of it, as if her muted terror were a whim or a passing mood. Momma could not help me with Casard's curses because she was helpless to stave them from herself. And I would end up just like her—alone—unless I chose.

"Momma," I said, "I'm not going to be like you and Casard."

It took her a moment, but finally she nodded.

"Do you understand, Momma? I'm not."

"Mmm," she answered. "I think you're right. Now, what do you say we go back to the car?"

Kna merir yegooz sirem, the old ones said. Go die, come back I love you. The old ones knew that only death makes us truly wise, while mortification teaches us to love, and by loving become new.

As I watched her, Momma mindlessly dug her toe into the hard ground, ruining her shoe. "Hmm? Can we please go to the car?"

When the human heart finds it is about to run out of hope, it madly searches for another guarantee. That night, after we came home, Frank's mother called and invited me for dinner. I accepted eagerly, anticipating the warm hearth, the silver plate and lace tablecloth, the happy family gathered round.

That next evening Frank and I sat in his living room, making small talk with Mrs. Agostini, a plump, handsome woman with dyed auburn hair she teased into a nest on top of her head. When we heard the garage door, we all rose.

"Your father's here," Mrs. Agostini sang. "Here we go." She ushered us into the dining room, where the table was set with linen and silver plate.

"Looks like Rio," exclaimed Frank's little brother, Jake, as he plucked a fork from the table and waved it in the air while doing the shimmy. "Hey! It's a party!"

Mrs. Agostini motioned for Frank and me to take the chairs by the banquette. "Jake," she said, "it's not always Seta joins us." Her smiling gaze turned from me to three large serving spoons set in a tidy row.

"Seta, you like nice things, don't you?"

"Yes, I do."

We took our seats as Mr. Agostini's steps thundered across the kitchen linoleum. Mrs. Agostini gave us each a look to let us know we were in for a big surprise. We all looked to the doorway expecting to find Mr. Agostini, and then we heard the door to the bathroom close. Mrs. Agostini frowned. Clearing her throat, she leaned toward me and whispered, "He likes to wash up before coming to the table."

I nodded to indicate that this was reasonable, this was what all fathers did. Frank held my hand under the table, and then we heard the toilet flush. When, at last, her husband appeared in the doorway, Mrs. Agostini pressed her lips together. "There you are."

"Here I am," he answered, raising glistening fatherly hands for us to see. Mr. Agostini took his seat at the head of the table, and, smiling, gave me a wink. He was a balding man, with a thick, pleasant face and three chins.

"Ah, Seta," Mr. Agostini began, digging a spatula into a dish of lasagna, "help me out here. What do girls eat? Big or small?"

"Give her plenty," Mrs. Agostini answered.

"Medium," I said.

"Don't forget the salad"—Mrs. Agostini waved. "Frank, start the bread."

When everyone had been served, there was nothing left to do but eat.

"Seta?" Mrs. Agostini said. "How's your mother. She getting along all right?" Her brow furrowed. "I think about her."

"She's OK," I said, and to fill the space, I added, "She's very involved at our church." This was a lie, of course, since Momma went to church only on holidays or to pick up Haig, but something in Mrs. Agostini's tone sparked a certain defensiveness.

At the other end of the table Mr. Agostini wiped his mouth.

"She's a beautiful woman, your mother," he said. "Beautiful woman." Mr. Agostini shook his head. "She's held up. Not like the rest of them. No sir. They all look ten years past their age. What a waste."

"Paul—"

"No!" Mr. Agostini insisted. "Don't listen to any of them, Seta. Your mother was the best-looking girl to graduate from that high school. She burned up the place. I was two classes ahead of her. Us boys—cripes—us boys used to stand with our backs to our lockers, taking in the view when she walked down the hall." Mr. Agostini passed his hand through the air to show Momma's parade. "Your father, I tell you, he had more than a few thinking he had caught the cat's meow." Mr. Agostini chuckled.

"Paul, I don't think—" Mrs. Agostini protested.

"What."

"I don't think this is the kind of thing—appropriate—now."

"Oh." He paused. "Oh, you mean"—he puffed his cheeks and fell silent.

We all fell silent, everyone pretending to be deeply interested in the food. I told myself I would not blush—that was something no one wanted.

Frank tried to act upbeat. "It's all right. Seta's mom *is* beautiful. I certainly think so."

"Yes!" Mr. Agostini affirmed.

Across the table his wife said, "Don't bother with him, Seta. Frank's father always liked the ladies. He always did."

"Delicious." Mr. Agostini said and raised his eyebrows as if about to do a trick, and then he shoveled a forkful of lasagna into his mouth.

We all focused on our food, except for Mrs. Agostini; her job was to monitor the meal. Somehow, we had gone off course, and she was doing her best to effect a correction.

"Your father, Seta," Mrs. Agostini began, trolling her spoon in a line beside her plate. "How is he?"

"He's OK. Busy."

"Is that so?"

"He has a lot of prospects, right now. You know, homes."

"Well, that's good. That's very good. Isn't it, Paul?"

Mr. Agostini nodded. "Good for him. I just ran into George the other day at the bank. Nice man. Looks good."

"Oh, they're nice people, Seta. Both your parents," Mrs. Agostini assured me, as if settling a question.

She looked to her husband. "It's such a shame what's happened, Seta. Mr. Agostini and I think it's a real shame. You hear about these things and you wonder what can you do?" Mrs. Agostini thought for a moment. "Seta, we want you to know you're welcome in this house anytime. Anytime. We're glad that you and Frank make such a nice young couple. Don't they, Paul? And we want you to feel welcome anytime. Will you do that? Will you do that for Mr. Agostini and me?"

They were looking at me. Mrs. Agostini's meaning was clear: she had invited the daughter from the broken home for a hot meal and what she asked for in return was assurance that she had done right.

"Seta?" she asked.

"OK," I said.

"Oh, good." She beamed. "Good for us. Frank," she said, "now pass that bread."

After dinner, Frank and I went outside for a walk. It had rained during dinner, and with the temperature falling, the road and sidewalk were a sheet of ice. Frank and I held on to each other as we slipped to the end of the driveway. Frank pulled me to him, his breath white plumes, and drew the wings of his parka around me.

"There," he said, quieting. "Let go of those shivers."

At times Frank spoke to me with a certain authority—the voice of the man he one day pictured himself becoming. At times I liked this older tone, believing it engaged us in a more grown-up exchange. But in other circumstances it irritated me, and I had to tell him to knock it off. Tonight, with my lips resting on his warm neck, I decided to ignore him.

"Frank. Your mother thinks I'm an orphan."

"Shh. Come on, Seta. Don't start," he said.

"No, Frank. She does."

"No." He propelled me toward the house. "Come on, you're freezing. Let's go downstairs."

I walked stiffly to the back door, into the kitchen, then down the cellar stairs. When I reached the bottom, I turned to meet him. "She's right, Frank. I am."

"Come on," Frank said and snapped off the light. "My mother likes you."

The only light left in the room was a dim beam passing from the street through the cellar windows. We blinked as the room slowly revealed itself: the brown sofa, the pool table in the center and, over by the corner, Jake's set of drums.

"Why does she like me, Frank? Because you like me?"

"That's not so bad, is it?" He guided my hands to his back pockets—"I'm gonna especially like these once they're warm." He ran his palms along my arms. "Better?"

"Mmm. Not much."

Frank, determined to keep things moving, led me to the pool table. "Don't worry," he said, hopping onto the table. "I'll be the floor." He spread his jacket over the felt, and then, leaning back, held his arms open for me to crawl inside. I stared at the outline of his body and was amazed at how much, at that moment, I hated him. One minute Frank was great and the next he seemed like the ultimate jerk. I stood over him, waiting for something to say. The whites of Frank's teeth and the stripes in his shirt glowed like X-rayed bones.

"You won't listen to me," I said.

"Yes, I will. Come on, I'll listen." He patted the table. I waited for a wave of good feeling to overcome me, and when it did not, I removed my coat and climbed on top of Frank so we matched, knee to knee, chest to chest. I lifted my head, and peered into his face, which I could hardly see. "Frank, tell me what I'm talking about?"

"What?" He grimaced, dropping his head against the table so I would not be so close.

A siren shot down the road, and for a moment we turned to the window. "I'm talking about me, Frank."

"I'm sure," he said, "your Mom and Dad would appreciate you calling yourself an orphan."

"They know," I said.

"They know?"

"They are too."

Frank sighed and rolled me over so he was on top. He gave me a furtive look. My mood was making him irritable and nervous, and he could not find a way out, short of an argument. He had been patient during dinner, with his mother and me. Now he was searching my face, willing it to open and give him a break.

"What do you see," I asked.

He smiled. "Serious Ates Nool." Then he kissed me, sliding his hands under my shirt. He had made the decision to bulldoze his way through. Unsnapping my bra, he murmured, "You. You," as his fingers walked back down my spine, around my hips, to my zipper.

"Shh," he cautioned, hot breath in my ear, "Seta. You feel my hand? You feel that. That place? There. Wait a sec—there. Your slidey slick bump? Tell me you don't."

"I don't."

"That?"

"Stop—OK?" I pushed him off.

"Christ!" he protested, and hurtled a cube of chalk against the far wall. "What are we doing here, Seta? What am I doing here if you're just gonna go off alone? Answer me."

I got up on my knees and faced him. "You never listen, Frank. All dinner you're quiet as a mouse. You let her talk to me that way. Why would you let her talk to me that way?"

"Oh, is that it. All right. Here's what I won't listen to. You say you're an orphan. Well, I don't buy it. I think it sucks what's going on at your house, but that doesn't make you an orphan. And I don't understand why if you feel so alone, you can't trust me. I tell you I love you. You say you do back. What's the problem? Why can't we just be together and you trust me?"

I paused. "Because your mother and father are condescending idiots."

"Fine." He chortled. "That's great. That's a beaut. Now what. Huh, Seta Loon? If I'm going to be judged by my parents, what does that say about you?"

Smiling, I nodded. "Exactly. Now you've got it."

His brow knit with confusion. "This makes no sense. Seta, this makes no sense."

"Frank, my mother still sleeps with my father. Do you understand. She goes over to his apartment—she told me this—and after all that's happened she fucks him."

"So?"

"So? You ask 'So?' " I cried.

"What does that have to do with us—" He shook his head with confusion.

"Think about it," I said, and zipping my pants, I fell back on the table like a corpse. Another fire truck roared past the house, its strobe pulsing red across our faces and the dark paneled walls.

Frank gazed at the window. "What do you bet another drunk crashed at the reservoir," he mused.

"Yes," I said, crossing my hands over my chest to monitor my beating heart.

"Seta, you forget—" Frank began. "Your Dad. Maybe it's him who fucks *her*."

"What's that supposed to mean."

"It means there's two of them, Seta. What they've got is between them. You don't know, so how can you judge. Maybe this is just their way of working it out."

I brought my face close to his. "What about Haig, huh, Frank? What about Mr. Haig."

His pupils ticked back and forth, studying me. A smile ripened on the salesman's lips. He tasted the word before pronouncing "Goof."

"Goof!"

"Yeah. He's a goof."

"You're crazy, Agostini," I said, swatting him.

Frank beamed. "Dropped my watch in water for you."

"For you."

"No. You." He pulled me to him.

We began to wrestle, gripping, pulling, rolling like a sack of potatoes on the pool table. When we neared the rim, Frank sank his weight onto me and the balls in the well below knocked together, a sound much like elements shifting deep in the ground. Frank kissed me and I imagined I heard him whisper, All the way.

"OK," I said.

Frank froze, unsure. So I guided his hand. That first time, it was like this: Frank filling the shallow bowl, while in the dim light we looked into each other to see if it worked, if it was good. We were solemn, we were tender, we were pioneers. And it did not hurt the first time, not like they tell you, but was as smooth as the back of your hand between the knuckles, the place you kissed not knowing why.

After, we curled like spoons on the bed of coats.

"Agostini," I murmured, stretching the syllables of his name. "A-a-gos-t-i-ni. How long have you been carrying around that rubber?"

In my back I felt him smile. "Not long."

"How?"

"Since I was twelve."

"Twelve!" I howled. We fell quiet then, smiling, thinking our own private thoughts that had to do with not waiting anymore. My mind flashed on all kinds of things, and then, briefly, I thought of Casard.

Frank primly kissed my hair. "Sweet."

I popped his pinky from my mouth. "Frank. Remember the fire downtown?"

"Mmm. You mean D and L's?"

"Yeah. Did you see it?"

"My father and I parked on the hill and watched it from the truck."

"Those sirens reminded me. We drove to see it too."

We had stood—Van, Melanie, Dad, Momma and me—with the crowd on the grass divider next to Squaw. Everyone was silent, transfixed by the awesome spectacle of flames and black serpentine smoke. The fire, greedy as a mouth, leaped from D&L's department store to the bank, its illumined tongues scouring the walls and ground for food. When it became unbearably hot, the crowd moved back, but one man refused to budge. He grabbed the arm of the woman standing next to him. "I have money in there," he said, waving at the bank. "There's our money. Look at it now."

It took all night to contain the fire, and when it was over, three city blocks were gone.

"What did you think of that fire?" I asked Frank.

He licked my ear. "Not better than this. Why? What did *you* think."

I closed my eyes, trying to recall what it was I could not grasp. I recalled the embers and the heat rising like soapy film in front of my face. We had hugged each other—Melanie, Van and I—as the walls of the buildings popped like kindling. When we returned home, the phone was ringing. I answered it, but before I could say anything, Casard cried, "I couldn't find you. Are you all right? I couldn't find you."

"Grandma?"

"Honey, put your mother on the phone."

Momma got on the phone and the two of them digested the fire, embellishing, gasping at the spectacle. At the end of the call Momma said in Armenian, "You're all right? You sure? Mayrig, I love you. You know, Mayrig." Then Momma nodded, as Casard said it back. They never used such words, except for funerals and near misses. Only then was it safe. The two of them hunched over the phone, exaggerating the danger, feeding on it, the way the fire took air and wood into its hungry mouth.

Frank asked again, "What about the fire?"

I rolled over to look at him and smiled. "It made me think: I wish I had a lover. I wish I had a lover. I wish I had a lover and he loved me."

At midnight I went home to soak in the tub. Afterward I climbed into bed, my skin steamy and pink, and drifted off into a delicious sleep, where Casard found me.

"Seta," she whispered. "My Seta, come here."

She lay in the mahogany box—her pearls, her best blue dress, her black tie shoes.

"Closer," she murmured. "Show your face."

I crept slowly, with reverence, to her satin bed. The inside of my face was peaceful and serene. Kneeling on the wooden pew, I peered into the coffin.

Her secret braid was longer than any of us had imagined. It dropped past her knees, curling, at her shoes. The secret hair inside her bun was not gray, as I had supposed, but black and luminous, the hair of a young girl.

"I'll tell you once more," she began, "but you must promise not to judge." She peered inside me, her gaze steady and unwavering.

I reached and touched a finger to her long, thick braid.

She smiled. "I held you in the church. You were just a baby. Now you're as old as those other girls."

"Yes, Grandma. I remember them."

"Those girls the Turks hung by their braids. What were their names?"

"Ani, Shushan, Chortz, Nevart," I said. "And the other one—"

"Jilla," she said. "It was Jilla."

She paused, her eyes lit like beacons. "What's my name!" she cried. "*My* name!"

I stroked her braid, trying to calm her. Her intensity frightened me and I wanted her calm. "I know," I said. "At the river—you couldn't help it—you let go."

"Yes!" she cried, amazed. "And all these years, cursed!"

"No," I said, looking at her, seeing that she was just a tiny, tiny baby.

"Oh, yes, cursed," she whined. "My own Araxie thinks I abandoned her. Look at her, so troubled. I see her struggle; ah, on this side I see too much. Maybe she was right, marrying outside. I could never allow her, though. Her with him and then you babies, so beautiful. But me, I could never touch Araxie. We had the river between us, don't you see? That curse. My beautiful, beautiful girl. What a waste I made. I could give her nothing." Casard tucked her chin and sobbed.

"Medz-mayrig?"

She sniffed, her voice squeaky and childish. "Medz-mayrig you say?"

"Yes." I paused, and speaking firmly, added, "What do you want?"

She closed her eyes and began to unwind her secret braid, her fingers darting nimbly like knitting needles. Her lips quivered with all that was said and unsaid. At last she spoke. "You. You."

I awoke to find that I was shivering. I yanked at the covers and, wrapping them around me, pulled my knees to my chest. Slowly, I rocked. OK, I said to myself, Here you are in your room, it's OK. I tried to forget about Casard and recall what had happened earlier, with Frank. But Casard and the dream pulled at me. And so I rocked as, first, panic, then utter calm passed through my bones. Waiting for one or the other to take hold, a thought came to me that seemed remarkably clear: in spite of all that had happened, Casard was right to let go of her mother's hand; letting go was what any reasonable person would do.

Lying in the dark, I found myself greatly relieved. Of course she had been right; it was so obvious. Suddenly, I felt light-headed and giddy. What a night: first Frank, then this. Grinning, I felt oddly at peace. This golden light, I thought. This wonderful, wonderful life.

Happy images skittered through my mind, and then my thoughts turned to Theresa. I saw her playing the duduk: her face singular and true, like her note. It occurred to me that I wanted to do something for her. I wanted to give her a gift. I lay awake for another hour, trying to think what that gift could be, and then it came to me: with her mother gone, I would bring Theresa food.

On the first of December, Theresa returned home from the hospital. The attacker had left her for dead, but with physical therapy her body would heal. Theresa's soul was a different matter.

I arrived, as the old ones would, wearing wool. I stood in the driveway waiting for a sudden compulsion to propel me up the steps. When none came, I set the basket of canned tomatoes and corn, sliced roast beef, bread and chocolate bars in the grass alongside the shrubs. Then I turned away and went home.

For seven days and seven more I attended to Theresa's care and feeding. Each morning, before school, I rode the public bus to her house and dropped food into the basket. I gave her all the flavors I could think of: savory, salt and bitter. For sweet I gave her chocolates and hard candies, and then I went hunting for something sour.

I rode my bicycle to Casard's. After she died, Dad sold the house to a Puerto Rican family with five children. Poppee said she would never forgive him for selling Casard's house to lowlife. The havoc that family had wreaked in four short years was certainly evident from the road. Boxes, metal scraps, rusted car parts and other miscellaneous junk lay piled in heaps in the garage and along the front porch. The flower beds were full of litter, broken twigs and leaves. But the final blow was the birds—they had vanished. The multitude of winged creatures that had once splashed in Casard's birdbaths and nested in her trees—the wren, the jay, the oriole, the cardinal and the sparrow—all had taken flight. It was quiet along the street.

I parked my bike in the driveway, and since the house seemed empty, I strolled into the backyard, not a little curious to see whether I would find my grandfather hiding in the lemon tree.

To my amazement, the tree had flourished, despite the absence of Casard's digging rituals and fervent prayers. It had grown half again as large in four years. Because it was December the tree was without fruit. I clipped just a thin branch, and finding neither my grandfather nor any other sign of welcome, I hurried away.

I rode quickly back to Theresa's, carrying the branch aloft. By the time I reached her yard I had decided to plant the branch in the hard caked dirt behind the garage, where I first saw Theresa with Bob Humms. Why not, I thought, why not? And retrieving Casard's trowel from my basket, I dug a hole and covered the branch with frozen dirt.

I did not linger; I did not ring the bell. I gave Theresa privacy with both hands, as Casard had taught me. Standing over the uprooted mound, I made a brief wish regarding Theresa's soul, which I saw as round, with many chambers, similar to a hive.

I left the yard feeling cleansed, buoyant. As I rode home I thought of Theresa and of my grandmother, who loved her. I recalled the time I went to the house with Casard and met Mrs. Vartyan, and then she and Theresa had played the duduk. It was the first I could remember spending time with Theresa, though now that I thought about it, there were other occasions, too. Those Sunday mornings, beginning when we were five, we threaded single file past the vats and stainless-steel sinks of the Armenian church kitchen, down a narrow corridor lined with paintings of grimacing kings and pale priests, to Grandma Casard's Sunday school classroom.

The room was small, with a window in the back and a blackboard in the front. Five wooden benches lined the room. I sat in the first row; Theresa waded to the back, to the bench no one raced for because it was hers.

We began each class by reciting the numbers in Armenian: *Meg, Yergu, Yereg.* Casard led the count from one to one hundred, as we followed along, droning like bees. Each time we stumbled over a hard consonant or gaping vowel, Casard corrected us, enunciating the language that always made me think of hands in rich dirt.

We droned on—except for Theresa, who refused to speak. Only her eyes participated in the lesson. Round and silent, they roved the classroom, focusing on parts. First they landed on Joanie Hosepian's mole, making the girl itch; then, on Casard's gold rabbit brooch; and finally, they focused on the heel of my shoe.

Casard addressed Theresa by her Armenian name. "Shushan. Repeat after me the days of the week: Ger-a-gee, Yer-goo-shap-tee, Ye-rek-shap-tee. . . ."

We swiveled in our seats, not wanting to miss Theresa's latest stunt. There was no telling what she might do. That day she was ignoring us, but another day it was something else. She trained her sloe-black eyes on the pin anchored to the teacher's breast.

Theresa shifted her gaze, narrowing on Casard's mouth. She fixed it there for an obscenely long time, until it seemed that she had explicitly stated, Teacher, you have a very wet mouth.

Casard's tongue darted from its chamber and the class broke out in giggles. Casard ignored us. Peering lovingly at the girl in the back row, she asked in a soft, girlish voice, "Shushan? Inch ga chi ga?" What's new?

Theresa stared assiduously at Casard's mouth and refused to answer. Casard gave her more of our time. This time we had earned by mouthing silly foreign phrases while the backs of our thighs scratched against our crinoline slips. We had been good and for our goodness had to endure our teacher's attention being doled out to another.

"Shushan, inch ga chi ga?" Casard implored.

Theresa's gaze fell dramatically to her lap, where all her fingers had twined themselves into knots.

"Shushan?"

"Pan chi ga"—the girl said: Nothing. And with this declaration she tore her fingers apart to reveal something hidden in her palm. A pink spotted seashell dropped to her lap—the kind of shell one could put to one's ear and hear the ocean.

Her greedy eyes had taken our time, our teacher's attention, and to this she added the miracle of a shell. How it got there, from what ocean, from what adventure, she would never think to share, and we would never ask.

Sitting in my plaid navy dress, fresh from beating Van to the car and thereby capturing the window behind Momma all the way to church, wearing a bracelet of cheap gold with two charms—a skate and an otter—I thought I was better than Theresa, simply because I fit in. I could not have known then how much we were alike. Two girls, one in front, one in back of Mrs. Essayan's classroom.

I stowed my bike in the garage and went inside, then up to my room. Closing the door, I reached into the closet and took down the box of gifts I kept hidden on the shelf. That morning, as usual, I found the basket in the grasses near the shrubs, exactly where I had left it. In the bottom she had placed a lock of her hair. There were other gifts, too. During the two weeks, she proffered a slip of lace, a small soap, a comb, ribbons, a dried rose and, the day before, a foot from her lavender hose. Theresa scented these treasures with herbs: rosemary, basil, cinnamon, clove. I believed she intended them as keepsakes, and so I saved them in a box on my closet shelf. Whenever I felt inclined, as I did then, I took down the box and counted my gifts.

Momma was rarely home. She would return just before dinner, breathy and spent. We stepped around her, granting her the room one extends to the afflicted, so as not to disturb, so as not to touch. As revenge, we dubbed her condition with his name. "She's Haiged." Or, "Don't bother her, she's on a Haig."

Dust balls ran like miniature tumbleweed in the foyer. The next morning, a Saturday, Momma was in the kitchen by nine o'clock. I came downstairs to find her with Casard's box of recipes open on the counter and each burner on the stove covered by a simmering pot. She was dressed in slacks and slippers that looked like ballet shoes and an old white apron with blue lace trim.

"Look at this," I said, lifting the lids to find pilaf and kuftah soup. "Would you look at this?"

She was rolling dolmas on the counter. "Do me a favor," she answered. "Open up the oven and check on the meat."

"What is all this, Momma? What's it for?"

"Church."

"There's something going on at the church?"

"Don't be ridiculous," she playfully scolded. "If you thought about it, you'd know. Tonight? The supper to raise money for Theresa's hospital bills?"

"What supper. There's a supper?"

She lifted a lid on a pot. "Stand back. Can't you see I'm busy? I've got to hurry, get this done before I'm too tired and have to sit down."

"Are you tired now?"

She eyed me carefully, considering the offer. "Don't you have plans with Frank?"

"No," I said. "Not until one."

When Van drifted downstairs at eleven, he found the two of us bent in silent communion at the kitchen table, our hands rolling hatsig dough. He stood in the doorway watching. We glanced at him once, then returned to our work, rolling and knotting the dough. We placed the rolls on cookie sheets and left them to rise. When they were ready for the oven, we brushed their tops with egg, then sprinkled black and white sesame seeds over them.

Van watched, his arms folded, a curious smile on his lips. He was unsure of what to make of this irregularity, this curious normalcy that had entered his house. It was perplexing, possibly a new kind of feminine ploy. Then again, he felt left out. "Where's Mel?" he asked.

Momma and I looked up, surprised to find him still standing there.

"At the Y," I said.

"You want to pick her up?" Momma asked, eyeing him, though her hands never stopped moving.

"What time?"

"Noon."

"OK," he answered. "Sure." Thus released, he lunged toward the refrigerator. "I'm starving," he said.

After Van left, Momma and I fixed kebob sandwiches and ate them at the table. Except for practical exchanges regarding the meal, we never spoke. What there was to say had already passed between us. When I left at one, she was in bed, exhausted. Archie would come by later and pick up the food and bring it to the church.

In the evening, Momma had a date with Haig. She floated down the stairs like a lounge singer in a silk dress. Haig kept the engine running and tooted the horn, and when she approached the car, he walked over to her side and handed her in.

That night, Van, Melanie and I returned from our separate evenings and watched the late movie in the den. At one o'clock Melanie gave up and went to bed. At one-thirty Momma waltzed through the front door, breathy and excited. She placed a program, flattened like a keepsake, by her purse.

Van retrieved it from the table in the foyer. "What is this. You didn't go to the church supper, did you? You went to the symphony! Seta, look at this. She went to the goddamn symphony."

Van shook the incriminating evidence.

"Oh, Van," she said, "you remember." Her eyes, bright as sequins, her pink dress matching her frosted lips.

"Van," I cautioned.

"Stay out," he barked.

It was too much to ask of Van to understand the business with Haig. Nearly every night Haig pulled up in his car and collected our mother and never once did she speak his name or bring him in the house for an introduction. This way, Haig was forced to the shadows of Van's imagination.

We were all standing there in the kitchen when the phone began to ring; Van fumed at the clock.

Momma caught the phone on the second ring and laughed into the receiver. "Yes," she said, "oh yes, what a good time."

"Who's that?" Van barked.

"Oh, Van," she called over her shoulder, the pearl earrings Dad had given her dangling from her lobes.

"Who—"

She paused, looking at Van, trying to think of what to tell him. "Archie, all right? Can Archie call me now or since when has that become a crime?"

"Liar!" Van hissed.

She held out the phone. "Fine," she said. "See for yourself."

"Oh, come on," he grimaced, stalking to the phone. "Hello?" he barked. And when he heard the voice on the other end, my brother's face pinkened, and I thought he was going to cry. "Dad?" he said. "Is that you?"

Christmas trees filled the bay windows along our street. Night closed like a drawer after school. In another week the sun would reach the nadir of its southerly decline, dropping to a longitude of 270 degrees. The winter solstice, which marked the darkest day of the year, would also mark the beginning of the sun's northerly climb to longer days of light.

One night Frank and I rummaged in his garage and found the cans of spray paint he had used to paint his valentines to Seta Loon. We stowed them in his mother's trunk and drove to the reservoir. And clutching each other, we skated across the black ice. When we reached the round house, we tried the door and found it locked. We circled the foundation, stopping at LULU SUCKS; we obliterated the words with paint. Then Frank handed me the can. "What are you going to write?"

I shrugged. "Theresa's name, I guess."

He put his hand out to stop me. "Not her name. Do something

else. Something, you know, in code, that only she'll understand."

I thought about it for a minute, and then a picture Mrs. Vartyan had in her living room came to mind, the one of the twin-capped mountain in Armenia. Carefully I spelled out the words FREE ARARAT. Frank gave me a puzzled look. "Don't worry," I said. "She'll know."

Then taking Frank by the hand, I led him to the window of the round house. Frank smashed the glass and we climbed into the small space inside, and laying down our coats, we made love on the cement floor.

Later that night, on the library wall and on an overpass leading to the capital, we wrote: FREE ARARAT.

That weekend Dad and I rode under the overpass on our way to a fancy dinner in the capital.

"What do you think of that," he asked.

I shrugged. "What do you think?"

"Probably the work of some zealot, or a kook." He cleared his throat. "You know, in Canada, a couple of Armenian nationalists recently shot the Turkish ambassador." He shook his head. "I don't deny they have cause. But killing Turks, what good can that do?" He nodded at the windshield. "I don't know about you, but I don't care much for vandals, either."

I shrugged, keeping my eyes on the road.

My father, thinking that talk of vandals and murderers disturbed me, patted my leg. Dad wanted us to pass quickly through the disagreeable parts of our lives, relegating them to the back of our minds, thus freeing ourselves for better times.

"Why don't you find something on the radio?" he said.

I pushed the buttons until I found a song we could both agree on. A Joni Mitchell tune. Joni's lilting voice relaxed Dad, clearing the words on the overpass from his mind. But Free Ararat I would not forget. Smiling, I closed my eyes and gave myself over to the locomotion of the car.

• • •

On the night of the solstice I rode my bike to Theresa Vartyan's. I had fed her body, I had prayed for her soul. Now it was time to claim her.

In the yard I paused, to see if she would come out on her own. The front door and all the blinds were closed. I walked over to the shrubs and found the basket; in the bottom, she had left one of the duduks. I picked it up; the instrument was freezing cold. Warming it in my hands, I carried it with me to the front door.

I turned the handle, it was unlocked. I went into the dark living room and, standing still, gave my eyes time to adjust. Everything was much the same: the religious paintings on the walls, the carved wooden tables, the picture of Mount Ararat, the photographs of Theresa. I raised the duduk to my lips. Noise erupted: ugly, blunted sounds, sharp as a goose's honk. I tried several times, until finally I was able to produce one clean blast.

Climbing the stairs, past the portraits of the saints, I let my instincts guide me. I went down the hall to the farthest door and opened it. Books, leather-bound and paperback, lined the walls of the room, and more books were piled on the floor. In the center, there was a walnut library table with a thick leather-bound atlas set open, its binding split in half. From the bulb in the ceiling hung a large globe. The room was filled with a golden haze. Theresa lay on a cot in the corner, curled toward the wall.

I walked over and took her hand. Without a word she floated to her feet and went with me, down the hall and the stairs, past the relics of Mary and Jesus.

When we reached the living room, she kicked open the front door and inhaled the icy, salubrious air. On the stoop, she glanced at the neighboring houses, and at the cloudless sky and the bare branched trees. I handed her the other duduk and she took up the instrument and breathed into it.

This was the second time I heard her play; only this time, instead of the solitary note, Theresa chose the melody.

On the front steps she began to dance the shourchbar, the circle dance we had learned as children. Raising her palms to the sky and lifting her heels, she danced around me, smiling through her funny gapped teeth. A long scar ran across her forehead and a bandage covered the top of her head where her hair had been shaved. I reached into my back pocket, took out a rumpled Kleenex and handed it to her. She pinched the white tissue between her thumb and forefinger, and dangling her wrist, she danced: the official leader.

We are never more ripe than beginners nor wiser than fools. Watching her, the two of us bathed in golden light, I knew that Theresa and I were always meant to dance the shourchbar, the circle that is death and birth. When we were children, we understood this: in the schoolyard we played ring-around-a-rosy and duck, duck goose, circle games in which the beginning promises the end.

It was not so late. We were young, though in some ways, at fifteen, we would never again be so old. At fifteen, we could see the past behind us, and in front of us the future. In our bodies we were girls and yet we were grown. And in our dreams we drew wisdom from old ladies and made love to faceless men. Wild, delirious, triumphant, we laughed like women and danced like girls.

Later, we became aware that we were being watched from behind the shrubs, and so we went inside. As we stepped into the house the air we left was replete with mumbling and muted sighs.

It was the elders, of course, their curiosity compelling them to see for themselves what other tricks destiny had planned for Theresa Vartyan. This was their sport: to watch the future unfold. They had studied the signs that spring, beginning with the gypsy moth; Poppee had come to the house to tell Momma she smelled death. Poppee knew something had to die but she did not know what. The elders endured a relentless summer and a colorless fall, waiting for that evening, when they would lean forward in their chairs, as the white whir of the milk truck passed by carrying Theresa Vartyan. They did not see her, of course, but in their bones they felt a change. They would not for anything miss her rebirth.

We went into the house, while behind us we heard fluttering, like the flapping of wings, and then whooping and patting hands.

We stood in the living room facing each other, while all that had happened in our time and in the time before us passed through our bones.

Later, as I said good-bye, I turned to her. "*Anooshig,*" I said, Pretty, returning to her what she once gave me.

Theresa laughed, tipping her head back to reveal a neck of rubies.

And turning, turning, I went back to my room, climbed into bed and closed my eyes. I was no sooner asleep than the women came to me. There was Poppee, Archie, Auntie Vart and Auntie Sarah; there was Aunt Sue and the slave girl Ani Baboostian; and there was Momma, Sweet-Rueful Momma. There were the women from church and about town, each dressed in a bright colored robe. The Italians, blacks, Puerto Ricans, Irish, Poles, Chinese, and Jews walked on together, a veritable parade. The Armenians approached like floats, with their red lips, their flying-buttress noses.

The ritual was a solstice rite of absolution. On this night the women gave me a new story, not of Indignities, not of shame, but a story for the day after the solstice, for the journey back to light.

I followed them, fortified by their strength. They walked, heads high, their knowledge pulled up from their bellies, and the wisdom of their ancestors and their children and their men. We walked together, on the longest night of the year, to Squaw, and assembled at her hem, wet-eyed, nervous as goats.

Downtown was deserted, just a few cars parked in front of the bank. Plastic wreaths and Christmas lights winked from the telephone poles around the center square. The streetlamps illuminated the sides of the buildings, while over our heads, the statues shone like mythic constellations, stark and white as bone.

I could barely move, the crowd burgeoning. Then the women began to speak.

"There was the river. The Euphrates."

"We went down into the water where we could not breathe."

"We had nothing to eat, not even a potato."

"Is this all, is this what I asked for?"

"The soles of our feet bled. Our rags were not enough to cover our bodies. Under the sun we were—indecent."

"Dignity, that is what it comes down to."

"You had none. Your mother neither. For her it was not an option."

"I am a shard of her life. A tiny piece."

"When are you going to be free of her, when are you going to let go?"

"But my mother said 'No!' At the river, Mayrig refused. Her refusal is something I must carry. The shame."

"She wanted to live!"

"Why? Why did she want to live?"

"Because it is what you do—whether you have everything or nothing—it is your job. For the children you live and you make the house round."

"I hurt her."

"Of course you did."

"And then?"

"That's for you to decide. When are you going to get on with it?"

"I am."

"Not until."

One voice spoke above the others: "Over the bridge the Unborn will rise, she will conduct a symphony." The women turned toward the voice and found Theresa.

"Oh, not her. She's crazy," someone said.

"Quiet. Let her speak."

"I'm not going to listen to her crazy talk. She wasn't there."

"Shut your mouth. Let her speak."

"No. She is dangerous, that one. So free."

Theresa continued: "The river bends low at its seam. We will thrive there. We will float on the backs of the animal. Come. My kerchief, my bit of dress will raise us. You'll see, we will float like the music."

"And then?"

"Yes, tell us."

"Then we'll rise."

I knelt in Squaw's shadow and spread the box of treasures Theresa had given me at Squaw's feet. The elders stood back to show respect. They winked at each other as I put Theresa's lace in Squaw's Bible, wrapped Theresa's ribbon at Squaw's feet, and scented Squaw's ragged hem with a rose. As I moved around the statue, I recited these words: "The daughter assumes what is unfinished in her mother's life. The unanswered questions become her work. She spins, turning the questions upon herself. Generation after generation, it is a spiraling."

The women stood by me in a circle. One by one the elders approached, to touch my face. "How much longer," they murmured, "till it's done?"

I awoke, the streetlamp lighting my room. Momma was sitting in the chair by the windows.

"I heard you," she said, coming closer. She sat on the bed and peered into my face, her expression curiously serene.

"Momma, I dreamed—"

"Yes?"

"I dreamed about Theresa and me. And Poppee and Archie and you—"

"Shh, now. I'm right here."

At that moment, looking at Momma, I knew. "Momma?"

"Hmm, Seta-Sue?"

"I think I found Grandma's name."

Momma leaned over me, her face pale. She bent so close her sweet breath passed between us. And though we were both smiling, our eyes brimmed with tears.

"*Garod,* Momma. It's Garod."

She thought about it for a moment and then she nodded. "Yes," she said, rolling her lips and closing her eyes. Sighing deeply, she pressed her palm to her belly and breathed. "Oh yes. Of course. Yearning—Garod."

• • •

I see that night: Momma perched on my bed, as she was the night Casard died. On both occasions I recall Momma's shoes, the buttons of her dress, and my own face mirrored in hers, pale and utterly serene. Both nights were preceded by an eerie calm that made a hallowed place of my room, the way an empty church draws one inside to find comfort in what is incomprehensible and vast, and, in that vastness, be hushed. This calm, illumined space between what we know as earth and what we assume is spirit was with me that night. And I saw my tiny inward life draw away, and in its place was choice: there was the path Momma and I knew, and over by the window, escape. Did Momma know? Did she feel the rise in her heart like a lifting bird?

With Casard, we had not looked for joy, so joy we did not see. But the night of the solstice, as I spoke her name, it was as if I had known this joy forever. I spoke the word and the dry, velvety hands around me loosened, releasing a tremendous weight, until I thought I would cry out, Oh that is what it was! Momma, look: all this time, hands. Yet, I did not cry for fear the hands might change their course and descend upon me like a noose.

But oh, when they lifted, that was freedom. My hair spilled from its clasp as the cool weights dropped from my shoulders and limbs, as a great maw rose from my chest like a universal heaving. Finally, there remained just a circlet of thin, translucent fingers clinging to my ankle like a garland of leaves. When these gave too, I knew I could fly, I knew I must.

I had done my work, I had given Casard her name. And I was still young, still virtually new. Yearning was the word and by sending it out into the world, by speaking the very name, its power over me was released.

I reached for the window and Momma murmured, "There you go."

What were her words anyway but permission? She might have said nothing, or denied the vision, or attempted to pull me back. But hers was a generous heart, whose dreams had inspired and damned her to a life unfulfilled. By naming Casard I named the thing that had brimmed in Momma, too, the thing so obvious we could never see it. She whispered, "There you go, Seta-Sue. There you go!"

With her blessing I slipped through the fenestra where all things become desire, and all desires locomotion. Any flight would do: a fast car, a nameless man, days and nights replete with humidity, a slip of feeling, wind. I measured my life by the quickening of my heart and the reckless dizzying pace. Years would pass before I proved to myself and to Momma just how well I could take back the dozen arms she hated, how willfully and finally I could pluck them from her, one by one.

I would travel far, but Memorial would always follow me. Only a fool thinks she can leave behind what has come before. We are of a knit. We are, as Poppee said, bound of the same thread. Mother begets daughter, father begets son; on a Naugahyde couch two teenagers hump and grind, thereby discovering the strings, which for countless generations have pushed and tugged at the species since we were swimmers in the sea, our gills and our fins.

Before I ever was a seed in Momma's womb, the women of the church prepared me, as they prepared the lavash and hatsig rolls in their white floured palms. I was then and am now their Armenian girl. The men and women with their sad, croaky tunes of deeds and misfortunes, massacres and floods, kneading their bread and counting their sheep; the innocent boys, the girlish brides arriving in the new land, with its factories; my grandfather moiling on the assembly line, a necktie the emblem of his pride. The music of this tone-deaf choir no car can outdistance, no anonymous fucking can quell. The weary, arthritic men need only murmur in their armchairs late on a summer afternoon, or wipe their galoshes on a mat in the hall, or tap a razor against the steamy surface of a porcelain sink; or the women let go a sigh from deep in their bosoms, or carry a platter of meat to the table, or place a cool palm on a child's sweaty neck, or hoist tired stocking feet onto the rung of a kitchen chair, or lick their fingers to tame their man's hair with spit and they pull me back, marionette on strings, so I might be going about some business in my new life, say, walking to my car, or in the drugstore aisle buying shampoo, and way a ways in Memorial they give a gentle tug and, far away in the aisle of shampoos, the bottom drops out of me, and the River, that riparian ache that is in me always and forever begins rising, just as it did when Seta, the first, felt her dress rise over her head, as she dropped under the muddy water like a stone, and Yearning, Yearning is her name.

Epilogue: Unborn

The old ones find me before the airplane from California touches ground. I am flying over New York, on my way home. "Here she is," they murmur, "look at that." They assembled at my leaving, and now at my return. "That was some trip," they say, of the fifteen years since I first left Memorial for college. "She's no longer young."

I have come as soon as I felt able, with a little extra in my heart to spend. I have a new life now, rich with possibilities and joy. I have good work, life with a good man, and friends, all of whom I bring with me, folded in my pocket like policies of insurance. I have brought my new life to show to the old, and when I feel afraid or stuck, I will take my lover, Lou Prince, from my pocket and remember what we say when we first awaken and the rich smell of our life, which draws me home at night.

For Momma—it seems so little—I am wearing a dress. It is a floaty number Lou bought me, liking the way it cups my breasts, then sets off on a gentle swoon above my knees. The dress is green with gold buttons, and each time I wear it Lou swears I do the walk of the goddess.

It is afternoon, they are having tea. Rose-milk hands cradle cups and saucers in a living room where the sun's rays are mitigated by ivory lace and mauve damask curtains. Poppee, the left side of her face slack with palsy, tips forward in her seat. The others bend toward her, spokes to hub. As Casard's oldest friend, Poppee will speak my story. Slowly, deliberately, she begins.

"*Gar oo chugar,*" she says. There was and there was not.

"There was Seta Loon, born in Memorial, daughter of George and Araxie Loon, granddaughter of the late Vrej and Casard Essayan. On the other side, Theodore and Bette Loon, also deceased. The child was odar, on the father's side.

"She was George and Araxie Loon's second, their first girl. She was an unremarkable child, special only to the ones who knew her well. Hers would not be the first face you would find in a room. But speak to the child and you would notice those two black eyes, pinning you, memorizing your clothes, your face, the blemish on your forehead.

"Such intensity in a small child is difficult—Seta always worried me. The tragic accident which killed our dear friend Casard Essayan, God rest her soul, occurred when the child was eleven. Casard favored Seta but she did not have time to finish with her."

The plane banks north over Long Island Sound. Perhaps I have come too soon. It has been fifteen years and the place still haunts me. I have promised myself that by coming to Memorial I will not regress; yet, as I fly over, the muted colors of New England pull at me and make me small.

We are flying over houses where children will grow up having to wish for things to happen; they will play their games in fenced yards that mark the modest dimension of their elders' lives. We are passing over shady trees, then downtown, where the stores and post office border a central patch of well-tended lawn. I see that this town, too, has a monument, a soldier on a horse. The soldier is the man of honor, the man whom the children once yearned to become. Now he is out of place. From high up on his steed he is meant to look out over the new, promised land, but in fact what he sees are abandoned warehouses and railroad yards, a chain-link fence running the length of the tracks and, beyond, a field of poison sumac and scrub. His view is of weeds growing brilliant and lush in the yellow, yellow sun.

My heart cramps. It occurs to me that I am looking at a town on the other side of celebration, and that, by the measure of the great civilizations, two hundred years is an awfully short time to verge on collapse.

"Seta Loon," Poppee continues, "turned thirty-three last month. She has reached an age of no significance, in the store there are no special, funny cards for her. She is on the other side of potential now, where everything counts. Enough with her search, her relationships, her schooling. She has sampled life from her generation's fancy buffet. She has abandoned her good instincts and her home for yet another experience; another morning she wakes up and finds herself uncertain of what room she's in, what bed.

"But Araxie tells us that Seta has now put an end to such activity. She has scrubbed that tired skin and started new. Yet she continues to live far from home. So and so. Araxie tells us Seta has started her own business: free lance. She has moved in with a man who is not her husband. A month ago she phoned her mother to say she is expecting a child with this Lou Prince. Already she is in her fifth month."

As Poppee speaks, the others cast seeds of doubt and recrimination onto the curly vines and petals of Lila Bedrosian's Persian carpet. They themselves might have sprung from this carpet, their knotty limbs and stalwart trunks, their roots crossed at the ankle, the deep crimson dye that flows through their hearts.

I have come to Memorial with a new life in my pocket, but the ladies I carry with me like chromosomes. As far as I travel, they remain, tilling the bed. Their voices and the voice of Casard guide me now. As I plan for this child, for whom I want choice, the old ones remind me of what has come before.

Poppee does not speak of the brevity of my visit, nor does she linger on the fact that I am unmarried and pregnant—the women already know. These difficulties are present in the room, in every sigh and gaze. The women do not disclose their secret thoughts; their movements are slight, seemingly invisible: a tinkle of bracelet, an adjustment of lapel, a tongue stealthily moistening the inside seam of a firmly closed mouth. Beyond these, they will not commit.

Who can blame them? I have gone beyond the horizon of their imaginations to trade my family for a life of newness. I have cavorted and filled my pockets with plenitude, all the while thumbing my nose at my elders, who, I must believe, have nothing better to do than spend their afternoons sucking on pearls of massacre and heartbreak and discontent. I have left these women like so many suitcases in the road.

The plane prepares for its final approach. Hartford lies just beyond the rolling, tree-covered hills.

Poppee dips her chin and continues: "As for the baby, well, Araxie wished to act pleased. When she could not, she did the next best thing—she showed her worry. She says, 'How about your legs? You're going to be careful now, huh? Nighttime, prop them up. Have that Lou Prince bring you a chair. Seta, don't be a fool and later be sorry.'

"At night Araxie lies awake. She cannot understand how her child got so far from her, so far she cannot picture what Seta's rooms look like. What color are her plates? From what cabinet does she take down her dishes?

"Araxie lies awake listening for a key in the door. She pleads with a daughter three thousand miles gone. For now Araxie is the one who needs. Araxie imagines Seta very worried and she wonders why she did not tell Seta something to comfort her. Araxie blames herself for the questions she never heard. 'I am not a bad woman,' she reminds herself, 'I was a good mother, there were mistakes, but in my heart, Seta, please, don't blame. We have done all right. Look: your father and I, back together. You forgive him and not me? We've done all right. The best we could do.' Araxie turns to George—he stays with her most nights." Poppee pauses and presses her lips together for emphasis. She waves bad thoughts away with her hand. "Who's to judge? This is still the girl's home.

"So and so. In the morning Araxie draws open her curtains and looks out in the direction of California, where it's still night and her daughter sleeps, and the child in her womb. Araxie remembers how it was with her first. At six months, Van turned inside her and Araxie thought her organs were being yanked from their walls. In the middle of the market, she collapsed. At seven and a half months, he slammed a leg against her ribs and she carried him to term unable to draw one good deep breath."

The women shake their heads, smiling, shrugging off the pain. "It never mattered."

"Never did."

"They were ours."

Poppee nods and waits for the women to settle down. She continues. "Araxie looks out her window and sees that Seta, now that she has her own, no longer needs her mother. What a shame, I want to tell Araxie, that two people can't seem to need each other at the same time. It's always one coming towards, one backing away. Does Araxie remember her own mother, sitting in the dark the night George Loon proposed?

"So and so. Araxie makes up the bed. As she tucks a corner, her eye catches a glimpse of the closet door. In that moment she sees through the wood and the clothes to the box with the wedding dress she saved for Seta, then Melanie's turn. She straightens up, running her hand through her hair, the coarse gray against her palm. Well, she thinks, maybe Melanie? And it's just another compromise, a compromise she will have to live with. But as she leaves the room and makes her way down the stairs, it is the one who got away who grips her heart. She clutches the railing with two hands as the lost child turns inside her. It is the same turning, whether they be unborn or grown. *Gar oo chugar.* Her girl, Seta Loon, is thirty-three and gone.

"Look now, here she comes. What is it Seta wants: a priest or a judge?"

Did I imagine celebrations, did I imagine a host of open arms? Did I come expecting Memorial to anoint this one lowly departed daughter?

When we were children, it was Van who imagined driving West, his fantasy centering on a beach, a convertible and sun, while Melanie and I swore allegiance to foreign cities or the farm of our imaginations—mine with a stone house and brindled cows.

Van lives in Boston now, with his wife and son. Melanie lives in New York City; they see each other in Memorial on holidays, or when Van passes through New York on business.

Of this family of birds, I alone flew West. Eleven years ago, after college, I rode over the Golden Gate Bridge and settled in a place that reminds me somewhat of Memorial. If I squint, I see Memorial's shade trees and thick, well-tended lawns; in the autumn I drive an hour to where I know the leaves will be turning red, yellow and orange, their scent twining in my hair, the way sleep and dusk cleave to the skin of a child.

I have stayed for what reminds me of Memorial and for what is new. For a sun that rises through the fog, a white circle illuminating the clouds. The sun of my childhood is yellow, and each morning it is what I expect to see. But the Western sun denies me, rising white and round as a moon. All morning she reveals herself through veils, and then, at noon, she suddenly breaks free of the dry umber hills that lie on the land, the burlap breasts of a sleeping giant.

Gar oo chugar.

The ceiling inside Bradley International Airport hangs low. The people of New England seem heavier to me, their winter faces doughy and tired. It is April and I suppose they have had enough of cold. A family huddles by an Arrivals monitor, the mother dressed in a powder-blue parka and stretch nylon slacks, the father in a tartan sports cap and windbreaker. They await their son, who has arrived on my plane. When his mother sees him, she turns shy and, tucking her chin, diverts her radiant smile to the carpet.

Momma waits for me at home. Even so, as I walk from the gate, I look into the crowd expecting to find familiar faces.

And then I am in a car, a compact rental, merging onto Highway 91, into a sea of large American-made boats. I am a Japanese Toyota among Buicks and Chevrolets. We ride along in three lanes of traffic, assuming a moderate speed. The police are cagey here, they hide in unmarked cars and radar-infested trees. Everyone knows this, and we drive slow.

I reach the capital just as the insurance companies' first shift is letting out. A half an hour and we crawl just three miles. Then, mysteriously, the block of cars breaks apart. We glide past West Hartford, then Farmington, where the remainder of the traffic drops off, and I go it alone the next three exits to Memorial.

"There is no center anymore," Momma complained. "People shop at the malls in West Hartford or Meriden, instead of downtown."

I have imagined Memorial fallen like thin bones into an early grave. I have imagined the call of Bob Humms greeting me as I turn onto Corbin Avenue.

I have imagined the cobbler's sorrowful call, but not the slow hum of suburban traffic and the gentle shaking of trees. The underlying stasis gives me a chill. I pass Washington Elementary School and across the road, St. Mary's Catholic Church; I recall the afternoon I visited the Catholics and swished my fingers in the holy water. I drive on, the suburban landscape—the trees and bushes—all overgrown, enveloping me in silence. I pass through as though leaping through hoops of flame. This silence, I tell myself, is what, thank God, I escaped.

• • •

Gar oo chugar.

In the town where Lou and I live, a bookstore café is the central meeting place. The café sits at the bottom of the mountains, in the valley's crotch. The café patio, filled with white garden tables and chairs, looks out in three directions onto the hills and beyond them, the sea. Midmorning, after the children have gone to school, the adults gravitate to the café in their blue jeans and bright knit sweaters. Tanned and fit, they assemble on the patio, their hair tousled as though they have just risen from a collective sleep, the whole town communing after a pleasant slumber party. Those arriving first choose seats nearest the door; this is a place to come to be seen. Any sudden movement—a rattled dish, a bird swooping for crumbs—and all eyes lift, as though an invisible conductor has raised his wand. The newcomer is greeted with smiles, polished like white plates and white garden chairs, smiles hungry for entertainment and buzz.

I walk by the café on my way to work, but at that hour I rarely go inside. Even so, I like to glance at those sitting at the outdoor tables. It is an amusing sight: couples huddling close, wooing over coffee and the newspaper.

I walk by, my heels tapping on the brick walk. I am the pregnant woman in palazzo slacks. I am smiling, asking myself the question: Seta Loon, how did you get so far from Memorial?

Some days the answer comes. Some days it does not; on those days I arrive at my office as though someone has plucked me up and landed me there. I fall into my chair and begin again, reminding myself that this is my office, my chair. Look: my hand on my phone. On such days I must imagine my life, to believe that it is real; and the fragility of this life tears inside me like a tender leaf.

My office is located in a brick building leased to small proprietors of the commercial arts. Next door is a printer, and beside him a technical writer, and above us all, a video production house. These more artistic enterprises are topped, on the third floor, by an accountant, a software outlet and a lawyer who specializes in divorce (he has had three himself).

I am on the ground floor. My room is small but it opens out to the garden. I work the hours I want, and, often, they are long. Some days I do not answer the phone. This too: sometimes, when I glance up from my work, I expect to find a stranger in my doorway, asking me, Who do you think you are? The voice is matter-of-fact and chilling. This is no job, the voice says. This life is flimflam. Where is your home? The voice is Casard's and she condemns me with a word: store-bought.

Gar oo chugar.

In my mother's house.

In my mother's house time never moves. As I pull into the driveway Momma rushes out of the house to greet me. On the lawn, we hug, rubbing circles in each other's back.

"Momma," I say. "Hi."

"Seta-Sue," she murmurs, and all the other names she gave me run through my head: Missy. My girl. Princess-Sue. Dreamer. As we pull apart, her fingers fly to her mouth and, for a moment, she hides. She has turned gray at the temples and around her eyes are dark rings; still, she is lovely. She glances at my protruding belly and, behind those fingers, she smiles. Then Momma cries and I cannot help crying, too.

Tomorrow Dad and I will spend the day together, but tonight is Momma's and mine. We make dinner and, afterward, Momma drapes a coat over my shoulders like wings and sends me outside while she does the dishes. I offer to help but she refuses—she says with the baby and all I should rest. So I sit in the yard, watching Momma through the kitchen window; she runs a yellow sponge through scalding water, then wipes down the table. Cleanliness, I see, has become her new obsession. She sterilizes and wipes, and I cannot help thinking that Casard is looking down, well pleased.

The hemlocks have grown, their crowns brush the telephone wires. Dad planted the trees so that they would create a wall, but he never imagined they would grow above the house, shading it and making it cold.

Momma comes toward me, across the lawn, rubbing cream into her hands.

"Momma, what were we so afraid of?"

"Afraid of?" she says.

"The hemlocks. Why didn't he just put up a fence?"

"Your father wanted privacy but we didn't want a fence."

"Why? What were people going to see?"

Momma looks at me. She is a remarkably handsome woman of sixty, more beautiful with the lines in her face and the salt in her pepper hair. She sighs and folds her body into the chair beside me. We are cozy, having gotten over the strangeness that years apart put in our minds. We sit next to each other, our bodies, our breath, kin.

"Actually, I was the one," she admits. "When we first moved in, I asked your father to put in the hedge because I felt exposed, on the corner."

"Momma"—I laugh—"that's what curtains are for."

She shrugs. "I suppose we wanted some kind of buffer. Don't forget, we were worried about you kids running into the street after a ball."

I nod, a know-it-all. "You passed your fears on to us kids. You felt people were looking at you, so you told yourself that you were worried about us getting run over."

Momma smiles. "Your time will come. The day that baby is born, you'll know what it's like to worry." She pats my stomach as if making a pact.

As it gets dark we sit and contemplate the future. We envision children running through the yard, children who look a lot like Van, Melanie and me.

"Momma, did you think it would be like this?"

"What?" she asks.

I peer at her.

"No."

"Me neither, Momma."

She sighs and I feel her breath in my belly. "Your father and I,

Seta, since that business with Haig, we've been OK. We've had our truce." Brushing my arm, she adds, "A man and a woman don't have to spend every day in the same house to prove they love each other, do they?" The way she leans back in her chair, I know she has been waiting a long time to say this, and so I nod.

It occurs to me how much my absence, though necessary for me, has hurt her. I cup both her hands in mine. "Momma, it takes a long time, but I think it's possible to forgive one's parents. I think we've got to, before we can ever forgive ourselves."

Her fingers fly to her lips, but she nods. She gets a far-off look and I suspect, like me, she is thinking of Casard. We are both thinking that Casard died without forgiveness, the thing she wanted most.

We watch the street. We watch the heavy limbs of the hemlocks brush the telephone wires.

"I realized a while ago," I begin, "we never learned to be happy. Sometimes, when I'm the most pleased, I seize up, and I have to find one small grain of discontent so that I can be at peace."

Momma runs her nail along the metal seam in the chair's arm. "You going to solve the world, Seta-Sue?" Her voice is playful. "You gonna have some joy?"

"I want to, Momma."

She gazes at our roof. "Don't focus on the bad. You kids did fine." She nods at the bushes. "And you, you were smart to leave. Downtown, they're trying to rebuild, but they should just let it go. It'll never be the same. Piece of garbage." She turns and looks at me, and it occurs to us both that she sounds an awful lot like Casard. Momma mimics the old woman's pursed lips and we both laugh until tears pour down our cheeks.

"So Mr. Lou, huh?" she says.

"I think so, yes."

"He's the father."

I nod.

"Seems like a nice man."

I glance at her, she glances at me, her eyes full of mischief. "Oh, the other day, we talked on the phone. You were out. He had just come in the door. He was unpacking the groceries, imagine that. That was when I knew this one might stick." She laughs. "Next time, why don't you bring him with you."

I smile, rubbing my belly. "Momma. When you called, I was home."

She turns and looks at me, her brow furrowed. "You were?" I nod once, and then I tell her: I was upstairs, taking a nap, when I heard the door open. Lou kicked it closed, his boots heavy on the linoleum. He set his bags of groceries in the sink. I asked him once why the sink and he answered: "On the way home, your food gets ruined—eggs break, tomatoes ooze, milk cartons sweat. Your good food ends up debris seeping to the bottom of a paper sack." Lou Prince has beliefs about such things.

The phone rang and I would have let it go, but he answered it. He talked as he unpacked groceries. Without calling out, he knew I was home but did not wish to speak. I knew that whenever he was finished he would come up and bring me a surprise.

But the caller was keeping Lou on the phone. I tried to imagine who it could be, Lou's voice sounded so formal. I smiled, imagining his trying to make small talk as he chased spills.

When at last he hung up, Lou hurled himself up the stairs, as though he were an anchor, landing in the doorway of our room.

"My mother," I said, my face buried in the pillow.

"She tells me that you're going there for a visit." His voice carried an edge. Without looking, I knew he was standing by the bed waiting for me to explain why, after all this time, I had finally decided to go back to Memorial, and why I had not told him. And I knew he was not about to reward me with the chocolate egg he had hidden in his fist.

"With or without me?"

I sighed and rolled over. "Without."

"Why?"

I reached for his hand. "Lou, come here."

The first time we made love it was like falling into snow. And then the snow turned to water and he washed my limbs until they did not ache anymore. Lou. In my mind I call him This Man or Lou-Lou when we play. He paints me up and down with his eyes each time he sees me. Say my name, Lou. He says Seta. Call me what you call me, and he says, Sunshine. Say it again, say it until I grow tired. And he says Seta, Se-ta, Seta oh Seta come here. Sometimes he says, My Lady.

But he is no fool, this Lou. He leaned away. "Seta, what's going on?"

"I guess Momma won't believe in this baby until she sees me. In a way, it makes sense that I go. I think it's time I stop running from that place."

"How long will you be away?"

"I don't know. We haven't gotten that far."

Lou winced at a "we" that did not include him and I wished I had said it differently. Sighing, he dropped the chocolate egg wrapped in yellow and purple foil on the bed.

Telling Momma, I leave out the part about the chocolate egg, and the audacity with which I unwrapped the foil and slowly nibbled the chocolate. Momma would just think I was spoiled. And I leave out the part afterward, when Lou and I talked, and with words and then touch, we stumbled back from the edge.

"Well," Momma says, smiling, pointing her chin toward the road. I know she has a feeling about Lou and me, and of our future, though she is not going to spoil anything by talking about it.

"He lets me be, Momma," I tell her.

"Hmm," she muses and I know by that sound she is no longer thinking of me. I want to know whom she is thinking of.

"Dad," I say, guessing, and I am greatly relieved when she nods.

Gar oo chugar.

There is a crazy woman in our town, and every morning she finds her way to the bookstore café. She is the one I look for, the former wife, they tell me, of a rich lawyer. She sits at a table by the large tree, her expensive sweater the color of her blue milky eyes. It slinks off her shoulder, as though the garment were rigid and her bones fluid. She mumbles into her café mocha and tugs at her sleeve. She picks at her scalp, she picks at her cinnamon roll. She rattles a newspaper, a dish, and when the others do not look at her, she begins to shout.

From the sidewalk I watch her, until I am late and have to hurry to my meeting.

My client is rich and miserable. As he reviews my designs for his office, he talks about his girlfriends and his upcoming vacation in Europe. In college, he tells me, he majored in art history, but at our meeting he discusses name brands and award-winning advertisements as though they were the bedrock of civilization.

My client was raised in Michigan, but of our pasts we do not speak. I tell him that I am from Connecticut, and I know he pictures the rolling lawns and Tudor estates of Greenwich and Darien, while I see a brown Colonial house, with the reservoir to the west, and to the east the empty mills and the rotted cars and tenements along Arch and Pearl and West Main. I see those who are alive and those, like Casard, who are not, and a population of ancestors raised on pedestals of granite, alabaster and marble.

Each year, in the summer, I make a large feast for my friends; I serve the old food: butterflied lamb, dolma, pilaf, eggplant and salad with mint and scallions. For dessert there is paklava and strawberries and tea from Casard's silver-plated samovar. Along with dessert I set out my inheritance: Casard's silver spoons. When it gets very late and the wine's been drunk, my friends and I hold up the spoons and laugh at our distorted faces.

Gar oo chugar.

Momma and I talk until we are exhausted. She goes to bed early, and before I head up, I dial Theresa's number. Through the years we have kept in touch. She lives in the Vartyan house with her Armenian husband and their two adopted children. In our letters and phone calls she tells me of the changes she has made. She has pulled up Mrs. Vartyan's shag carpets and packed away the effigies. She has painted the living room, each wall a different color. I imagine the colors of her hose: lime, magenta, teal, fuchsia.

I know from our letters and phone calls that Theresa is active in the community; she, Garin, and their two little girls, Sona and Hasmig, regularly attend church. Theresa is a leader in the Armenian Relief Society; she raises money to help the diaspora. Last year, as recognition for her efforts, she was part of an international delegation sent to Yerevan.

She says she has pictures to show me. She says she has hope that at last our tiny country may stand on its own. "But then, you predicted it," she says, and laughs. "You're the one, Seta. Free Ararat."

"Yes," I reply, and across the phone lines we smile.

Theresa warns me that the situation over there is in constant flux, and that they are hungry and desperate in the troubled country of our hearts. As she talks I close my eyes and try to imagine Armenia.

At night the men are rounded up and taken over the border. They are put in cells without food or water. Not even a hole in which to shit. The women are left in the villages, subject to frequent and brutal searches. A child cries out in the night and is silenced. A lone man stalks the shadows outside his home. Inside, his wife blinks at the night. What about Noah? she asks. What about the first Christian nation on earth? Where is God? Her hungry children hope for peace. They are certain of violence: by guerrilla soldiers and nature, too. They watch adults act helpless during the earthquakes and the shelling, the walls of the houses tumbling down. The children believe it is nature's way that there will be earthquakes and artillery fire, that even the ground shall not be firm. Across the border, a man cries out from his cell, "Why—O God—are we always the martyrs?" Another prisoner answers, "If you see yourself as one, so you will be."

• • •

Gar oo chugar.

On the phone I say to Theresa, "You'll never guess, last week, who went to church."

She laughs, a crazy hyena. "Did you bring him, too? No, Seta Loon went alone. Am I right?"

I nod into the phone, recalling the church filled with the same diminutive ladies and men in ash-colored suits. They watched me enter, fresh as a secret, and greeted me with a silent question: Whose am I?

At the back wall I lit three candles: one for the family, one for Casard, one for Lou and me. The Der Hyre priest marched down the aisle, chanting in the ancient tongue. An altar boy followed behind him, swinging the lamp of incense, keeping his eyes on the Der Hyre's miter. At the altar, the Der Hyre, because he himself is a sinner and his hands are sinner's hands, used a blessed handkerchief to remove his miter, which is God's crown.

In the church, I was reminded of what it was like to lose one's country, one's family, one's hope; to be the real odar, that is something the elders in the pews cannot forget. Year after year they gather at the church, to remind themselves of where they have been; to tell stories on us all. On my way out, I heard the elders whisper: *Gar oo chugar:* there was and there was not. Stopping in the back, I lit a fourth candle for Unborn.

Theresa sighs into the phone and then, as she did long ago, she proclaims me: "Seta Loon has made her home."

Gar oo chugar.

Momma is in her room, and I lie awake in my girlhood bed, thinking of where I have been: the early places I have not thought of, though I see them now as clearly as though someone has wiped a hand across the rear foggy window.

In my belly Unborn kicks and will not let me sleep. I find myself wondering what the fetus knows. The book says that at twenty weeks the ovaries or testes establish themselves and the tubules of the kidneys branch. I lie awake in my girlhood bed, wondering the exact date when the miraculous cells, with plans for eyelashes, a nose and a heart, release the record of memory. I wonder: Will the binding between Lou and me hold? Will there be enough? When we fail this child, and, inevitably, we will, what then?

It occurs to me that each of us is many people, and there are many lives in time and space we hold. I am Seta Loon, daughter of George and Araxie Loon, granddaughter of Casard Essayan. I am the lover of Lou Prince. I am the woman in palazzo slacks, passing by the bookstore café window, a child pushing out from under my shirt. I am a designer. I am the keeper of Garod's song.

She will not leave me. There are sounds with which you enter the world and those with which you leave. Casard has taught me much, but much I have learned on my own. I have learned to walk in the world without shame.

And I am not so lonely anymore. My family has found its names and by our names we live. Lying in my girlhood bed, I am all the people, and all the places I have known and seen. I am in my old room, yet I am also in my California house. Downstairs, Lou waits while I finish dressing, and, later, we will go out.

I am sitting at my vanity, putting on makeup, when the baby starts to kick. I glance in the mirror and, suddenly, I see her. I see both our faces, Casard's and mine, together. And I watch as the years flip through my mind: she is taking the dog for a walk and I am in the window seat, watching them through the glass. Casard has on the peach housedress and her gray tie shoes. Sonny, here Sonny, yes Sonny, pulls and sniffs beside her.

It is August, and the air is thick with dusk and everything is moving slowly. Everything is winding down like a lullaby. Here there is no teacher, sister or brother, there is only Grandma Casard, in whose house the light of day comes filtered through venetian blinds. In her house there is no risk in saying No, since there will always be time.

I have been sitting at the mirror for an hour, it must be an hour. Any minute Lou will call up the stairs and ask—does he know what he asks?

In my belly, you kick and then turn. And I feel the spiraling—the wondrous spiraling—I have waited for all my life. And I am full of questions. What will I give you? How will my song differ from the song of Araxie and Casard? What burden will I pass on? I will do my work and be responsible, yet still you will feel the weight of a question I never thought to answer. Looking in the mirror, I see Casard, her furry cheeks and her gray tie shoes. And I recall that summer, her last, and the days we spent, when it was hot and then it got even hotter, and then, in August, she died.

And I wonder, what do you know of your grandmother and great-grandmother, and what do you know of me? I wonder, as you grow, which part of me you will cleave to, the woman sitting across from your father at dinner, the woman in the black dress with the wide cream collar, or that lonely girl—daughter of Araxie, granddaughter of Casard—who dreamed of Turkish bloodswords and a muddy river and a hand letting go, the girl who ate shish kebob sandwiches in a kitchen of the past she holds in her heart, so reverent and blind that she cannot hear him calling, I can almost hear Lou calling, "Are you ready?"

About the Author

Carol Edgarian, a graduate of Stanford University, lives on the West Coast with her husband. *Rise the Euphrates* is her first novel.

About the Type

This book was set in Baskerville, a typeface that was designed by John Baskerville, an amateur printer and typefounder, and cut for him by John Handy in 1750. The type became popular again when the Lanston Monotype Corporation of London revived the classic Roman face in 1923. The Mergenthaler Linotype Company in England and the United States cut a version of Baskerville in 1931, making it one of the most widely used typefaces today.